'Combines the ironclad plotting of Sansom with the artful recreation of Mantel'
Independent

'Such is the quality of the recre[...] and flow of everyday life but a[...] easy to believe Satan is walki[...] thought-provoking'

'A fine, rich, beautiful historical thriller – literate, engaging and moving'
Manda Scott

'MacLean has the first-rate historical novelist's gift ... communicates her passion for the period without downplaying its brutishness'
Daily Telegraph

'A substantial story, well researched, never slackening pace'
Scotsman

'What a find this book turned out to be. It has a unique setting and a strong narrative voice'
Eurocrime

'A multi-layered and satisfying read'
Crimepieces

'A satisfying, skilfully constructed mystery with richly developed characters ...A truly memorable and exciting read'
Historical Novel Society

'Intelligent, enthralling and beautifully written'
Crime Review

Shona (S.G.) MacLean was born in Inverness and brought up in the Scottish Highlands. She obtained an MA and PH.D. in history from Aberdeen University. She began to write fiction while bringing up her four children (and Labrador) on the Banffshire coast, and has now returned to live in the Highlands. *The Redemption of Alexander Seaton* was short-listed for both the Saltire First Book Award and the CWA Historical Dagger; *The Seeker* was winner of the 2015 CWA Historical Dagger.

By S. G. MacLean

THE ALEXANDER SEATON SERIES

The Redemption of Alexander Seaton
A Game of Sorrows
Crucible of Secrets
The Devil's Recruit

THE CAPTAIN DAMIAN SEEKER SERIES

The Seeker
The Black Friar
Destroying Angel
The Bear Pit

A GAME
OF
SORROWS

S. G. MACLEAN

Quercus

First published in Great Britain in 2010
This paperback edition published in 2019 by

Quercus Editions Ltd
Carmelite House
50 Victoria Embankment
London EC4Y 0DZ

An Hachette UK company

A CIP catalogue record for this book is available
from the British Library

PB ISBN 978 1 84916 244 9

10 9 8

Typeset by Jouve (UK), Milton Keynes

Printed and bound in Great Britain by Clays Ltd, Elcograf S.p.A.

MIX
Paper from
responsible sources
FSC® C104740
www.fsc.org

To James

The wild or mere Irish have a generation of poets, or rather rhymers vulgarly called bards, who in their songs used to extol the most bloody, licentious men, and no others, and to allure the hearers, not to the love of religion and civil manners, but to outrages, robberies, living as outlaws, and contempt of the magistrates' and the king's laws . . . For the mere Irish, however . . . they nothing so much feared the Lord Deputy's anger as the least song or ballad these rascals might make against them, the saying whereof to their reproach would more have daunted them than if a judge had doomed them to the gallows.

Fynes Moryson, hostile commentator
on Ireland, 1617

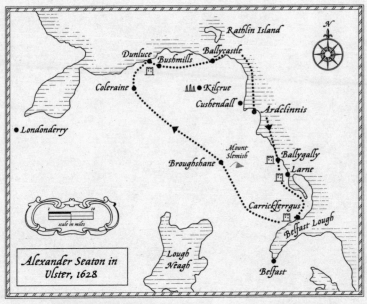

Alexander Seaton in Ulster, 1628

Rathlin Island
Ballycastle
Dunluce · Bushmills
Coleraine
Kilcrue
Cushendall
Ardclinnis
Londonderry
Broughshane
Mount Slemish
Ballygally
Larne
Carrickferrgus
Belfast Lough
Lough Neagh
Belfast

scale in miles

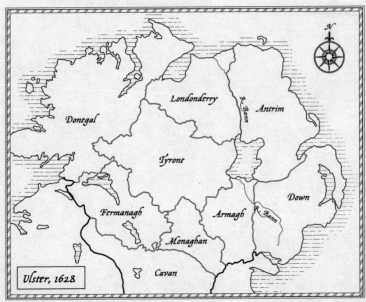

Ulster, 1628

Donegal
Londonderry
R. Bann
Antrim
Tyrone
Down
Fermanagh
Armagh
R. Bann
Monaghan
Cavan

Historical background

In the early decades of the seventeenth century, Ulster was a province undergoing tremendous change. From the time of the first Anglo-Norman incursions in the twelfth century, English power and interest in Ireland had fluctuated significantly, but the 'Old English', as they became known, never left, and over the centuries became deeply rooted in Irish society, at times marrying into the native Irish aristocracy and adopting their speech, manner and way of dress. In the course of the sixteenth century, the Tudors under Henry VIII and Elizabeth I made resolute efforts to extend English royal power throughout the island. The greatest obstacle to their plans was Ulster which, under its native families, remained the most thoroughly Gaelic part of Ireland, with distinct language, dress, landholding and economic practices, cultural and religious beliefs and loyalties. The most powerful of these native Irish families was the O'Neills.

It became clear to the administration that for English power in Ireland to be assured, Ulster must be brought under control. This was not simply a question of political or military conquest, but of cultural assimilation. The native Irish leaders of Ulster must be brought to acknowledge the sovereignty of the English Crown, and the people under their authority brought into conformity with English mores.

While the native leaders appeared at first to be willing to

secure their own title to land in return for acknowledging royal authority, increasing awareness of the concomitant assault on the Gaelic way of life brought them to rebellion. The most significant of these rebellions was that led by Hugh O'Neill, Earl of Tyrone, in what became known as the Nine Years' War. The brutality and hardships of this war devastated Ulster. Tyrone's ultimate submission in 1603, followed four years later by his flight to the continent with the Earl of Tyrconnell and other native Irish leaders, left Gaelic Ulster open to what English advisers had been urging for some time – not the Anglicisation of Ulster, but its colonisation.

Following 'the Flight of the Earls', the Crown initiated mass confiscations of native Irish land. Those who retained their lands held them on terms which greatly circumscribed their power and standing. Others, whose loyalty to the Crown was judged suspect, faced imprisonment, exile or death. Ulster was to be secured by the granting of the escheated lands to new landholders whose loyalty to the British state and the Protestant religion would not be in doubt. Pre-eminent in this new order were to be the 'New English' settlers, especially the 'London Companies' who were to re-establish and 'plant' the towns of Londonderry and Coleraine and vast tracts of land in the North with well-affected, mainly English or Scots, tenants. Only those judged most 'well-affected' amongst the native Irish were acceptable as tenants, generally on the poorest land and at the highest rents.

These 'New English' planters were distinct from the Catholic, Hibernicised 'Old English', having more in common with the Scots, who had been colonising areas of Antrim and Down for decades. Four peoples – native Irish, Old English, New English and Scots, with all their cultural, political and religious differences – were now left to forge a new society in what until the turn of the century had remained the most thoroughly Gaelic part of Ireland. Tensions and resentments were inevitable, and would eventually find expression in the carnage of the 1640s and the Wars of the Three Kingdoms.

Despite references to some actual historical figures and events – Randal MacDonnell, Earl of Antrim, James Shaw of Ballygally, Julia MacQuillan, the disaster of Kinsale, the abortive uprising of 1615 – and although the vast majority of locations mentioned in the text exist or existed, what follows is an entirely fictional account of how these tensions might have affected one family in Ulster in 1628.

Shona MacLean
July 2009

Prologue

The bride's grandmother smiled: she could feel the discomfort of the groom's family and it pleased her well. This wedding feast was a sickly imitation of what such things should be – her father would have been ashamed to set such poor fare before his followers' dogs. But no matter. The music had scarcely been worthy of the name, and of dancing there had been none at all, for fear of offence to their puritan sensibilities. It was a mockery of a feast; she should not have permitted it, regardless of what her husband had said. It might well be politic to pander to the ways of these new English settlers, but it was not the O'Neill way, not her way. She should have insisted that the marriage took place in Carrickfergus, and according to her own customs. But the girl too had been against it – like Grainne, she would reap what she had sown, and she mattered little, anyhow.

Maeve looked down towards the far end of the table – they should not have put him there; he should have had the place of honour – these people knew nothing. Finn O'Rahilly was resplendent in the saffron tunic and white mantle, bordered with golden thread, that she had gifted him for the occasion. He would be paid well enough too, although it was not seemly at such times to talk of money. Regardless of all that her granddaughter and her new husband's English family had said, on this one point the old woman would not be moved. There had been a poet at every O'Neill wedding through all the ages and, despite all that had happened, there would be a poet at this one, to give his blessing on the union, to tell the glories – fallen, broken though they now were – of the great house of O'Neill. As Finn O'Rahilly rose and turned to face her, Maeve felt the pride of the generations coursing through her: her moment had come.

He spoke in the Irish tongue. Everything was still. All the guests, even the English, fell silent as the low, soft voice of the poet filled the room. Every face was turned towards the man with the startling blue eyes whose beard and long silver hair belied his youth. No hint of the chaos he was about to unleash escaped his countenance, and it was a moment before any but the most attentive auditors understood what was happening. But Maeve understood: she had understood from the shock of the very first words.

Woe unto you, Maeve O'Neill:
Your husband will soon lie amongst the worms and leave you a
  widow,
You of the great race of the O'Neills,
Woe unto you who lay with the English!
Your changeling offspring carried your sin,
Your son that died, with the earls, of shame.
Your daughter, wanton, abandoned her race and her name and went
  with the Scot.
Woe unto you, Maeve O'Neill,
Your grandchildren the rotten offspring of your treachery!
Your grandson will die the needless death of a betrayed Ulsterman,
Your granddaughter has gone, like you before her, whoring after the
  English – no good will come of it, no fruit, only rotten seed.

Your line dies with them, Maeve O'Neill.
Your line will die and the grass of Ireland grow parched and rot
over your treacherous bones.
And the O'Neill will be no more.

The poet turned and left, without further word, and all for a moment was silence, save the sound of Maeve O'Neill's glass shattering on the stone floor.

ONE

The Taste of Tomorrow

Aberdeen, Scotland, 23 September 1628

I had waited for this moment without knowing what it was that I waited for. The college was quiet, so quiet that the sounds of the life of the town and the sea beyond permeated its passageways and lecture halls unopposed by scholarly debate or student chatter. The shutters on Dr Dun's window, so often closed at this time of year against the early autumn blasts of the North Sea gales, were open today to let in the last, surprising, golden glows of the late summer sunshine. The rays lent an unaccustomed warmth to the old grey stones of the Principal's room, less austere now than it had been in the days of the Greyfriars who had walked these cloisters before us, in the time of superstition. The Principal's words were as welcome to my ears as was the gentle sunlight to my eyes.

'It is in you, Alexander, that we have decided to place this trust. It is greatly at short notice, I know, but you will understand Turner's letter only came into the hands of the council yesterday, and response, not only by letter but in the form of the appointed agent of the town and college – yourself – must be aboard the *Aurora* by the turn of the tide on Thursday. We met in the kirk last night to discuss it, and our choice was not long in the making.' He named a dozen names, all that mattered for learning and the word of God in our society. There had been a time when knowing that I had been the subject of such a conference would have engendered apprehension in me, for there could only have been one result of such a council then – censure, condemnation, exile. But that had been a long time ago, and in another place, and these two years past I had lived quietly and worked hard at my post in the college. My students in the third class, where I taught arithmetic, geometry, ethics and physics, liked me, I knew. I passed myself well enough with my fellow regents, and from Dr Dun, from the beginning, I had known nothing but kindness. My friends were few, and I did not seek to add to their number. William Cargill and his wife, friends both since my own college days, George Jamesone the painter, Dr Forbes, my former teacher and my spiritual father, and Sarah, since the day I had first met her, there had been Sarah. I seldom travelled, and rarely returned to Banff, the town of my birth, where I had friends also who were truly dear to me, and all the family I had in the world. Yet I did not like to return to the stage of failures past, so I did not go there a tenth of the times I was asked. I had had no fear, then, on being summoned to the Principal's presence. Neither had I had any inkling of the news, the great prospect that awaited me there.

'You are well versed in the German tongue, are you not?' enquired the Principal.

I asserted that I was. My old friend Dr Jaffray, in Banff, had insisted on teaching me the language. He had spent happy years of study on the continent in his youth, and having no one else to converse with in that tongue, he had decided he would converse with me. Despite the ravages of the war which now raged over so many of the lands he held dear, he never lost sight of the hope that one day I would follow where he had first walked. And now, at last, his hope was to be fulfilled, but not, perhaps, in a way he might have foreseen. I was to sail on Thursday for the Baltic, and Danzig. From there I was to travel to Breslau and then Rostock.

'Our brethren in the Baltic lands, in northern Germany, in Poland and in Lithuania, suffer greatly under the depredations of Rome and the Habsburgs: the King of Sweden struggles almost alone in their cause. Our brethren thirst for the Word and for their own ministers. Turner has written here, as the town of his birth, asking that we might accept two Polish students to study divinity for the next three years, that they might be sound and strengthened in their doctrine, and when they return to their homeland to fulfil their calling and spread God's word there, that they should be replaced by two more. He has mortified to that cause the sum of ten thousand pounds Scots.' Dr Dun paused for a moment to allow me to contemplate the incredible vastness of this sum.

'Praise be to God for such a man and for such a gift,' I said.

'Indeed,' said the Principal.

'You wish me to escort the two students to Scotland?' I asked, for the Principal had still not made clear what was to be my role in this enterprise.

He shook his head. 'No, Alexander, some returning merchant or travelling townsman of good report could have performed that task. I wish you to travel to Poland to meet with Turner, and with his assistance, to seek out and find the two most worthy young men you can to fill these two places. I wish you to travel to the universities, to question the young men you find there on their learning, their soundness in doctrine, their strength of heart in adversity, their love for the Lord. When you find the two young men you know in your heart to be fit and right for this ministry, then you are to bring them back here with you. The council and the college will give you four months for the fulfilling of this task. Will you take up this trust, Alexander?'

The sounds from outside the open window were shut out by the contending voices in my head, all my own. Here at last, after false trails and false dawns, was the chance I had never believed I would be given. Here was the moment where Dr Jaffray's hopes for me could be fulfilled. I would at last travel beyond the narrow bounds of our northern society, and all in the work of God and for my fellow man. Here was a chance fully to justify the kindnesses and the faith in me of Dr John Forbes, my mentor, and of Dr Dun himself, who had plucked me from my self-imposed obscurity in Banff for something better. Here was the moment, and I was as an idiot, in a stupor.

Dr Dun smiled kindly at me. 'Do not tell me you mislike the commission, Alexander, for I can think of no other better suited to it. The loss of your own calling to the ministry – and I know you suffer from it yet – will make you a better judge than any other of those who would aspire to it. Will you go, boy?'

At the age of twenty-eight, it was a long time since I had been called boy, and never before by Dr Dun. The warmth unlocked my seized tongue. 'Aye, Sir, I will go.'

There was much to be done and less than two days to do it in. By midday on Thursday, I would be aboard a merchant ship and bound for the Baltic. Many had gone before me, to increase and pursue their learning, to better master their trade, to escape present drudgery in the hope of a new and better life. I was not to be embarking upon the journey of a new life, but I felt that what the next few months would bring would change the life I had to come. There were letters to write, bills to pay, and farewells to make. It would be another week before the students began to arrive back in the town after their long vacation, and Dr Dun already had the matter of my temporary replacement in hand. I almost flew to my own chamber on leaving the Principal's study, taking the granite steps two at a time and nearly knocking over the old college porter as I did so.

'You're as bad as the lads, Mr Seaton. I swear before God this place will be the death of me yet.'

'You'll be here when the sky falls in, Rob,' I said, and ran on. The bare little chamber at the top of the college, looking out over the Castle Hill to the North Sea that would soon transport me to unseen lands, was all my own: I was not, like some of the younger unmarried teachers, constrained to share, and the solitude and simplicity had suited me well these last two years. The stone walls were unadorned, as was the floor. The only colour in the room came from the subtly hued books along the shelf, and the brightly coloured bedding which every married woman of my acquaintance deemed herself obliged to furnish me with. My unmarried state was a matter of great concern to all save one of them, and that one, the wife of my good friend William Cargill, had, I believed, guessed my secret. I had resolved in these past few weeks that it should remain a secret no longer, and was determined that what business I had to transact before I left for the eastern sea would be done with by tonight, so that I might devote tomorrow to persuading Sarah Forbes, servant in William's household, mother to the beautiful, illegitimate son of a rapacious brute, that I truly loved her and that she must become my wife.

The remainder of the afternoon was spent on the necessary preparations for my departure, but by six o'clock most had been done and, as was my habit on a Tuesday evening, I threw on my cloak and went down through the college and into

town, to William's house on the Upperkirkgate. I did not go
in by the street door but went instead by the backland. As ever,
I was greeted first by Bracken, William's huge and untrained
hound, bought in the mistaken belief that he might one day
again hunt as he had in the days of his youth. As he had learned,
a busy young lawyer with the demands of wife and family
hunts only in his dreams. The huge dog pressed me against the
wall with his paws, and administered a greeting more loving
than hygienic. I pushed him off, laughing, to attend to the
other urgent greetings taking place around my knees. Two little
boys, one as fair as the other was dark, clamoured loudly and
repeatedly for my attention. It was little effort to sweep both
of them up in my arms.

'Uncl'Ander, Uncl'Ander,' insisted James, the white-haired,
two-year-old joy of my friend's life, 'make dubs.' And indeed,
the hands which he pressed to my face were covered in the
mud the children had been playing with.

'And what would your mothers say if I was to come into
the house covered in such dubs?'

'No tea till washed,' said the serious little Zander, shaking
his dark head. I kissed the hair on it. How could it be that I
felt such love for another man's child? But I did. I had loved
him from the moment his mother had held him out towards
me and, without looking at me and almost with defiance, told
me she was naming him Alexander, Zander, after me. The child
of a rape, the son of a filthy, bullying brute of a stonemason.
It had been she, and not he, who had been banished the burgh
of Banff in shame when her condition could no longer be
hidden; she who had been sent to a loveless home where she
was not welcome. And alongside the stones and the abuse
hurled at her as she had crossed the river had been me. I had
not known it then, I am not sure when I did finally know it,

but at some point on our silent, reluctant journey together that day, she had utterly captivated me. Bringing her to the home of William and Elizabeth had been the best thing I had ever accomplished in my life, for them, for her, for her child, and for myself. But two years had been long enough; too long, and I was determined that on my return from Poland Sarah and Zander would leave the house of the Cargills and make their home, for life, with me.

The boys were wriggling down and began tugging at my sleeves to pull me after them into the house for supper. I stopped them by the well and we all three of us washed, although in truth my hands were dirtier after cleaning the two boys than they had been to start with. I steered the children past the still bounding dog, through the back door, and right into the kitchen. Lying in a large drained kettle on the table was a huge salmon, freshly poached and cooling, its silvered scales dulled and darkened, its flesh a wondrous pink, full of promise. It must have been one of the last of the season. I would relish it, not knowing what manner of food I might have on my travels to come.

At the other end of the table, bent over her flour board where she thumped with an unnatural venom at the pastry for an apple pie evidently in preparation, was Elizabeth Cargill. Instead of putting down her rolling pin and coming over to greet me by the hand as she would usually have done, she looked up tersely, gave a pinched, 'Well. Mr Seaton,' and returned with increased vigour to her thumping. Davy, William's steward, sat in a wooden chair by the fire, plucking a bird. I looked to him for some explanation but was rewarded only with a narrowing of his thunderous brows and a muttered quotation from the book of Deuteronomy. The boys themselves seemed taken aback at my reception, but before we could make any sense of it, I heard the soft familiar brush of Sarah's habitual brown woollen work dress against the flagstone floor. I turned to look at her, and she stopped stock-still where she was, her eyes those of one in shock. Her lips started to form some words and then she drew in a deep breath and stepped resolutely past me without a word.

I had had this treatment, or the semblance of it, before on occasion. One such incident had arisen from my failure to notice a new gown for the Sabbath, of a rich black stuff with white Dutch lace at the collar, sewn by Sarah's own hand of gifts brought back to the family by William after a trip to The Hague. My protestation later to Elizabeth that Sarah was always beautiful to me had been to no avail, and the thaw of the women had been near two weeks in the coming. Another time, worse in that I knew it truly affected her more deeply, and that she had cause, was when Katharine Hay had passed through the town, staying a night at her parents' town house in the Castlegate, on her way to Delgattie. I did not lie when I told Sarah that Katharine Hay, married now and with a child also, could be nothing to me, but I could not pretend that she never had been. This episode had been made all the more diffi-cult by the fact that there had never been – and indeed still now there had not been – any open expression of love, any acknowledgement of expectation, between myself and Sarah. But I did love her, and I could not believe that she felt nothing more than gratitude towards me. I could not, in fact, believe that the desire I felt for her and the conviction I held to that she had been put on God's earth to be my wife could have the strength they did were she not indeed meant for me. And once I had discussed my plans with William tonight and settled what business I needed him to perform for me, I would come here again tomorrow and tell her so. What this evening's misdemeanour was, I could not even begin to guess, but I was confident that, as it had those other times, it would be carried away on the wind.

When she caught sight of Sarah, Elizabeth gave over her thumping and, passing me also, took her friend and maid-servant by the arm and proceeded with her out of the kitchen, though not before having said, very audibly, to Davy as she passed, 'Would you tell Mr Cargill that Alexander Seaton is here, Davy, for it is surely not to see us that he visits.' Davy favoured me with another glower as he rose stiffly from his chair and went to do his mistress's bidding.

I stood alone in the centre of this well-loved room, silent now save for the crackling of the fire in the hearth, with the two small boys who now regarded me cautiously, in no possible doubt that I, Uncle Alexander, was the cause of their mother's displeasure and therefore of all disruption of the usual life of the house. They said nothing, and the accusa-tion of it burned into my confusion. The silence at last was broken by the arrival of William, the ageing Davy hobbling behind him.

'Alexander,' my friend said, smiling awkwardly. 'It is good to see you. I had feared you might not come.'

'Might not come?' I enquired, confused. 'I have been here to my dinner every Tuesday and Saturday evening for the last two years, and many another in between. Why in all the world did you think I would not be here tonight?'

'Well,' said William, hesitant and looking sideways in the direction of Davy, then down at the two boys. He looked away from me. 'Davy, will you take the boys to get washed, and tell the mistress Mr Seaton and I will take our dinner in my study.' The boys made to protest that they were already clean, but their protests were to no avail. I felt like protesting myself, but instead followed William silently through the house to the sanctuary of his study.

Once we were in, he shut the door firmly behind me and then turned to look at me, a weariness in his eyes. 'What in the Devil's name has been going on, Alexander? What were you thinking of? This house has been as the eye of the storm all day, and I dare hardly mention your name without my dear wife bringing down all the imprecations of Hell upon both our heads.'

'William,' I said, shaking my head, 'I have no idea what you are talking about.'

He strode across the room and sat down heavily behind his desk, evidently angered. I had seldom seen William angry in the fourteen years I had known him. 'What I am talking about,' he said, enunciating each word clearly, 'is you taking leave of your senses. It is all around the town, and not only amongst the women, that you were in not one but two drunken brawls last night, and that there was not a drinking house in the town where the serving girls were safe from you. I had it on authority that you kept low company the whole night, and that only the quick thinking of the ill-favoured Highlander you were with kept you from the sight of the baillies. I was half astonished not to find you in the tolbooth.'

I sat down, though unbidden, and tried to disentangle his words from what I knew to be true. 'William,' I said, screwing shut my eyes for hope of greater clarity, 'I still have no idea what you are talking about. I spent last night in my room in the college, burning the candle low and deep into the night, alone, with a Hebrew version of Paul's first letter to the Corinthians. I have not been drunk since you and I sat up half the night with Jaffray and his *uisge bheatha* when he was here in March, and the only Highlander I know is Ishbel, the wife of our friend the Music Master in Banff, and I believe were you to call her ill-favoured, he would run you through, he and Jaffray both.'

William's face began to lighten a little. 'So you were not at Jennie Grant's place near the Brig O'Dee last night, gambling and getting into fights with the packmen?'

'I have never gambled, as you know. And why on earth would I go to the Hardgate for food, drink or company?' I asked.

'And you were not at the Browns' place, nor Maisie Johnston's either?' he asked.

'No,' I said, shaking my head, perplexed.

'And there were no brawls, no bridling of serving girls, no Highlander?' he persisted.

'No,' I said.

'I have your word?'

'You have my word, although I am not a little astonished you should need it.'

He sank back in his chair, convinced at last and visibly relieved. I myself now felt convinced of little, and a good deal unsettled. 'William, what is all this talk?'

My friend took a bottle of good Madeira wine and two glasses from a press behind his desk that he thought Elizabeth was unaware of and poured us each a generous measure. He handed me my drink and smiled ruefully.

'Alexander, I should not have doubted you, but this house has been in such an uproar of female fury all day that I had no peace even in my own head to think. Sarah returned from the morning market on the verge of tears and stayed there a good hour, apparently, before Elizabeth was able to draw from her what was upsetting her. The girl had been told by not one but half a dozen of the burgh's finest scolds that you had been drinking and pestering women through the town half the night. She would not have countenanced their scandalmongering had she not had it from some respectable matrons too.'

He looked up at me, a little uneasy, and half looked away.

'You know, Alexander, there are many in the town, and that number growing, who suspect you have a partiality for the girl. Och, Heavens, Alexander, I know it well enough myself; I see it in your face every time she walks into the room. But there are petty minds aplenty who would take little pleasure in seeing a servant girl, a fallen woman at that as they see her, being raised above her degree by a marriage to you. They would have been tripping over each other this morning to reach her first with the news of your carry on.'

I could feel the anger raging in my chest so I could hardly breathe. 'Aye,' I said, 'tripping over each other and landing in a midden of their own making.' I stood up. 'So they think she's beneath me, do they? Well, William, do you know why I have never yet spoken to her of it, of my feelings? Do you, William?'

My friend shook his head wordlessly, somewhat taken aback by the force of my rage. I took a breath and spoke slowly, deliberately. 'It is because I know her to be so far above me in every way, other than that of the station that fate has thrown her to, that I am too scared to speak lest I hear her say she will not have me.' At that moment there was a firm knock at the door, and Davy entered with a tray bearing our dinner. William had long assured me that Davy was not as deaf as he pretended to be, and I suspected from the look on his face that he had heard every word of my outburst. As he turned to leave us he gave me a look I had rarely seen from him before: it was something approaching respect.

'Sit down, Alexander,' said William after the old man had gone.

I did so slowly, looking all the while at some spot beyond my feet.

'Would you not look at me?' he said in frustration. So I did, and saw that his eyes were kind and there was a rueful smile about his mouth. 'I would be the first to agree that Sarah is a much better person than those who would calumniate her. And remember, I myself married a maidservant. Since you brought her to our home, she has been a better help and friend to Elizabeth than I could ever have hoped for. She nursed my son when my wife was too ill to do it herself, and we both thank God every day that He sent her to us, through you, that our boy might live. Young Zander is as a brother to James, the brother he will never have.' This I knew already, for Elizabeth had come so close to death in bringing James into the world that William had sworn he would never risk her in childbirth again. 'No one knows better than I her qualities. And of course, she is beautiful too, which will not help her cause with many of the beetroot-faced dumplings of the burgh.' I laughed, against my will, as did he. 'But,' he continued, 'there are few know you better than I do either. And I tell you you are the best of men, whatever may have happened in the past; I know you to be the best of men, and so does she. Tell her of your feelings, before you are both too old and too set in your loneliness to live otherwise.' He filled again the glass I had emptied, and lifted up his own towards me. 'And do I have your word on *that*, Alexander?'

I returned his toast. 'You do, and I will do it tonight. I was – and believe me if you will – going to ask for an hour alone with her tomorrow, although after tonight's reception I was near enough resolved to put it off again.'

'Aye,' mused William, 'if you approach her before this misunderstanding – though whence it proceeds I don't know – is made clear, there is no telling what harsh words might rain upon your ears.' He glanced at me. 'Women have a pride and a stubbornness that is beyond all comprehension, you know.' I knew. 'Let me talk to her tonight, talk to Elizabeth first, in fact. It must be that there was some visitor in town who looked very like you, who caused this rumpus last night. If I can persuade Elizabeth of the logic of that – and God help me for a night's sleep if I cannot – then she will smooth your way with Sarah.'

'Do you not think this tale has been spread about as an act of malice,' I asked, 'by some indweller who wishes me ill?'

William shook his head again. 'No. If it had just been the women at the marketplace, I might have thought so, but Davy had it from a crony of his who claims with his own eyes to have seen you hurled, indeed rolled, out of John Brown's with curses at your back. There has been much muttering about the fall of man in general and the stool of repentance in particular from that corner today, let me assure you.'

My heart warmed more than ever to William, as I saw in my mind's eye the day he had endured in his own house, all at the cause of my supposed misdemeanours. 'And you will set me right, with the women, and with Davy then?' I said.

'Aye, I will,' he answered. 'And now let us eat, before I starve to death at my own table.'

We made a fine supper of the salmon, and of the apple tart. The bell of St Nicholas kirk struck eight, and I realised with some sadness that Sarah had not sent Zander through to bid me goodnight as she usually did. Something in feeling that little head pressed to my chest, the sleepy murmur of goodnight, gave me a strength that little else did. I would not dwell on it, for I would see him tomorrow, and not many tomorrows after that I would call him my son.

The house was quiet by the time I left, the women, children and servants all long asleep. The autumnal mildness of the day had given way to an early frost and the silent heavens were bejewelled with a thousand stars. I did not hold with the corruption of the proper science of astronomy peddled by the astrologers who cast the horoscopes of the foolish, but I felt a power, a sense of foreknowledge in the heavens of the destiny I set out towards. The next night I looked upon these heavens above this town, it would be with Sarah's pledge in my heart and the prospect of peoples and nations over the sea before me. I was filled with gladness and the knowledge of the spirit working within me and powering me towards my destiny. It is what they call happiness.

The College gatekeeper grunted as I passed that at last he might get some sleep, that I was always the latest of the regents abroad. I would have felt greater guilt at his sleeplessness had I not had to waken him from his slumbers to let me in. There was little noise save that of my own feet on the stone flags and the gentle breaking of the waves onto the darkened shore beyond as I mounted the chilly steps to the chamber that would be mine for only one night more until I returned. I murmured a curse at myself as I saw from the light beneath the door that I had left a candle burning. The folly and thought-lessness of it angered me. I pushed open the door and stopped. The light from the candle was not bright, but there could be little doubt as to what I saw. There ahead of me, no more than four feet away, was my own image, as in a looking glass. Yet there was not and never had been a looking glass in my chamber, and as I stood dumbfounded and still, the image that I looked upon came towards me and offered me its hand.

TWO

The Man in the Mirror

'Alexander Seaton,' said the man, and my name echoed in the room as if my own mother were calling me. He grasped me by the right hand and threw his left around my shoulder, encircling me in his grip and holding me fast. He stood back to appraise me. 'I had begun to think I would never find you.' His face was suffused with such affection and joy that my own initial shock and apprehension began to subside. The eyes that laughed in mine were the same grey-green as my own, the lashes as long and dark. He had the same straight nose, the same set to brow and chin that my father had called arrogant and my mother manly. His hair, I would have said, was a little longer than mine and darker, almost black, but all in all, I doubted whether more than a handful of people still living could have told us apart. I knew before he released me and spoke again who he was, for there could be no other explanation.

'Sean O'Neill FitzGarrett,' he said with a flourish. 'Son of Phelim O'Neill FitzGarrett, and grandson of Maeve O'Neill of the O'Neills of Ulster, who has sent me here.'

'My cousin,' I said, sitting down at last on the bed.

The face smiled a mischievous smile. 'None other.' He pulled over the chair from my desk and turned it around to sit astride it. It was only then that I noticed, lurking in the unlit corner of the room, a stocky form, with eyes that moved as much as his body was still. He was wreathed in some sort of Highland garb, a yellowed linen shirt wrapped over faded red trews of a rough woollen cloth, the whole swathed in a long brown blanket edged with goats' fleece. 'That's Eachan,' my cousin said. 'Pay him no heed. He's a dour fellow but will do you no harm, unless you would wish to injure me, and then he would kill you as soon as look at you.'

'"The ill-favoured Highlander",' I murmured.

My cousin glanced at me quizzically but said nothing.

'When did you come here?' I asked.

'Into the town? We arrived last night. Half-starved and exhausted, the pair of us, by the time we got within the gates – which was when, incidentally, cousin, I learned of our resemblance to one another. The fellow on the watch mistook me for you and let me pass without question. Eachan gave him more trouble, until I intervened – under guise as yourself; the watchman seemed more at ease with that arrangement than any other, and I judged it best not to antagonise him. Aye, half-starved and exhausted we were, and our object nowhere to be found. This is not a hospitable place; I will be glad to be home.'

'You are a long way from home,' I said. 'Carrickfergus.'

His eyebrows rose. 'You know that much then.'

Still watching my cousin's servant, I said, 'My mother spoke of you sometimes, her brother's child. I have often wondered about you. As a boy I used to wish . . .' I stopped. It was pointless to remember that now. 'It was a great sorrow to her that she did not see you grow to manhood. She is dead now. I think she grieved for her homeland until the day she died.'

'Ah, did she? I think I have some memory of her yet, Grainne. Of her hair, the scent of her skin, her face sometimes. There has not been a day that our grandfather has not mourned her loss.'

He said nothing of our grandmother, Maeve: there was no need. My mother's every letter to her had gone unacknowledged, unanswered, until at last she had written no more letters home. I had sometimes wondered how many kind words from the stern old Ulsterwoman of my childhood dreams would have been needed for her to leave my father and this cold and wind-blasted coast of Scotland to return to the land of her birth. I might have grown up all but a brother to the man seated across from me. But there had been no such words, she had never returned home from this place, and the man before me was a stranger.

He regarded me a few moments, as discomfited as I, I think, to learn of another who lived his life in his own exact image. 'You have no brother or sister?' he asked.

'None,' I said. 'Nor mother or father either now. And you?'

'I have a sister,' he said, 'Deirdre. Four years younger and twenty wiser than I. Our mother died when she was born, and our father left before she was five years old or I nine, in the train of Tyrone; he fled to the continent.'

'Tyrone?' I said, stupidly almost, as some image from my childhood stirred in my memory. A memory of my mother weeping, as I had never seen her do before nor indeed did I ever afterwards.

'Aye, Tyrone,' said Sean with some bitterness. 'My father fled Ireland with the Earls of Tyrone and Tyrconnell, when they took fright at only they and God alone knew what. They left their people and their lands to be parcelled up amongst the English and the Scots as your king and his deputies saw fit, and Deirdre and I were left to be brought up by our grandparents, to inherit our grandfather's wealth and our grandmother's dreams.'

'I think my mother was saddened that she had not known her brother better.'

Sean sighed. 'It was not our grandmother's way. She insisted that Phelim be brought up in the Irish fashion, fostered with her O'Neill kindred in Tyrone. Our grandfather was much against it, I have been told, but in the end he gave in to her, as he always has done. Our grandmother fell in love with an Englishman and she never forgave him for it.'

'But our grandfather's family have been settled in Ireland for many generations, have they not?' I said.

'Yes,' said Sean. 'And they have our Irish tongue and can ape our Irish ways when it suits them, and they have not, thank God, embraced the Protestant heresy that has infected these shores.' Here he crossed himself and it sent a shiver to my soul to see my own image do so. 'But for all that,' he continued, 'they are still the English, no more accepted by my grand-mother and her like than she was accepted by them. She married for love, the one weakness, the one mistake of her life. To our grandfather's wealthy family in Dublin, a marriage alliance with the O'Neills was potentially useful for business in the North, where Maeve's family held sway, but in other ways it was beyond their powers of acceptance and they never did accept her. As for Maeve's family, the O'Neills were well used to accommodations with the English for their own benefit, but for her to marry into a trading family was almost beyond disgrace. She soon gave up trying to find favour with her husband's family and instead set herself to salvaging some with her own.'

'And did she succeed?' I asked, becoming interested, in spite of myself, in this woman who had been little more than a shadow in my life.

'Oh yes, she did. And the fact that her son Phelim rose with the Earl of Tyrone against the English, and then went in to exile with him on the continent, has given her much honour with the native Irish of our land, but it is an empty honour.'

'An empty honour? What do you mean?'

Sean's face became grave. 'Because the Irish have no honour in Ireland any more. Tyrone's rising was the last hope for our people – for our language, our laws, our customs. Perhaps even our religion. The lands the earls left are being settled now by the English and the Scots. The native Irish are being pushed to the margins – untrusted and yet needed still for their labour. Those who had honour amongst their people must now till their scraps of land like beasts, and pay the English Crown for the privilege.'

'I am sorry for that,' I said, 'but what has it to do with me?'

Sean got up and walked over to my bookshelves. He picked up an edition of Horace and leafed through it a few moments before putting it back on the shelf and turning to me. 'Nothing, cousin, it has nothing to do with you. With your books and your pen and ink, and your drab Presbyterian garments in your cold northern town. Your mother went far to ensure that your life should be free of such concerns, and had it not been for the happenings of Deirdre's wedding, I think she would have succeeded.'

And here, I saw from his face and from the increased tension of Eachan by the door, we had come to the point.

'Tell me about Deirdre's wedding,' I said.

Sean stretched out his feet towards the fire which had also, I only now noticed, been lit. I wondered how long they had been here waiting for me, whilst I, unknowing, had whiled away the evening with William. I saw, hanging where my own cloak would normally have done, another mantle of the sort his servant wore, but of much finer stuff and trimmed with fur. Over the back of the chair, a jacket of a soft, dark brown leather, quilted and stitched with gilded thread, had been hung. My cousin was evidently a man of wealth. He said something to Eachan and then asked me if I kept glasses in my room.

'The life of a college regent is not that of an Irish gentleman,' I said; 'but I do have beakers.' I took down the two pewter beakers I kept with my own plate and knife on a shelf, and the unspeaking servant poured into them some amber liquid from a flask he had hidden somewhere in the folds of his clothes. 'Are you having none yourself?' I asked, as he stoppered the flask. He answered me in words I did not understand and returned to his place by the door.

Sean smiled. 'Eachan could drink us both under the table and through the floor, if he had a mind to. But of late, he has not been of a mind to. He prefers to keep his wits about him. Do not be fooled by his sullen looks – he has wits enough for both of us, and at times has needed them.' He downed the liquid in the beaker and formed a resolution. 'Deirdre's wedding. Where do I begin? You will think me biased in her favour, but I assure you I am not. My sister would have been a prize for any man in Ulster, and many sought her hand, but two months ago she turned her back on everything she had been brought up to, taught to value, and had herself married to the son of a wealthy London planter at Coleraine, on the north coast of our province. Her new husband's father is a builder, a master mason, and in great credit with the English author-ities there, for that he has built many of their properties and walled their town of Londonderry for them.'

'Then our grandmother must have been well pleased at the match,' I said.

'Pleased?' he said, incredulous. 'Maeve was about as pleased as you would be by a visit from the Holy Father, I suspect.

No. She was not pleased. She was almost unrestrained in her fury that her granddaughter had chosen the same path in marriage as your mother and indeed she herself had done.'

'What do you mean?'

Sean regarded me for a moment. 'She taught you so little then, that you do not understand even that?' He held out his beaker without even looking at the servant, who again silently filled it. He drank a little, then spoke again. 'My sister married outside the blood of the Irish, the Pure Irish. She married an Englishman, a newly settled planter, worse still than your mother having left Ulster to marry a Scot, and worse than our grandmother's crime in having married into the Old English.'

'And our grandmother could not prevent it?'

He shook his head. 'For the one and only occasion in my lifetime, our grandfather overruled her. He said he would not lose Deirdre as he had Grainne, he would not demand that they sacrifice their love to her pride. There were such storms in the whole of Carrickfergus over it that I was surprised to see ships still put to sea. But in the end there was something, I think, that may have made her come to believe it was in her interests to let the match go ahead in any case.'

'What was it?'

He shook his head. 'I cannot be sure . . . Anyway, it does not matter; that is a tale for another time.'

I looked at the candle, which had spluttered low in the sconce. I took another from the shelf and lit it, for it was clear that Sean's tale was not over. He told me then of my cousin Deirdre's wedding, of the English solemnity of the service and the imagined propriety of the celebrations afterwards.

'It was not to my taste, cousin, I'll tell you that. Such long faces and at so cheerless a feast I have rarely seen. The Blackstones could scarcely content themselves between showing their shame at their son's marriage to a common Irishwoman as they see her – for these people understand nothing of lineage – and their fear of opening their purses for the sake of it. Had I not taken precautions on my journey north to the "festivities" I would surely have died of thirst. My grandmother was in a triumph at the utter Protestant misery of it.'

'And what of Deirdre?' I asked, feeling something already, some care and kinship for this girl I had never seen, nor known existed until less than half an hour ago.

'Deirdre sat still and determined throughout it all. She held herself with such a grace – it is something that the women of her husband's family could never muster. I fear this marriage will bring her much grief.'

'But if her husband loves her?'

'Her husband? Perhaps, who can tell? He has little enough to him. I do not know why she married him – I had thought her eyes were turned elsewhere. Perhaps it was to spite our grandmother.' He mused a moment on this and then brought himself back to the point. 'Anyhow, the dreary feast eventually approached its end and it was time for the one thing they had not been able to prevent: the poet's blessing. Now, Alexander, I know that this is not a land of poets, but ours is, or was. I am not talking here of men who compose pretty sonnets.'

'I know that.' My mother had spoken often of the poets, learned men who spent years in their training and were greatly honoured. Like the castes of genealogists, doctors, lawmen, their knowledge passed down their families for generations in the service and under the patronage of the powerful. Their word could legitimise, glorify a leader and his line or cast his name for ever into the ashes.

'This man's name is Finn O'Rahilly, the last of a long line of poets who served the O'Dohertys of Inishowen. He claims to remember our parents, your mother and my father, but he can have been little more than a scrap of a thing in the days when they travelled in those parts. He was still hardly more than a child when Sir Cahir O'Doherty's rebellion was crushed, but he found refuge in Donegal and had some schooling amongst the last of the poets there. Finn O'Rahilly lives in the hills above the north coast, making some sort of living as a hireling poet for those who would keep to the old customs. My grandmother sought him out herself, and hired him to declaim at Deirdre's wedding, much against my sister's own wishes and those of the Blackstones.' He paused, remembering. 'And such a declamation was never heard at any wedding in my lifetime.'

'What do you mean?'

'He gave no blessing, but a curse. He damned Maeve for her own marriage outside the blood of the pure Irish, and your mother and my sister for theirs; he taunted her with the loss of her children; he told her our grandfather would soon be dead, and myself also, and that Deirdre's marriage would be barren. There would be no great rising of the O'Neills from the line of our grandmother, for her line would end before her own eyes. He . . .'

'Stop!' I said. 'You begin to lose me. What "great rising" are you talking of?'

He looked at his servant, who shrugged his shoulders, and then he looked at me.

'You know that the land of Ireland is under the control of the English Crown?'

'I know,' I said, 'that the king has striven to bring peace and civility to that . . .'

But this time it was he who stopped me, waving his hand as if to dismiss an importunate dog. 'Spare me that, for the love of all that's holy. To be preached civility by brutes without culture, with no notion of hospitality and with the manners of the sty, is too much in my homeland. I will not hear it in the mouth of my own cousin.'

'I only meant . . .'

'What? You have no notion of the slaughters and barbarity perpetrated on our people in the name of civility. The burning of crops, the starvation, the massacres of women and children that sent men half-mad with grief.' He turned away as if he did not trust himself to master his passions.

'I am sorry,' I said. 'Go on.'

He took a moment to compose himself. 'The tale I have to tell you is one that requires subtlety, but I have little of that. Hear me out, and I shall tell you in fewer words and less time than is needful, for time is short tonight.'

I nodded my acquiescence and he continued. 'The last of Ireland to submit to the English was Ulster. The Old English – our grandfather's race – have held the garrison at Carrickfergus for centuries past, and there are many Scots and some English settled in Antrim and Down, but as to the rest, it was, until twenty years ago, the preserve of the Gaelic Irish, much of it under the control of the O'Neills, our grandmother's family.'

'Yes, my mother told me something of that.' In truth, my mother had told me very little of her heritage and even less of my grandmother, despite all that my youthful curiosity would have had from her. In time I had learned not to ask her about that other family, and to keep my thoughts of them to myself.

'While the rest of Ireland fell under the heel of the English, Hugh O'Neill, Earl of Tyrone, stood out against them. For nine years he rallied others to his cause, and fought in the name of Gaelic Ireland and Holy Mother Church. After nine years of warfare that brought Ulster to its knees, they submitted at last to the English Crown, and all might have been well enough, but then they had some intelligence of conspiracy against them, and fled for the continent, in the hope of rallying support. They never saw Ireland again, and their lands and the lands of all their kindred were claimed in escheat by the king, and parcelled out amongst English planters, old soldiers, Scotsmen – Protestants all. Such is the breed that my sister has married into. They work daily at the degradation of the people, the native Irish, reduced to the worst land, our laws and customs disregarded and our religion trampled upon. In truth, Tyrone himself is much to blame, for he traded the rights of the kindred to increase his own, and now they have been abandoned. Anyway,' he said, as if he had been wandering from the subject, 'our grandmother will hear nothing against Tyrone, and has spent every hour of her life since the day my father fled with him in praying that the O'Neills will rise once more and drive the English from Ireland. And at my sister's wedding, the poet cursed her, and Deirdre, and myself, before all the company, and told her that her dreams could never be.'

He finished his drink and relaxed himself, as if the telling of his tale was done.

I got up and poured some water from the pitcher by the window into the basin below. A struggle was rising within me, for these were not the dreams I had planned to dream tonight, although often enough they had filled the lonely nights of my childhood. For the sake of kinship and hospitality alone, I could not dismiss my cousin now, and besides, I could see there was something yet in his tale to be told. But despite the better self that counselled tolerance, the bitterness of years got the better of me. 'And it is for this that you have crossed the Irish Sea? To tell me of the demented ramblings of a mercenary poet and the deluded dreams of a bitter and superstitious old woman? What does she want me to do that you cannot? Should I go to him and declaim to him in Latin that he is wrong? Proclaim to him in Greek the honour of the O'Neills – of which I know little and care less, let me tell you? No, cousin, you have had a wasted journey.'

He took a step towards me and I registered Eachan's hand going to the dagger at his belt. 'You care nothing for your mother's people?'

'They cared nothing for her. She died to them the moment she set sail with my father. And what do you think she found here? Poets ready to sing her praises and her beauty? Followers to do her bidding? A cold place and a cold welcome she found, and it never thawed. She died dreaming of a homeland that had long forgotten her. Do not play my mother's people on me. I have had long to reflect on my mother's people.'

Sean reached out to my arm. 'But I told you, our grandfather . . .'

'Our grandfather is a man, is he not? You say he grieved for his daughter? Why did he not come and find her, bring her home? You cannot lay everything at our grandmother's door.'

My words shocked even myself. I had not known there was such bitterness in me. Sean let his hand drop and shook his head slowly. 'How little you understand. I had been foolish, perhaps, to believe that Maeve's reputation would have reached even to here, but no, you do not know her.'

'I do not know her,' I said, 'and I am astonished to find that she knew if I lived or died.'

'Oh, she knew of you, all right,' said Sean. 'Of your birth, at least. But she told not one other living soul of your existence, not even our grandfather. Until five weeks ago, I never knew I had a cousin. Our land was in the midst of war when your mother left her family – a long war that all but destroyed Ulster and her people. Men, women and children starved to death on the roads, disease was rife and slaughter everywhere. Three weeks after your mother left Carrickfergus, Maeve told our grandfather his daughter was dead, drowned in a shipwreck off the western coast of Scotland. That is the manner of woman I am telling you of, and the man whose heart has been broken thirty years. He does not know yet that she lived, or that he has another grandson.'

As his words fell in the silence of the room, I felt a wave of desolation surge through me, a desolation for my mother and what might have been and for an old and disappointed man I had never met. Finally I was able to look up at my cousin.

'So this is the truth of the woman I dreamed of as a child, when other boys had a grandmother's love. A woman who could deny her daughter, torment her husband and deceive her whole family. A woman who gives credence to the rambling of half-wild poets. Her cruelty is matched only by her madness, I think, and yours in being of her embassy.'

He paced the room and turned to face me. 'No, Alexander, I am not mad, and no more is she. It is not madness for one brought up as she was to believe in the word of the poets. To Maeve, it would be madness to ignore the terrible doom that has been pronounced upon her.'

'It is godless superstition to believe in it,' I said.

My cousin's face was still and his voice deadly serious. 'We are not a godless people and we look with horror upon your abandonment of the faith. That our grandmother is superstitious I will grant you, but I am not. I would have paid O'Rahilly's malediction little heed, other than as a curiosity, were it not that some of what he foretold has begun to come true.'

The fellow at the door seemed to straighten his stance, seemed to stare ahead with even more determination.

A horrible dread filled me. 'What has happened? Is our grandfather dead?' I was gripped by a sudden fear at the prospect of the loss of a man who had been lost to me long ago.

'No,' said Sean, 'but he is gravely ill. He is an old man who has seen near enough eighty summers. It would take no great seer's gift to tell that he had not many years left on this earth.' His words failed him a moment, and he looked away to some point in the distance that only he could see. He breathed deep and went on. 'And yet he was strong, you know, strong.' He flashed a sudden smile. 'You and I, we get our eyes, our dark hair from our grandmother's people, but our height and our strength, it is all his. Aye, he was strong, and he has seldom laid any store by the myths and legends, the beliefs of our grandmother and the words of the poets. But he loves Maeve yet, you know. He has told me that for all her difficult ways, all her angers and her dreams, he loves her as much now as he did the day he first saw her. To see her cursed because of him, to be reminded of the loss so long ago of his son and daughter and to have his hopes for Deirdre's happiness dashed, were too much for him, I think. We will see him in his grave before many more dawns have broken.' At this Eachan murmured something and crossed himself. To see it done did not trouble me now as it had done before.

I looked at Sean. 'You have more to tell me, I think.'

'Yes,' he said wearily, 'there is more. Three weeks after Deirdre's wedding, somebody tried to murder me.' He looked up and smiled, but the word had chilled me. I knew something of murder and of the chaos and the tragedies it could bring with it. 'Now, do not mistake me, cousin. An attempt is made on my life nigh on every day of the week. Indeed, your fellow townsmen would have had me dispatched three times last night at least, were it not for Eachan here. Is that not right, Eachan?'

The man gave an uninterested grunt in response and continued to gaze over my head at some space beyond the flickering candle on the wall.

Sean laughed. 'Eachan has little patience and less sympathy for me in my nightly scrapes in taverns and their courtyards. He has had to pull me from them too often.'

'I had heard something of your adventures last night,' I said. 'But you were talking to me of murder.'

'Pray God it will not come to that. But this attempt on my life was something different from what I have experienced before. It was not in some brawl over a woman, or for a gambling debt. It came in the dark and silence of the night, many miles from any witness or help. I was riding home alone, down the coast between Ballycastle and Cushendall. I had been visiting – friends. Dusk was coming on fast as I rounded Tor Head and I was thinking of pulling up somewhere for the night. The cliffs are treacherous; they are not to be negotiated in darkness. For some time I had had a sensation that I was not alone – but it is not unusual in such places to feel that way. All the reason a man might command begins to fracture in the face of what he knows of the darkness, of the spirits of the world beyond our control.'

My feelings must have registered in my face. 'Do not scorn me for a fool, cousin,' he said. 'These forces may have retreated from this your land in the face of your ministers and the narrowness of your minds, but they have a home yet in ours, and they are not ready to be vanquished.'

'I think you delude yourself,' I said.

'Then may you always think so,' he said, before continuing. 'Just as I was turning off the bridle path to make for a steading I know of some way inland, a musket shot rang through the dusk. The shot missed me, though not by much. And it startled my horse. I had the Devil's own job to keep the beast from careering over the cliff's edge and breaking both our necks. By the time I had mastered and calmed him, there was no sign of musket nor marksman, no sign of life other than the screeching of the startled gulls and the scattering of the creatures of the night.'

'Where had the shot come from?'

He laughed, a laugh with little humour in it. 'I cannot say for certain, but I thought, and you will not understand the irony in this, for the present at least, but I thought it came from the burial place of Shane O'Neill – a great rebel and hero of our people. I did not tarry long to search. I am no coward, but a sword avails little against a musket ball out of the dark. I turned the beast's head and we rode for our lives. At length we came to a road that led us back out to the coast at Cushendun. I spent the night in a hidden chamber beneath the church of Layd, near the cliffs above the bay. No one troubled me in the night, and in the morning I found my horse still tethered and unharmed where I had left it. I think my precautions may have been unnecessary.'

The Irishman at the door said something in a low voice, as if to himself. His words did not escape his master. Sean uttered something, laughing, to him and turned to me. 'Eachan does not agree with me. He thinks me a danger to be let out on my own, and it took little effort on his part to persuade our grandmother of the same. Much to the chagrin of many a maiden, I have not spent a night without him since.'

My cousin sought to make light of the situation, but I

thought I could judge enough of him already to know that he was not a man easily frightened. That he was here, many hundreds of miles from his home, and with his guard dog at his back, bespoke how seriously those around him took the threat.

'And what explanation do you have for all this?' I asked.

'Very little, and that not poetical. Not that our family has been cursed for the honour of Ireland, that is for sure. Someone wishes very real harm to our family, and there is only me to protect them. I do not like being so far away from them at this time of trouble.' He took a deep breath and looked directly at me. 'Maeve sent me here because you are the only one of her line, of our blood, not encompassed by the curse of Finn O'Rahilly. He pronounced a special fate for each of us in his prediction of the end of the O'Neills, but you he did not mention. Alexander Seaton, the son of Grainne FitzGarrett and grandson of Maeve O'Neill – he does not know of your existence. She believes that only you can break the curse, that the very fact of your being saves her line.'

'Then she must tell him so,' I said flatly, for I was tired and I had little desire to hear more of this woman's wishes.

'Alexander,' he said gently, 'the woman has spent the last thirty years telling people her daughter died before ever she reached Scotland. Who would believe her now were she to say no, Grainne lived, bore a healthy son? No one. No one.' He waited a moment, for me to understand. Through the darkness, the bell of St Nicholas kirk tolled the advancing night. 'I am here to take you back to Ulster, to the land of your forefathers, to save the name of your mother's people and the mind of your grandmother, and to ease the passing of an old man with a broken heart. You cannot deny them, Alexander, you cannot deny your blood.'

I got up from the bed and turning away from him, went to the window and looked out on to the night sky. The stars shone as bright then as they had done an hour ago, but something in the world beneath them had changed. The lack, the emptiness I had felt my whole life was calling to me, and I wanted to deny it. I turned back to face him. 'I have had to make my own way, without my family's blood. I am not so callous that I care nothing for their troubles, but my life is turning now, and in a direction I have long prayed it might take. God has shown me His grace, and I cannot flout it to calm an old woman's superstitious mind.'

Sean eyed me levelly. 'I do not ask you to, cousin. I ask you as a man to help me protect our family against a very real, human agency that means it harm. Whoever paid the poet to lay this curse aims to fray our grandmother's mind, my sister's too, perhaps, and to remove me altogether. That attempt at my murder failed once – it may not do so a second time. Our grandfather is old and ill; I have Eachan and a few other good men that I trust, but of family there is none, none but you and I. We have lost a day already – there is a boat making for Leith and I must be on it. I had thought to have another day to persuade you, but the captain tells me the weather is to turn, and that we must leave on tonight's tide. We have less than an hour, for he goes whether we are aboard or no. I can tarry here no longer. I ask you again, Alexander, will you come?'

THREE

A House of Tapestries

There was little to be heard save the sound of the oars and the soft lapping of the water against the sides of our boat as we made slowly towards the shore a little to the north of Carrickfergus. It was a frosty night, the sky not quite black but a dark blue. The meagre light of the new moon, assisted by its retinue of stars, gave us all the guidance that was needed to complete the last few miles of our long journey. Eachan read the constellations like a man born to the sea, and besides, he knew the coastline between here and Olderfleet, where our ship from Scotland had landed, so well that he had little need even for recourse to the sky to steer him.

From across the boat, Sean watched me. 'Well, Alexander, are you ready?'

For a moment I could think of no answer. Within a few hours of our ship docking at Leith, almost all I knew with any sense of familiarity had been behind me. We had pushed relentlessly onward, to the south and west, giving little respite to the hired horses Sean had left stabled in Edinburgh. It was then that I first witnessed for myself the remarkable endurance of the Irish of physical hardship, an endurance the sheltered life of the philosopher had never required of me. The endless cold and rain and the harshness of the terrain as we pressed further into Galloway had little impact on my companions, who slept on open ground, amongst moss and fern, with an ease that only sheer exhaustion allowed to me. And with every mile we travelled I had felt more of an alien in a strange land. There had come a point at which I'd realised that the Scots tongue was no longer spoken around us, in the inns, the farmsteads and the hovels we stopped at for water, food, and, very occasionally, rest. All about me spoke in the same Gaelic tongue now familiar to my ears in the voices of Sean and Eachan. King James had gone far to bring this part of his Scottish kingdom under his heel, but his son would have to go further still, I thought, for there was greater kinship and nationhood between my cousin and his servant and the people we met on our journey than there was between those same people and me.

When at last we had crossed Scotland, from one coast to the other, I no longer had any feeling that I was still in my own country. And what greeted us on that southwest seaboard were not the dramatic cliffs, the crashing oceans I had imagined, but a gentle shore and a calm sea, beyond which, only a few miles away, past the great rock of the Ailsa Craig, I could just discern the recumbent form of my mother's homeland: Ireland.

We left the horses at Ballantrae, at the inn from which Sean had hired them, and although we had ridden for the best parts of two nights, he would allow little rest before we were on the move again, boarding the boat which would take us to the home I had never seen. It was a fair crossing, and we had reached Olderfleet, in Larne, shortly after dusk. The same purse, Sean assured me, that had oiled our way past the customs there would see us safely through the gates of Carrickfergus. We had passed the cliffs and the daunting promontories of Whitehead and made our way down the side of Belfast Lough towards the old English garrison town and the castle that had guarded it for four hundred years. Nothing of what Sean had told me of the country I was now about to set my foot on, of its history and its present situation, had prepared me for this sight; nothing of what Eachan had told me, of the myths and legends of his people, had done anything to ease my apprehension of what I might now encounter.

We were now at the walls of the town itself; they stretched away in the darkness to the Norman mass of the castle, not hewn, grown almost from the rock as our sea fortresses were, but set imperiously upon it, not overlooking the sea but jutting aggressively into it. Above the castle walls towered the keep – grim, square, unyielding. For so many years the only foothold of the English beyond the Pale in the North, and now presiding, as my cousin had told me, over a different kind of occupation of his homeland.

Summoning a reply in the Irish tongue they had earnestly been teaching me since we had boarded ship in Aberdeen, a lifetime ago now, I said,

'I am ready.'

Eachan brought the row boat to a halt at a gate in the town wall and hailed the watchman, who had evidently been sleeping. They exchanged a few words in Eachan's peculiar English, coins were transferred, and then an Irish voice was heard. A moment later the gate swung open and a small, stocky fellow descended the stone steps towards the boat. He nodded to my cousin's servant and inclined his head more deferentially to Sean, but studiously averted his gaze from me. He steadied the boat as we three disembarked with what little baggage we had, and then took it to tie up at the shore as we went up the steps and through the wall, past the watchman, who kept his back turned to us, and into the town of Carrickfergus itself.

Within the walls it was even darker than it had been outside them, and I would surely have stumbled or lost my way had

I not kept my hand on my cousin's shoulder until my eyes became accustomed to the greater darkness and my feet to the feel of solid ground beneath them once more. Despite the darkness though, the smell of beasts, waste, trade and humanity that now assailed me told me I was once again in a town. We weaved at first in between some curious and noxious forms raised from the ground to a height not much greater than my own; only later would I discover that these windowless mounds of clay and thatch were the habitations not of pigs but of people. A few yards beyond these miserable dwellings loomed much larger, more solid shapes, but we did not turn our steps towards them, instead keeping amongst the hovels and within easy reach of the sea wall. There had been no speech between the three of us after we had left the boat, and I understood that there would be none until we had reached safe to our destination. We followed the line of the walls southwestwards until suddenly Sean broke off to the right and headed in towards what I took to be the centre of the town. Within moments we had scaled a wall and traversed a garden, and were standing at a broad oak door to a tower at least four storeys in height, and Eachan was growling something in a low voice to an unseen person at the other side of the door. A key was turned and several bolts pulled and then the door stood open. Eachan took a step inside and, having seen to it that the doorman had found other duties to attend to, pulled me swiftly in after him. Behind me, Sean pulled the door to and locked it again. He turned to face me.

'Well, Alexander; I have brought you home.'

We were standing in darkness in what appeared to be a large vaulted storeroom.

'There is no time,' said Eachan, before I had any chance to speak or even to begin to look properly about me.

Sean nodded curtly and spoke to me again. 'Come on, follow me.'

And so I did, up a narrow, winding flight of stone steps, past the door to the floor above, which I surmised from the lingering smells to house the kitchens, and upwards to the second floor. Emerging from the dim light of the turret stairway through a door on the second landing, my eyes smarted as they were greeted by a blaze of light. We had come into a hall, almost square, overlooked on three sides by a wooden gallery. Above the gallery, arching from stone corbels, oak beams supported a high vaulted ceiling. In the sconces by each of the long, narrow slit window embrasures burned huge candles, and a large fire roared in the open hearth at the far end of the room. The stone walls were hung with no paintings, but fine tapestries depicting battles, feasts, trysts, strange creatures, great beauties and heroes. The legends, the tales I had been brought up with by my mother, those same tales with which Eachan had beguiled the long night hours of our journey, rendered here in fabulous colour. And waiting for us in the centre of the room, as if she had emerged from one of the scenes hung on the wall, was the woman I knew must be my grandmother.

I had thought I was prepared to see her, to meet with her. On the days and nights of our journey from the northeastern corner of Scotland to this coast of Ireland I had schooled myself as to how I would carry myself, what I would say, but all that deserted me now: what I was looking at, had she lived beyond the age of thirty-eight, was an image of my mother. Maeve O'Neill must have been almost seventy years old, but there was no stoop, no concession to age in her manner of holding herself. She was dressed in what I thought must be the fashion of another age – a linen shift with long, wide sleeves, covered by a tunic of red velvet, and belted with a girdle of gold. She wore a headdress of many folds of white linen, and her thin neck and bony wrists were bedecked in more chains of gold and beads of coloured glass than I thought seemly. But for all the strange clothing, the extra thirty years of life she had lived that had been denied her daughter, there could be no doubting that this was my grandmother. My throat was dry and I did not trust my tongue to move in my mouth.

Sean did not go to her, but addressed her from where we stood. 'And so, Maeve, I have done what you asked of me. I have brought Grainne's son to you. And now I must go to my grandfather.'

He made for the gallery steps but Maeve's voice stopped him. 'Sean! Stay a moment. There are things we must talk of first.' There was nothing pleading or wheedling in her voice: it was a simple order from one who was accustomed to give them.

'All that can wait. I must go to him.' He had his foot on the stairs and had not even turned to look at her.

'Sean,' she said, more insistent this time. 'Your grandfather does not know.'

He stopped where he was and turned slowly to look at her. 'He does not know?' The colour was draining from his face. 'Do not tell me I have travelled all these weeks, these hundreds of miles, dragged my cousin in the night practically from his own bed, and he does not know?'

'Come and sit,' she said. 'Eat something.'

'Eat?' he asked, incredulous. 'Woman, do I understand you right? That you have not yet told him, even now, that he has another grandson, that his daughter lived?'

Her eyes were hard. 'Do not think to judge me,' she said. 'I will not be judged. To have told your grandfather before you returned, before I could know that you were not both lying dead on the sea bed, would have been to kill him. And besides, the priest is with him. Sit and eat, calm yourself. And then you will come with me, and we will tell him.'

Sean's anger did not subside, but he did not argue with her further, and did as he was bid. She put her hand to his face a moment. 'You have been away from us too long.'

'Where is Deirdre?' he asked.

She let her hand drop. 'She is where she has chosen to be. Kept like an English housewife in some hovel in Coleraine.'

I could see by the widening of his nostrils that he was struggling to keep his temper. 'And have you even told her?'

'She will be told, when the time comes.'

'She should have been here,' he said, slamming down his hand.

My grandmother's face became as fixed as granite. 'Time enough when he has gone: she would bring him no comfort, and I will not have her husband's people under my roof a moment longer than I must.'

And now, at last, she spoke to me. Her eyes, like green stone, had hardly left my face since we had entered the room. 'Alexander Seaton.' She nodded slowly. 'This is why Grainne left; this is what was meant to be.'

'I do not understand you.'

She held out her hand towards me, beckoning. I walked towards her. She was not tall, but something in her presence gave an impression of stature. Beneath the white linen head-dress some wisps of hair were visible at the sides and at her forehead – a dark slate-grey, no longer black, but far from the white of most women of her years.

I came to a halt two paces from her – there was no inti-mation that I should approach any closer than that. She searched my face. Her mouth smiled though her eyes did not. 'You are no Scot. Your mother ran as far as she could from her own people, but she could never have got far enough. She carried them in every part of her being and she gave birth to them in you. It was meant to be.'

I looked to Sean for some explanation but he, ill at ease, said nothing.

'Are you saying Andrew Seaton was not my father?'

She shook her head impatiently. 'Andrew Seaton was the name of the man she abandoned her home and name for, and he was your father, no doubt, for she fancied herself in love, for a time, as I had warned her it would be. But I should not have been angry with her, for she could no more help her leaving than I could prevent it. I should have seen it. It was meant to be that she left this place and gave birth to a son far away from here where he would not be known, that you might return one day to break your family's curse.'

It was clear she was in earnest, and I knew I could not listen to this from her. 'It is as well that you understand now, Grandmother' – for I did not know how else to address her – 'that I have no belief in your superstitions. I am here because my cousin asked me to help him in whatever danger threatens him and this family. I have come for the sake of my mother's love for this place and people, but this is not what I was born to, and when I have done what I have to do, I will return to my own country and people, for they are not here.'

Her only response was in her eyes, whose contempt said I would do whatever she required of me, and that whatever I thought I had been born to was no concern of hers, or mine.

Eventually she said, 'You sit and eat also. Sean, I will take you now to your grandfather.' My cousin got up, draining his glass in one. 'And then we must talk, for Roisin's father has become anxious, and the girl herself is getting restless.'

Sean glanced at me. 'Another time, Grandmother. Another time.' He followed her up the wooden stairway to the gallery above, there to disappear from view.

Although I had not eaten for many hours, my appetite had gone completely, and the wine, fine though it no doubt was, tasted sour in my mouth. I put my glass down and looked around me. The furnishing in the room was solid work, of good quality, not shabby but well worn. Chairs, tables, cabinets, settles, had all been here a long time. But how long? Had they been here thirty years? Had my mother known them? I could not tell. But the hangings on the walls, those had been there more than one lifetime, I was sure of it. I looked more closely and saw what I knew my mother must have seen as a young girl, standing where I now stood, and again in her mind's eye many years later as she told those stories to me. As I looked on them I began to recall the tales again, of Lugh and Balor, of Niamh and Oisin and of Cuchulainn. Images of feastings, battles, shape-changing heroes and tragic lovers were in my mind and before my eyes. It might have been a matter of minutes, or it might have been an hour, before Sean's voice interrupted my reverie.

'Alexander, will you come now?'

He stood behind the carved wooden balustrade and waited for me. As I drew nearer it seemed to me that his face had aged ten years. Beneath his eyes were shadows that had not been there before, and his mouth was drawn tight in an effort to keep his composure.

'Is he still living?'

He nodded, once. 'But it cannot be long now. I think he will be gone before morning. Come.' I followed him to a small arched doorway set back in one corner.

The room we passed into was very dimly lit. Despite the

early frost that had taken hold outside, it was almost over-whelmingly warm, like a place that had known no true air or light for days. Maeve was there, and in a corner, only just illuminated by the meagre light, was a dark-hooded figure, mumbling in Latin as a set of beads moved though his hands. I did not care. My only interest was in the figure lying propped against the pillows in the centre of the heavily canopied bed. That he was very ill was clear even from where I stood, but so too was a light in his eyes that could not be mistaken, a light I had last seen ten years ago, before my mother had left this world. Maeve started to speak but I ignored her and went to him.

'Grandfather,' I said.

He reached out a hand and I took it in mine. Two hands, the fingers the same length, the same shape, but separated by fifty years of time and life. What would I have given to have had the hand of my four-year-old self in the firm grip of that man in his prime? To have been embraced by those arms when they were still strong, to have known him a lifetime?

By some great effort he spoke. I bent closer. 'Alexander. My Grainne's child. My boy, my boy. That I lived to see this day.' He gripped my hand more tightly but the effort of speech was too much and he sank back into the pillows, exhausted. Maeve left the room, but the mumbling priest did not, and I understood that he would remain until my grandfather passed from this world into the next. Sean came over to the bed and sat down on the other side. He gently stroked the old man's forehead and took his other hand in his. Our grandfather smiled one last time and closed his eyes, to begin a sleep from which we two who were with him knew he would not wake. I would have waited until he made that final crossing, but I did not, for I had not been that four-year-old boy, that strapping youth, that young man sharing hopes; I leaned over and kissed his forehead and then got up and left, leaving him with the one who had.

I was taken by Eachan to the top of the house, up a narrow, almost hidden set of steps from the balcony, to a kind of attic behind the vaulted ceiling. We passed from the top of the steps through a walkway, jutting out from the parapets and open to the elements – the machicolation – from which overhang any enemy approaching to the tower house could be watched in safety and, if necessary, dealt with. I was hurried along the walkway to a small door in the other corner of the parapet. Eachan knocked on the door and spoke in a low voice to the person on the other side.

The man who opened the door was older than me, older than Sean too, thirty-five, perhaps. His straight blond hair came halfway down his neck. He glanced at me only for a moment, green eyes in a strong-boned face assessing me before he turned to Eachan and said, 'By God: he is like Sean after all.'

Eachan said nothing, merely nodding before he left us alone in the tiny chamber. There were two beds in it, and some plain furnishings – a chest, a stool and small table with a chessboard on it, wooden candlesticks with cheap-smelling tallow candles – but after the travels and discomforts of the nights on my journey from Aberdeen, its cleanliness and simplicity were things of luxury to me.

The other indicated one of the beds. 'You can sleep there. I will not disturb you, but if you want anything, food, drink, the latrine – you are to ask only me. You are not to wander the house yourself.'

'Am I a prisoner?'

He seemed to consider a moment. 'No, but aside from your

grandparents, Sean, Eachan and myself, no one knows that you are here, or even of your existence. The mistress would have it kept that way.'

He turned his back, our conversation over. I didn't even know his name. He carried himself with some authority, and I wondered if he was Deirdre's husband.

'Who are you? What is your place in this household?'

'My name is Andrew Boyd. My father was your grandfather's steward. I work in your grandfather's merchant business and travel for him throughout the province. I have the status of a servant in this house.'

He did not have the bearing of a servant, or of one who would remain a servant long.

'I am Alexander Seaton,' I said. 'But you will know that already.'

He looked up from taking off his boots and shook his head, the trace of a smile for the first time showing on his lips. 'Until an hour ago, I knew nothing of your existence. In the last hour I have learned that my master's dead daughter did not drown within days of leaving her home, but went to Scotland and there bore a son, who was the living image of Sean, and of his father Phelim before him, an O'Neill to the marrow of his bones. I have learned that Sean was not away in the south, on what we are constrained to call "his business", but in the far reaches of Scotland, to fetch you here because your grandmother believes you can lift the poet's curse by which she and her kind set such store. You are to remain here until she is ready to present you.'

'You set no store by such curses then? You are not of my grandmother's kind?'

He stopped in his work. 'You don't know much about this place you have come to, do you?'

'Sean has told me much about this country and its different peoples, but I am not so well versed in it all that I can place someone on a moment's acquaintance.'

He sighed, as if tired already of my intrusion. 'I was born in Galloway, but my father brought us here in the Nineties, after the third harvest failure in a row. He found employment with the FitzGarretts. I was brought up not to masses and incense and bells, but to the word of God, given freely to all men. I have no time for curses and incantations and give no credence to them.' He turned back to his boots. 'But I would ask you one thing. And you may think it is a thing a servant has no place to ask of one whose family he serves, but there are some matters that go beyond worldly standing.'

'Whatever you think of the family my mother came from, I am a craftsman's son. My father earned his living by the work of his own hands, and after she left here to come to Scotland, my mother knew no servant but herself.'

'Oh?' He appraised me again. 'What I ask is this: that you would not set up your crucifix nor work at your beads when I am in this room.'

Before I could prevent myself, I laughed out loud. 'You think me a Papist? You are as like to find John Knox still living and playing at his beads as you are to see me set foot in a mass house. Have no fear, there will be no Latin mumbled here.'

He nodded, evidently satisfied, and with little interest in learning any more about me, lay down, fully clothed, and closed his eyes. I lay down also, exhausted, and thinking to make sense of how I had come to be where I was now, and of what I must be in the eyes of those I had come to and those I had left behind. The hastily scrawled notes I had left to Sarah, to William Cargill and to Principal Dun can have done little enough to explain my sudden night-time disappearance from

Aberdeen. Regardless of what words I had scribbled down, my abandonment of my friends and my responsibilities so soon after Sean's escapades could be seen only in one way: the grace-less dereliction of duty and friendship by a thankless man. I had never spoken to Sarah of the aching loss I had carried all my life for the world my mother had come from, and the certainty of her hurt and anger, Dr Dun's disappointment and the utter bewilderment of William Cargill kept me awake for some time, until at last fatigue overcame the restless wander-ings of my troubled mind.

At some hour of the night I was aware of the door being opened and Andrew being called quietly from his bed. I knew it meant my grandfather was dead. I huddled myself more deeply in the blankets and willed myself not to think of it until daylight. Eventually I slept again, trying to remember the feel of my grandfather's hand in mine. I may have dreamt, but any dreams I had were lost in the violence of my waking. It was still night, and I thought for a moment that I was still on my journey with Eachan and Sean, sleeping out with little shelter as we had done on more than one night, for I became gradually aware of water dropping on me, on my face and hands. I felt for my cloak, to pull it over my face, and as I did so, I realised someone was leaning over me; there was a pressure on my forehead, and as I struggled to consciousness, words in the Latin tongue snaked into my mind. Then the door of my room was thrown wide open and there was a flood of light. Someone shouted and the figure leaning over me was pushed away. I opened my eyes to see Andrew Boyd standing above me, his hand at the priest's throat. My grandmother was also in the room, pale and shaken, with her grey hair loose down her back.

'Leave him,' she said, although I could not tell at first if it was to Boyd or the priest that she spoke. The two men stood back from one another and regarded each other with unconcealed contempt.

I sat up, remembering now where I was. 'What is happening here?'

It was Andrew Boyd who spoke first. 'They were trying to claim you. They had their water and the priest was at you with his oils. They were baptising you into the Church of Rome.'

I looked to my grandmother in disbelief, waiting for a denial. None came. 'My husband is dead,' she said. 'God knows, I may follow him soon enough. Your mother was lost to us and damned herself when she abandoned her family and her faith to go with your father. I will not have her son, my grandson, lost in the same way.'

'And you think your holy water and bells and oils can overcome my faith? Come to my chamber every night with your unction and incantations: you will not change my soul.'

Maeve came closer to me, and her eyes were fearful. 'Child, I beg of you, let the Father do this. It will protect you against whatever dangers we face, and give you merit in the judgement to come.'

I took her old, veined and bony hand. It was frozen. 'You must understand,' I said. 'I give no credence to such merit, and neither does my God. Only my faith and not some token like this can save me. Only the life I live can show my faith, not these trinkets.'

If I had hoped to reach her, I failed. She let her hand slip from my grasp. 'Then you will go down the same path to Hell that your mother walked before you. Do not say I did not try to prevent it.' She left the room, taking the dark-hooded figure with her.

Andrew Boyd bolted the door behind them. He sat down on his bed, his head in his hands.

'Thank you,' I said.

He looked up, surprised, vulnerable for a moment, a man who had dropped his guard.

'I am not often given to fearfulness, but this has been a hard night. And this will be a different house with your grandfather gone. But you were right, none of their ceremonies could have imperilled you.'

'All the same, I am grateful.'

'Aye, well . . .' Not finding the words that suited him, he was silent.

As we both lay down again in the darkness, I thought of this strange new companion, and wondered what it was of him that he was so reluctant other men should see. There were many things about this house that I wanted to ask him, but they would keep for the daylight. We would each take what respite remained to us in the hours of the night.

Andrew went early to his duties and it was Sean who brought me my breakfast a little before dawn. He unlocked the door and came in bearing a tray of beer and warm bannocks. He sat down and let out a great sigh.

'You know our grandfather is dead?' he said. Even in saying the words, something in him seemed to crumple.

I put out a hand to him. 'I am sorry. So sorry.'

'He was the best thing in my life, Alexander. The one true thing.'

'I would like to have known him better.'

'And he you. You would never have had a greater friend than Richard FitzGarrett. He was everything a man, a grandfather, should have been, and more than that. He was a better father to me than my own.' Sean had been only ten years old when his father, Phelim, had left Ireland for exile with the earls, and had scarcely known him before that, for my uncle had always been in the train of the Earl of Tyrone, always on his business, in his wars. Had it not been for the troubles of the time, Sean would have been fostered out within the O'Neill kindred as Phelim had been before him, but he had been born in the middle of Tyrone's great rebellion, the Nine Years' War that had devastated the country and meant the end for many of her great Gaelic families. It had been judged safest for Sean to remain with his grandparents, at the very heart of the English administration at Carrickfergus.

'I was fortunate. Others were not so.'

'But you were only a child.'

'And do you think that would have mattered to them? The Flight of the Earls was so sudden, so rushed, so unplanned, that one of Tyrone's own sons was left behind. He was six years old. That boy rotted his life away a prisoner of the English. He died in the Tower of London at the age of twenty-one. It was my grandfather's name and his usefulness to the English that helped them gloss over the fact that I was Phelim O'Neill's son.' And so he had been brought up by Richard FitzGarrett and by Maeve, and had had, from birth as he told me, 'a foot in both camps'.

'And now our grandfather's duties fall to you.'

'What?' said Sean, startled out of some memory. 'Yes. Yes, that is what they tell me.'

'And are you ready for it?' The man I had come to know over the last few days and nights was not one I could see easily bound to a desk, tallying his accounts, or at the harbour checking grain and hides, negotiating with other merchants and traders or overseeing the distribution of stock. He was a man who would be happier on horseback, with a hawk on his arm, with men at his command whom he might lead, and with whom he might joke, sing, drink.

'I am as ready now as I will ever be, but that is saying little. Andrew Boyd will deal with all of that nature that needs to be dealt with. The tradesmen and merchants here and in other towns respect him. I will keep out of all that for a while.' He gave a wicked smile. 'The traders do not like me – I have been too much amongst their daughters, and I am a little too Irish for the tastes of the new settlers along the coast and in the North. Besides, Maeve has need of me. There is the funeral to arrange and there will be many people coming here over the next few days.' He regarded me uneasily. 'I am sorry Alexander; I wish you could stand by me as I welcome them to our house, but Maeve is determined that none shall know of you until she has brought you to Finn O'Rahilly and had the curse lifted. I have spent much of the night in trying to persuade her otherwise, but once she is set upon a thing there is none can shake her from it.'

'And what about Deirdre?' I said.

'Deirdre? Three letters from her arrived for me while I was away: each speaks of a greater degree of frustration and misery. She had thought to free herself from our grandmother, to become a woman of means and position in the new Ulster, rather than be a brood mare in Maeve's dynastic plans. Instead she finds herself incarcerated in a miserable tradesmen's house in Coleraine, with women of little conversation and less wit, expected to play the housewife and dutiful daughter-in-law. She who grew up hearing daily that she was of the blood of Irish princes now has that blood-line cast before her as if it were no better than that of a dog. I don't know how she stomachs it, but she will not give my grandmother the satisfaction of knowing it.'

'Does her husband do nothing?'

'Her husband has very little about him. I think – no, I know it: this Blackstone marriage has been the biggest mistake of her life. She might have waited here and run our grandfather's business, and married where her heart pleased her better, had she only had some patience.'

'And where does her heart please her better?' I asked.

He hesitated a moment. 'That . . . that I cannot say. But she does not love her husband, that I know, so she could scarcely have placed it worse. She wanted to come back from Coleraine when our grandfather's health worsened, but Maeve, fearing – as indeed she well might – that the Blackstones had nothing in mind but to wrest my dying grandfather's business from him, would not permit it.'

'Surely she will be allowed to come now?'

'Oh yes,' said Sean. 'Maeve is one for the proprieties. Deirdre has already been sent for, and her husband, too, on sufferance. The rest of the Blackstone crew have been politely informed that they need not trouble themselves with such a journey at this time of the year.'

I could not help but smile with him. In spite of her coldness, there was something almost admirable in my grandmother's monstrous pride, for I knew already that I did not like these Blackstone upstarts. 'And she will be told of me then?'

'Yes,' he said, 'but Maeve will only tell Deirdre face-to-face, alone – even her husband, Edward, is not to know.'

'This is more secrecy than I am used to.'

Sean laughed. 'Then you have not been long enough in Ireland. But in truth, what you must understand is this: Maeve fears you will be killed if your existence is known before the curse can be lifted. Whoever has made this threat to our family has made it clear that I am to be disposed of. How then do you think they would react upon learning of you?' He looked at me, now very serious. 'When I first saw your face, Alexander,

I saw in it the answer to questions that have haunted me my whole life, but I saw too answers to what besets this family now. Maeve and I differ on many things and always have done, but on this I agree with her: there are risks we cannot take with you. You hazarded a great deal to come here, I know that.' I had told him about Sarah, about the second chance for happiness God had given me in bringing her into my life. I had told him also of the trip to Poland, that would have fulfilled so many youthful ambitions. I had told him about the tatters my name would now be in. 'But, God willing, you will win back all you think you have lost. The funeral is to be in five days' time, and then I am to take you to Finn O'Rahilly. After that this secrecy will end, and this place will be a prison to you no more.'

We talked on until long after the food and drink were gone. He reminisced about his childhood, our grandfather, and made much of what our grandfather would have made of me. There was regret, sadness, humour and bravado, a kaleidoscope in one man about to shoulder responsibilities he had long avoided. I was reminded of my last night with Archie, my bosom companion from boyhood to manhood. Archie who had hunted, fought, drunk, laughed, loved to the full, who had coloured my life where there might only have been shade. Archie, who was now dead. I had not thought to feel such a bond with another man again: I had not thought ever to know the bond of blood that can bind like no other, and yet I felt it now, with Sean.

As he was about to finally leave, he surprised me by asking suddenly, 'How do you find Andrew Boyd?'

'He has been – courteous to me, more courteous than I would be were the roles reversed, I think.'

Sean nodded. 'Perhaps so. But his is a cold courtesy, full of resentments.'

'You do not like him?'

'It is not a question of liking,' he said. 'Born in another time, another place, things might have been otherwise, but there is nothing in him for me or in me for him. We are just different.'

FOUR

Deirdre

The next five days passed in great activity in the house beneath me, and in near-silence in my own chamber. I had brought with me no books of my own in that rushed departure from Aberdeen, and so my only reading was in Andrew Boyd's bible. I sought assurance in its pages that I was in the right place, that I had not wandered from the right path, but all I found there were reminders that I should have been in another place, I should have been making my way to the Baltic, searching for ministers of the Word, rather than hiding in a tower house in a town I did not know, in a land still awash with priests and poets.

The near-endless hours of darkness from early evening until sleep would finally take me were spent in trying to write to Sarah something she could understand, believe, forgive, but the words came slow and awkwardly, and lifted dead and cold from the page. I closed my eyes and tried to see her. In the silence I tried to hear her voice. Sometimes I would catch a fleeting glimpse of her smile and then it was gone, leaving me with nothing but a searing emptiness, as if the essence of her had been clawed out of me. Each day ended with the burning of the letter in the flame of the candle by which it had been written.

My daylight hours were spent in watching. Musket loops and arrow slits on the walls gave perfect views down the high street of the town. It was broad and long, flanked by the great stone sentinels that were the other tower houses of wealthy aldermen and burgesses. The governor might have his palace, but the old families of Carrickfergus had each their stronghold. Only from the open parapets, from which I had been forbidden, might I have seen the castle, or the church or Irish Gate behind us, but all the life of the marketplace, courthouse, jail and any travellers who entered the burgh from the North or Sea Gate, or from the Scots Quarter outside the town walls, could be seen by a watcher at one of my windows.

In the evening, Sean would come and spend a half-hour with me and elaborate for me on what I had seen. Mourners had been called and were gathering. I had learned from my mother not to believe the tales of the Irish peddled by those who had no interest but to denigrate them, and so it was no great surprise to me to see the mourners from the West who brought their magnificent horses to rest at the gateway to my grandparents' tower house; they bore themselves with a sense of their own dignity that would not have shamed an earl. With them came their retainers, their humbler mounts heavy-laden. Sean knew them all, went to greet them all, and in the evening would regale me with tales of every tragedy, scandal or feud they had ever laid claim to. Between mouthfuls of food and drink, he could reel off levels and generations of cousinage more complex than any mathematics I had ever stumbled over, and the next day would express genuine astonishment that I could not remember my exact relationship by blood or marriage to every soul who had the previous day passed beneath the portals of the house.

Late in the afternoon of the day before the funeral, a party arrived from the direction of the Irish Gate, five well-mounted and richly clothed riders and their followers. Of the leading group, four were men, attired much as Sean had been when he had come to fetch me from Aberdeen, and in their midst, as if cordoned off from the lesser beings inhabiting the world outside, was one woman. I could not see her face and her head was covered by the hood of her furred cloak, but the tendrils of pale gold that escaped from it were those of a young woman. I had been so entranced by the sound and sight of the new arrivals, I had not heard the footsteps come up behind me. I spoke without realising I spoke or knowing I would be heard. 'Deirdre.'

'You should stay back from there. You might be seen.'

It was Andrew Boyd. He had often passed me in this attitude before, without remark. I ignored his warning. 'I have been watching my cousin arrive; she travels with a larger retinue than I had expected.'

He came towards the opening and I stepped aside to afford him a better view. His eyes can scarcely have lighted on the party below us when he turned away again. 'It is not Deirdre,' he said, without looking at me. 'It is Roisin O'Neill.' He went past me into our chamber and closed the door behind him.

I continued to watch. Of the four men, the leading rider was perhaps about fifty years of age: the others were around my own age, and enough alike each other and the older man to be his sons. Their arrival before my grandmother's house had not gone unnoticed in the marketplace and the high street; of the many arrivals over the preceding three days, none had occasioned as much interest as this. Traders left off their business and turned to watch, wary. Two English soldiers who had been flirting with a girl at a vegetable cart gave off their attentions when they saw the party come to a halt, and soon left at a brisk jog in the direction of the castle.

If the riders noticed any of the interest they had occasioned, they showed no sign of it. The stillness of their waiting contrasted with the noise and busyness I could hear rising from the floors beneath me. Doors banged, orders were shouted, and feet flew up and down stairs. At last the entrance door to the tower was opened and my grandmother emerged. Sean was a step behind, and while she went towards the main rider, he went directly to Roisin's horse and took the bridle from the servant who held it. The older man dismounted and his three sons did likewise. My grandmother gave him a long greeting, which I could not hear, and received an equally long response. When it was over, and acknowledged, the two embraced warmly. It was only now that Sean helped Roisin dismount from her horse. He was stiff, formal, and did not look directly at her as he spoke.

This was a new guise to me, my cousin's incarnation as a courtly gentleman. This was not the man who had brawled and debauched in the inns of Aberdeen; who had sung to me, with me, on our journey from Scotland and who, despite the shortness of our acquaintance and the sadness of the time, could make me smile simply at the sight of him. I wondered how many guises he had. Roisin stood before him, tall, slender and still. Her composure masked some great uncertainty that her eyes could not quite hide. I felt something in my stomach, a pull, a kind of shock, like a ghost of something: she was like Katharine, that was all; she reminded me of Katharine. The feeling passed as quickly as it had come, and I watched Maeve go to her and kiss her on both cheeks, before slipping her arm through the young girl's and leading her into the house. I stayed where I was, pondering the arrival of this party, unannounced to me and so formally received. And I wondered about the girl, so beautiful and so sad, whose name I had first heard on the night of our arrival from Scotland, and why, in the long list of loves and conquests with which he'd regaled me for much of our journey, Sean had never mentioned her once.

That night there was to be a great feasting before my grandfather's burial the next day. Each night since his death there had been a wailing and keening of women such as I thought could not have issued from anything human. 'It is their way,' Andrew Boyd had said. 'Their excess in grief is matched only by the gluttony and drunkenness of their funeral feasts. You will never know anything more pagan given a Christian name. Their enjoyment of it would shame Lucifer himself.' On this final evening there was a constant rumble of feet back and forth from the kitchens to where the mourners were to gather for the last night of waking over my grandfather.

I had returned to my chamber at around five, to begin my nightly letter to Sarah, as if putting my feelings into words now could somehow reclaim for us all the time that had been wasted. I hardly noticed the footsteps on the stairs, so many comings and goings had there been in the house that day, and I didn't lift my head when the door opened, thinking it was only Andrew. Only when I heard the sharp intake of a woman's breath, a surprised 'Oh!', did I look round and see, standing in the doorway, in front of Sean, a vision from my own dreams. She was like a spirit, a princess, a myth from the whispered bedtime tales I had gone to sleep to. She was like a story in herself, a fable. The hair that hung down her back in waves of red and gold was not the black of myself, or Sean, or our grandmother, but the face illumined by the arc of light thrown by Sean's lantern was the face of my own mother. My heart was thumping and my breathing came hard to me. I looked down at my hands and realised they were clenched in determined fists. At last I stood up and went towards her; I felt barriers begin to break and crumble: the barriers erected by the cold heart of my grandmother; by the priests and the beads and the incense and the oils; by the Irish tongue I tripped and stumbled over; by the sea separating me from all I had ever cared about. For here was my family, the only blood relations who remained to me in this world, and I knew in that moment that what they wanted me to do for them, that would I do.

'Did I not tell you then?' Sean's voice was warm and happy.

The girl continued to gaze at me, as if she could not believe what was in front of her eyes. 'I could not have . . . I would not have . . .' And then she smiled, a smile that reached out and held me, and sent warmth to every part of me. She took my face in her hands and was gazing up into my eyes with love that lighted the room. 'Alexander. I could not have believed it. Alexander.'

I could find no words, and stood there as one struck dumb, until a mighty slap on the shoulder from Sean brought me to my senses.

'Do not tell me you don't know your cousin, man. All I have heard since the day she was born is how like your mother she is.'

'Yes,' I said, stuttering a little, 'yes . . . she is.'

'Then I am glad,' the girl said, 'for you will have to love me now.'

'You must never doubt that,' I said. And I knew it was the truth.

She searched my face as if seeking out the differences between myself and her brother. Each feature was studied, memorised.

'It will take some of the pressure off me, I don't mind telling you,' said Sean. 'He is not so handsome, of course, and his manners are utterly beyond redemption, but no doubt the ladies of Carrickfergus will not be altogether disappointed when they eventually lay eyes on him.'

Deirdre gave her brother a withering look. 'Are there ladies left in Carrickfergus? I am glad to hear it. You have surely been occupied elsewhere this last while, Sean. What ladies there are will not be allowed within a hundred yards of you, Alexander, if their fathers have any say in it. He ruins the family name nigh on every week.'

Sean laughed. 'Did I not tell you she was a shrew, Alexander?'

'You said nothing of the kind, and I would not have believed you in any case. Deirdre, I am glad to see you at last.'

'And I you. You cannot know the blessing it is to us that our grandfather lived to see you.'

'I would have liked to have longer.'

'You must not grieve over what has passed and cannot be changed. The sight of you will have healed a wound he carried with him thirty years.'

We were all three silent a moment, before Sean spoke. 'And yet we should not be sad, we three. He would not wish us sad. We are his legacy, and let it not be one of sadness; this is a joyful moment.' He looked around him. 'I suppose it would be too much to hope that Boyd keeps a drink in this room?'

'I have never seen it if he does.'

'All that Protestant discipline of his. It cannot be good for a man.'

'You think your Catholic indiscipline keeps you in better health?' Deirdre's tone was severe, but her eyes were laughing.

'I will go to my grave having known what it was to live.'

It was as if a cold breeze had travelled through the room. 'Please do not speak of it, Sean. You must take greater care.'

His face became tender. 'I take care where I must, little sister. You should not give so much credence to poets and their curses.'

'And what of men and their muskets?' she asked.

'You know about that?'

'The whole of the North knows about that, Sean. By the time the rumours of it reached Coleraine the tale was of twenty men with muskets, and that only some bewitchment, some pact with the fairy folk, kept you and your horse from death at the foot of the cliff.'

'And do not tell me you believed any of this, you who laughed in the face of tales that sent me to my childhood bed in terror?'

'Sean, I could sit here a month and still not have told Alexander of every escapade you have been in. There is no tale of you I could hear that I could discount at first hearing, other than that you had settled to a life of business and piety. But I took the precaution of speaking to our grand-father's agent. He is the only man in Cóleraine whose word I trust. He told me the truth of it. You must be careful. Murchadh . . .'

He glanced at me. 'Not now, Deirdre. Let us talk of pleas-anter things. It will not be long until the wake begins. Time enough for sombre thoughts.'

'But the curse . . .'

'Ach, the curse. Do not trouble your head about that. After the funeral, I am to take Alexander to O'Rahilly and . . .'

Her face paled at the mention of O'Rahilly's name. 'You cannot be thinking of that. You cannot place Alexander in that danger.' She gripped my hand again. 'You must not go. Please, you must not go.'

Before I could answer, the door to the room opened and Andrew Boyd walked in. He stopped short when he saw that I was not alone. Sean stepped back and Deirdre stood up. Boyd muttered something that sounded like, 'I am sorry,' and left as suddenly as he had come.

Sean looked to Deirdre. 'Come on, your husband will be wondering where you are.'

'I am his wife, not his lapdog.'

Her brother grinned. 'I do not think Blackstone knew what he was about when he married himself an Irishwoman. But it is time for us to get ready, all the same. Alexander, Maeve has some plan for you for this evening. We will talk later.'

Deirdre kissed me on the cheek. 'And you and I also will talk, and talk, for there is a lifetime of you that I must get to know.' And then they were gone, and something of the light inside went with them.

It was not long afterwards that my grandmother entered the room. We had not spoken since the night of the strange, aborted baptism. There were no preliminaries.

'Your grandfather will be buried tomorrow.'

'I know that,' I said.

'No doubt. You should be there, by Sean's side, at his funeral. It is your place, but it is not yet the time to make you known.'

'I will do him honour here, in prayer, in scripture reading. I would like to have known him better, but I will pray to take example from what I have learned about him in life.'

Maeve's mouth contorted slightly. 'How Grainne must have suffered with such people,' she said. 'But you are in my house tonight, and there are none of your ministers here. It is my desire, and he would have expected it also, that you watch over your grandfather's body tonight.'

'You wish me to sit in the chapel with his remains?' I asked.

She looked at me as if I were lacking in something. 'His remains rest in this house. I wish you to be at the wake.'

'How can that be if I am not to be made known? Is the house not full of people?'

'There is a place in the gallery that you can watch from.

Andrew Boyd will show you where. You must take great care not to be seen.' Her voice was low and soft, as my mother's had been, but there was no warmth in it for me. I still gave little credence to her worries, but I assured her I would be cautious. Her business finished, she made to leave, but paused a moment when I spoke again.

'Tell me, who is Roisin O'Neill?'

She appraised me, interested.

'Roisin O'Neill is the only daughter of my cousin Murchadh. Through the duplicity of others, Murchadh fell out of favour with the Earl of Tyrone in his youth, and had made his peace with the Crown before the end of Tyrone's rebellion. The earl never forgave him, and Murchadh was not with him when he and the others, my own son Phelim amongst them, left for Spain, to seek help for our plundered land. But there was a blessing in it, for the English trust Murchadh, and he has managed to hold to some of his lands where others have had them wrenched from them.' My grandmother seemed pleased with this, what must have been a well-rehearsed justification of her cousin's prosperity where so many others had been driven to poverty and dishonour.

'And Roisin?'

She looked at me, surprised that I had more to ask. 'Unlike Deirdre, she knows her duty, and her worth. She is a true Irish-woman. Roisin will be Sean's wife. After a decent period of mourning for my husband has passed, they will be married, and Sean will at last begin to take his place amongst our people.'

I thought of the scene I had witnessed outside the house earlier that same day, and my heart sank for my cousin and the beautiful woman who would be his unloved and unhappy wife. I thought my grandmother was finished with me, and I prepared to take up my pen again. But she was not finished.

'And you?' she said.

'Me?'

'Yes. Are you yet married?'

'No,' I said flatly, 'I am not married.'

The trace of a smile appeared for a moment on her lips. 'Good,' she said, turning to make her way back down the corridor. 'That is good.'

FIVE

The Funeral Feast

Andrew came to fetch me just as I had consigned my letter to Sarah to the flame. I had struggled in the candlelight and failed to write on paper words I had never been able to say to her when she was standing before me. I did not have the words to tell her of the emptiness, the ache within me the lack of her caused. All I had, night after night, were ashes. He looked from the ashes to me as if he would say something, but thought better of it, not yet ready to breach that barrier.

The place he led me to was a broad stone pillar at the far side of the gallery. All along the rest of the gallery, torches burned in the sconces on the wall, but there was no sconce here.

'All of these houses have such a place,' he said, 'where people may watch, listen, unseen. None of these people trust one another.'

'In the mix of all the races?'

'It is the Irish themselves I am talking about. They live to fight. There is not an insult or an intrigue they will let pass for an excuse to go to feud. They would spend all they had on hospitality for a man one night and slit his throat the next if they thought themselves slighted.'

'I will take care to watch my tongue, then,' I said, laughing.

He turned his startling green eyes on me, and his face was

deadly serious. 'Watch everything. Always. Do not let up your guard for a moment. With anyone.'

He left me, and I edged forward to peer through the wooden balustrade down onto the hall below. It had been transformed since last I had seen it. The comfortable settles and chairs had either been removed or pushed back against the walls. In their place was an array of long trestle tables, arranged with benches for the seating of over sixty people. The top table was backed by seven carved, high-backed oak dining chairs upholstered in red velvet. Three more tables ran down the room from this one, set out with good pewter whilst the ware on the top table was of fine silver. Candelabra blazed at each table, casting a burning sheen of light upon already unimaginable quantities of food. Baskets of oat bread and towers of fresh autumn fruits contended for space with platters of salmon, majestic-looking still, gutted and poached in their entirety. Tureens of shellfish simmered on each table, sending up aromas that brought to me memories of the best of student feasts. Dishes of nuts and dried fruits were set on the side tables. Pungent rounds of cheese, bowls of bonnyclabber and mounds of butter, already beginning to glisten in the heat of the extravagant candlelight, were set at intervals from one end of the tables to the other. Every manner of fowl and game bird was represented, roasted and stuffed, on the boards. And then, just as the guests were about to enter the hall from the top of the main stairway, huge salvers of hot roasted meats began to appear from the kitchens below.

The musicians had assembled themselves at the far side of the gallery and had begun tuning their instruments. A piper set up his drone, but it was as nothing to the monstrous dirge from the drones of the pipes of the Highlanders from my own country. Another player had a bag of flutes and whistles of varying sizes, playing a few notes on each one before trying the next. Two fiddlers scraped their bows across different tunes, before one set his instrument down to try his tabor. Below, in the hall, I noticed a huge harp had been set up in a corner, near the stair head. At a signal from the piper all noise stopped, and then he began, alone, in an assured, almost defiant, march. As he grew in confidence, and I realised my foot was tapping, almost of itself, against the floor, he was joined by a whistle and then the bodhran, beating out the pace.

Now the guests emerged from below and began to flow into the hall, where they waited, expectantly. At the top of the balcony stairs, on Sean's arm, my grandmother finally appeared. For all her coldness, I could not help but admire the stately old woman my cousin led to her seat at the top table. She was clad in a gown of the deepest green velvet, her head still covered in the habitual linen headdress. At her neck was a heavy gold chain and cross, garnished with emeralds and pearls. She walked upright, without a stoop, and looked neither left nor right, betraying not the slightest trace of emotion or grief. She had all the bearing, not of a merchant's wife but of a queen from the ancient tales, and the people assembled around the hall acknowledged her as such.

Andrew had appeared quietly beside me. 'The old woman plays her part well, does she not?'

I murmured my agreement. Behind them came Deirdre on the arm of Murchadh O'Neill, Roisin's father. In contrast to Maeve's sparkling magnificence, Deirdre was dressed entirely in black, save for the simple white lace at her neck. In her hair and at her throat were beads of jet that shimmered in the light as her dark silk skirts moved through the hall. She also looked straight ahead of her as she went to take her place at the top table. Murchadh O'Neill, on the other hand, inclined his head, bestowed smiles, or uttered words of greeting to all who caught his eye. I wondered for a moment if he thought to take my grandfather's place in this household, but only for a moment: he must have been almost twenty years younger than Maeve, and Deirdre's hand was already given elsewhere. Next came Roisin herself, on the arm of one of her brothers. 'That's Cormac,' said Andrew, as the oldest-looking of the three took up his seat to Deirdre's left at the principal table. He was tall, like his father and brothers, but serious and watchful, like darkness to Sean's light, with none of my cousin's ready smiles or easy grace. His younger brothers disposed themselves happily among the upper reaches of the lower tables.

Amongst the leading party, there was no sign of Deirdre's husband. 'Where is Edward Blackstone?' I asked.

Andrew Boyd did not even bother to look at the top table, but instead scanned lower down the hall.

'There,' he said finally, indicating a place about midway down the table furthest from Deirdre herself.

My eyes followed the direction of his hand to the two young men dressed in sober black, their whole aspect proclaiming them Protestant.

'Which one?' I asked.

'The older,' replied Andrew, indicating a broad-built man with close-cropped brown hair and a wide, pockmarked face. 'The younger is his brother, Henry.'

'Why so far down the table?'

He looked at me, feigning incredulity, something approaching humour appearing for the first time in his eyes. 'The woman in green is your grandmother.'

'Surely, now that they are married, she would not slight Deirdre's husband so publicly?'

Andrew merely raised his eyebrows. 'Would she not?'

I looked again at Deirdre. She was deep in conversation with Cormac O'Neill. Murchadh's oldest son had scarcely taken his eyes off her since they'd been seated. There was something in the intensity of his demeanour that held her. She gave never a glance to her husband, though he looked often at her.

My grandmother surveyed the scene before her, and her eyes glowed with satisfaction. She nodded to her steward, who filled her glass. And then she rose, and as one the conversation in the hall was hushed and the musicians fell silent.

'Welcome, my friends. Be truly welcome. You do honour to this house in your coming, and honour to my husband who was its master and lies here one last night.' At this many mourners crossed themselves, and there were murmured invocations of the saints. 'Often, in more joyful times, you have known our hospitality; you have been welcomed in this place.'

'That is a lie.' Andrew Boyd's low whisper cut into my mind. I turned to look at him. 'Your grandfather would not permit half of that crew in this house. Murchadh O'Neill never set foot over the door in his life before.'

'But I thought . . .'

He held a finger to his lips. Maeve was in full flow. 'We have known laughter here, and nights of triumph. But there has been weeping also, and tragedy. And tonight there will be weeping, for Richard FitzGarrett is dead.' She meant to go on, but I could see that, for a moment, she could not, and I understood then what I would otherwise have doubted: Maeve O'Neill had loved her husband. She gathered her strength and continued. 'The man who for fifty years shared my bed, my troubles and my joys is gone. He was the master of this house and the father of my children. He grieved with me over those children, both lost to Ireland, though for very different causes. He was the best of his race, that breed of

Englishman who came here so many generations ago, to conquer our land, and could not. They stayed, and were conquered by it. He was as Irish as he was English. He spoke our tongue, gave due honour to our ways, and died in the true faith. He fathered an Irish hero in our son, and will be grandfather, God willing, to many more.' She held high the glass in her hand, the candlelight dancing in its ruby wine. 'Drink with me to Richard FitzGarrett, my husband. Father of Phelim, grandfather of Sean, the last of his race.' As the company loudly proclaimed my grandfather's name, I drained my cup to its depths.

Maeve's was the first of many toasts made, as the musicians took up their playing once more and the company set to the food before them like hounds at a kill.

It was not long until Andrew realised he would be needed below. 'They will be needing more casks up from the cellars.'

'But there are casks everywhere they can be fitted.'

'Have you seen how much they are pouring down their throats? I tell you, Bacchus himself would not outlast some of those beneath you. What would kill many another man is to them but a taster for what is to come.'

Unmarked by the players as he passed behind them, he went down amongst the company. He walked behind the tables rather than amongst them as the other servants did. But then, he was not quite a servant here. If not a servant though, what? He appeared to know little better than I what his place here really was. He spoke to a few of the merchants and aldermen at the lower end of the tables, but made no contact with Deirdre's husband or his brother. Now and again, he would issue instructions to the other servants when he noticed something was required, but there was no ease in his bearing, and to the native Irish, Maeve's relatives and their retainers, he spoke not at all, nor even approached the high table where the principal mourners sat.

My gaze drifted to Deirdre, whose eyes were searching the room. It was evident that she was not looking for her husband. She was drinking little, but the point came when she had finished the wine in her glass. Murchadh O'Neill noticed and called for more to be brought. One of the kitchen boys stepped forward with a jug, but Murchadh shook his head and pointed at Andrew instead. 'Him. Let him bring it.'

Andrew flinched for a moment and I thought he would refuse, but he took the jug from the boy and walked slowly towards where Deirdre sat and began to pour. Murchadh seemed to take a peculiar pleasure in watching the act, but Deirdre stared ahead of her, not acknowledging the man she must have known her entire life. I thought for a moment that Andrew would allow the wine to spill over the edge of the glass, but at the last moment he tilted the jug upwards and walked away. My cousin carefully lifted the glass to her mouth, her hand very steady, and only a trickle of the ruby liquid overflowed the rim and dropped on to the white linen tablecloth below.

The harper was playing now, and conversations in the hall gradually came to their end as all around turned to listen to the melancholy notes issuing from his strings. I closed my eyes and leant against the cold stone of the pillar. There was a grace in the music rising towards me that brought to my mind images of the seas and land separating me from all that I had understood of the world until a few weeks ago. What was Sarah doing now? The melody that insinuated itself into my mind was beckoning me, telling me this was the place now, that it was the other that was the dream. I caught sight of her, her hair blowing across her face, at the other side of the Irish Sea.

She would not cross, I knew that; she would not exist here. I allowed the music to take me where it would.

'You are a true Irishman indeed, cousin. But take care your snoring does not drown out the harper.'

I came to with a start and was relieved to see Sean's face looking down upon me. 'How long have I been sleeping?' I asked.

He raised an eyebrow. 'I have been here two minutes, and you have been dead to the world all that time. And they say we are lazy.'

I smiled sheepishly. 'The music and the warmth and the wine overcame me. I had expected Andrew Boyd by now.'

He squatted down beside me and sighed heavily. 'Andrew will have taken himself off somewhere to seethe in private. Murchadh does not realise when he overreaches himself.'

'What was that about?'

He moved uneasily. 'Ach, it is not worth talking about tonight. I will tell you sometime, when you know him better.'

I indicated Deirdre's husband. 'Your brother-in-law seems ill-at-ease.'

He snorted. 'As well he might, in this company.'

'Cormac O'Neill seems much taken with Deirdre.'

'She is like an illness he cannot shake off. I fear for him because of it.'

'And his sister?'

'Roisin?' He looked away from me. 'She too has placed her heart where it does not find a welcome, and in one much less worthy.'

'She is very beautiful.'

'Yes,' he said heavily. 'She is very beautiful.'

'But that is not enough?'

'No, I do not think it is. I would to God that it was.' He would tell me about it when he was ready to. For now there was sadness enough between us. Andrew returned with more food and drink for me, the two nodded briefly to one another, and Sean took his leave.

The harper came to the end of his final air, and was hugely lauded. As the tumult died down, Murchadh O'Neill rose to his feet and addressed the company. 'Drink to the harpers,' he said. 'And to the poets, and the lawmakers, for Ireland has no heroes any more. Drink to Richard FitzGarrett, the last of his kind, as different from these new English who have come to wrest our lands and ways from us as the stag is from the stoat.' Some of the traders and merchants at the lower tables began to murmur amongst themselves and to shift uncomfortably on their benches. Murchadh afforded them little notice. 'Richard FitzGarrett has gone, and there is no place for his sort of honour in Ireland. There can be no accommodation now for his race or mine with the godless heretic interloper who would rape our land. His passing is the passing of the time of compromise. We have been butchered, starved, harried and robbed, and our time is coming. The day is not long when we will make a new Ireland out of the ashes of the old.'

A pallor had descended on the faces of many of the guests, and principally the English, for what in Murchadh's mouth was a rallying call to the Irish was in their ears nothing less than sedition. Henry Blackstone stood up. His brother tried to pull him down, but the younger man struggled free, knocking over a tankard of ale as he did so.

'Do you think we have come here to listen to this, you old Irish goat? Your poets and your harpers are gone, and your days are gone too, you and all your kind.'

All along the principal table, and at the upper ends of the

side tables, hands went to hilts. There was a dead silence. Andrew Boyd whispered to me, 'At a word from Murchadh, they will slit his throat.'

Edward Blackstone made another attempt to pull his brother down. 'Henry, you make a fool . . .'

'No, Edward, you are the fool. Do you allow yourself to be treated like this by your own wife? Having your family and your nation insulted in this way? Consigned to the lowest tables like an inconvenient stranger? Your wife's lover flaunted in your face . . .' Half-a-dozen Irishmen leapt from their seats; Sean was only kept in his by the firm hand of Eachan, who had rarely left his side all evening.

Edward Blackstone let go his brother's arm: he looked utterly defeated. He pushed his plate away and got to his feet. He ignored his brother now, and looked past him to Deirdre. 'Well?' he said to her.

'It is not the place . . .' she began.

'No. It is not. And I will not stay here.' He took his brother by the arm and began to walk from the hall. As he came to the stair head, he turned again to his wife. 'Well? Do you come with me?'

She had not moved. 'My grandfather . . .'

'Your grandfather be damned,' he snapped. 'You are my wife. I return to Coleraine two days from tomorrow; you will come with me then or not at all.' Without waiting for her reply, he left.

All eyes were on my cousin. Her long, loose hair glinted brilliantly like the red leaves of autumn in the candlelight. Her composure had not faltered, but I could see that she breathed deeply, and that her fingers gripped hard to the goblet in her hand. Cormac O'Neill stared long after my cousin's husband, and I would not have slept easy in my bed had I been Edward

Blackstone that night. Further down the table, Sean's face was like thunder, and I noticed Eachan's hand still pressed hard on his shoulder. At the centre of the table, Maeve had never wavered, and only a slight smile at the corner of her lips betrayed what she felt. She lifted high the glass in her right hand, and again her steward filled it.

The players had their pipes and bows flying in a jig within minutes. The tension was broken, and soon all around the hall there was movement, music, the clamour of talk between old friends and the exchange of wary or defiant glances between old foes. Andrew Boyd had told me the names of as many of the mourners as he knew, and I had tried in my head to match them to Sean's stories of rivalries and feuds between families and neighbours. Everywhere was brilliant light and warmth, yet when I looked at Roisin O'Neill I saw she sat alone, unreachable in her stillness and silence. I wondered what it was in her that my cousin had no interest in knowing.

'What did Henry Blackstone mean,' I said, 'when he spoke to his brother about his wife's lover?'

There was no response from Andrew Boyd and for a moment I thought he had not heard my necessarily low whisper. I repeated my question. 'Who did he mean by Deirdre's lover? Is it Cormac?' Murchadh's oldest son was tall, striking, with a strange beauty to him that might dazzle man or woman.

Andrew Boyd followed the direction of my gaze. 'Your cousin has no lover,' he said, in a tone that suggested that should be the end of the matter, but there was more I wanted to know.

'Even so . . .'

He turned exasperated eyes on me and waited.

'Even if that is so,' I continued, 'could no one have stopped her throwing herself away on Edward Blackstone? She clearly does not like him, still less love him.'

He looked away from me, his voice hardened. 'I am not made privy to such matters.' And in that moment, I heard the answer to all the questions I might yet ask: it was not Cormac O'Neill who had been Deirdre's lover.

I could say nothing, but after a moment something in him relented. 'Maeve tried, of course. You know that already. But she was not dissuaded. She did it to defy your grandmother, to throw off her Gaelic roots and to find herself a place in this new Ulster.'

The woman I was looking at was an Irishwoman in every part of her being. 'I think she is wasted with him.'

'A pearl before swine,' he murmured, and then he looked at me, a light in his eyes that I had never seen there before. 'She told me once that she wanted to escape, as your mother had done. But I think your father was a better man than Edward Blackstone, and that your mother chose a better path. Deirdre would have done well to have fallen in with Maeve's plan that she marry Cormac.'

When I looked again at the man she had refused, and thought of him she had chosen, I realised that my cousin's abhorrence of our grandmother's world must be great indeed.

As Andrew was showing himself more inclined to conversation than he had ever done before, I thought I would try my luck a little further. 'Why will Sean not defy Maeve in the same way? It is evident that he does not love Roisin O'Neill.'

He squatted down on his haunches and regarded me as one would an inquisitive child.

'You really do not understand these people yet, do you? But Sean does, for all his careless manner, he knows what is expected of him. Roisin is an O'Neill, and her father, by conforming to English law, has held on to some of the old O'Neill lands. With your grandfather's money now coming to Sean, and trading on the FitzGarretts' good standing with the English administration, they will buy into more lands. Sean will take his FitzGarrett name and his FitzGarrett money and dazzle the English with them. He will be given some of the old O'Neill lands in return, he will promise to nurture his tenants in loyalty to the Crown. The English will think themselves well served in this bargain.'

'And will they be?' He did not answer me at first. I persisted. 'Will they be well served?'

He considered a moment and spoke slowly. 'About as well served as a coop of chickens by a starving fox.'

I looked at Murchadh O'Neill and his sons. They might have kept their peace and kept their lands for twenty years, but everything in their bearing, their appearance and their speech told they were Irishmen, through and through. As Roisin's brother called to the players for a livelier air, I suspected they would not dance to the English tune much longer.

Andrew got up. 'I am needed downstairs,' he said. 'You should forget what we have spoken about tonight. And take care you do not move into the light; I thought I saw you once.'

As he was going down the steps from the gallery, I heard a shout from somewhere outside. Few in the hall appeared to notice it. After a moment it came again, and then a third time. Andrew had heard it too, and started towards the ground floor, taking the steps two at a time. It was a few minutes before he returned, his face set and determined. He went directly to Sean, whose expression darkened as he listened. Then they went to Maeve. Whatever message they brought had only a slight effect on my grandmother's countenance, the briefest flicker of something – fear, surprise – then a deepening of its habitual resolution. She said a brief word to Andrew and took up her seat once more at the centre of the table. He hesitated a moment, but it was clear that Maeve was not going to give her order twice, and he went to do her bidding. After standing a moment in a kind of shock, Sean began to speak urgently to her. Maeve rewarded him with a few words only and continued to gaze straight ahead, a picture of composure. With a great reluctance, Sean took up his seat beside her once more. Both now watched the head of the stairs, waiting.

I too turned my eyes towards the stair head, wishing Andrew Boyd was still by me to tell me who the new arrival was. The man he led into the hall was like no one I had ever seen; he was a figure from an earlier age, from the age of the heroes. His garments were long, his mantle reaching almost to the floor; his tunic was gathered at the waist by a strong belt with silver buckle, and ended just above the knee, its sleeves wide and long, and bordered with threads of blue and gold. His long silver hair hung loose. His beard, like his eyebrows, was not silver, but dark, and his skin was that of a man not yet thirty-five. A silver bangle was at his wrist, and in his hand he held a long staff, tipped with a carved head. The room fell to complete silence as he walked to the head of it and came to rest in front of Maeve, who stood up and bowed her head slightly towards him.

'You do honour to this house and to my husband's name. Be welcome as an honoured guest.' She indicated the seat to her right, which Sean at once vacated. No one in the room moved until the stranger sat down and was given wine. I could see, but not hear, much low whispering taking place amongst individuals and small groups. Food was brought to the newcomer – he was not left to help himself from the platters on the table as everyone else – even Maeve and Murchadh – had been. Sean stood behind our grandmother, never taking his eyes off the newcomer. The harper was called back to his instrument, and

gentle airs soon began to rise from his strings, a contrast with
the lively jig that had been taken up only a few moments ago
and that had been so suddenly stilled. The stranger ate and
drank his fill as muted conversations rose and died around the
room. No one at the upper table spoke, but all watched or cast
glances they thought unseen at the newcomer. Maeve had lost
none of her composure, but Deirdre was pale, as pale as death.
There was not one of the O'Neill men in the room who did
not have his hand on the hilt of his dagger. I felt my own
breathing come deeper and harder, for in this place there was
a reckoning coming, and it would be soon.

At last the stranger stopped eating and had had his fill of
wine. He closed his eyes, pressed clenched fists to the table
and took a deep breath before standing up. The harper fell
silent and even the movement of the servants in the hall stopped.
It was only when he began to speak that I realised at last who
he was: Finn O'Rahilly, the poet who had placed my family
under the curse that had brought me here. My grandmother's
resolve was more than I would have believed even her to be
capable of: she showed no trace of fear, but I could only guess
at what turmoil the sight again of this man must have caused
her. His words rolled through the house like a quiet thunder.

Hearken to me, you band of the O'Neill;
Hearken to me and hear your fate,
You who have betrayed Ireland and now think to enjoy her
favour,
The hour is fast approaching.

It has come to pass, Maeve O'Neill, as it was foretold:
The Englishman is dead; do not pretend ignorance at the
cause.

His leaving does not cleanse your guilt;
In English whoredom you have lived and so shall you die.

The daughters of this house have traipsed wanton in your
    wake,
They have their reward:
Grainne lies dead, at the ocean's depths, claimed by the sea-
    god Manannan
For her treachery to Erin.

Fickle Deirdre, dead already in her heart,
Will share her barren fate,
For no child shall she bear
To claim her English gold.

The line of the O'Neills has abandoned Ireland,
Your honour gone with Phelim and the earls.
Think not your grandson can restore your fortunes,
A harder path he has taken over tainted ground.

You think to make a union with the line of the Rose,
But the Rose will wither,
And bear no bud,
Its blossom poisoned by a bastard child.

And you, Murchadh O'Neill,
Who kept to your fold when the wolf devoured your
    brothers,
Do not think to redeem your honour with the Irish here,
For Shame is all your bounty at this table.

Now the poet turned and spoke directly to my grandmother, who sat aghast, her hands gripping the table.

I have spoken and you will heed my words,
For all these things will come to pass.
Your grandson will soon lie with his fathers,
In the cold chambers of the dead,
And your line will be no more.

Cormac O'Neill leapt from his seat, his knife in his hand, but was caught and held by his father and his arms bound behind him in Eachan's firm grip. Finn O'Rahilly left the place unmolested, and nothing was heard save a thin, rising wailing of a woman, joined soon by others as the wake for my grandfather truly began.

SIX

Conferences in the Night

Only the dead slept in Carrickfergus that night. An endless eerie wailing of women, the keening, echoed through the house and the tolling hours of darkness. I felt myself the inhabitant of some pagan nightmare. Within half an hour of the departure of Finn O'Rahilly everyone who was not related to my family by blood had gone. I began to make my way to the balcony steps. As I did so, Andrew looked up. For a second, his face froze, and then he made the smallest movement of his head. The muscles in his face and neck tightened, and he formed his lips into a silent 'No' that brooked no misapprehension. I slunk back into the shadows, into my secret place.

Soon, he had appeared beside me. 'You were about to do something very foolish.'

'There are none left in the house that are not friends or family.'

He shook his head almost wonderingly at me.

'Did you understand any of what the poet said?'

I nodded. 'Most of it, I think.'

'Then you need to understand that behind the face of every friend in this house may be the face of a foe. These people play a long game: they have been playing it since before you were born, or your mother either. I would not trust one of them with my horse, never mind my life. I advise you to adopt similar caution.' He turned back down the steps. 'Come with me; your grandmother is asking for you.'

As we approached my grandmother's room, I discerned the sound of raised voices intermingled with the weeping of women from other places in the house. Eachan opened the door to us. Inside it was much more brightly lit than on the night of my grandfather's death. Deirdre sat on a footstool by the fire, crouched over the embers as if she would never get warm, and Sean and Maeve were on their feet in the middle of the room. Sean was in a fury. 'He has no knowledge of the country or the people. How should he begin to discover what we wish to know? Send me and I will soon bring you an answer, on the end of my sword if need be.'

Maeve remained calm. 'You cannot go; I will not permit it. Too much rests on you. You have been cursed, to the risk of your life. You will stay here, until the curse is lifted.'

He shook his head in frustration and spoke with near contempt. 'Curse! The man has been paid to do this!'

'The poets have always been paid,' she said calmly. 'They have never been the less honoured for that.'

'Finn O'Rahilly is the dregs of the poets. He will take his coin from whoever will pay him. He has no honour. You can lift the curse tomorrow; you can lift it now. Tell everyone of Alexander, tell them what nonsense this charlatan speaks. And then let me find who it is that has set him up to this . . .'

Her face was grey with anger now. 'What do you know of the poets? "Dregs"? He sat as a boy at the feet of Mac an Bhaird himself! He might have accomplished many things; all you see is what he has been reduced to. Lift the curse? He has made it and only he can lift it. And I will send Alexander to him, to show himself, and to show the curse is ill-founded.'

'Please, Grandmother . . .'

Maeve turned with venom upon her granddaughter. 'You dare to speak? What is this to you? You have turned your back on this family. I have only allowed you into my house because your brother insisted upon it!'

Deirdre stood up now and showed herself the equal of the old woman. 'You could not have stopped me. He was my grandfather. There are things I know that you would not wish to have known. You could not have stopped me coming here now.'

Maeve had opened her mouth to speak, but something in my cousin's words silenced her. She looked at Deirdre with something approaching hatred.

Sean took a step towards his sister. 'Deirdre, there are other forces at work here. O'Rahilly has been put up to this. I will . . .'

'I will go to him,' I interjected. 'Just tell me where to go.'

Only now did any of them notice me. Sean opened his mouth to remonstrate, but my grandmother held up her hand. 'You have had your say. Let your cousin speak.'

I spoke directly to Maeve. 'I will go to this man and tell him he is wrong. I will tell him that my mother did not drown, but lived to bear me. Let him make what protest he likes then – his "curse" can have no validity. And when that pretence is stripped from him, he may be better induced to reveal who is behind this.'

Deirdre came over to me and took my hands in hers. 'Alexander, you have only just come back to us. We have so much to put right, we three. You do not understand the risk you will be placing yourself in. Sean, who knows this country so well, was very nearly murdered by an assailant in the darkness. His life is still threatened, endangered. How could you, a scholar and a stranger here, hope to go where you must go, do what you must do, and return to us in safety? Do not risk your life on this fool's errand.'

She had almost persuaded me. The call to me in her eyes, in the face that I had known a lifetime, almost reached me, but then her last words overturned the rest. I sought to reassure her.

'It is because it is a fool's errand that I go. The charms and incantations of your poets cannot touch me.' I turned to my grandmother. 'I suspect your purse will also be needed.' Maeve nodded her agreement. 'But understand that I do this for my mother's sake, to find out who is threatening her family, who has such malice for you, for Sean and for Deirdre.'

She regarded me in her accustomed cold manner. 'Do it for whatever reason pleases you. Eachan will go with you, to show you the way and to help you find O'Rahilly. His whereabouts are secretive, but messages can be got to him if you make yourselves known at Bushmills.'

Sean was prepared to countenance this, but his better mood was short-lived.

'I will not go. Curse or no, Sean's life has been threatened. I will not leave him. You must find someone else.'

Maeve was struck motionless in astonishment.

'You'll go where you're told to go,' said Sean.

Eachan looked him full in the face. 'I will not,' he said, and went to sit on the floor in a corner by the door, arms folded across his knees.

Sean cursed him and all his line in English and Irish and some hybrid of the two, with such vehemence that I almost expected one or other of them to have a seizure, but Eachan was not to be moved. 'Then you cannot go,' said my cousin, finally turning to me in frustration.

'I will go with him.' It was Andrew Boyd who had spoken.

'I will take him by the new settlements, where you are not known, Sean, and where we are less likely to meet with the Irish. He can masquerade as a Scottish planter seeking his fortune, and I will play his servant. We will reach Coleraine safely that way and take our chances from there to Bushmills.'

Nobody said anything for a moment, but Deirdre's face was ashen. Eventually she spoke. 'Why are you doing this?'

'Because I have had my fill. The sooner this is ended the better. It will be the last service I do this family. When it is over, I go my own way.'

Maeve looked at him. 'Go with my blessing. You have never shown your father's loyalty, but you might prosper, for a while. Now, I must go to the other women. Deirdre, you will come with me.'

'No, not yet.'

'As you please. You will hardly be missed.' She did not look at me as she left; there were no parting words of love or farewell from my grandmother.

Sean ranted a few more minutes, at Eachan for his obstinacy and parentage, at me for my lack of gratitude – for what I do not know – at Andrew Boyd for his duplicity in taking my side, but eventually he ran out of curses and causes, and began to think. He told Eachan to make ready the two best horses from the stables, and fetch money for our journey, and then he turned to Andrew, and the curses of only a few moments ago were forgotten. 'Pay no heed to my grandmother,' he said. 'She is an old witch. It is an honourable thing that you do and you will always have my gratitude for that.'

But there was no gratitude in Deirdre's eyes. She stood before Andrew, looking at him a long moment before finally speaking. 'Do you really hate me so much?' Without waiting for a response, she went in the way of her grandmother. Andrew stood there, unmoving, unflinching, but I saw something in him break.

After she had left, Sean went over the plan for our trip. I was of little consequence for the most part of this, that was until my cousin revealed a plan that would require more audacity and a stronger nerve than I possessed: when we arrived at Coleraine, we were to go to the home of the Blackstones, where I was to be presented as Sean himself.

This took my attention. 'Have you taken leave of your senses? No, but have you? These people will know within minutes of looking at me that I am not you, that is if their credulity survives the opening of my mouth.'

He laughed. 'If I can be taken for you in Aberdeen, you will pass for me in Coleraine. These people do not know me from my grandfather's horse. Other than Edward Blackstone, who is to be in Carrickfergus another two days, I met them only once, at Deirdre's wedding. I arrived late. There had been more interesting – distractions – eh, Eachan? – on the road. I made my bow to the father, paid my compliments to the mother, and attempted to dance with each of the sisters, who were evidently half in fears, half in hopes that I would ravish them. The temptation was not great, I will tell you that. Not one of them speaks Irish, and your northern tones will sound little different in their ears from what they hear from the Ulstermen hereabout. The idea that you might not be me will not enter their heads.'

'And what – for the sake of conversation – am I to tell them I am doing there? From what you have told me of them, I hardly think they will know the whereabouts of a Gaelic poet.'

He moved closer to me. 'You are to say nothing whatsoever about the poet. I am not convinced that they are not behind the thing somehow. Tell them you have come with your steward to see to our late grandfather's business in the town – for he had much trade with the planters at Coleraine. The Blackstones have no notion of hospitality, but they will have to let you stay. Andrew can go into the town and find out more about them, and you can observe the family itself.'

'For what?' I asked.

Sean raised his hands in a gesture of indifference. 'Signs. Indications. Slips of the tongue. Anything that suggests they mean our family harm, or look to wrest our grandfather's business from us. They will know well enough that I have no business head. Taking you for me, they may try to draw you into some swindle. Of course it may well be that they have nothing to do with it. Whoever is behind this clearly seeks to send our grandmother from her senses and see to it that, should I dodge further musket balls, I have no friends left.'

'And to prevent your marriage to Roisin.'

He waved my words away. 'That is something different. Remember: Edward and Henry Blackstone will leave here in two days' time, so you must not tarry in Coleraine any longer.'

'And then?'

'I will get a message to a person who is known to me at Bushmills. He will take you to Finn O'Rahilly. Show the charlatan to his face what falsehoods he peddles, and with the contents of your purse you will learn something of who set him to it. And yet I doubt you will get as much from him as I could have done. I fear your techniques of persuasion will be more subtle than my own.'

I did not need to ask him what he meant. I looked at Andrew. 'Can it be done?'

Andrew had been thinking it through. He did not take long to answer. 'Yes, I believe it can be done.'

Sean raised an eyebrow. 'This is how things stand, is it? You have roomed together five nights and now my place in my cousin's esteem is usurped.' He was trying to make light of it, but I could see in his eyes that he was hurt. It was the kind of hurt I used to see in the eyes of Archie Hay, if I should take myself off with other student friends for a day, to speak of things of scholarship in which he could feign no interest. Sean and Archie, they were the gilded ones. But there was a little truth in what he said, for I was beginning to feel that beneath the stubborn indifference to the world with which Andrew carried himself, there was a warmth and a well of friendship waiting, for those whom he might come to trust. And he was a man of integrity in whom sense would always be the master of emotion.

'You cannot blame me, Sean,' I said, 'for seeking sound counsel of a fellow Presbyterian, and a Scot at that, against the schemes of an adventuring Irish scoundrel like yourself. What to you is a mere diversion might be a matter of some difficulty to more cautious men.'

He broke into a gradual smile and then laughed, slapping me on the back. 'Caution be damned, Alexander. Two men who can face down Maeve O'Neill as you have both done care little for caution.' All was well with him again, and even Andrew smiled, a smile that lifted five years from his face and showed a glimpse of the young man he must, not so long ago, have been.

Our humour was broken by the sound of approaching voices. 'Murchadh,' said Sean. I felt myself being bundled towards the garderobe and pushed through its door. 'Under the seat,' was all Andrew had time to hiss before pulling it closed behind me. I was in complete darkness, with very little room even to turn. I could hear Sean greeting Murchadh and his son Cormac by name in the room next to me. I groped around, almost knocking over the water-butt, until my hand found a lever under the lid of the seat. I depressed it and instantly a panel behind me opened and I was facing a recess in the wall. I stepped into it and pulled the panel shut behind me. A narrow slit in the stone afforded what meagre light the stars could offer, and all the air I had. There was not room to turn or sit, and the cold and damp had reached into my bones in moments.

Murchadh and his sons made very little effort to lower their voices, but they spoke quickly, and in the Irish tongue, and often more than one of them at a time, so I found it hard to follow what was said. That there was bad feeling between my cousin and Roisin's father was evident. Her name was mentioned at an early point in their conference, the resolution of the matter was put off to another time. The younger men talked of harsh justice for the poet, but their father counselled caution, talking of honour, and his name, and disgrace and greater cursing. Sean kept his peace on the matter. It became clear that despite the current of animosity between them, Murchadh treated him as an equal and would not allow any of his sons to have the upper hand over my cousin. There was much talk of the kindred, of messengers, of 'the Franciscan', and of Dun-a-Mallaght, a name repeated several times, in lowered voices. It repeated itself in my head, against my will. My mind was translating where I would have preferred to remain in ignorance. Eventually, the name came to me in my own tongue: Dun-a-Mallaght: the Fort of the Curse.

After perhaps an hour, someone came into the garderobe to relieve himself. I was in terror that he would find and press the lever, by accident or design. I hardly dared breathe until I heard the waste washed down the outlet channel and the garderobe door open and shut once more. There I stood, freezing and numb, nauseous from the odours assailing me in that confined space, until the first hints of dawn began to filter into my tiny window, and Andrew Boyd came at last to release me from my prison.

'I had begun to think I would never be let out, that my bones would be found many years hence, walled up in this privy.' I sought to make light of it, but there had been times through the night when I had wondered if I should ever be taken from my recess alive, if the ghost of my mother's child would haunt this house for ever.

'Murchadh, Cormac and the rest have only just gone to their beds,' he said.

'What did they want?'

He shrugged. 'I was dismissed as soon as they appeared.'

'By Murchadh?'

'By Sean.'

It was clear he would talk no further here, and when we re-entered my grandfather's room, Sean was still there with Eachan, who was holding a bundle of clothing – finer by far than my own – for me. Sean handed me a long mantle of sheepskin and a pair of good boots. 'They are my own, but they will fit you well, and I cannot send you out in the country in your scholar's shoes.' I looked down at my feet. William had berated me for some time about my want of elegance – a message, I knew, from his wife. The money was given to Andrew. Sean smiled. 'These Scots will never waste a penny. You have too much of my Irish blood to be trusted with the purse. Boyd fears you will be induced to gamble it away, or worse.'

Andrew's face was severe, but his eyes were crinkling in a smile. I was as anxious as any to lighten the mood of our parting. 'I have never gambled in my life.'

My cousin looked genuinely appalled. 'Then when you return to Carrickfergus, you must give me two weeks. Two weeks of your life before you return to your dour Scottish town and your teacher's robes, and I will put right all that you have missed in your life, all that you have neglected, for who knows after that when we will meet again?'

I laughed. 'I will give you two weeks, cousin, and perhaps it is I who will change you.'

'And what I lack, you will be to me, and what you lack, that will I be to you. Keep safe, Alexander.'

He clasped me round the shoulders as he had done on our very first meeting, and wished me good fortune. 'I wish Eachan was going with you, but he is a recalcitrant troll and you will have a pleasanter journey without him. And, withal, it is a good man you have with you in his place. Play my part well, but steer clear of those sisters for my sake: they are foul of face and ill of humour. Make no promises to them on my behalf.'

'I will study to resist the temptation.' And then, promising that I would be returned within the week, to share with him my adventures, I bade farewell to my cousin.

SEVEN

Tales of the Dispossessed

We left Carrickfergus very soon afterwards, as the dark crispness of the night faded in the face of the coming dawn. There was an early frost still on the ground and we headed to the northwest. When we came to the common grazing grounds I looked behind me. The walls of Carrickfergus stretched far to the east and west, flankers jutting out into the land beyond. Behind the walls clustered a hotchpotch of rooftops, thatched, slated, or bright with red pantiles. To the west was the spire of the church of St Nicholas and to the east the gaudy palace of Joymount, at odds with the stoic tower houses that lined the high street. Finally, closest to the sea, were the rounded gatehouse towers of the castle. The town that had been the stronghold of the English in the North for centuries remained a formidable sight. Every pace of my horse took me further from its solid outline and the protection it offered me, and I advanced into territory unknown.

Andrew sensed my apprehension. 'Come on, you have been too long shut up, and so have I.' He dug his spurs into his horse's flank and flew. I followed his lead and soon the cold morning air in my lungs and the wind in my hair blew from me the fears of the dawn. I could see him up ahead of me as he unfolded himself into the air and the open spaces, and threw his head back, a man released. I caught up with him, but this served only to spur him on, and we raced until the terrain became too rough for the gallop, and we had to pull up, at the foot of a small glen, laughing like two boys truanting school.

'It is good to be out of that damned town,' he said.

I took a moment to get my breath. 'Why have you stayed so long?'

'It had claims on me. No more.' And he went on again, more carefully now, as the road had grown worse, boggy in parts and narrow, twisting round the bases of ancient oaks or by crumbling stone bridges, and at times disappearing altogether. The sun was not yet high enough in the sky to glimmer through the turning leaves of yellow, red and gold that made a canopy over our heads and shrouded us in a strange half-light. The leaves already fallen softened the sound of the horses' footfalls, making me all the more aware of the silence around us.

'This is an eerie place.'

'There are too many of these places hereabouts; I would have avoided it if I could, but the other routes are worse.'

'For what?'

'The woodkerne,' he said. 'Dispossessed natives who lived in the armed retinues of the old Irish lords. The native Irish must toe the English line to be awarded even the poorest land, but these kerne will not submit to the new order; they cite their pride and their lineage, which makes it a disgrace for them to turn their hands to a day's work, and prefer to live in the forest, ambushing and attacking travellers and new settlers. Some are as poor as common vagabonds, but there are others, of your cousin Murchadh's ilk, who are not.'

'For all I dislike him, Murchadh O'Neill is a man of wealth and standing. He is no forest-dwelling bandit. He has kept his lands.'

'Oh yes, he has kept them, and he will never be caught with

the bands of riders and woodsmen who terrorise so many, and neither will Cormac, the first-born. They know how to play to the English rules. I told you that.'

I remembered what the poet had said of Murchadh, who had kept to the fold while the wolf devoured his brothers.

'And the rest?'

'Murchadh's younger sons and his followers?' His face was a picture of contempt. 'They ravage the country up and down and gather tribute for their father.'

'And Sean?' I could not believe he would ride with such men.

His face was stony. 'I am not privy to his counsels.'

'Does Deirdre know what Murchadh and his sons are? Is that why she rejected Cormac?'

He looked straight ahead of him. 'I am thirty-four years old. What do I know of what is in a young woman's heart?' He picked up his pace. 'Come on, let us get out of this infernal woodland. I am determined that we should put up for the night before dark. There are places in this province where the ground itself cannot be trusted. Further north there is a lake, Loughareema, they call it the vanishing lake. The track skirts its edges, but on most days there is no water to be seen and you would think the land sound for miles around, but then, of a sudden, the water rises bubbling out of the ground and the place becomes an impassable lake. The people say it is the water spirits, come to claim the souls of those who have scorned them, and that the ghosts of those who drowned there haunt the place at night. It is not a Christian place.'

I looked around me and began to understand how a man of so firm a faith could still talk of spirits, ghosts, things of super-stition. As we left the woods, the land became desolate, devoid of all signs of life save my companion and myself. The wind that had not found us in the glen blew harshly in this exposed land-scape, bringing a promise of winter from the north. Everything was dun, brown. Everything looked dead, the occasional wild cherry or hawthorn standing as old and dry as stones. In a place like this a man might lose his reason, forget his faith. As a child I had believed every word of the stories my mother told me, of kings and princesses, giants and gods and messengers of the spirit world, fairies, banshees, changeling children. When I had grown to manhood, I had let these beliefs slip into memories of child-hood, knowing they were the superstitions of the godless and the pagan, forgiving my mother what many around me could never have forgiven her, for conjuring tales of the spirit world, of her own country, to entertain her child. But now, in this place, so expressive of the ageless powers and harsh beauty of the earth and the elements, I began to see how it was that men and women of sound mind and good faith could hold these tales as truth. I spurred my own horse on, anxious as Andrew to reach the secu-rity of one of the new settlements soon.

We stopped at last outside an inn, a squat place of clay and thatch with only two windows and a smoke-hole in the roof, giving little promise of hospitality. A traveller would be desperate indeed before he consented to spend the night in such a place. As we slid wearily from our horses, a young woman appeared in the doorway. She was thin but strong-looking, brown from outside work. Her hazel eyes were lit with warmth at the sight of Andrew.

'Margaret,' he said.

Flustered, she straightened her apron and tried to tidy the hair from her eyes, and then her glance fell on me, and her face froze for a moment in a shock of disbelief. Andrew had not noticed, busy as he was greeting the older woman standing behind her.

'Jenny, it is good to see you.'

'And you, my boy,' she said, reaching up to embrace him. 'It is too long since you have stopped at our place.' She looked old and weary, but her joy at Andrew's arrival took years from her face.

'I am kept busy these days.' He gestured towards me. 'This is Alexander Seaton, new arrived from Scotland. I am taking him up to the north coast.' I noted the care he took not to lie to her, and I warmed to him the more for it.

She turned her smile on me. 'And yourself, Andrew?'

'I have some people to see near Ballymena, before I make up my mind. My old master is dead now, and there is little to keep me in Carrickfergus. It is the right time for me to move on.' She nodded, a little pleased, it seemed, and ushered us inside, calling to her young son to bring more peats for the fire as she did so.

'How do you fare now, Jenny?'

'Oh, we . . . we fare as you see.'

Inside the dwelling, it was hard to see anything. The small windows in the thick walls afforded very little light, and the woman had pulled the door shut behind her, to keep what warmth there was in the place. My eyes smarted in the smoke that pervaded the building, only some of it finding its escape by way of the hole in the roof. Gradually, I became accustomed to the shadows and the grey, and saw around me a picture of abject poverty. The floor was of beaten earth, with rushes at the far end and two recesses in the wall, covered in some rough-looking blankets. There was a table with a wooden bench at the end nearer the door, a couple of flimsy stools and a well-worn rocking chair. A cumbersome chest, stacked with simple earthenware bowls, beakers and dishes, completed the house's furnishing. Suspended from a beam running the length of the roof was a pulley with pieces of dried meat, a few shrivelled onions and some battered copper pans hanging from it. It was like no inn I had ever set foot in before, but Andrew had warned me it would be so. 'The people here live more roughly than you will ever have been used to; they have none of the luxuries of your grandmother's house in Carrick-fergus. There are many places called "inns" where you would be lucky to find a pallet on the floor, or a blanket to cover you. Jenny is a Scot, a distant cousin of my father's, long settled here. She is a good woman, but poor. Do not be put off by the meanness of her home: we will find a warm welcome and hearty food to sustain us on the rest of our day's journey.'

The warning had not been enough – some misgivings must have shown on my face, for the girl Margaret saw them, and went to the defence of her home. 'We can fare no otherwise,' she said pointedly, directing her comment, it was evident, at me.

I struggled for a response, but her mother, shocked, was there before me. 'Margaret! Mr Seaton knows nothing of our troubles. Andrew has brought him here as a friend to our hospitality. We will not be found wanting.'

The girl bit her lip, and I thought her eyes threatened tears, but she mastered them. 'Yes, Mother. I am sorry.'

Andrew gave me an annoyed glance, and then took the girl aside to talk to her, while her mother prepared our meal and talked to me of Scotland. Margaret said little else for the remainder of our stay as she moved quietly around us, serving us coarse oat bread and mutton broth, the bubbling fat in which the barley swam pervading the place with its smell of old, dead animal. She did not look at, or speak to me again, and I was glad when the meal was over and we were able to leave, but not before I realised that always, when his gaze was turned elsewhere, her eyes were on Andrew. I saw a longing in them that had not been born today, or yesterday. I wondered how long this girl had been in love with my sombre companion, and why he had not noticed it.

After we had left, into the welcome fresh air and pale sunlight of the afternoon, I asked him about her.

'Oh? What's your interest?'

'I am just curious,' I sought to reassure him. He did not look convinced. 'She seems – in the wrong place.'

'We are all in the wrong place, here. But Margaret, yes: she's better than her surroundings. She deserves better. They all do, and might have had it one day too, had it not been for the woodkerne.'

His voice had hardened and I was not sure I wanted to know what he was about to tell me, but I could not go back now.

'Tell me what they did.'

'They . . .' He swallowed and started again. 'Jenny had another son, Margaret's older brother, David. He was murdered six months ago, in the prime of his life. The kerne wanted Jenny to pay tribute, but she could not, and David told them so. They cut his throat and hung him from a tree. It was Margaret who found him. She had to cut him down herself, for such was the fear of reprisals by the woodkerne that none would help her.'

My mind went back to the glen we had passed through earlier, to what he had said of Murchadh's sons. 'Who were they?' I asked quietly.

He did not look at me. 'I cannot be sure. Anyhow, now they are near to destitute. Margaret is leaving in search of work, that she might earn some money to support her mother and young brother. I have written her a testimonial.'

'She's a pretty enough girl; perhaps she will find a husband.'

He raised a quizzical eyebrow at me, a smile at the corner of his mouth.

'Are you looking for a wife, Alexander?'

I shook my head. 'I thought perhaps you might . . . she looked often after you.'

This was not a surprise to him. 'Aye, but I would not make her happy. I do not think I am the stuff husbands are made of.'

'I thought that, once. But now I know I was wrong.'

He pulled up his horse and regarded me with puzzled amusement.

'I did not know you were married. Indeed, your grandmother was congratulating herself last night that you were not.'

I did not dwell on why that might have been. 'I am not. But if God grants that I set foot in Scotland again, it is the first thing I will make certain of.'

He laughed. 'Then shall we tell the ladies of Ayr and Stranraer to prepare themselves?'

'I mean home, to Aberdeen. There is someone there I should have married two years ago. But I did not have the courage, and now I am afraid that when I return to Aberdeen I will find I am too late.'

'I hope you are not, Alexander. If you truly love her, I hope you are not.'

We walked our horses on. I should have left it, but I could not. 'Andrew, I know what it is to love, and to think you can never love again, but . . .'

I could not see his face, but I could see the muscles in his jaw working, the tendons on his hands tense at the reins. 'I have thought of it,' he said at length. 'But I am resolved that I should think of it no longer.'

'That is a hard road for a man to take.'

'I have the option of no other.'

I felt surrounded by desolation as we made our way in the last glows of the fading autumn light across the plateau. The gentle curves of Slemish rose a little to the north of us, and we cast shadows on the occasional granite rock that jutted oddly from the earth or lay recumbent on it. Every few miles a solitary hawthorn would be standing, windblown and gnarled, in a landscape scattered with the stumps of other trees.

Andrew spoke again as we passed one such. 'None will touch the hawthorn. To the Irish it is a special tree, protected by the spirits. It is believed that great misfortune will befall anyone who dares to cut down the fairy tree.'

'Surely the new planters do not give credence to such superstition.'

'They learn to,' he said.

We passed through Broughshane as the shadows of the night lengthened and took the last of the day. Andrew had a destination in mind and was determined to reach it before we might lay our heads in rest. Thoughts of the woodkerne were beginning to play on my mind, and I could feel the first stirrings of night-fear, when at last he stopped.

Before me rose a strange fortress, the stone walls over twenty feet high, with rounded flanking towers at each corner topped by conical slated roofs. Narrow windows were cut at intervals into the upper storeys of the towers, and the front was breached only by a huge set of oak doors. The night-fears tied themselves into a knot of apprehension in my stomach as my companion dismounted and began to hammer on the door.

EIGHT

The Franciscan

It took almost two minutes of hammering before any reply came from within the strange fortress. An anxious voice called out gruffly, and in plain English, that we should state our names and our business.

'Mr Alexander Seaton, a Scot, making his way to Coleraine, and Andrew Boyd, Scot, his servant.' A shutter was opened then closed again, and a moment later a lighted torch appeared at the top of the wall above us.

'Let them in.'

The doors swung open and I followed Andrew under the archway and into the courtyard beyond. What greeted us as the bolt was brought to behind us was not a fortress or castle but a farmstead, and the gatekeepers looked to be cottagers or craftsmen, not soldiers. The stockier of the two came to take my horse.

'Welcome, friends. You are late abroad. You should not travel in these parts after dark. The woodkerne are about.'

'Are you much troubled by them?'

'We keep watch night and day.' The man jerked a thumb eastwards. 'There, it is safe enough, but they roam almost at will from the northwest. You are fortunate to have reached here in safety.'

More torches had been lit about the enclosure as curious inhabitants came out to view the foolhardy visitors. A long stone-built house was set at the far end of the homestead, and three squat, thatched timber-framed cottages ran up the west wall of the place. Two women, an old man and half a dozen children had straggled out of the buildings and were watching us from a distance. When the women saw that we posed no threat and were welcomed, they went back into their dwellings, leaving their children, under the eye of the grandfather, to come and look at us more closely.

There was a bakehouse on the eastern wall and to the right of the entrance doors on the outer wall was a small clay cabin that passed for the guardhouse. Next to it were the stables, in the loft of which Andrew and I were to spend the night.

The place was filled with animals. Goats were tethered near the cottages, and some sheep were penned in a far corner. Between the cottages and their well was the hen house, its inhabitants at rest for the night. A few small, black, Irish cattle lowed in another corner. A couple of friendly dogs came bounding up to us, and to my surprise, Andrew knelt down on the ground to greet them: it was the first time I had seen him show affection to anything. As I bent towards them, something caught my attention, a slight movement at the edge of my vision. A man had moved out of the shadow of the bakehouse door; his eyes were fixed on me as if they were looking at a dead man.

Andrew straightened himself at last and asked if we might have some refreshment after we had seen to the horses.

The older gatekeeper nodded. 'After you have finished in the stables, go to Stephen and he will see you all right with food and drink – will you not, Stephen?'

The expression on the face of the man who had been staring at me changed swiftly, and the grimace broke into a broad smile. 'Oh, I will that, don't you worry. You gentlemen just come over here when you are ready, and I will have fine warm pasties and ale waiting for you.' Nodding cheerily to us, he returned to his bakehouse where a faint golden light still glowed. I shivered now, conscious of the approaching coldness of the night.

Once we were safely in the stables, I quizzed Andrew. 'What is this place?'

'Armstrong's Bawn. It's a Scotsman's estate but the lands were formerly in the O'Neill kindred – they raised cattle and lived here for much of the year. When the lands were seized by the Crown those amongst them who could not be trusted were executed, imprisoned, banished. And so they have a great grievance, and they show it by attacking and despoiling the settlements while they can. Like many others, Armstrong is obliged to defend his land, his tenants and their livestock, and because they have not yet built suitable houses themselves, they come and live here, within the safety of the walls.'

One of the gatekeepers had come in while we had been talking. 'It would be madness for us to live outside the bawn by night. I have been here three years and have never yet been inclined to build my own house further afield. Though God knows, there will be little enough safety here if they put their minds to it. Their leaders play their hand so close and clever. If once they should rise against us, they will tear us limb from limb and feed us to their dogs. This is a barbarous country you have come to, Mr Seaton, and godless too.'

Later, as we crossed the yard, I spoke quietly to Andrew. 'Have you been here before?'

'No. That is why I chose this place. I am too well known in the inns and villages on the road. There would have been too many questions about you, and always the chance that someone might have taken you for Sean. It will be safer for you here.'

His words brought home to me what I had tried to ignore: out on the road, away from all the safeguards of my grand-mother's tower house and of the town, it was not Sean's life that was in danger from this curse but mine. There had been a time when I would not have cared about that, but now I did, for now I had a life, the promise of a life with Sarah and Zander, that I wanted to hold on to. 'There is no chance that Sean would ever have been here?'

Andrew laughed. 'Do you see a tavern somewhere, or a whorehouse? Besides, your cousin has no need to seek shelter from the woodkerne.' The meaning of this was plain enough and I asked no more about it.

Neither of us had noticed in the gloom, but the baker was waiting for us by the door. He thrust out a hand to greet us. 'Gentlemen! Welcome, welcome. Come away into the warmth and take a seat. It is a bitter night, and you will be tired after your long riding.' Andrew stepped back to let me pass ahead of him under the low doorway. As he did so, I caught for a moment a look of unease in his eyes that had been wholly absent until the baker had spoken.

The bakehouse was warm and welcoming, and only once seated on a straw pallet that passed for the baker's bed did I realise how weary I was. The baker was pulling a pan with half a dozen pies on it out of the oven. The smell alone made me ravenous. While the pies cooled he poured us each a jug of ale. Andrew watched him all the while. The baker held his drink up. '*Slainte!*'

Andrew nodded. 'And to you.' He took a drink and set down his cup. 'You are Irish, then.'

The baker looked at us, conspiratorially, his eyes dancing. 'I am that, but you gents need have no fear, for I am as English and well-affected as the Irish come. I know the scriptures from back to front and could recite the oath of allegiance at the drop of your hat.'

Andrew was not altogether reassured. 'Have you been here long?'

'Ah, not long, sir. I travelled many years and learned my trade and only now am I ready to settle back in my home-land, in these new times. I offered my services here and they were taken. The master has trouble finding men and women enough to work the land, and a baker and brewer in the bawn frees others to go out and work in the fields and woods. I can see to the stores and buy what is needful at the markets, and the native Irish cannot cheat me as they would others, for I know all their ways.'

I could believe this; he must have been fifty, but he was of burly build and strong still, and the ready humour in his speech could not quite mask the busy intelligence of his eyes. This man was thinking, thinking all the time.

'You have travelled far today?'

Andrew spoke before me, which was as well – my answers were ill-prepared. 'We landed at Olderfleet this morning, and have been travelling ever since.'

'You would not have gone by Carrickfergus, then?'

'Why should we have gone by Carrickfergus? Our journey takes us north, to Coleraine.'

The man nodded. 'Coleraine. Of course. But you met with no one from Carrickfergus on your way?'

'No one.' Andrew's voice was becoming harder.

'There was a party passed by here yesterday on the way from Coleraine to Carrickfergus. They were making for the funeral of some great merchant that was to be held there today.'

'Deirdre.' It was on the tip of my tongue to say it, but I managed, at the last, to keep my mouth shut.

The baker did not seem to have noticed, and continued. 'I thought you might have heard something of it on your travels. A funeral always makes for an interesting gathering, and we get so little news here.' He had been careful to speak to both of us, but he turned his full attention now to me. 'And so you have come from Scotland, Mr Seaton. Whereabouts in Scotland might that be?'

'The North, the town of Aberdeen.' I hesitated. 'Do you know it?'

I was relieved to know that he did not. 'But I have heard that they are not so well affected there, to the Reformation of religion. Would that be right, sir?'

'All that was long ago, before my birth,' I replied. 'But now the controversies are over the forms of worship. They will be settled soon.'

'Pray God they are.'

I did not think it would be profitable to spend my evening explaining to an Ulster baker the disputes over the liturgy that inflamed the pens of the divines of Aberdeen.

'And what is your business here in Ireland, sir? Have you come for the plantation?'

Andrew spoke for me while I struggled for an answer. 'My master has a mind to buy into land from the Irish Society and to ship willing settlers from his home to this province. I am to be his agent here.'

The baker turned interested eyes on Andrew. 'You know this country well, then?'

'Very well.' The two eyed each other steadily, until the baker returned to the business of feeding us. Venison pasties and a pigeon pie were produced, much finer fare than we could have

expected in a roadside inn. There was little further conversation as we ate. The baker was busy about clearing up his work
for the night and preparing for the morning. He hummed a
tune I did not know, and some snatches of Irish escaped him,
but for all the aura of casual contentment and busyness he
sought to give off, I could not escape the feeling that he was
calculating something all the time.

As we were finishing our food he came with another jug
and two goblets. 'Mead,' he said, 'from our own bees. A fine
thing to warm and rest a traveller for the night.'

The warm, sweet liquid curled down my throat and the
baker opened the conversation once more. 'Where will you
lodge, once you reach Coleraine? Have you acquaintance there
already?'

Before Andrew could warn me otherwise, I had begun to
speak. 'We are to lodge with Matthew Blackstone, master mason
in the town.'

'Ah, Blackstone, is it? He has built half of Coleraine and
Derry City too, so they say. A man of means and influence.
Now tell me . . .'

But the baker did not get to finish his question, for Andrew
had stood up and hauled me up unceremoniously with him.
With a curt, 'Thank you for the food and drink,' he took me
out into the darkness of the bawn, the baker's murmured Irish
'Good night' dying at the door.

'That fellow asks too many questions,' said Andrew, after we
had clambered in the pitch dark up a stepladder into the stable
loft.

As he laid himself on the straw, I pulled Sean's sheepskin
mantle round me, and did what I could with a blanket on the
straw beneath my head. My body yearned for sleep, but my
mind had unfinished business and rebelled against it. I felt

myself to be the plaything of the malicious Irish gods: Alexander
Seaton who had no place in the stable loft of an Ulster bawn,
removed from everything I understood, a life in Scotland so
far away now that it seemed almost to be the life of another.
The image of the family I had been brought to and told 'This
is yours' was unravelling in my mind, the strange and ragged
threads of it losing their colour and eluding my confused grasp.
Sean, Deirdre, Murchadh, my grandmother, Roisin – they
seemed little more to me than players who already knew the
end to a tale I was only beginning to listen to.

It was deep in the windless night that I heard a creak of
wood below me. My bones were too cold to allow me the
sound sleep that Andrew was in, for he had scarcely moved
since he had first lain down. I lay still and listened as the horses
shifted in their stalls: another movement, a rustle of straw, a
heavier creak on the stable steps. I was rigid, trying to control
the unnatural heaving of my chest. Slowly, I moved my foot,
and gave the back of Andrew's leg as hard a kick as I could
manage in the silence. There was no response. I tried again:
nothing. Nothing but the creak of a closer rung and the unmistakable sound of another human being breathing heavily. Only
the merest suggestions of shapes made themselves known to
my eye in the blackness of the loft, but at last I caught some
slow movement from the direction of the steps, and the light
brushing of straw across the floor. The form of Andrew beside
me was kicked, then more closely inspected, and made no
response. I had no weapon and readied myself to grab the foot
of the night-time visitor when he kicked me. But no foot shot
out, and I had no time to understand the sudden dancing light
that made its way towards my neck, until the prick of the
blade's edge had found my throat.

'Who are you?' This in Irish.

I thought as quickly as I could as the knife played against my skin. 'I am not – I do not . . .' I stumbled to find the words in the Gaelic, the fear numbing my tongue.

Again in Irish. 'Who are you? You are no Scot. You are of the O'Neill. Who are you?' The baker leaned over me, his eyes only inches from mine, and I had no doubts that should I make a wrong move, I would be dead. I took the only route open to me.

'I am Alexander Seaton, a Scot, son of Grainne FitzGarrett, grandson of Maeve O'Neill of Carrickfergus.'

The man sat back on his haunches and let the knife fall softly to the floor. 'Well, well, well, by God!' he said at last. 'Grainne's son? So the old besom lied after all.'

I could make out the knife now, lying a hand's span away from me, but I dared not move. The fellow seemed to have forgotten my presence for the moment, as he took in what I had said. 'Grainne's son,' he repeated. 'Well, well, well. The good Lord has his reasons indeed.' He struck flint expertly against his knife and lit a small candle he had brought from the folds of his tunic. In the ensuing light I saw that he was smiling.

I sat up, pulling up the mantle against the cold. 'Did you know my mother?' I said it in English, for that was the tongue in which he now spoke to me.

'Oh yes, I knew your mother, although she could scarce have told you who I was, just another of her brother's companions that would have wooed her if he could. If she had glanced my way but once, she would almost have driven me from my vocation.'

'Your vocation?' I said stupidly.

He laughed. 'Yes, boy, my vocation.' A strong hand was held out towards me. 'Father Stephen Mac Cuarta of the order of

St Francis, late of the Irish College in Louvain, and now of Bonamargy Friary in the county of Antrim.'

'But why . . .?' My mind still sleepy. I struggled to make sense of his words.

'A long story for another day,' he said, with a resolution that brooked no argument. 'But now, tell me why you are here, instead of being at your grandfather's funeral.'

Questions. Too many questions, as Andrew had said.

'What have you done to my companion?' I knew Andrew was not dead, thank God, for I could see his chest rise and fall in the pale light of the candle's flame.

He held up his hand in a gesture of appeasement. 'A sleeping draught, a little decoction in the mead. He will wake at dawn after the best sleep of his life and bless the very straw he lay down on, and no harm to him.'

I looked down on Andrew's sleeping face, at the vague smile that played about his lips. The priest was right: I had never seen him so contented.

Father Stephen drew closer to me and his face became serious. 'Tell me then, what are you doing here? Did Sean bring you? You should know that I am a friend to your family and have been forty years at least. I left Ireland with your uncle in the train of Tyrone, and swore to him that when I returned I would watch over his children's interests. You must believe me in that. You are the very image of Phelim and of his son. I mean you no harm.'

The knife, whose blade sent small darts of light dancing and flitting on the timbers of the roof above me, assured me of that. If he had meant me harm, I would have been dead by now. I took the decision to trust him. 'I was called to Ulster by my grandmother. She sent Sean to Scotland to find me. At my cousin Deirdre's wedding, our family had been cursed by the poet who had been hired to honour them.' He nodded at this, evidently familiar with this part of the tale at least. 'The curse predicted a swift end to my grandmother's line, but as no one but Maeve knew of my existence, I was not encompassed in it. An attempt was made on Sean's life and my grandfather fell gravely ill. My grandmother believed that if she could reveal me to the poet then the curse would be lifted.'

'And so you came to Ireland.'

'With great reluctance, and after a deal of persuasion, yes, I came to Ireland.'

He looked directly at me, searching for something more. 'And yet, on the day your grandfather is buried you are not in Carrickfergus, but journeying north, and not with Maeve, or Sean, or Deirdre even, but with a servant, and masquerading as what you are not. Something else has happened.'

And so I told him of the events of the wake, of Finn O'Rahilly and his renewed curse. His face grew more troubled as I went on, and darkened considerably when I repeated O'Rahilly's words on the union with the Rose and the bastard child. He asked me to repeat what the poet had said of Murchadh O'Neill; the words seemed to afford him a certain grim satisfaction.

'He will not have liked that. No, Murchadh will not have liked that. He thought that no one but the English noticed the care he has taken to worm his way into their favour. But go on.'

'There is little more to tell,' I said. 'My grandmother is convinced of the power of this curse; I think my cousin Deirdre too is affected by it.'

'And what do you think?'

'That O'Rahilly has been paid to do this, and what threat comes to our family will be the deliberate policy of a human agency.' To my surprise, the priest nodded. I was only just beginning to understand that one form of superstition does not of necessity encompass all others. 'Maeve insisted I should travel to O'Rahilly and thus "break" the curse, but she would not permit Sean to travel with me, for fear of another attempt on his life. That is why Andrew Boyd is here instead.'

Father Stephen looked at the recumbent figure of my fellow Scot. 'Do you trust him?'

The question had never till now entered my head. From my arrival in my grandmother's house I had accepted Andrew's place there as more valid and permanent than my own. 'Yes,' I said at last. 'I trust him. A little more than he trusts you, I think.'

'Then he will do well enough,' he said. 'But why do you go to Coleraine? O'Rahilly is not there.'

'Sean suspects the Blackstones of some design to get hold of our grandfather's business. I am to present myself there as him, and get what intelligence I can on the matter, which will be little enough, for I am no spy.'

The priest laughed heartily at this. 'No, but Sean's very walk proclaims him to be Sean O'Neill, of Ulster, and mindful of the censure of no one, and you walk with the same pride, which I think cannot sit well with your Calvinist countrymen. But you think, I would say, before you act, not afterwards. Am I right?'

'Now I do. Yes.'

'But tell me,' he said, digressing. 'You are truly from the northeast? You did not lie about that?'

'No, I did not. I was brought up on the Moray Coast, and teach now in the Marischal College in Aberdeen.'

'A dangerous work for you. And do you win minds for the faith? How does our Church fare in those parts? There are great hopes of your bishop and your university doctors. And the Jesuits are busy out in the country.'

I realised with a growing sense of apprehension that he did not understand. I glanced again at the knife: it was closer to me than it was to him – I could reach it first. 'You have misunderstood,' I said, edging my hand very slightly closer to the hilt. 'I am an adherent of the Kirk of Scotland. I was never a Romanist in my life.'

He sat back, visibly deflated. 'But your mother . . .'

'My mother gave up her faith when she came to Scotland. I have never been brought up to anything other than the Kirk.'

He closed his eyes and, crossing himself, uttered a prayer in the Gaelic, my mother's name passing his lips several times. The only phrase I could properly make out was the last one he said: 'Dear God have mercy on her tortured soul.'

There was an uneasy silence between us for a moment. 'It is late,' said the priest eventually, getting heavily to his feet, 'and you will need your rest and your wits about you for the days to come. Come to me in the morning for your breakfast; take your companion with you – you may tell him as much about me as you wish.' And then he was gone, and his light with him, and I lay in the dark many long hours until the first stirrings of the dawn.

NINE

A Thing Foretold

Maeve wanted to retire to her room, she was tired now, oh so tired. But she could not, for she was Maeve O'Neill, and she had played that part well seventy years now. A little longer yet, just a little longer and she could rest. She did not know half the people in the house and cared for fewer of them. How many people did she care for? Not many. On this side of the grave, there was only one, only one who mattered, and within him he held everything.

She watched her grandson as he danced, talked, made a friend at every turn. Half the girls were in love with him – a few who were no longer girls, also. But they would not have him. She recalled the hour, twenty years ago, when she had witnessed the birth of the girl who she had chosen to be Sean's wife. Murchadh had fathered many fine sons, but it was a daughter Maeve had waited so eagerly upon, and when that daughter had drawn her first breath, it had been Maeve who soothed the laboured mother's brow, whispered sweet comforts in her ear and handed her her child. And she had chosen well, for Roisin was everything that she should have been. A pale beauty, but healthy: she would be as good a breeder as her mother had been. And she was compliant, she knew her place, knew her duty, would serve it without murmur or complaint. What could she have had to complain of, with a man like Sean handed to her?

Not like Deirdre. Maeve shivered. How the gods of her fore-fathers had punished her in her daughter and granddaughter. She had sullied the purity of her line with the taint of English blood, and they had made her pay, first in Grainne and now in Deirdre. Oh, but Richard FitzGarrett had been a fine man, and they had known passion. And in their grandson her debt would be paid, her line redeemed.

The young people were enjoying themselves: they had paid her husband due honour, as was right, but now the night was theirs. She allowed herself a smile, gracious, if one of them should catch her eye. Murchadh's sons were fine men, all of them, like their father, but stronger. He had been foolish in his youth, weak. His resolve had not been strong enough, but he had learned, and surely he had paid for it now? But it was only the weak that had survived that killing time, those days of exile. The heroes, like Phelim, were dead. Cormac would have been such a hero. That Deirdre had rejected him was beyond her comprehension. There was a madness in the girl that went beyond dishonour, ingratitude, spite: it was the taint.

The taint. Grainne. Grainne had been the warning. An aber-ration she should have been, but she was not; she had continued into the next generation. And now God had gifted her Grainne's heretic son, and he had come to play his part, pay his due to his race and his name. But he did not matter: only Sean mattered.

A servant filled her glass again. She had had a lifetime with her glass full, but the wine often bitter. No more. A boy came from the lower floor, a note in his hand. Pray God not the poet; she could not withstand him a third time. The lad searched the room and found Sean soon enough. He took the note from the boy and read it in a moment. His countenance changed, the mask slipped. The mask that faced the world, day and night. But she knew that other face. She had seen it sometimes in the boy he had once been. Grainne had known it in his two-year-old face. Deirdre had seen it all her life. He had hidden it from Maeve, but that did not hurt. Not so much. She would accomplish in him what must be accomplished, and if her grandson's love be the cost to her, then so be it.

She watched as Sean left Roisin's side, murmuring some politeness to her and seeking out Eachan. He had not long to look, for the man from Tyrone was never far from his master's shadow. Again, in that, she had chosen well. Eachan was not well pleased at the content of the note, but Sean laughed, slapped him on the shoulder, sought to reassure him, and then downed his drink and descended the stairs, calling for his mantle. Not the poet, then, but a woman. Some town whore, no doubt. It would do no harm, it was natural, after all, and Roisin knew the way of the world of men. Even so, he should not go out in the night alone, not when the threat to him had been made so clear, and public. But she need not have concerned herself about that, for as she had known he would, Eachan had gone out after his master, a minute or two behind.

She could sleep safe now. She was in truth very tired. Deirdre had already gone to her bed, long before she should have done, feigning grief for her grandfather. What did she know of love? Maeve's bile rose to think of it. She should bid goodnight to Murchadh, but she had had enough for the day, and did not want the whole company called together to watch her retire. She would slip away unnoticed. She was an old woman and it was her right. But she took the longer way to her chamber, seeking out the serving boy. He trembled to see her coming, and it reminded her weary bones to straight – themselves.

'The note for my grandson – who brought it?'

'A girl. She covered her face.'

'A whore?'

The boy stammered. 'No, Mistress, I do not think it. Just a girl. I could not see her right.'

'Very well. Now see to my guests' glasses. This is a house of hospitality, not a Protestant church.'

The boy ran to do her bidding. It pleased her. She was Maeve O'Neill.

It cannot have been two hours later that she was woken by a hammering, a kicking at the door, a howling that was not of human born. Half the house had not yet been abed, and yet the noise overpowered all their laughter, their singing and their music. It pierced the doors, the walls, and found its way through stairways and along corridors to meet every terror in her heart. By the time she had reached the balcony, the whole house was up. Deirdre, in her nightclothes, was running down to the hall. From below, Cormac had bounded up to meet her and sought to hold her back. She pulled against him but he smothered her head in his shoulders and would not let her look on the horror.

But Maeve saw. As the household parted like the sea in front of Eachan, she saw. Sean's servant, whence the howling came, had dropped to his knees at the entrance to the hall and lifted his hands in tormented appeal to a relentless God. Before him, on the floor already staining dark, was the body of her grandson.

The world had stopped. There was no sound or movement save the animal cry of the man from Tyrone, echoing through the house, reaching to the other world. No one put a hand out to her, sought to stop her as slowly, she descended the stairs.

Eachan had laid him like a child, carefully, on the ground, as if fearful of hurting his head. He had closed the eyes that had lighted every thing they had ever looked on. He might have been sleeping as a child sleeps, a day's labours done and with no fears for the morrow. But his face was white, the white of death, and already the blood was drying at the cut in his throat. For a moment, she feared she might not find her voice. 'Take him to my chamber,' she said at last.

There were six of them in the room: herself, Eachan, Cormac, Murchadh, Deirdre and the priest. Eachan had laid him on the bed – he had carried him up alone, allowing no other to touch him. Maeve had ordered more coals to be brought, as if the warmth of the fire could ever reach him now. The priest was at his offices, and the servant was prostrate at his dead master's feet, but none of the others were on their knees. Murchadh was breathing heavy, his fingers clenching and unclenching over the hilt of his sword, and Cormac was as white as a winding-sheet, beads of perspiration on his brow. Deirdre was staring at her grandmother, all insolence, all defiance gone: nothing left but a sheer and complete hatred.

'You have killed him,' she said.

Cormac laid a hand on her shoulder but she shrugged it off.

Maeve kept her voice steady. 'Not I.'

'You would not leave it. You would never leave it, and now he is dead. You have murdered my brother.'

Maeve spoke slowly, for the certainty had only now come to her. 'Deirdre,' she said, 'you know who murdered your brother.'

TEN

Revelations

'You should have woken me.'

'I couldn't; I tried: you were dead to the world.'

'You should have tried harder.' Andrew's good humour after his sound sleep had disappeared entirely when I'd told him the cause of it. 'You think I am here to take the country air? You are as bad as your cousin. As bad as them both. The O'Neills always know better. They can manage on their own. Who would lay a hand on an O'Neill?'

'But I am not . . .'

'And he was a crony of Phelim's? Well, there can be little better to recommend him than that.' He was striding resolutely towards the bakehouse and I struggled behind, still trying to get on my boots. 'I was to return to Carrickfergus with your corpse on my back, was I?' He raged on, then brought himself to a halt, spun round and looked very close in my face. 'Have you any idea who this man is? What he is doing here? I should never have brought you here.'

'Andrew, what do you know?'

He looked at me a moment, still seething, his nostrils widened and his chest heaving as he tried to master himself. 'Nothing,' he said eventually. 'I know nothing. But I will have answers.'

We had by now attracted the attention of one of the young wives out seeing to her hens. I gave her a cheery wave and bade her good morning, propelling Andrew towards the bakehouse as I did so. 'This is hardly the place to discuss it. You can find your answers once we are inside.'

'Oh, I will, never fear for that. I will.' He strode through the door ahead of me, and it was only as he disappeared inside that I realised he had taken his dagger from its sheath.

Father Stephen was going cheerily about his business, and clearly had been for some time. He showed no sign of fatigue after his night ventures, and greeted us heartily.

'Well, Alexander Seaton! And Andrew Boyd, is it not? Well rested, I'll wager.'

'Too well,' said Andrew, with little heartiness and no attempt to hide his anger.

'Ah, now, you must forgive me, my young friend. For I thought I knew this fellow, or something of him, but of you, or why he was with you, I knew nothing. We live in dangerous times for the O'Neills and their friends. And those of my order must take special care who they make themselves known to.'

'For the O'Neills who will keep the law, these are no more dangerous times than any other, and as to your order – you are out of Bonamargy, I take it?'

The priest nodded, watching Andrew carefully, watching too the hand on his dagger.

'Then you have the protection of Randal MacDonnell, although I doubt whether even the Earl of Antrim could explain what you were doing in a Scots bawn, disguised as a baker.'

Mac Cuarta looked at him carefully but said nothing, only closing and bolting the door, before he brought us fresh bread and milk.

Andrew inspected his bread carefully and sniffed at the milk. Father Stephen laughed. 'Eat your breakfast, boy. There's nothing in it the cow didn't put there. I will trust you now, and you will trust me. You know too much about me already for it to be any other way.'

He sat down beside us, and all the humour had gone from his face.

'Have you brought any message from Sean?'

Andrew bridled. 'Do I look like a message boy?'

The priest appraised him carefully. 'Not much.'

'Our commission is to Coleraine, and to Finn O'Rahilly, nothing more. Sean was to send a message to Bushmills, that someone might guide us to O'Rahilly, but he mentioned no name.'

'It will be waiting for me at Bushmills, and then we will see what is to be done.'

'There is nothing to be done but that you should take us to the poet.'

'That remains to be seen,' said the priest, looking at me. 'But how is it to be done? Where do you fit into things?'

'In a philosopher's robes in the Marischal College of Aberdeen,' I said, 'for after this nonsense of the poet is done with, I have no place in any scheme here.'

He shook his head. 'The matter of the poet cannot be dismissed. That his words have been spoken, and so publicly, matters greatly. Our leaders have often rested their reputation on what the poets say of them, their name honoured or damned by generations according to the pronouncement of the bard. This common law of the English might be blown away soon enough in this country, like a weed on the wind, and what will be left, and how will a man like Murchadh legitimise himself and his claims then, if not by the word of genealogists and the poets? No, the curse cannot be dismissed. Perhaps it would be better that you had no place in the scheme. God grant that it might be so.'

Andrew was in no humour to listen to a mass priest speculate on what God might grant. 'If you have some intelligence of Sean's "business", or this curse, I would thank you to share it with us. We have little time to squander.'

Father Stephen's face hardened. 'No more do I. I am fifty-seven years old. I have worn the robes of my order over forty years. I have seen our houses in Ireland dishonoured and destroyed, the succour we gave to the people taken from them. I have said mass in a morning and stained my sword on the blood of Ireland's enemies in the afternoon. I have seen our great leaders degraded and die far from home, the glory and hope of our people gone. I have travelled and studied in Spain, France, Italy and the Low Countries and I am on my last mission. The man before me is the image of one whose last confession I heard in a filthy alley in Madrid. I do not take his presence here at this time lightly, and neither should you.'

Andrew drained his beaker and stood up abruptly. 'I don't. Come, Alexander, we must lose no more time.'

The priest took hold of my wrist as I got up, and held it in a firm grip. 'Give me ten minutes. Your friend can play the servant he is supposed to be and see to the horses.'

Andrew very pointedly handed me his knife, before going out once more into the courtyard and letting the bakehouse door bang shut behind him.

Stephen Mac Cuarta's face was deadly serious, his eyes searching mine. 'Tell me again what the poet said. Tell me what he said of Roisin, and of Macha.'

'He made no mention of Roisin, and of Murchadh he said . . .'

'Not of Murchadh, of Macha.' He gave emphasis to the last word.

I shook my head. 'I know no Macha; he spoke of no Macha.'

'He spoke did he not, of the union with the Rose—'

'The union with the Rose' – Roisin. 'Poisoned by a bastard child.' I looked up. 'Who is this Macha – is it Sean's child?'

He hesitated a long moment, then spoke. 'No, she is not Sean's child, she is his wife; I married them myself, when he was on his way to Coleraine for Deirdre's wedding. She is almost nine months gone with child and under my protection.'

'He would have told me.'

'There are things that . . .'

He had placed a kind hand on my arm but I brushed it away. 'He would have told me. He is my cousin: we talked of such things.' A heavy emptiness was dragging itself down to my stomach. 'He is like my brother.'

'He could tell no one. You know of your grandmother's plans for him. She looks to join these two branches of the O'Neills, and with them your grandfather's money and lands to Murchadh's, and to see her family a force to be reckoned with once more. If Sean has a bastard child, Roisin might not like it – although, in truth, most of the Irish of his rank will have – but it would make little difference to her and any child she might have by him in wedlock in English law. But if Sean is already married, and has a child of that marriage, that child, and not any from a bigamous marriage to Roisin, would inherit all he has.'

'So why would O'Rahilly have talked of a bastard child?'

'Because he does not know. He does not know Sean is married.'

'But if, as you say, such things are common, can he have really hoped to put Murchadh off the marriage by talking of a bastard child? Under the law, Murchadh has nothing to lose by that.'

'Under the English law, perhaps, but under our old ways, our old laws, the brehon laws, a bastard child has as much right to his father's property as a son born in wedlock, and as much call on the loyalty of his father's followers.'

The significance of this was beyond me. 'But Murchadh has woven himself into the fabric of the English occupation, he has danced to the English tune over twenty years now, has he not, in spite of what his sons might do? Why should the old Irish laws bother him now?'

The priest got up and began to tidy up the breakfasting beakers and bowls. 'Aye, you are right. Think no more on it. Now go you to Coleraine. When you are finished there, I will meet you at Bushmills, and take you to Finn O'Rahilly; I know his lair. But if you meet with any difficulties or dangers on the way, make straight for Bonamargy Friary. Whether I am there or not, you will be given sanctuary.'

I was about to leave but Andrew's voice, repeating itself in my head, stopped me. 'Tell me,' I said, 'since we are to trust one another. What are you doing here, in this bawn, and under this guise?'

'My master's bidding,' he replied, in a manner that invited no further conversation. He blessed me, and trying not to flinch I emerged into the welcoming sunlight of the waking morning, where Andrew was waiting with my horse.

He brooded quietly a good two hours or more until some time before mid-morning we stopped by a stream at the edge of a birch wood that had struggled up the hillside as high as it could before it surrendered the ground to heather, moss and stone. Andrew filled his flask and then let the beasts drink. I leant against a lump of granite, higher than myself, that jutted from the earth like something left over from the Creation. Towards the east, at the edges of the great plateau beneath us,

I thought I could discern the sea.

'Well?' he said at last.

'Well what?'

'Your priest. What did he want of you that I was not to know?'

I felt a trickle of amusement to see him so riled, but I judged best not to take it further. 'What do you know of Macha?' I said.

'Macha?'

'Yes. What do you know of her?'

He frowned, wrinkling his nose in a beginning of disgust. 'There is a legend of a woman, many centuries ago ... Has the priest been telling you stories?'

'Not that kind of story. Did you know Sean has a wife?'

'I'd sooner believe the Pope has a wife.'

'The priest says he has a wife whose name is Macha. He married her two months ago, and she is at this moment under the protection of the priests at Bonamargy Friary. He says she will very soon give birth to my cousin's child.'

All humour went from his face. 'My God – if Murchadh should find out ... But Sean cannot hide them for ever.'

'I do not think he intends to hide them for ever.'

'Then may God help them when he brings them before the world. Come on, let us get on.' But it was not long before he resumed our conversation. 'What did he have to say of Deirdre?'

'Deirdre? I ... he said nothing of Deirdre.'

'He must have said something.' There was an edge to his voice, an effort at self-control he could not mask.

I scrambled through my mind. 'He told me he promised Phelim he would keep an eye on both his children. I should have thought to ask him more, for there is something far wrong in Deirdre's marriage. I would hardly have thought a few weeks of marriage enough time for the breeding of such resentments.'

'Resentments here can be roused in seconds and last for centuries.'

'I am coming to see that; and with the sons of Murchadh stoking the fires of those resentments, they will burn a long time after the passion between Deirdre and Edward Blackstone has cooled.'

I saw him swallow, look straight ahead of him as he spoke. 'There never was any passion between them.'

I looked at him. 'Andrew,' I began.

'Do not ask me, Alexander. Do not ask.' He dug his heels into his horse's flanks and rode hard for the northwest. I thought again of the night of the wake, of the trouble between Deirdre and her husband. And I wondered how many, when Edward Blackstone's brother had shouted that Deirdre's lover was flaunted in her husband's face, had thought as I at first had thought, that he meant Cormac O'Neill. I wondered also how much of the truth Cormac O'Neill knew, and what it would mean for Andrew should he ever find out.

ELEVEN

Coleraine

By the time I caught Andrew he had reached a forest, where woodcutters felled and sawed relentlessly. I tried to talk to him, but he made it clear he would not hear what I had to say, as if our conversation of earlier had not taken place at all. 'The planters are stripping these woods to the bone to build their towns at Derry and Coleraine, and making a nice profit on the side with illegal exports.'

I looked around me. 'There is enough wood in these forests to build ten towns.'

'But not to satisfy the greed of those who live in them. They can hardly find the time to build their houses, so busy are they sending this wood to France and Spain for making barrels and building ships.'

'But the king is at war with . . .'

'I know that and they know that. But the king is in London – he'd be as well on the moon, for all the heed his Irish Society's agents here pay to the good of their nation.'

We came to the river Bann at last, and kept close to its banks from then on. The light was beginning to fade and the day had grown much colder, a wind from the north bringing with it the smell of the sea. A mile or so after we had left the salmon leap behind us, I began to discern a large mass, like a stunted hill leaching out from the riverside up ahead in the gloom.

Andrew stayed his mount for a moment, and held out his hand towards the mass. 'There it is: the city of dreams; the Promised Land.'

As we approached closer to the gates of Coleraine, any optimism I had felt seeped out of me. I had expected stone walls, towers, magnificent gatehouses: a shining citadel of this new-made civilisation. What was before me, across the broad, water-filled ditch that served as a moat for the enclosure, was a fortification of earthworks, perhaps fifteen feet high, jutting out at angles into the ditch and towards the surrounding countryside, for the walls and flankers of the London Companies' new town at Coleraine were, like an ancient compound of savages, made entirely of earth. To our right they reached massively northeastwards. To our left they came to an abrupt end at the Bann, with only a flimsy wooden palisade stretching down into the fast-flowing waters.

Andrew had come to a halt across the moat from a timber gatehouse. He shouted our names and our business, and I heard myself for the first time announced as Sean FitzGarrett. I did not need to ask Andrew why in this place, this great enterprise of the new English occupiers of Old Irish land, he had omitted the 'O'Neill' from my cousin's name. Now the time had come to play my part, and for every moment until we left this place I must think myself Sean FitzGarrett, Catholic gentleman, grandson of a wealthy Anglo-Irish merchant and of his noble native Irish wife. The bearing of a Calvinist scholar, the son of a poor Scottish craftsman, must be left at the gates. The watchman let down the timber drawbridge and we crossed, the sound of the horses' hoofs jarring hard and clear on the wood after their two days travelling overland.

Andrew asked the gatekeeper for directions to Matthew Blackstone's house. The man laughed and said we knew little enough about the town if we could not find it for ourselves. 'There are two decent houses in Coleraine: there is Sir Thomas Philips' house, within the walls of the old abbey, down towards the river; Matthew Blackstone's is the other.'

'And in which street is that to be found?' Andrew had no patience for the gatekeeper's humour.

The man smiled, a row of rotten and missing teeth coming into view behind his grey lips. 'The only street with a decent house on it.' He turned to his companion, and both roared with laughter as they went to pull up the drawbridge behind us.

It was almost dark, and Andrew had asked the watchmen for a torch, but they had laughed again and replied scornfully that they'd as well set fire to the town themselves as give a lighted torch to a stranger with an Irishman in tow, however grand he might carry himself. When we were far enough out of earshot of the gatekeepers, I asked Andrew what he was smirking about, for that was the only way to describe the look on his face when the watchman had thrown his last insult.

'Do I smirk? Indeed I might.'

'Why?'

'Because he took you for an Irishman without question. You are as much Sean FitzGarrett to look at as I am Andrew Boyd. You sit your horse with the same look of entitlement on your face, the same arrogance in your bearing. Pride. A good pride, I think. But how our kirk ministers in Aberdeen have tolerated it in you, I do not know.'

It was my turn to smile now. 'Often they have not,' I said.

The street leading into the town from the southern gate was straight and broad, and utterly deserted down one side. On the other, a mixed row of squat, shoddily built houses, mainly timber-framed and plastered, with thatched roofs, faced out onto the emptiness of the untenanted plots across from them. At the end of the row of about a dozen such houses, the street was bisected by another, just as broad and straight, but this one utterly devoid of habitation. There were some rigs of land on either side, some showing signs of cultivation, of pig- and hen-keeping, others dead and sterile. In time, the street came to its end in a broad open square that must have served as the marketplace. There were no signs of any activity whatsoever. Of the houses on the square, none could remotely have been imagined to belong to the family of Deirdre's husband.

A smell of smoke wafted up to us from brick kilns near the river, and as we drew closer mingled with that of fresh-sawn wood and baking clay. A group of thatched cottages had been fenced off within a large wooden enclosure, the builders' yard forming its own village within the town. An exhausted-looking man, his face red with brick dust, came to the gate when Andrew hammered on it. A look of momentary curiosity crossed his face at the sight of us, but passed when Andrew spoke. Oh, yes, he knew Matthew Blackstone. It was clear from his tone that the overseer of the brickworks had no great opinion of the master mason, but he was civil enough in pointing us in the direction of Blackstone's house.

As we went back through the market square, a small herd of black Irish cattle was being driven to a pen in the north-west corner of the marketplace, a herd of sheep bleating and calling to each other close behind them.

'It is not safe for them to leave the beasts out in the fields at night,' Andrew told me, 'nor anyone to guard them, so they bring them in here.'

I looked around me wondering what kind of place was this I had come to, what desolate half-built, half-empty world where too-familiar dangers lay a few yards across crumbling earthen ramparts.

The Blackstones' house, we had been told, lay off the other side of the marketplace, towards St Patrick's church. In common with some of the better houses in the market square, many on this street had pent walkways, like little wooden cloisters, along their front.

'Piazze, they call them,' said Andrew, his face showing his distaste at what he saw as a Romish affectation.

'I suppose it must be pleasant enough, in the summer evenings, to walk there, or for the women to sit out with their work.'

'And look out on the dust and the mud and the empty streets and wish they were somewhere else?'

'Well, we will find out soon enough I think.'

He followed my line of vision to what was, by far, the grandest house we had yet seen in Coleraine.

'This is it, sure enough. Are you ready?'

I took a deep breath and lied. 'Yes, I am ready.'

He lifted the brass knocker on the door and banged loudly, three times.

Footsteps came hurrying along a corridor and as they did so, Andrew took two paces backwards and stood deferentially behind me, an amused smile on his lips. A girl's voice called out, tremulously, 'Who is there?'

I looked to Andrew and he kept his mouth resolutely shut.

'Sean O'Neill FitzGarrett, brother of Deirdre FitzGarrett, wife to the son of this house. Also my. . .' I stopped short at 'servant', '. . . my steward, Andrew Boyd.'

One door slowly opened, followed by the other. In the meagre light of the candle she held in her hand I could see warm hazel eyes in the face of a young woman of about twenty.

Her dress was of a coarser brown stuff, the apron less assidu-
ously bleached and pressed, but for a moment my heart misgave
me and I thought I saw Sarah standing there. All words stopped
themselves in my mouth as my heart pounded.

'Sir?' she said, and the spell was broken.

I recovered myself quickly enough. 'Is your master at home?
There is business I would discuss with him.'

'He is not yet returned from his day's business. He is expected
back in the next hour.' She stepped forward a little and made
to close the door. I turned helplessly to Andrew, who pushed
past me to stand right in front of her.

'Fetch your mistress, girl. We have not travelled all the way
from Carrickfergus to stand like hawkers in the street.'

Little more than five minutes later we were seated on an
uncomfortable carved oak bench in front of a not very
welcoming fire, and the still less welcoming lady of the house
with her two daughters. 'You will understand, sir,' the matron
was saying, 'that with my husband and sons away from home,
we must take the greatest of care in allowing strangers across
our threshold. This country is not . . . that is, not all of your
countrymen are . . . that is to say . . .' The woman was becoming
ever more flustered, her round cheeks growing redder, her
fingers twisting a linen handkerchief in her lap. I found myself,
unaccountably, enjoying her discomfort, as if Sean's very spirit
had inhabited my being and was sitting in the room, laughing.

'As the brother of your son's wife, I am hardly a stranger,
Mistress. It is scarcely two months since I sought to dance with
your two lovely daughters here at my sister's wedding.' I inclined
my head towards the two rather plain, pale-eyed girls sitting
across from their mother; one looked at the floor, the other
directly at me with something like contempt in her eye.

'Of course, of course. But your servant . . .'

'He is my steward,' I said.

'And a more fitting companion, I might say, than he who accompanied you the last time you travelled here.' I pictured Eachan in the company of this humourless dame and her daughters and stifled a smile. 'Nevertheless, there are proclamations out against Scots hawkers. Your "steward",' and here she favoured Andrew with a look of some distaste, which was not, I noted, echoed by her daughters, 'might well have been one such lawless vagabond.'

I resisted the urge to laugh. Although he did not open his mouth, I could see Andrew's entire body bridle with rage; to be compared to a shiftless vagabond was an affront almost beyond endurance to him. Had the insult issued from a man, the offender would now be flat on his back, nursing a broken jaw.

Although uninvited to do so, I removed my cloak. The heat from the fire was now reaching to every corner of the parlour that evidently served also for dining. Across the narrow entrance hall was the kitchen, whence aromas of roasting meat and boiling vegetables snaked their way to my nostrils. I was ravenous: it had been a hard enough day's riding, but we had not been offered as much as a beaker of water since we had entered Deirdre's husband's home. It was evident that the mistress had no intention that we should be encouraged to linger. Her daughters, by the glances they cast in Andrew's direction from time to time, were of a different opinion. Inhabited by Sean's mischief, I gave them my most becoming smile. They avoided my eye entirely.

A fine clock ticked on the mantelshelf. The matron looked periodically and with increasing agitation at this clock. 'My husband should be home soon. Mary, should not your father be home soon?'

'Very soon, Mother,' said the older and paler of the two girls. 'Do not agitate yourself. The Merchant Taylors' proportion is vast, and it may be that he has had to wait on the other side for the ferry.'

Her sister, of the more direct look, now opened her mouth for the first time since our arrival. 'You told the girl you had business to discuss with my father. What nature of business is that?'

'It is . . .' I stopped, looking to Andrew.

'It is business between men,' he said.

She appeared to be little chastened by the rebuke, for a retort was ready at her lips. 'My sister-in-law does not scruple to talk of the business of men.' Turning from Andrew to me, her every word dripping contempt, she added, 'I thought it was the way of you Irish.'

I let Sean choose my words. 'Women whose place it is to know of business know of business; the others keep to the hearth.'

As the clock ticked resolutely over the crackling of the fire, it came as a relief to all in the now overheated parlour to hear the front door thrown open, and a hearty voice announce his homecoming. I stood up, as did Andrew, and Matthew Blackstone's wife went quickly out to the hall. I heard urgent female whispers and then a loud laugh as hands clapped together. In a moment the master of the house strode into the room. Edward Blackstone's father was as tall as his sons, but broader in shoulder and neck. He was sandy-haired and ruddy of face. Nodding to Andrew, he came directly over to me.

'I offer you my hand and my prayers on the death of your grandfather, FitzGarrett. He was a fine man, and knew his business. A great loss to you all, but a long life well lived is not to be mourned. And how fares your sister? And my sons? She was much affected by her grandfather's death, I think.'

'They all arrived safe. My sister has been a great comfort to my grandmother.'

'Aye? Good girl. Though the old woman has never struck me as much affected by sentiment.'

'Matthew!' interjected his wife.

'I give that as a compliment, woman. Your sex is too much prone to weeping and wailing at the merest thing. Although I think I am right in saying that the women of the Irish do their mourning loud?'

I remembered the hellish noises I had heard in Carrick-fergus on the night of my grandfather's death, and again on the night before his funeral. 'Yes, they honour the dead in venting their grief.' I almost thought I saw Andrew smirk again as I said this.

'Well, well, so your grandfather is buried, and you come away so soon on business?'

Andrew had coached me on the road, and I knew what to say. 'With no disrespect to yourself, we know there are merchants in Coleraine who would not scruple to wrest my grandfather's trade from his dead hands, and with the pirates constantly operating along the north coast it seemed as well to re-establish my family's name and control as soon as was possible.'

'You do right. And any way I can help you in, so will I do.' He turned then to his wife, and asked why our places had not yet been set at the dinner table.

'I had not thought – I had not presumed to. I do not know where the gentleman and his servant are staying, or if they have yet eaten.'

I had been in the humblest cottage, the most austere manse, the sparsest garret, but rarely in my life had I been offered such poor hospitality as in this rich planter's house in Coleraine.

The blood was running into Matthew Blackstone's face. 'Do you tell me you have not asked? Elizabeth, make two more places ready at the table.'

'But surely,' said his wife, less able to read her husband's humour than I was, 'the servant will eat in the kitchen?'

'What, are you so dainty, madam?' Blackstone exploded. He held up two huge, grimy, calloused hands. 'These hands by their labour have built your fortune and put the lace and pearls at your neck. None of your niceness here. FitzGarrett's steward will dine at my table.' He looked at Andrew, whose jaw muscles were twitching, the rest of him motionless, as he stared straight ahead. 'I daresay you have much knowledge of your master's business?'

'Aye, sir, I do,' replied Andrew, continuing to stare straight ahead.

'More than I have myself,' I said.

'It is often the way,' said Blackstone. 'But you should not persist in such ignorance. Only a man you can trust with your life should be trusted with all your business.'

Further enquiries established that we had arranged no lodgings for ourselves in Coleraine: at this, the master of the house was well pleased, and the expected invitation was not slow in being issued. We were given a room at the top of the house. 'The garret room has no great comforts, but you Irish do not bother yourselves overmuch about comfort, and I daresay you have slept in worse.'

'Much worse,' I assured him.

By the time we had washed and changed and descended once more to the parlour, complete darkness had fallen, and more candles had been lit around the room where our host and his family were waiting for us. A brief grace was said, and before I had settled my quandary about whether to cross myself or no, Blackstone was decanting a ruby liquid into the crystal glass in front of me and urging my health. I held it up to him, the light dancing in and out of its many red faces. '*Slainte*,' I said, before helping myself to a thick slab from the haunch of venison in the middle of the table, and ladling onions, leeks and some crimson jelly onto my plate. Andrew followed my lead, and as the master of the house ate heartily, the ladies ate but meagrely and cast sly glances at my hands, a little surprised, evidently, that I could handle a fork. I wondered just what kind of account Sean had given of himself at his sister's wedding, and what price I was to pay for it. The lady of the house cast a parsimonious eye on my plate; I smiled at her, and served myself another piece of meat.

'You will find things well ordered here,' said Blackstone. 'Your sister has looked to your grandfather's interests; there are not many who will have cheated her. She has a better mind to business than many a man.'

'She would do better to set her mind to a more womanly calling,' said the mother. 'She thinks herself above the duties of my son's wife. She has so little notion of embroidery, or spinning, or the making of preserves . . .'

'She was brought up in a houseful of servants, to better things. She has Latin and Greek, and mathematics. She will converse with you in French as easily as in English.'

'Much good may such learning do in the face of slothfulness.'

'But it is the nature of the people, Mother, they have such little inclination to industry.'

Her father brought his glass down slowly, and deliberately. 'I will not have you insult the guests of this house, Elizabeth. Guard your tongue better.'

'I take no insult,' I said. 'Our people have no compulsion to labour when labour is not required. There are higher things.'

'Perhaps. But you will find me a common man, FitzGarrett, and I have brought my family up to be so too, although their mother would often enough have them forget it. There are many fine things in this house, and will be many finer still in the house I am building on my estate, not ten miles from here, but they have all been won by the grace of God and the labour of these hands he gave me. I have little time for your higher things. There is much work on the plantations, and opportunities too, for men of calibre.' He appraised Andrew a moment. 'Are you content, sir, to remain in FitzGarrett's employ?'

Andrew looked at me, directly, as if it was I who had put the question. 'I will stay in the employ of the FitzGarretts as long as I am needed, but then I have a mind to invest in a mill, and the linen trade on the Braid.'

'And I wish you good fortune in it. You may have started life the son of a steward – I myself am the son of a brick-maker – but you could finish it a man of land and means, if you took the right turn. The son of a brickmaker I am, but I have built half the walls of Londonderry, many of the houses within those walls, castles on two plantations and bawns on many more. I will have me a title and see my wife "ladied" before the Lord calls me to that better place. All by the grace and gifts of God and the work of these hands.'

'If the king does not take it from us,' said the sly-eyed sister quietly.

'Hush, girl,' said her mother.

'Why should the king wish to take it from you, when you do his work so well?' I asked.

Matthew Blackstone drained his glass and filled another. 'Because he thinks we do not do it well or fast enough. The

London Companies cannot work the lands they have been granted without granting leases to many of your people. And truth to say, the Irish will pay higher rents than anyone else to get access to the land that they once thought theirs. But this does not conduce to the king's plans of civilising this province, of spreading the true faith, and the tongue and customs of the English. What is more, it is an arrangement potent of great danger.' He looked hard at me. 'I will not dally with pretty words, sir. There are many of the Irish who have not accommodated themselves so well as your grandfather or some of your grandmother's people have been willing to do, to the king's arrangements for the tenanting of his land.'

'The place is alive with savages,' said his wife.

'With men who had their land taken from them,' I said.

'It was forfeit by the treachery of O'Neill and O'Donnell.'

I began to respond in defence of the Earls of Tyrone and Tyrconnell, as I knew Sean would have done, but was interrupted by the younger girl. 'We have heard such politics often enough at this table from your sister, sir. It is a wonder, if she had such leanings towards the way of the savages, that she does not . . .'

'Elizabeth!' said her father sharply. 'I will not have that talk at this table. You will hold your tongue, or you will oblige us by going to your chamber.' Blackstone did not notice the resentment that burned in his daughter's eyes as he settled again to his former conversation. 'The king and his agents are not sufficiently pleased with the speed and manner of our plantation. There are those in London – and some of the disaffected English who were here before us – who have been urging him to revoke our grants.'

'Matthew! No, it cannot be.' His wife's face had gone the waxy yellow of old linen. 'We could lose everything.'

'Not everything, but much.'

I contemplated the matron opposite me and wondered how she might enjoy life as a brickmaker's wife.

'But it will not come to that,' her husband reassured her. 'Our detractors will overreach themselves, and the king must know that should he throw us from this land, after all the time, money and labour we have invested here, not a soul in their right mind would be willing to take our place.'

'But we could return to London,' said the slower girl, who had been less forward with her opinions than her sister. 'If we were forced to leave here, we could go back to London, to the old house there. What would it matter not to have an estate, a grand house, if we could have company, and some semblance of a life, instead of withering in this half-empty town on the edge of a wasteland where wolves and savages roam?'

'It would be a shameful thing to go back now, Mary. We have moved beyond those people and that company. And there is nothing to be bought in the streets of London that your father cannot have sent to us here.'

'But to what purpose, Mother? To what purpose?' And in those words I saw played out before me the tableau of her life in this place. Few friends, little entertainment, and even less chance of finding a husband. Of what her life in London had been, I knew nothing, but it must surely have been something better than this.

Once the women had retired, we moved towards the hearth and Matthew Blackstone took out his pipe. Within a few moments, the smell of burning peats in the fire was joined and mingled with an unmistakable aroma of Virginia leaf that took me back to another place and another hearth. How Jaffray would have relished drawing Andrew out of himself, and

intriguing on the mission before us. I had not been in Banff
for many months, but I could have wished myself back there
now, with the doctor and Charles Thom and Ishbel, and the
cares of that small town. My host's voice broke into my reverie.

'Your sister gave us to understand that you had no great
interest in matters of business.'

'I am more at home out on my grandfather's estates in
Down, or with my grandmother's people in Tyrone. The charms
of the marketplace hold little attraction for me. But I cannot
shirk my responsibilities for ever – they are finding me out.
Without Andrew, I would be lost.'

'Well then, after you have spoken to your agents in town
tomorrow, you must come with me to the port. A ship from
Bristol has been trying to dock these three days, but the seas
have been so bad of late, and I fear there will not be many
more before the year's end. My work at Monavagher is held
up for want of nails and bolts, and I have two good carpenters wasting their time and losing their stomachs on that barque
while wood lies idle in Londonderry city, waiting on them to
turn it into house frames. But if it should happily dock
tomorrow, you may pick up some bargains at the customs
house, and no little experience either. Or perhaps you already
have some interest in its cargo?'

Before I could form a reply, Andrew was there with his own.
'My old master had ordered a consignment of good Madeira
wines for Sir James Shaw of Ballygally. It was sent by this ship,
since the vessel it should have travelled on met with mis-
adventure on the way out to Spain.'

'Piracy or tempest?' asked the old man.

'Piracy. Basques.'

'Ach.' Blackstone spat. 'A plague upon the seven seas, they
are.'

We spoke an hour or so longer, although in truth most of the conversation was between Andrew and the older man. Their topics did not stray far from business – trade, investment, expansion, the scarcity of coin – and I soon stopped attempting to follow them. The role of Sean came easy to me on this point. My mind drifted to other matters. It had been three weeks now since I had left Aberdeen, three weeks since I had set sight on a face that wanted something from me that I also wanted to give. What would they think had befallen me, or that I had done? William Cargill, Sarah, Dr Dun, would they comprehend my hastily scribbled notes, or would they believe that I had left the town after my denied debauches of the previous night, fled of my own accord with the 'ill-favoured Highlander' whom I had denied having known? Or would they think that I had been taken in the darkness, against my will? I looked into the cooling embers of the fire and wondered if they thought I was dead.

'That is the case, is it not, Sean? Sean?' Andrew was looking at me meaningfully. It took me a moment to come to myself, or rather to that other that I was supposed to be.

'I am sorry. I got lost in your talk, I was dreaming.'

Blackstone looked at me curiously. 'You are a people much given to dreaming, and wandering in realms of the mind that are best left alone. This business of the poet for instance . . .'

'Yes,' I said, 'my grandmother has been greatly distressed by it; my sister also. But I am not inclined to wring my hands over O'Rahilly's words. He has betrayed his learning and his heritage in what he has done. He has sold his honour somewhere.'

'That may well be so. You honour heritage and learning more highly than do I, FitzGarrett, or than your steward here does either, I suspect, but I know a charlatan when I see one, and you are right: that fellow is a charlatan. As are all of his kind if you seek my opinion, but we shall not quibble on that. Your sister had been much against engaging him, but your grandmother would hear of nothing else, and so brought the trouble down on her own head, and much embarrassment upon ours.'

'My sister told you this?'

'She did not need to. We saw it all for ourselves when your grandmother accompanied her on a visit up here about a month before the marriage took place, to see to the arrangements.'

'Of course,' I said. Sean had told me none of this. Perhaps, in his roving the country with Eachan, he had not known.

Blackstone continued. 'There were dark clouds over Coleraine on those days, let me tell you. My good wife and your grandmother saw eye to eye on precisely nothing. The girl herself was seldom consulted as to the matrimonial arrangements, and I not at all, thanks be to God. By the afternoon of the second day there was such a freezing in looks and words in this house that you would have thought us caught in the grip of winter. Your grandmother declared that she had no further interest in our "petty proceedings" and would happily cede the "shameful event" to my wife, but that she would have one thing, and without that thing there would be no marriage that she or her husband ever saw: she would have her poet. My wife was too much in a glow at her triumph to protest, and nothing your sister said had any moment with your grandmother.'

'Did my grandmother go to O'Rahilly from here?'

'She and Deirdre both. Your sister was determined that the poet should not be engaged to perform anything – what shall I say? – outrageous, or offensive to the sensibilities of others who were to be present at the marriage.'

'Then she failed in her part,' I said.

'Indeed she did. That rogue managed to affront everyone at the table. But something went wrong on their way back here from seeing O'Rahilly. I cannot recall precisely, but your grandmother was much shaken by it.'

'Something the poet had said?' I asked, fearful that Blackstone was about to drift to another topic again.

'Eh? No. Not that: it was later, on their journey back from engaging O'Rahilly. Some nonsense about a woman Deirdre had seen at a window, at Dunluce, or Dunseverick or some such place.'

Andrew looked up with interest. 'Maeve MacQuillan?'

'Aye, that was the name, I think. I paid it little heed – there is enough woman's prattle about this house at the best of times, without adding your Irish superstitions to it.' He sucked deeply on his pipe, but it had gone out and he did not light it again, instead heaving himself to his feet with a sigh. 'Well, gentlemen, I must leave you, for these old bones grow weary at their work, and I must rouse them fresh and ready for the labours of the morning. Come down to the port after eleven, sir, and you may see the *Carolina* dock then. There is wine on the sideboard, and tobacco on the mantelshelf. Have what you will and then rest yourselves well. I bid you goodnight.'

We finished our wine in silence. Genial though our host was, we did not yet trust the inhabitants of the house. We had got candles from the girl and reached gladly to our chamber in the attic before the bell of St Patrick's church tolled ten.

I lay on the truckle bedstead with its feather bed and bolster while Andrew made do with a coarser arrangement of blankets and pillows on the floor, having dismissed my offer of tossing a coin for the comfort with a curt, 'I play the servant, you the master; the master does not sleep on the floor.'

The window of our garret was unshuttered, and in the frosty and cloudless night the moon cast an eerie illumination around the room, enlivening minds that should have rested.

'What think you to our hosts?' Andrew asked eventually.

'That bitter wife and those stranded girls – such a powder keg of resentments. I am not much surprised that Blackstone spends his days in the outposts of the plantations. I would be in no hurry home to such a welcome. And it is a cramped house for a man of wealth.'

'Do not be deceived. When his house at Monavagher is finished, it will be one of the grandest in the province. For all his pride in his workman's hands, Matthew Blackstone does not intend that his family should go down in the world come the next generation.'

'Unless the plantation falls out of favour with the king.'

Andrew drew in his breath for a moment, considering his answer. 'I think he takes precautions to insure himself against it.'

'What kind of precautions?'

'Deirdre is his precaution. Deirdre and what she might bring with her.'

'What do you mean?'

'Your grandfather was of the Old English. He was well respected and trusted by the English administration, and rich. His business had brought him a large estate in Down, to which my father drew many Scots settlers: the king will have no cause to escheat the lands of Richard FitzGarrett, unless they fall into the wrong hands.'

'Sean's,' I said, things beginning to become clearer to me.

'Blackstone knows rightly that Sean has no head for business, nor mind to it either. I suspect rumours of Sean's sympathies have also come to his ears.'

'His sympathies?'

Andrew drew in his breath, impatient almost. 'A man who has been known to ride with the sons of Murchadh O'Neill, who is married secretly by a disguised Franciscan priest, treads a dangerous line. And should he cross that line, there will be plenty ready to swoop, and who better for the king to grant the estates to than the obedient English planter family of Sean FitzGarrett's sister? Could the native Irish even complain? A just and satisfactory conclusion for all. Blackstone talked also tonight of the shortage of coin. When your grandfather's debtors are called to account, there will be a great deal of coin available to whoever controls his estate.'

'Do you think Deirdre knows any of this?' I said quietly.

'She is too proud to see herself a pawn in anybody's game. The walls of this house and the lives of the women in it must be like a slow death to her.'

There was one more thing I needed to know before I could shut my mind on these matters for the night. 'Who is Maeve MacQuillan?' I said. 'And why should the mention of her have upset my grandmother?'

He sighed and opened eyes that had not long since closed.

'Long ago, before the power of the MacQuillans on this coast was usurped by the MacDonnells, the daughter of the MacQuillan chieftain was locked up by her father in a tower at Dunluce Castle, until she should come to her senses; she had refused to marry the man he had chosen for her. But the girl showed no intention of coming to her senses, and while her father paced the sands below and raged at her obstinacy, she spent her time in the tower in knitting herself a shroud. Eventually, the father relented and arranged the girl's escape with her lover across the sea to Scotland, but their boat foundered and the pair drowned. When the father looked up at her window, he saw his daughter's ghost look down on him; she held up her shroud and said, "See, Father, it is finished." It is said by the superstitious that the ghost of Maeve MacQuillan still paces the room of that tower, and if anyone should chance to glance up at the window and see her there, holding her shroud, they will be dead within the year.'

'And Deirdre saw this vision?'

He was quiet a long moment. 'I asked the servant girl about it. She said that when your grandmother and Deirdre returned from their visit to O'Rahilly, the old woman was in a state of some distress, and little your cousin could say would pacify her. They had travelled by Dunluce on their journey back to Coleraine, and stopped there to dine. The castle is the seat of Randal MacDonnell, Earl of Antrim. Your grandmother is a distant cousin of MacDonnell's wife, and finds a welcome in all such houses. The earl gave them a guide back to Coleraine. As they left the castle, Deirdre turned back to wave to MacDonnell's wife, and your grandmother said she stopped cold. It was only once they were back through the gates of Coleraine and MacDonnell's man returning to his master that she eventually broke and told the old woman what she had seen: Maeve MacQuillan at her window, holding up her shroud.'

I had no more time for superstition and tales of ghosts and their threats and promises than did Andrew, but I felt I would sleep better for the reading of the scriptures, as we had done together on occasion since my arrival in this country. Our choice had fallen on St Paul's letter to the Romans, but the seventh chapter, where Andrew had last set his marker, gave little comfort to either of us, with its words on the law regarding married women.

'Well, that is clear enough, I think,' said Andrew, shutting his bible after only three verses. 'Adultery or widowhood, the alternatives for a woman who has married where she does not love.' His words were clipped and bitter.

I raised myself on my elbow to look at him properly. 'Andrew,' I began hesitantly, 'you must believe me, for I know it for a certainty: there is a madness in men sometimes, in women too, that makes them reject what they love.'

'Then they do not truly love.' He turned his back on me and laid himself down to sleep.

When at last I also closed my eyes, it was with my cousin Deirdre's face before me, her hand reaching out to me from a tower window, offering me her shroud.

TWELVE

Cargoes

The warmth of our welcome from the ladies of the house did not improve in the watery sunshine of the late October morning. While the night candles in the parlour had endowed the edges of their mother's face with folds and shadows, they had lent a sort of golden glow to her daughters which was utterly dissipated by what daylight found its way through the window panes and into the house. Pasty faces and dull eyes greeted me when I went to make my breakfast. Andrew had declared his intention of breakfasting early in the kitchen and then going to the stable, to see what further information he might glean from the maids and stable-boy. I was therefore constrained to make an uncomfortable breakfast myself in the cold parlour with the three women, the master having gone early to see to business across the river at the Clothworkers' Hall. There was little conversation, but when they did speak it was to ask insulting questions, dressed as apologies for their ignorance, about the life and habits of my family. I learned in the course of the half-hour I was able to sit there that 'I', and those they supposed to be my 'sort', were commonly believed to live a life of licentious sloth in conditions of filth the masters of Bedlam would have baulked at.

'I am sorry you find my manners and person so offensive to your expectations,' I said. 'I am only surprised my sister has not disabused you of these notions.'

'Oh, no, your sister's manner had quite prepared us . . .'

I stood up. 'You must excuse my sister's manner, Madam: she is accustomed to the company of ladies.' Putting my knife in my belt, I left the frozen room.

What Andrew had learnt from the servants told us little new: Matthew Blackstone was a good master, but not a man to be crossed; his wife was a harridan and the daughters vessels of bitterness and misery. The sons were better but not well liked, and my cousin Deirdre was disdained by all in the family save her husband, who seemed genuinely to love her, and her father-in-law, who treated her as more worthy of conversation than he did his own daughters. Blackstone's position in the plantation was sound, and his grip on building works throughout the London Companies' proportions and the City of London-derry tightened by the day. What he made, he invested back in land. Should the king declare the plantation forfeit, Black-stone's losses would be incalculable.

Andrew did go to meet with my grandfather's agent in the town and I made a show of going with him. The man was a little surprised to see Andrew and more to see me, but beyond some words of sorrow at the passing of my grandfather found little further reason to talk to me. I showed an appropriate level of interest in their conversation, and in the role of Sean as I was, spent more time admiring servant girls and young wives out about their business on the vast and empty streets of this new town. On our way down to the ferry afterwards, Andrew told me the gist of what the man had said.

'The position of your grandfather's business in the market here is assured. However, he says the greatest threat to the Fitz-Garretts' prosperity lies in Edward Blackstone – within an hour of the news of your grandfather's death reaching Coleraine, the leech was at the shore, claiming to act in your grandfather's behalf, and that all FitzGarrett business here should henceforth be conducted through him.'

'What did the agent do?'

Andrew shrugged as if my question had been unnecessary. 'He told him to take himself off and comfort his wife, of course. That only your grandfather's seal or my word was any currency to him.'

As Matthew Blackstone was not expected back in town until almost midday, and neither of us had any desire to return to the house, we made our way towards the quayside for want of anything better to do.

We passed the smithy to the west of the market, and the smell of the furnace and clang of iron on steel brought me back to another smithy, only ten years ago, where my father had worked and hammered almost until his last breath, pounding out his pride and his disappointments.

'I was brought up at a forge,' I said.

Andrew raised a surprised eyebrow. 'And now you are a philosopher.'

'I don't know what I am now. I do not know what I will go back to. I do not know if my night flight with Sean will have closed those doors to me that had not long begun to open.'

'And if they are? What then?'

'I do not know.'

He pointed to the cluster of the old abbey buildings, where a school was planned for the townsfolk's children. 'I know they have no proper schoolmaster as yet.'

How clean a new beginning it would be, to be part of a society that was itself only just beginning. But I still wished with every ounce of my will and strength to hold on to the life I had, and was determined to do so until it was shown to me for certain that I had lost it.

We stopped by the jetty where the ferry from Kilowen would dock. A small barque from Ayrshire was disgorging its load of coals, bolts of Scots cloth and whisky on to the side, its master and men declaring loudly that they were damned if ever they tried to make port at Coleraine again.

The workers ashore had heard the like before.

'Then you are twenty times damned, the whole crew of you, for you have been uttering your threats six times a year these last three years and more. And who else but the desperate and stranded would pay as we do for your shoddy wares?' The ensuing scuffle was brought to an end with little more than bloodied noses on each side, and the dropping of a flagon of whisky which was declared to have a crack in it.

The load fully landed and accounted for, the antagonists betook themselves and the damaged bottle to a corner of the abbey grounds. As I watched them, a movement at a door in the abbey wall caught my eye. He must have been a hundred yards or more from where I stood, and he was no longer clad in his baker's garb, but I would have sworn the fellow behind whom the small wooden door now swung shut was the Franciscan, Father Stephen. I hardly had time to gather my thoughts before Andrew took me by the arm and pulled me towards the dock.

'The ferry is coming, with Blackstone on it. Let us see who he is with and who he talks to.' I tried to tell him about the priest, but my voice was lost in the crush towards the quayside, for beyond the ferry could be seen, still a little way down river, the masts of the long-awaited Bristol vessel, her sails being furled as men and boys ran like monkeys over her decks and rigging. A cheer went up, and frantic work began at the harbour to make ready for the arrival. Shouts and signals were sent to the ferryman, but he had already seen the ship, and had begun slowly but deftly to guide his craft towards the far side of the jetty. Within minutes he had docked, and his passengers – a woman holding an old hen under one arm and a small child in the other, an Irishman with three stout black cows, and two Englishmen with their horses – noisily, and with some difficulty on the part of the cattle, disembarked.

'Who is that with Blackstone?' I asked Andrew, for the man looked familiar.

He glanced for only a moment at Blackstone's companion. 'I don't know. I have never seen him before.'

'No, wait,' I said, forcing him to look again, 'is that not the overseer of the brickworks?'

Andrew looked at the man for longer this time. The other's face and clothing were clean, no trace visible of the gritty red dust that had encrusted itself into every line in his skin last night, but as he removed a coarse leather glove to take Blackstone's change from the ferryman, I saw the redness in his hands and nails. In his eyes was the same disaffected expression we had seen before.

'Yes,' Andrew said at last, 'I think you are right.'

Blackstone hailed us warmly across the throng. 'Well, gentlemen, is this not a fine sight for a morning? She'll pass the bar this morning and be unloaded before dinner-time, I'd stake my horse on it. Is that not so, Dunstan?'

'Aye, sir, no doubt,' said the overseer, with little enthusiasm.

'Now, then, get you to those brickworks and see if you can't wring some work out of those lazy dullards. We'll need eight hundred more for Monavagher than that idiot Cookston told me.' He turned his attention to us, the smile re-forming on his face. 'And now, gentlemen, you have had a pleasant morning I hope?'

'We have found plenty to occupy us,' Andrew answered. 'But

now I must seek out my old master's agent, and give him instructions about the Madeira about to be landed.'

Blackstone clapped him on the shoulder, looking not displeased that Andrew would be leaving us. 'Aye, quite right. Very good, very good.'

Andrew had warned me that he might have to leave me with Blackstone a while, and had counselled me not to leave the public view in the docks until he had returned. I wondered for a moment why he felt the need to give my grandfather's agent his instructions again, for amongst what little I had caught of their conversation earlier in the morning were instructions regarding the Madeira. I knew enough not to question him on it in front of Blackstone, and so said nothing as he left us to make in the direction not of the agent's house, but of the brickworks. Blackstone did not notice, so engrossed was he in the attempts of the ship to negotiate the bar and ease herself triumphantly into Coleraine harbour.

Two great cheers went up, one from the crowd on the quayside, one from the ship. Scrawny men scampered like boys down the riggings, and others made ready the ropes, huge heavy coils waiting to be flung out to shore. Another cheer went up as the anchor was dropped, and then the ropes were caught on the quayside and tied fast to iron bollards. A gangplank was thrown down and soon a straggling troupe of weary and exhausted passengers was making its uncertain way on to dry land. Blackstone found his way to this group and detached from it his carpenters: he would have had two apprentices too, had not a tanner, in his apron and still reeking of the noxious fumes of his trade, claimed them as his own.

The passengers safely disgorged, the business of unloading the merchant cargo began. The customs officers, even I could see, kept a close eye on some loads but turned their backs resolutely to others, their palms no doubt already profitably greased by some merchant's coin. It took well into the afternoon before all the cargo was ashore, its contents and provenance verified, and allocated to its rightful owners. Amongst those checking and marking receipt of their goods was my grandfather's agent; of Andrew there was still no sign. The agent counted out three bolts of silk, two barrels of oil, and the cask of Madeira. It seemed a small enough item to warrant such special instruction, but then I knew little more of trade than did Sean, and I did not ponder it long.

Blackstone oversaw the landing of his goods with a degree of satisfaction and an eye that missed nothing. He took particular care over the loading on to carts of some cases of slates. 'For my own new house. The slates produced here are not of a quality I would happily use. I advise my wealthier clients also to spend the extra coin now to save them expensive repairs in the future. But do they listen to me? Ha! Not many. But when I come to the end of my labours, I'm damned if I'll sit under a leaking roof. Welsh slate, FitzGarrett. Welsh slate.' He glanced uneasily at the customs officers, but they fortuitously, it seemed, had turned their attention elsewhere, and showed no interest in the contents of the heavy cases loaded on to his carts. It appeared Matthew Blackstone was not above bribery when it came to his own interests.

There was a degree of relief in his face as the second of his carts was drawn away from the docks in the direction of his brickworks, and his good humour was such that he offered me a very favourable price on a sack of dates he had that morning bargained his way to, but I laughed and told him it would not be worth the wrath of my steward to make purchases without him.

'He is a good man, that one, but you will not keep him

long I think: he does not wait upon his opportunities. I will not beat about the bush, FitzGarrett. You need someone you can trust to manage your business, or you will not see one penny in two that belongs to you. To add an alliance in business to the one in marriage between our two families would do neither of us any harm. It would give me, and my son, greater trust amongst the Irish, and strengthen your support for the plantation in the eyes of the king. Neither of our families would lose by the arrangement.'

'And if I do not support the plantation?'

'Then the day will come when you will lose everything that was ever dear to you.' Blackstone then left me, urging me to consider his words.

Remembering Andrew's warnings, I would have lingered longer by the quay, had it not been for the young man I caught sight of, emerging from the abbey grounds and coming towards the river. He was dressed in the robes of a Franciscan friar and walking towards me with a purpose that left no doubt that he thought he knew me. I had not been prepared for this, for recognition as Sean by someone who might have been a mere acquaintance, a close friend, or a sworn enemy. The set of his face suggested the latter. Whatever this man was to Sean, it would soon become clear to him that I was nothing but a fraud.

As a paralysing panic worked through me, good fortune, in the shape of a recalcitrant donkey, came to my aid. The creature, a few feet in front of me and between me and the oncoming stranger, objected greatly to the attempts of its handler to encourage it away from the quayside with its load. The more he pulled and cursed, the firmer the beast stood, until at last, at the end of his patience, the man kicked it in its hind quarters. The thing let out a terrible screech and took off at a speed neither I nor the carter had thought it capable of, sending barrels of apples and fish rolling and sliding all over the quay, with merchants and shore porters alike running after them. I heard one barrel crash into the river, and that was enough to bring me out of my own stasis: I ran and I did not look back. I went through yards and behind walls, anywhere that I thought might shield me from the sight of my pursuer. When I was at last satisfied that I had lost him, I went in search of Andrew. It was almost half an hour afterwards that I found him, in a tavern close to the brickworks. It was a desperate place, where poor ale was served to poor men, and women of no attraction or hope sought to entice what remained from the pockets of those men. He was drinking alone, a jug of beer before him, and ignoring the efforts of a young but pock-marked woman to engage him with her charms. I thought of Margaret, in the inn we had eaten at two days ago, clean and lovely and unsullied, and still unable to interest Andrew, and I pitied this poor and hopeless creature.

He seemed startled by my voice. 'You have been dreaming, I think.'

'Dreaming? No, not dreaming.' He moved along on the bench and I sat down. 'Did you find much entertainment at the shore? How was Blackstone?'

'Eager for my grandfather's business, but he is a man who favours a direct approach. I think the subtlety of destabilising my family's position through an Irish curse would hold little attraction.'

'You are probably right,' he said, still somewhat distracted.

'What did you learn from the brickmaker?'

'The brickmaker?'

'That is where you went, is it not?'

'What? Yes, yes. He told me very little that I did not already know.' He pushed the jug towards me and beckoned to the girl for another tankard.

'Enough of them though. Did you see the priest?'

'What priest?'

'The Franciscan. From the Bawn. I thought I saw him this morning, in the abbey grounds, as we were waiting for the ferry to dock. And then there was another one, a young brother I think, that I am sure thought he recognised me. He was coming straight for me down at the harbour. It was only by the intransigence of a donkey in his path that I got away.'

Andrew pushed aside his tankard and gave me his full attention for the first time since I had entered the tavern. 'Are you sure of this?'

'I am certain.'

He stood up. 'Damn! I knew I should not have left you by yourself. I think we had better leave this place as soon as we can. I do not trust Mac Cuarta, and only something of great import would have brought him within the ramparts of Coleraine. As to who the other is, who knows what Sean might be to him? I am not inclined at the moment to find out.' He threw down some coins, more than were needed for his beer and bread, and ushered me out into the street.

Andrew strode determinedly through the marketplace, in no mood to browse the stalls and booths. What did take his notice, and dishearten him greatly, was the platform being positioned towards the far end of the square. He swore softly to himself: 'The play.'

A troupe of players had come into town, and were to perform that night in a work of the English playwright Shakespeare. It was to be the great event of the year, and Blackstone had made clear it was not to be countenanced that any guest in his house should miss it.

'I had forgotten about the play,' said Andrew.

'Would our absence be noted?'

'Oh, I think Blackstone notices more than he would tell you, or has it brought to his notice. We had better show ourselves here this evening, and first thing in the morning we will make our farewells and go.'

'To Bushmills?'

'We will have to discuss that tonight. Your sighting of the priest makes me anxious on that score.'

'Whatever might befall us afterwards, I will not be sorry to leave this town.'

'Nor I. It is a Godforsaken place.'

THIRTEEN

The Flight of the Players

The falling of night found us again in the marketplace, but it was a place transformed. Torches had been lit around the platform, a strange half-hexagon jutting into the open space, and also at intervals in a ring around the marketplace itself, so that the playgoers could see enough to put one foot in front of another without coming to grief in the mud. A canopy had been erected, so that the more exalted citizens amongst the audience might have some shelter from whatever of the elements might play upon Coleraine that night. Andrew and I preferred to stand in the open with the commons, the better to observe without ourselves being observed.

The platform was decorated with ribbons and streamers of many colours, and at its back was painted a scene that conjured up dreams of a far country, of warm winds, olive groves and vineyards, things I had heard of but would never see. Images of bright pink blossoms tumbling over balustrades of the whitest marble told us there was a place where mud and dirt and grime were not the constant lot of those who lived there. A brazier burned at the front of the stage, casting strange shadows on the picture. Other braziers had been lit where the greater dignitaries amongst the audience were to sit, but warmth found its way into the crowd in other forms, too. One vendor sold warm spiced wine from the frontage of his tavern, another hawked roasted chestnuts amongst the crowd come for the spectacle. A stand near to us sent out aromas of apples baked with figs, and hot plum tarts. The dancing anticipation in the eyes of the people as they began to fill the marketplace told its own story of how long they had waited for some entertainment, some festivity, to take them for a few hours from their endless endeavour.

Sounds of fiddles and flutes, not in any great effort at harmony, issued from taverns and the streets leading to the square as the populace streamed to their entertainment. There had been great commotions in the Blackstone house that evening as the women prepared themselves for this very public occasion. Andrew and I had happily taken our supper in the kitchen, as well out of the way as we could make ourselves, and left the house before the party of our host was ready to do so. We could stand, now, and watch as they arrived. Blackstone himself was the epitome of a sober and respectable English gentleman, but his wife and daughters had attired themselves as if for a ball at court.

'They sparkle somewhat amongst the dirt and mud, do they not?'

'Their finery only serves to render them all the plainer,' Andrew answered. I saw that the Blackstone women's treatment of Deirdre was something he would not forgive them. The family took its place amongst others of the officers of the London Companies. Lack of practice had left them doubtful as to the matter of precedence, and there was something of an unseemly scramble for what were evidently regarded as the best places.

Andrew settled himself, disgruntled, against a wall. 'I saw such a play once, in Carrickfergus, when a troupe come to entertain the Governor performed for the townsfolk too. The thing was lewd and ridiculous, and I have never bothered since.'

'You could still return to the Blackstone house. I doubt if it would be noticed now.'

'And leave you alone to get into an O'Neill's mischief? With a loose Franciscan on the prowl? I think not, my friend.'

A trio of musicians, with a singer at their head, entered the marketplace from behind us and led the players to the stage, to wild cheering and stamping from the gathered citizens, eager for the coming performance, announced by the leader of the troupe to be *Much Ado About Nothing*.

'I suspect it will be,' said Andrew, as we settled ourselves to watch. I made no sense whatsoever of what was going on before me for some time, so strange in my ear was the language and the frequent exiting and entering of characters. Andrew understood it little better than I did, and his impatience increased as the crowd laughed uproariously, and booed and hissed at those they did not like. I found in time that I began to know the characters and decipher their words for myself, but it put me in some discomfort to be a witness to so much practised deceit and, impostor that I was, to see the damage done when a man or woman makes claim to be what they are not.

As the air grew colder, Andrew and I found ourselves returning more than once to the vendor of warmed wine. As the honeyed liquid began to loosen his tongue he stepped off his guard a little and allowed, at last, that he might enjoy the play.

'A woman the like of Beatrice, though? Could a man find happiness with one who speaks her mind so freely?'

'Much more than with one who does not, I think.'

'And your Sarah? Does she speak her mind?'

'Only when she has finished blazing it at me through her eyes.'

He laughed. 'You do not fear that another will entice her away from you?'

'I fear it every night. I close my eyes and play out in my mind a parade of men I know would want her, and each night their attraction, the likelihood of her succumbing, seems to increase. In the light of day I tell myself it is nonsense: she will wait for me this one last time. But then, why should she? Why should she wait to know passion from one who has sometimes been almost unable to speak to her? Two years, Andrew. I have been a fool two years.'

'I have been a fool longer, and know from this fool that passion can destroy a man.' He finished his drink in silence, in one draught, and went to get himself another.

I noticed then that Matthew Blackstone was not in his place, but talking a little way off from the side of the stage with one of the players, the friar, who had been to conduct the marriage between Claudio and Hero. I could see little of their faces in the shadows as they were, and could get no impression of the tenor of their exchange. Then a second friar appeared at the first's side. Unlike the other pair, he was standing in the light of one of the stage torches. It was the young man whom I had seen making his way so urgently through the crowd to me earlier, the one I had taken such pains to avoid. It was a strange occurrence, and one made all the stranger a few moments later when, as the play was approaching its end, the older friar made his entrance on the stage once more. I could see him very clearly in the light – the shape and colouring of him – but I did not need such information now to tell me that this was not the man I had seen talking with Matthew Blackstone, for that man had now left the company of my host and was hurrying away in the darkness towards Church Street and out of my view. The light caught his face as he passed out of the square and I knew him at once: it was Stephen Mac Cuarta, the Franciscan. His young companion was now nowhere to be seen.

I pushed through the crowd at the wine-vendor's stall as the play reached its climax, but there was no sight of Andrew there. To call out for him would have been useless, as the audience cheered and stamped its acclamation of the players. The whole multitude seemed to be converging on me, determined on more drink and food to finish their evening off. The closeness of the tide of bodies, the smell of their sweat and their foetid breath, almost turned my stomach. I glimpsed again, briefly, the young friar who had been with Stephen Mac Cuarta, but the throng kept him from seeing me, for which at least I could be thankful. I got at last to the edge of the crowd and saw Matthew Blackstone escorting his wife and daughters back in the direction of their home: too genteel to take part in the public merriment that would follow the play, their night was over.

Still I could not see Andrew. I could not think he would have returned to the Blackstones' place without me. The only other people I knew him to be acquainted with in Coleraine were my grandfather's agent and the master of the brickworks, and I went in that direction. It was not a place through which I would have chosen to wander alone at night. What light there was from the marketplace behind me dwindled as I walked, until I could scarcely see my hand in front of me. Figures lurched past, revellers uneasy on their feet, or lovers looking for dark and secret places to play out their desires. About halfway down to the river, regretting with every step my choice of direction, but reluctant to turn back before I had assured myself that he was not there, I felt a hand grasp my shoulder. I spun round.

'What in God's name . . .'

'Alexander, it is only me.'

'I know that,' I said, my heart still pounding. 'What possessed you to wander down here alone?'

'I needed some air, and the play was not to my liking. How did it end?'

'How did it . . .? I cannot tell you. I was distracted; I think we may have trouble.'

'What sort of trouble?'

'The friar. He was here again tonight, talking to Blackstone, and had a brother of his order with him. It was the same young man I only just got away from earlier.'

'Did you hear any of their conversation? Could you judge their mood?'

'I was too far away.'

'Where are they now?'

'I don't know. I think Mac Cuarta may have been leaving town. The other is still looking for me, I would lay my life on it.'

His voice came quiet in the darkness. 'Let us pray you will not have to.'

We kept to the shadows where we could. The marketplace was emptying and we could see no sign of the young brother. We were soon making our way up Church Street, and were almost at the Blackstones' house when I noticed a movement at an upper window. Less than a moment later the front door opened and the master mason himself appeared in the doorway. He looked in our direction and turned inward to say something to someone standing in the darkened hall. I heard a shriek from within the house, and the kitchen boy ran out, stared at us a moment in terror and then shot up the other side of the street, shouting for all he was worth for the constable.

He was closely followed by two men I recognised instantly, and my heart gave within me: Edward and Henry Blackstone, Deirdre's husband and his brother. They were coming straight at us, both with swords drawn. From the house came a hellish womanly chorus of 'Murderers! Impostors! Murderers! Thieves!'

My mind turned quickly. 'Which way?' I shouted to Andrew.

'The church,' he said, already on his way. For a strongly built man who would not see thirty again he had tremendous speed; I knew that few could catch me on the flat – to their astonishment, I had beaten all my scholars in their summer races at the King's Links, despite the burden of my ten extra years – but Andrew could have come close. The Blackstone brothers were slowed in having to turn, and encumbered by the heavy riding cloaks and boots they still wore. The desolate spaces encompassed by the earthen walls of Coleraine closed to the brothers any advantage familiarity with the town might have given them over us, for we could see our way clear beyond the church to the ramparts themselves and the unmanned bastion beyond the east port. I cleared first one wall of the churchyard, then the other, heedlessly trampling the graves in between. Andrew was behind me, making the leaps with as much ease as I did myself. We were twenty yards from the bastion when I heard shouting coming from the guards at the east port, and saw a man running along the top of the earthworks – he would reach the place before us.

'There!' Andrew shouted, and pointed to a breach in the rampart where much of the earth and turfs had been washed away by rain. I was through it in moments and, almost before I knew it, up to my neck in the filthy, freezing water of the moat and swimming for the other side. I could hear shouts and curses and commands to turn back, but I did not pause to look behind me until I had scrambled up the opposite bank.

Some of the shouts were coming from Andrew, whose head appeared briefly above the water and then sank down below it. He emerged again, taking a huge gulp and struggling to speak before he went under again. Realising at last that he could not swim, I plunged back into the murky water and had reached him before the first of the guards managed to scramble down the outside of the rampier. I had Andrew under the arms now, and was pulling myself back as hard as I could towards the other side once more. Edward and Henry Blackstone appeared at the top of the wall, cursing the guards who pleaded fear of drowning. The men of Coleraine stood, momentarily frozen in impotence, as I for a second time reached the far bank of the moat.

'Where now?' I gasped to Andrew.

'The bridge,' he spluttered. And so we ran on, towards a distant bridge over the mill brook.

Halfway there I risked looking back, and already men with torches had appeared on the brow of the ramparts, shouting and pointing to each other the way we had gone.

'Why don't they come after us?'

'Horses,' Andrew panted, and indeed, within ten minutes I could hear the distant clatter of horses' hoofs on the draw-bridge of the east port. The bastion obscured them for a while from view but then I saw them – half-a-dozen horsemen, and at their head my cousin's husband and his brother. My heart and lungs were fit to burst, and Andrew could not speak, but I knew, however fast we ran, we could not reach the bridge before they overtook us. I knew also that the men of the town would never have gone to these lengths in the chase of a mere impostor, and the shrieks of Matthew Blackstone's wife and daughters echoed in my ears, – 'Impostors! Murderers! Thieves!' Oh God in His Heaven, of what did we stand accused?

FOURTEEN

The Dogs

I could almost feel the breath of the horses on my neck, and the voices of our pursuers were loud in my ears. I hardly dared to look round to see how far behind me Andrew was, in case I should find one of them upon me, but I did look round, and my stomach lurched as I saw that he was almost caught. I opened my mouth to call out a warning, and the sound I heard was not my own voice but a terrible crack from the direction of the bridge. I stopped in horror as the leading horse reared up into the air, then collapsed, writhing, onto its fallen rider. Andrew was frozen in shock also, only three yards ahead of them.

He came quickly to his senses and began to move towards me at speed, aware his life depended on every stride. Not knowing what I was running to, I fixed my eyes on the bridge and did not look behind me again. I reached it at last, feeling I would collapse if I had to go a step further. I leant, wheezing, against the cold stone balustrade for a moment, allowing Andrew to catch me up. He all but lunged into me, before pressing his hands against the opposite balustrade and taking huge lungsful of air. Before either of us could master ourselves sufficiently for speech, another crack, much closer to us this time, rang out, and the three riders – who after a pause had taken up the chase again – reared up on their horses, two of them losing hold of their torches and scorching their already terrified

animals, and wheeled back in the direction of the town and
their fallen companion.

'Holy Mother of God, thanks be to you.'

The voice came out of the darkness that enveloped the other
end of the bridge, then a figure emerged from beyond the far
parapet and began to move towards us. We both made for our
knives, but the figure held out a hand. 'Stay your weapons. I
have been left here to help you.'

As he came closer and I could discern his outline better, I
recognised the form of the tall young man from whom I had
run at the quayside. While I relaxed my hand, Andrew did not,
and I saw him very deliberately remove his knife from its
sheath.

'Who are you?' I asked.

'I am Brother Michael O'Hagan, of the friary of Bonamargy
at Ballycastle. I travel with Father Stephen Mac Cuarta, who
asks me to see you safe from the town and bring you to him.'

'And where is he?' demanded Andrew.

'On his way to a safe house in Bushmills.'

'Having first denounced us as impostors at Coleraine.'

'No, he did not.'

'I saw him myself, talking with Blackstone, not half-an-hour
before we were hounded from the town.'

'He did not denounce you. You must trust me.'

Andrew was scornful. 'A priest with a pistol? Why should
we trust you?'

Even in the darkness I could see a flash of brilliant white
as the young man smiled. 'Because I am of more use to you
than a priest without one.' He held his weapon up for us to
see; it looked to be one of the new flintlock types that I had
heard of but never before seen.

Looking back towards where the dead horse and its injured

rider still lay, Andrew nodded. 'We have no choice, do we?'

'Very little,' said the young man. 'Now please, we must make haste. Three of the riders have gone back towards the town. The confusions and drunkenness in Coleraine will gain us some time, but it will not be long before they have gathered a new search party, and we should not waste a moment.' He unscrewed the top of a flask of water and we both drank gratefully, I now very much regretting the amount of wine I had indulged in during the performance. 'Now, let us get on,' he said. 'A few miles will take us to Dunluce and we can rest again there.'

Guided by the stars in a sky from which the clouds had begun to clear, we headed due north, and it was not long before the boggy edges of moorland became drier under our feet and a tantalising hint of salt came to me on the cooling night air. We were moving at a slow jog, all three of us ever anxiously looking back towards the diminishing darkened mound that was the town of Coleraine. There was still no sign of light or horses coming from it, but we knew it could not be long. Brother Michael led us from the shelter of one rock or group of ancient trees to another, so that we were seldom crossing exposed ground.

It was not long before I could hear as well as smell the sea. The land had started to slope downwards slightly and the gentle approach of the waves to the shore grew louder in my ears in the empty night. One by one, we slowed our pace and at last came to a halt at the stunning sight the moon now illuminated before us. Pale blue cliffs of chalk descended gently to a near-endless sweep of sand bordering the midnight black of the sea. It was only a moment's respite, and soon we were moving again, keeping to the coast and heading east.

'How far to Dunluce?' gasped Andrew.

'About three miles.'

'You are sure we will gain shelter there?'

'In the chapel. They will have been warned to expect us.'

'Father Stephen?' I asked.

'Yes.'

I could not picture the sturdy baker of Armstrong's Bawn, who had seen thirty summers and winters more on this earth than I had, making the journey we undertook tonight.

'Is he on horseback?'

'We seldom travel on horseback, unless it is necessary. It is the rule of our order. He is on foot.'

And then I recalled to myself that the man who had ridden at the side of my mother's brother as he followed O'Neill to the ends of Ireland and back, through winter, who had gone into exile with him in Spain, and had spent the years since travelling in Italy, France and the Low Countries, would not have been much troubled by a night flight in a land he knew as well as his own hand.

I regretted my vanity in changing my clothes earlier in the evening for the performance – the clothes Sean O'Neill Fitz-Garrett would have worn for a night at the play were not those he would have chosen for a cross-country run through the night in the first stirrings of winter. Andrew was dressed in a more sensible fashion, but we had both been soaked to the skin in the moat and our clothes clung heavy to our legs. Brother Michael, his cassock hitched up around his thighs, ran like the wind. The colder air began to scorch my throat and lungs. I wondered whether our pursuers would catch us before we succumbed to certain fever.

The sounds of our footfalls beat out a pattern with the rhythm of the sea coming in to shore. Suddenly, Michael stopped and held up a hand to stay us, another to his lips. Unmoving, trying to silence our breaths, we heard what he had: the sounding of a horn and the yelping of dogs, somewhere to the south-west of us.

'What is it?'

'The wolf-hunt.'

'There are no wolves in these parts, surely.'

'Tonight, we are the wolves,' said Andrew.

Michael moved quickly. 'They are about a mile off. We have a mile and a half before we gain Dunluce. They will be on us long before we reach sanctuary if we stay on this path.'

'Where can we go?' asked Andrew. 'They will have our scent.'

Michael was thinking. There was little shelter here – few trees could withstand the blasts of the northern wind, straight off the sea, and the land behind us was flat and open.

'The cliffs?' I said, hoping I was wrong as I looked down on the massive, misshapen lumps of white chalk, tufted over with grass and moss, and frozen in their riotous collision over a bubbling sea. 'There is no shore beneath them.'

'There is, eventually, in the shadow of the castle itself, not far from Magheracross there,' he said, indicating a promontory a little way off to the east. 'They may be our only chance. They are by no means sheer, and will offer us many footholds and hiding places amongst the rocks and caves.'

'Will the dogs not find us there?'

Again Andrew answered, thinking more clearly than I was. 'Aye, but the horses cannot get down there, and if their riders dismount and come after us, well, it may approximate to a fair fight.'

We all knew it would not be, but we had no option and there was nothing else to say. Every second in debate was a second wasted, a second closer for the hounds whose relent-less barking was drawing inexorably nearer. Without further word, Michael led the way over the cliff's edge to a ledge of rock just below; Andrew followed and I brought up the rear, taking one last look behind before I went over, and catching the first distant flashes of the hunt's torches in the darkness as I did so.

The ledge was not wide, but led down to another, and then grassy tufts and rounded boulders offered us sufficient foot- and handholds to progress slowly about twenty feet below the level of the cliff path. Our eyes were well accustomed to the darkness, and the moon afforded us light enough to discern the edges of rocks and the grassy dips and mounds between them, but for what was below we had to trust to Michael, and he to God. We moved along and downwards slowly and in near-silence, save for instructions or warnings to one another of where to find a handhold, or where the rock was sheer. All the while we could hear the yelping of the hounds and the shouts of the men who drove them.

Our progress was slow, hand by hand, foot by foot, as we edged our way along our chosen path, trying not to think of the certain death that must await us in the boiling sea and merci- less rocks below, should we once lose our grip. The rock was black and slippery now, and the going a little harder. It seemed we had gone on in this way for hours, although it could not have been so, when Michael called something back to us, and my heart lifted, for at last, in the distance, I saw reaching out over the sea the great looming mass of what could only be Dunluce Castle. Andrew had seen it ahead of me, and was inspired by the sight to quicken his progress towards it. At that very moment a hunting horn sounded, closer now, and he missed his footing. His right foot slid down and caught in a crevice as he tried to steady himself. He let out a cry of pain, and just managing to grab on to a coarse tuft of grass above his head, slid down the side of the rock. I lunged forward to grab at him, and Michael turned backwards to do the same, but Andrew's weight proved too great for the tuft he had clung to, and it slipped through his fingers as his whole body slid down and through the darkness to land with a dull thud somewhere below us.

Before I could think what to do, Michael had scrambled over the ledge and was out of sight. I looked for a safe way down, and began to edge myself over, testing the drop to where Andrew lay groaning. Again came the blast of the hunt's horn, much closer now.

Michael's voice came to me through the darkness: 'A five-foot drop, that is all. Straight down, onto grass.'

He had reached Andrew and was gently passing his hand over Andrew's head. 'You have taken a bad bump there,' he said.

'Do you tell me so?' said Andrew, laughing in spite of himself.

Michael took his hand away and held it up for me to see. I moved closer, and by the light of the moon I saw a dark stain running down the palm of his hand, a mirror for the stain that had spread from Andrew's temple to the side of his face.

'Where else have you pain?'

He gritted his teeth. 'Every part of me, but I think my foot may be the worst.'

I knelt down and passed my hand over his foot and around his ankle. 'I do not think the bone is broken, but it is badly twisted. You will not be able to walk on it.'

'Then you must leave me here.'

'That will not happen, whatever else befalls us tonight. You will not be left here.'

'You have no option. I cannot move and the wolfhounds will be on us in minutes.'

I looked at Michael and he shook his head. 'I can go for help to the castle.'

'It will be too late by then,' I said.

'Then you must leave me.'

I knew that if he was not torn by the hounds, Andrew would succumb to a fever or freeze to death on the rock if we left him there. 'And would you leave me?' I said.

He turned his head away. 'That is not the question.'

'It is the question I am asking.'

He said nothing, and I moved closer to Michael. 'How far now?'

His voice was lowered almost to a whisper. 'We are almost round the last headland, and then we can get him down to the beach. It is shingle, so not easy walking for him, but a hundred yards will take us on to the castle footpath. If we can get him there, I can scramble the rest and bring help.' He looked at me directly. 'If we leave him here he will not survive the night.'

The voices of the huntsmen and the barking of the dogs were now almost directly above us. There was no choice to be made. Michael took Andrew under the arms and I lifted his feet, an agony for him by the look on his face, and we carried him like that between us, but the passes where there was room to do so were few, and there were places only wide enough for a man's foot. Andrew had to stifle his pain and his cries and pull himself along and across the face of the rock as if there were no injury. For the rest, we dragged him. In this way, we somehow turned the final headland and allowed ourselves to slip ten feet or so down the rock to the black shingle beach below Dunluce. Michael signalled to me where the path began, little over fifty yards from where we were, and, pointing towards a recess in the rock that was almost a cave and would shield us from sight, ran for all he was worth in the direction of the great outcrop of rock that led up to the castle.

The huntsmen and their yelping dogs had come to a halt directly above where Andrew had fallen. A debate had ensued amongst the men, but I had not the time to listen. We could not wait for Michael, out of sight or not. Urging Andrew on, I began to drag us both after the young Franciscan, towards the path from Dunluce. We were making good progress, and although it was clear that every step was agony to him, Andrew made no plea for pause or rest. We can only have been about twenty yards from the foot of the path when there was a change in the sounds coming from above; I hardly had time to register it before Andrew said, 'The dogs!' I turned once more, and saw that three of the beasts had started to hurtle and scramble down the rock, barking as if to beat back the monsters of the deep. Those that had been kept with the riders howled their protests in return.

'Leave me,' gasped Andrew. 'You won't make it. Leave me.'

I took a decision there and then, and stepping in front of him, with my back to him, I told him to put his arms around my neck.

'No, Alexander, you cannot . . .'

'Just do it!'

In a moment, I had hauled him up onto my back, as my father had so often done to me when I was a young boy. The weight of him on me was more than I would have thought possible, but praying God for strength, I gritted my teeth and went forward. To my amazement, each stride seemed to give new force to the next, and within a few strides I had picked up a better pace than we had both had walking. A cloud had passed over the moon, and it was now difficult for me to see the base of the path I was making for. I dared not look behind or above me; all my strength and power were needed to drive me onwards. But the demented barking of the dogs had never ceased, and I knew it could not be long before they were on us.

From somewhere above came a shout, and then a terrible yelping; I turned in time to see the lead dog hurtling from high up on the cliff, through the air, and bumping and crashing against rocks as it made its way towards its death. Its mangled body came to rest on a stretch of grass just above the shingle. A strange, sickening, whimpering told me the poor beast was not dead. At any other time, I would have put it out of its misery, but I had to abandon it to its agonies.

Its companions on the cliff top were howling now, in great distress. The horses were whinnying and shying back from the edge, their riders having dismounted to try to make out what was happening below. The two other dogs, however, were progressing relentlessly on towards the shore, focused only on their quarry. Huge, lean shaggy hounds, beasts with no fear of wolves, they would be little deterred by two unarmed men, one of them crippled. I redoubled my efforts and forced myself and my burden almost into a run.

'Leave me, Alexander. Get yourself to Dunluce.'

I ignored him and went on, the foot of the path in clear sight now. And then I heard the crunch of huge paws on the shingle behind me. Andrew turned, for I could not. 'They are down. They are sniffing the fallen hound. Oh, good God!'

And now I did turn. One dog remained by its fallen companion, licking and nosing at it, and setting up a piteous howling, but the other was standing to point, its nose in the air and its tail erect, every sinew stretched in readiness. It saw us and it flew. I tried to run faster, but I could scarcely keep my footing. I stumbled once, twice, then felt Andrew drop from my back. He yelled in pain as his foot hit the ground. The beast was on him in seconds, its massive paws pushing him down onto the stones beneath, a demonic roaring coming from its throat. I grasped on the ground for the staff Michael had given me, and set about the beast's head and haunches with it. This only served to enrage it further, and it whipped its huge jaws round to me, snarling and baring its teeth, without for a moment letting go its hold on Andrew, who was struggling to get his hands up between his face and its jaws. I threw away the stick and launched myself at the animal's back. Again it whipped round, and I got my arm around its neck and pulled back for all I was worth. Beneath me, Andrew kneed it in the belly, and as it yelped and doubled forward, I wrenched back hard on its neck again. This time I heard a horrible snap, and the dog crumpled motionless from my arms. I pushed the dead weight off Andrew's body and started to pull him once more to his feet. His clothes were torn and his face was bleeding from where the animal had bitten into his jaw, but he was in a better condition than he might have been.

I did not take him on my back now, and at a slow trudge we reached the bottom of the path soon enough. The one remaining living hound on the beach was following us now, growling softly, but I sensed a wariness in it. Leaving Andrew to lean on the staff a moment, I picked up a rock and hurled it at the animal. It yelped and then slunk quietly away, to lie guard over its dead companions.

At last then there came the sound of voices, in Gaelic, and the glint of a light from further up the path. It was Michael, and behind him another man, in a priest's robes, and carrying a pallet of some sort. They were with us in minutes.

Michael surveyed Andrew's face and clothing. 'The dogs?' he said.

'One of them. They will not bother us any more.'

He nodded, and asked nothing else. Carefully, and with surprising ease and skill, they laid Andrew down upon the pallet, and with the older priest taking the lead and the lantern, Michael and I lifted it between us and carried Andrew up the narrow and twisting path from the beach to the rocky outcrop on which the castle stood. In the moonlight, through all the mess of blood and dirt, Andrew smiled at me.

'You are an Irishman after all. As good as the best of them.' He closed his eyes and his head lolled to one side, exhaustion and pain freeing him from further consciousness.

FIFTEEN

A Council of Priests

I had never set foot in a Romish church before, but I had never known such relief at entering the house of God as I did on crossing the threshold of the ancient church of St Cuthbert, in the shadows of the castle. The mingled perfume of damp stone and incense caught in my throat and set me to coughing. Burning candles spread circles of light and some blessed warmth around where they stood, in sconces in the walls and in candlesticks of gold on altars at the front and down the side of the small church. There were no pews, but some elaborately carved and sumptuously upholstered oak chairs near the base of the main altar. A brazier burned in the near corner, and we carefully laid Andrew down there.

'What is this place?'

The older priest took down his hood. He was tall, slightly stooping and with an aristocratic bearing. 'Father Fintan MacQuillan,' he said. 'You are in the church of St Cuthbert, anciently St Murgan's. You may take rest and sanctuary here for the night, until help can be brought to you in the morning.'

There was a comfort in hearing the old, old names. Despite the incense, and the golden candlesticks, and the ornate carvings, I felt I could rest easy a while in this place.

'Thank you. My friend is much in need of rest.'

'His wounds must be cleaned also. We can do something for

him tonight, but for the rest, he will have to wait until you get to Bonamargy.'

I looked at Michael. 'Why are we going to Bonamargy?'

'Father Stephen will explain. Fintan has sent to Bushmills for him, he will be here before dawn. Now, Fintan,' he said, turning to the old priest, 'have you dry robes for us?'

Within the half-hour, while Fintan attended to Andrew, Michael and I had stripped and washed every inch of ourselves in freezing-cold water from the chapel well, and before getting into the coarse grey robes the priest had found for us I had been persuaded to rub myself with pungent ointments from a box brought from the priest's own house.

'What are these for?' I asked, with less grace than I should have done. After my grandmother's nocturnal attempt to baptise me into her faith, I had little trust in priests and their ointments.

'They may do something to disguise your scent,' Fintan replied. 'Who knows, with their aid, and my old robes, you may throw them off yet.'

I felt something sink in my stomach. 'The hounds. They are still after us.'

'And will not give up,' said Michael, 'until they lose your trail.'

'That is why you have been brought into the church,' said Fintan, 'rather than to my own house.'

'Will they respect the sanctuary?'

'The dogs will respect nothing,' said Michael, 'but the huntsmen will not dare trespass on the sanctuary beneath MacDonnell's very walls. The town of Coleraine will take great care not to offend the Earl of Antrim.'

Andrew had woken while his wounds were being cleaned and dressed. He managed to sit up a little, and take some broth.

I ate hungrily everything that was offered me. Though I had dried myself thoroughly and was now in clean clothes – the priest's robe and thick woollen hose – I felt the cold and damp still to the depth of my bones. The stars tonight were much as they had been on my last night in Aberdeen as I'd walked home from William Cargill's house, promising myself that the next day I would secure my wife and set out on a mission to call others to the ministry of the Kirk. How then had that man come to be here, dressed in a priest's robes, with holy oils rubbed into his skin, a fugitive fleeing a wolf-hunt? The trappings and tentacles of the world my mother had known before she had ever known me were closing in on me, and I prayed God for the strength and the faith to withstand them. In the place I now found myself, it seemed the borders between the spiritual and physical worlds were blurring, eliding. I tried to pull myself back to the world of the material, to what I could understand. My eye lighted upon Michael, who had taken up a position by a southwest window and was peering into the night for signs of our pursuers.

'Why did you come to Coleraine? Why were you looking for me?'

He did not turn away from the window. 'It was not to give you up to the Blackstones, you must believe that.' After all that had just passed, I could not but believe him, yet I knew there was more. He breathed deep. 'I came to warn you that Edward and Henry Blackstone were on their way back from Carrick-fergus. And to tell you . . .'

He was searching for words he did not seem to have, and my patience was failing me.

'Michael,' I said, 'what am I running from? They would not have gone to these lengths to track and bring to punishment a man who had masqueraded as his own cousin.'

'No, they would not,' he said quietly.

'What then?'

He left off his window vigil. 'Alexander, your cousin is dead.'

The warmth that had at last started to come into my hands and feet went in that moment as a sickening chill spread through me.

'Sean?'

'Yes.'

'No.'

'I am sorry. The Blackstones knew you could not have been Sean, because they knew he was dead. He was murdered on the night after your grandfather's funeral. They rode hard for Coleraine as soon as the news became known. Deirdre refused to go with them.'

'Is she safe?'

Michael looked at Andrew. 'All I know is that she would not leave with her husband. Father Stephen will know more.'

I was shivering now, more than I had done on the cliffs, more than when I had first plunged into the moat at Coleraine. I wrapped my arms hard about myself but the shivering would not stop. I clamped my lips shut, tight, and bit down on my own cheeks to stop the scream that was rising from my stomach. Andrew lifted a hand but he could not reach me and it dropped again to the floor. It could not be so. God would not allow it to be so.

'You have been deceived,' I said to Michael at last. 'Sean cannot be dead.'

'Alexander, I am sorry . . .'

'He cannot be dead. He was so . . .' I could not finish it. Because he was so much alive. What cruel game of Providence was it that sent me on a fool's errand after poets and grasping men, when my cousin, who had been forced to remain in our grandmother's house, with his most trusted servant at his side, was murdered? How could Sean, who had Eachan, be dead?

Father Fintan was already lighting a candle at an altar, was already on his knees and praying, urgent words in Latin for the repose of my cousin's soul, and words in Gaelic that I could not catch. He begged favour and mercy on some 'cause'. I pulled my robe close and leant my head against the wall next to the brazier. Rest would not come, comfort would not come, only pain. I lay there, in a stupor of exhaustion and grief, hoping only for sleep or some other oblivion. As I passed into the world of dreams, my cousin's laughing face was in my mind's eye, and I drifted into sleep with the warmth of his voice wishing me a last 'goodnight'.

I was awoken from turbulent dreams by a cacophony of shouting and barking, and a loud banging on the door of the church. It was still night. Father Fintan, who had evidently not slept, was up and drawing back the bolt on the door, Michael behind him with his pistol ready. The door opened and in blasted Father Stephen, who hastily slammed it behind him, holding it fast with his powerful frame until Fintan got it bolted. 'Mother of God! The beasts would have had my throat.' He knelt then and crossed himself before the altar.

Michael had returned to his place at the window. 'They have been circling two hours, almost since we got here.'

I had come to myself fully now, and struggled to stand up. The old friar seemed to notice me for the first time. A light came into his eyes and was quickly extinguished; his face fell and he walked towards me, uttering some Gaelic prayer. He put his arms out and brought me into his huge embrace and wept, and I knew that for a moment he had thought I was Sean.

The dogs were still barking outside, and there came another loud banging on the door. I had been ordered down beside Andrew, and a blanket hastily thrown over the two of us, but I could still see something of what passed in the doorway. Outside was a man with a torch, more behind him, and baying hounds at the back. 'In the name of the city of Coleraine, I demand entrance here.'

Fintan raised himself up to his full dignity, and I would not have believed such a roar could come from the old man's throat. 'And in the name of God and of the Earl of Antrim, I tell you to remove yourselves and your pack of dogs from this hallowed ground. You trample on the graves of MacDonnell!'

The man took a step back, clearly shaken, then made another attempt to hold his ground. 'We have reason to believe that you harbour two fugitives from . . .'

'Off!' roared Fintan, and even the dogs jumped back with a yelp. 'The city of Coleraine has no jurisdiction here. If you doubt it, take it up with MacDonnell himself!'

I heard the horsemen outside, cursing, mount their beasts and call their dogs. I looked at the old priest in a wonder of admiration, then saw that he was breathing heavily and his hands were shaking. Stephen passed him a flask he carried at his hip, and the old man drank gratefully. When he had passed it back he spoke to Michael.

'Go through my house and take the passage to the castle. Tell them that we need a guard, one man on horseback, with MacDonnell's standard, at dawn, to take Stephen Mac Cuarta and others to Bonamargy.'

Stephen knelt down by me. He put his hand gently to Andrew's forehead, which was now cold and clammy. 'There is one of our order at Bonamargy who has the skills he needs. All will be well with your friend.'

I opened my mouth to speak but he shook his head briefly. 'And you and I will talk when we leave here. There is much I realise you want to know, but first there are matters I must discuss with Fintan that cannot wait. Take some rest now: you will need it for the days to come.'

It was good counsel, and I tried to take it. I lay down behind Andrew, for warmth for both of us. The beads of sweat that had formed on his forehead were cold to the touch, and his face and hands were like wax. The gashes on his face and temples had been cleaned, but gaped angrily, and I knew they would need to be stitched soon if the wounds were not to become infected. He was murmuring in his sleep, words I could not understand.

The two older priests were close to the altar, at the far end of the church. Stephen had also lighted a candle, and he too prayed for the repose of Sean's soul – as if the words of man, however earnest, could change the foreordained judgement of God. Through the pre-dawn gloom, in the light of the candles which were steadily burning down, I watched the two men draw their heads together and talk. The words I caught were words I had heard before: Murchadh, Louvain, MacDonnell, Deirdre, Rathlin, Macha, Dun-a-Mallaght. I could make sense of none of it, and was glad when Michael reappeared and told us to make ready, for our escort waited without in the burying ground, and it would soon be dawn.

An extra blanket was brought for Andrew, and Father Fintan laid a crucifix at his neck and tried to press on me another. I held it back out to him; the man had treated us with Christian charity, and we might have perished on the black, wet rock of Dunluce otherwise, but there was a limit beyond which I could not allow myself to go, and I knew in my belief that I spoke for Andrew also. 'I need none of your superstitious charms, and nor does he. The will of God cannot be changed by the wearing of a trinket.'

Father Stephen looked up from his examination of Andrew's ankle. 'It is not the will of God you need to concern yourself with. There are eighteen miles to Ballycastle. We will pass many people on our way. If they are to believe you to be friars of my order you must look like friars of my order. And if you think the crucifix but a trinket, it will cost you nothing to wear it.'

Michael had asked at the castle for a pony and cart also. 'Your friend is strong built. It is not a burden I would like to carry far.' Tall and slim, with shiny locks that were almost black covering a high brow, he looked to be of a studious disposition, better suited to the life of the Jesuit than the eternal roamings of the Franciscans, and although he could run like a deer, I doubted in truth whether he could have helped me carry Andrew five miles, still less the eighteen that we had to go. Father Stephen was a different proposition entirely: he might have been nearly forty years older than Michael, but he had the strength and the miles behind him of an old soldier, and I had the impression he could have carried Andrew to Carrick-fergus and back if need be.

The burial ground was deserted now, save the escort waiting at the porch. The tide was going out, and the sound of the sea was like a retreating horde. Looking back at the castle rocks, the massive gorges and gullies that had been cheated of their prey last night, I uttered another silent prayer of thanks for our deliverance. Andrew, on his pallet, had drifted back to wakefulness for a moment, and was mumbling, a run of words that made little sense. I went closer and told him to lie peaceful, but still he strained to sit up, to see something. He was looking upwards, at some point in the castle walls.

'Please no,' I muttered in spite of all I knew to be sane or godly. 'Please God, no.'

'Do you see her?' he said at last. 'Do you see Maeve MacQuillan?'

On the road to Bushmills a woman came out of her cabin and beseeched me to say a prayer over her sick child. 'A word to St Lucia, father, that she might beg the lord's mercy on my girl. Only a word, father.' I froze, held fast by panic and indecision, as she clung to my robe.

Stephen put up the reins and got down. Gently taking the woman's arm and leading her back towards her hovel, he said, 'That fellow's Latin is so bad, the saint would know not one word in ten that he says. Let me put up a word for your child – Lucia and I are acquainted of old.'

Three minutes later he was out again and we were back on the road.

'How is the child?' I asked.

'She will be in the arms of the Mother of God before darkness falls.' His face was grim, and he said no more until we had begun the gentle descent to the bridge across the river Bush. 'I have business to see to here; it will not want more than an hour or two of our time, but I doubt your friend can wait that long. There is one of our order who is of the caste of the *fir leighs*; his family have been doctors to Irish chieftains for many generations. What little their learning left out, he made up for in study while we were at Louvain. He will attend to the wounds and the leg injury, and see to the fever.'

We crossed the bridge and Stephen brought the cart to a halt at a stone mill on the right bank of the river. The smell of malted barley hung heavy in the air. The waters of the Bush flowed pure and clear past the mills and out towards the sea.

A man in a leather apron came out and greeted the two Franciscans by name, and nodded to me.

Stephen gestured towards Andrew. 'Michael will take this one, under escort, to Gerard at Bonamargy. There is no time to be lost.'

The still man nodded, the look on his face suggesting he thought there would be little Gerard could do for Andrew in any case. He stole another glance at me. 'I thought for a moment the dead walked. You had better keep that one out of sight.'

'Have no fears on that score. I value his life.'

Stephen gave his instructions to Michael, who had now taken up the reins, and to the escort, but when I set off to walk beside them he called me back.

'You must stay with me. We have much to talk about, and I have sent a message to Finn O'Rahilly; I am taking you to him at dusk. You will see your friend at Bonamargy tomorrow.'

I laid my hand on Andrew's brow. It was slicked with sweat and his cheeks were burning now. His whole body was shaking under its blanket, and he moaned and mumbled words that were not words.

'You can do nothing for him,' said Stephen. 'No more than he can do for you. You must see the poet, and O'Rahilly will consent to this one time. Let Michael take him now.'

With a heavy heart I realised I had no choice. I had to place myself in Stephen's hands, and leave Andrew, struggling for life as he was, at the mercy of subversive priests.

I rested while Stephen went in to talk to the still man, and wondered what his business with him might be, but I was learning that the Franciscan would let out knowledge like a length of rope. He would give me only what I needed to cling on to: the rest he would keep hidden in the robes of his order. I did not ponder it long, and passed into sleep instead. Drifts of their conversation came to my semi-slumbering mind, they talked of stores and supplies in the field, but I did not care enough to listen. The hours spent in sodden clothing began to exact their price, however, and I was taken with a coughing fit. The conversation stopped and the priest was through the door again in a moment.

'So, you are wakened? I would have thought you would sleep longer, but you Presbyterians do not much hold with rest and comfort, they tell me.'

'Then they tell you wrong. I crave both, but there is none here.'

He assessed me silently for a moment. 'Perhaps there is an aid to it though.' He called something to the still man and in a moment the fellow brought us two small glasses filled with a clear amber liquid. I let the whisky warm its way from my tongue to my body and mind, relax my bones, expand my thoughts.

'Tell me what happened to my cousin,' I said at last.

He sighed, and refilled his own glass from the flask that had been left with us. He sipped carefully, then he pursed his lips and sucked in hard, tipping the whole glassful down without giving it chance of pause in his mouth. And then he told me what had happened to my family on the night of my grandfather's funeral.

'No one saw the girl, but Sean took it into his head that the note was from Macha. He would not let Eachan go with him, telling him to stay with Deirdre and your grandmother. But of course, Eachan did go after him. He followed him until he saw him turn in to St Nicholas church. He would have followed him there, but a moment after Sean entered, he saw a young woman, heavily wrapped against the cold, emerge from behind one of the gravestones and follow him. Satisfied that all was as it should be, Eachan left and returned to your grandmother's house, to watch over the women there. He was not altogether easy at leaving Sean, and his unease grew as the night wore on. Sometime before dawn, leaving the house under guard of Murchadh and his sons, he went back to the church. All was silent, and he could see no one, but a light burned in the Donegall aisle and he went to it.' Here the priest filled his glass and emptied it again. 'There he found Sean's body sprawled across Chichester's memorial, his head almost severed from his neck.' Against my will, I pictured the scene. I had never set foot in that or any church in Carrickfergus, but my mind forced the images on to me; suggestions of candlelight, marble, blood and silence.

Stephen's voice grew bitter. 'Eachan lifted him in his arms, as if he had been a fallen child, and brought him home. He laid your cousin down on his bed, and cleaned his murdered body as he wept. And so was Sean betrayed.'

My voice was almost dead in my throat. 'Betrayed in what?' I asked at last.

He looked up at me from his empty glass and studied my face a long moment. 'In everything his life should have been. In everything that was before him to do. In everything that mattered.'

'How do you know all this?'

'Your grandmother's priest sent word to Bonamargy. He fears she will go out of her mind for grief. The Blackstones were declaring they would leave for the North in the morning – not a moment to lose in moving on your grandfather's business. Deirdre was in a hysteria, and refused to go with them. Cormac O'Neill and his brothers took her, in their protection, to one of their father's strongholds. Eachan was fit to kill any who tried to come near to Sean's body. The house is in a turmoil of despair.'

But there was something more. I asked the question slowly, afraid of the answer I knew would come. 'Why did the Blackstone women cry out that I was a murderer?'

He was hesitant to begin and poured himself a third glass from the flask and me a second. 'Your grandmother, as I told you, has been driven from her senses by the curse of Finn O'Rahilly and all that has followed. She has never been a kind or loving woman. Quick to suspect and slow to trust, swift to accuse and never forgiving. She was murmuring that she had brought it all upon her own head, and telling, to any who would listen, the story of Diarmuid and the boar.' He paused a moment, a sad smile on his face. 'Tell me,' he said, 'did Sean never tell you the tale of Diarmuid and the boar?'

'Never,' I replied.

He nodded, as if he had expected such a response. 'And I'll wager your mother never did either?'

'No,' I said, 'she didn't.'

'Then I'll tell you. Diarmuid was a warrior, of the *Fianna* of Finn McCool, the god-king. Diarmuid had a half-brother, the offspring of an illicit union of his mother and his father's steward. When the child was born, the husband took it and dashed it against the rocks. But Diarmuid's foster-father took pity on the bastard child, and through magic, brought it back to life in the shape of a boar. This creature dedicated the rest of its life to the pursuit and killing of its half-brother. There came the time when Diarmuid was tricked into joining the *Fianna* in a boar hunt. At the climax of the hunt, the boar fatally gored Diarmuid, just as he was driving his spear into its heart. At the moment of death, the beast transformed at last into its human form, and Diarmuid saw that it was his brother.'

'A fine fable,' I said, when I realised it had come to its end and its moral had not presented itself. 'But what is it to my grandmother? Why are you telling it to me?'

He looked me steadily in the eye. 'That you might think on it, as I have been.'

'I am not in the humour for riddles,' I said.

There was a long silence before he spoke again. 'Alexander, the reason that you were pursued from Coleraine, that you are pursued still, is that your grandmother has put it out, has called down judgement from the heavens, that it was you who murdered your cousin.'

I felt the glass drop from my hand and saw the golden liquid seep into the rushes on the floor.

SIXTEEN

A Woman Grieving

Carrickfergus

She was tired of walls: walls surrounded by walls, the damp cold of rooms that would never get warm. But here in her garden it was different. The slight breeze off the sea brought air that was fresh, not foetid. It was a clean cold that the rugs the servants had brought her, fussed around her with, kept from her bones. The wood of the bench was warm in the last of the autumn sunshine. A few blooms still clung to the stems of old roses that cloaked the western and northern walls, sending to her a faint scent of apricot and lemon. She closed her eyes and felt the hint of warmth on her cheek, and let herself think of Connemara, of fifty autumns past, and riding for miles along the endless sands with her mare, Emer, dancing in the spray.

The cook's child was gathering the last of the apples from the orchard. She remembered Grainne, on such an afternoon, running barefoot along the coast path at Whitehead, her small chubby fingers stained with the juice of the blackberries they'd been gathering, the startled delight on her childish face when a rabbit shot out of the bushes in front of them. When she had been young.

She called to the cook's child to bring her an apple, and the boy ran to her quickly with the best from his basket. She drew from her girdle the small jewelled knife she kept there and cut the fruit carefully, giving him a piece before dismissing him.

Murchadh had gone, at last. She was mistress in her own house once more. She should have mastered her grief quicker, held her tongue sooner. His rage, on learning of Grainne's Scottish son, had surpassed what even she had expected. It had taken some work on her part to convince him that she had no love for the boy, not a trace: he was not Sean. Perhaps Deirdre had been right, perhaps Alexander Seaton had not killed his cousin. Indeed, in her quieter moments she herself knew there could be little reason for him to have done so, but that he lived while Sean lay cold and dead, that she could not forgive. When Murchadh had been calmed, eventually, and begun to think, as Maeve had, it had not been a great work of persuasion to show him how the Scotsman might be of use to them, might salvage some of Sean's legacy and lay it at Murchadh's feet. What happened to the boy after that was of little interest to her. She suspected Murchadh had it in mind that he should not long survive his cousin. So be it: she had no further use for him, and greater concerns.

Word had come last night from the North, the word they had waited so long for, and Murchadh's dark mood had dissipated entirely on the hearing of it. He had thrown his arm around her and lifted her into the air, before shouting for drink, the best that was to be had from her cellars.

'By God,' he said, as he set her down, 'we have had little enough to celebrate these last days, but we have it now!' He appraised her, as if he had never seen her properly before, and shook his head in a kind of wonder. 'I'll own it to you now, Maeve: I thought you played too risky a hand, but you have known this game a long time and I should not have doubted you.'

She would not tell him how she had doubted also, that only a sort of desperation, a sudden madness had suggested to her the course she had taken. Deirdre had thought by her marriage to spurn her, but in so doing she had gifted her that unforeseen chance, the glimpse of a man's venality, and when Maeve had seen it she had taken it. 'It was the only way we would ever get the arms. We could not wait for Spanish help for ever.'

'And now we will do it without the Spaniards, because you did not flinch. Through all your losses, you have never flinched.' He laid a gloved hand over her cold, ringed fingers. 'I know your grief. Sean should have been with us, at our head. But his name will not be forgotten: in three days we will start our march; we will blast the English from Ulster with guns of their own making. They have "civilised" us more than they know. And the name of Sean O'Neill FitzGarrett will be written into the legends of Ireland. Three days yet, Maeve, that is all.'

It was a wonder to her that fifty years of life had not been enough to teach her kinsman how much might be lost in three days. 'Nothing must be permitted to go wrong, Murchadh. Deirdre . . .'

'You cannot be sure she knows.'

'She knows; she all but taunted me with it on the night I sent Seaton north.'

'Do not fear for her. Cormac has her safe; no one will be allowed near Deirdre.'

'Should the words of her loosened tongue reach the wrong ears, everything would be imperilled.'

'The preparations of your apothecary have dulled her mind and her tongue, and should they fail, Cormac has his instructions.'

'Murchadh, I have known your son all his life. He is the best of Ireland. Like Phelim, like Sean. But my granddaughter is his great weakness. Should the time come for her silence, we cannot rely on Cormac.'

He looked her straight in the eye. 'I have other sons, Maeve, and they will not have a lover's qualms.'

And so Murchadh had left, and she was alone again, and waiting. The clouds had gathered and obscured the sun. The wind off the sea had grown stronger and the garden was cold now. She got up wearily from the bench and began to walk back towards the house, the apple lying uneaten where she had left it, the white of its flesh already brown and rotting.

SEVENTEEN

The Cursing Circle

They had said it often enough: she was going mad. Finn O'Rahilly and his curses, Deirdre and her vision of Maeve MacQuillan, grief over the husband she had deceived for so long. And now the loss of Sean, her hope, her future. But what madness could create in her heart this hatred of me?

My mind was fracturing, and my head and eyes ached as I struggled to keep hold of what I thought I had understood. All my life, I had not known my cousin, and then I had known him, and loved him. I could look in a glass and see his living image, but he was dead. I had played his part, I had been Sean FitzGarrett in the eyes of others, I had walked in his very boots, and all the while he had been dead. The grandfather I had never known had loved me. The grandmother I knew despised me. I had come here for Sean, abandoned all that I knew and all that knew me, for Sean, but there was no Sean now, only Alexander. The grief that many years ago had threatened to rip me apart when I had learned of the death of Archibald Hay had hunted me down across the Irish Sea, and found me once more. And if ever Alexander Seaton saw Scotland again, it would be from Dunluce, from the Hanging Hill. I would never look again on the face of the woman I loved, never know what it was to touch her. Oh, God help me. The man in the clothes of a priest, hung round with the trappings of idolatry, calling on his God.

Stephen reached a hand out to my shoulder. His voice was gentle, but urgent. 'We must tarry here no longer, Alexander, if we are to be at Kilcrue before sunset.' And so, within the half-hour, I found myself on the road again. I had passed the middle of the day in sleep, and was again walking towards the night. Favoured words of my counsellor and friend Mr Gilbert Grant, late schoolmaster of Banff, came to me: 'Yet a little while is the light with you, Walk while ye have the light, lest darkness come upon you: for he that walketh in darkness knoweth not whither he goeth.' Blind at the end, these had been the last words to pass the old man's lips.

Upwards, away from the sea we went. The ground became difficult underfoot, bog and heather, and in time we entered woods once more, ancient woods of oak, hazel and willow. As I thrust my staff into the ground with every new step forward, I struggled to remember why I was here now, why I had come to seek out Finn O'Rahilly. My cousin was dead, and there was little in me that cared now for the poet's ramblings or his curses. And yet his voice came clearer to my mind, the words pulling at me. 'All these things will come to pass. Your grandson will soon lie with his fathers, in the cold chambers of the dead.' Sean was dead and the curse was no longer rambling, no longer a malevolent retelling of what everyone already knew: what O'Rahilly had predicted had begun to come to pass. I had to set aside my resentments and my griefs, and accomplish what I had come here to do. I must summon my determination and marshal my thoughts: what did I know, and what must I ask?

My grandmother had gone to O'Rahilly, to hire him to declaim at Deirdre's wedding. Maeve had insisted upon it, and, in the face of her own granddaughter's protests, her will had won out. The poet had accused and insulted Maeve, my mother, Deirdre, dishonoured Murchadh's name, derided his aspirations, humiliated his daughter. He had exposed Sean's secrets and foretold his death, and it had come to pass. And yet he did not know about me. Who had paid him, who had put him up to all this, and what was their end?

We came, at length, to a clearing in the wood, and at the edge of the clearing was the ruin of an ancient church. For the first time in many miles, I looked about me properly. What I had thought to be random boulders and stones were not – they were set, carefully, in a circle at the entrance to the overgrown burial yard of the church, and at their centre stood a stone, upright, thin, that came almost to my shoulder, inscribed on it a simple cross.

'What is this place?' I said. The birds were no longer in song or sight, and the air had grown cold and still.

'Kilcrue,' he said at last. 'The Cursing Circle.'

I put down my staff and walked towards the centre, to where the stone stood. The burial ground was so near and overgrown. I had never liked burial grounds. The place reeked of the knowledge of death: a once holy place that was holy no more. Unwittingly, I put my hand to my neck and felt for the coarse wood and moulded metal of the cross that hung there.

'Tell me about the Cursing Circle,' I said.

'There is little I can tell you.' I noticed he took care to keep outside the ring of stones. I was in too far now to do the same.

'Tell me why it is so called.'

He thought out his words with care. 'It is said that these places were used in pagan rituals in ancient times.'

'What sort of rituals?'

He caught a breath, and spoke again, slowly. 'It is said that the stone, the cross, before it became a cross, was perhaps an altar . . .'

A sacrificial altar. I felt the blood freeze in my veins. 'And the name?' I insisted. 'What is the meaning of the name?'

'It is the place of cursing, where curses are laid by the poets. It is the home of Finn O'Rahilly.'

The snap of a twig underfoot from the direction of the ruined church took my attention and I turned towards it to see Finn O'Rahilly, more gaunt than I had remembered, standing at the entrance to the circle. He looked at me and then at Stephen. 'What trick is this, old priest? What game is this you seek to play me in?'

'No trick, no game,' answered the Franciscan. 'Simply the man I told you wished to come.'

The poet stepped back, steadying his hand on a jutting rock and never taking his eyes from me. 'This man is dead.'

I advanced a step towards him. 'No, not dead. Death has not found me yet. I know it is a matter you take some interest in. What do you know of my cousin's death?'

He held his ground this time, but more colour drained from his face. 'You have no cousin.'

'My name is Alexander Seaton, and I am the cousin of Sean O'Neill FitzGarrett and of his sister Deirdre. I was called to Ulster by my grandmother Maeve O'Neill to tell you that your curse has no truth in it. I am the son of Grainne Fitz-Garrett and my grandmother's line will end not with Sean, but with me.'

He sat down, breathing heavily, on one of the flat stones of the outer circle. His knuckles were white as his fingers gripped the staff in his hand. 'I was not told this.'

'What were you told?'

He opened his mouth to answer and then thought the better of it. The silence was heavy in the stillness of the circle. Stephen spoke to me in a low voice. 'I have brought you here as I promised I would, but now I must go. I have business to attend to tonight that will not keep. I will return in the morning and bring you to Bonamargy. Use your time well. Master your anger and use your mind more than your tongue to draw out of him what you need. And remember the contents of your purse.'

I had not bargained for this. I did not greatly like the knowledge that I was in this priest's power, or that I had left Andrew Boyd to the mercy of his companions.

'Wait but half an hour and I will come with you; it cannot take longer to find out what this man knows. I have no desire to spend the night in this godless place.'

'Have you no faith, then?' he asked.

'I have faith in my God,' I said, 'but there are forces at work here that come from a darkness I do not comprehend.'

'Then you must pray for the strength to withstand them, and I will pray that also for you.' He said no more, and reminding me again that he would return for me the next morning, he disappeared into the trees.

A wind had got up, and the coldness of it whistled through the branches and around the stones that encircled me. Finn O'Rahilly had risen to his feet.

'Do you stay?' he said.

'I have no choice. I do not know this country in the light, never mind the darkness. I will trespass on your hospitality this one night. I have no greater wish to be here than you have to have me here. Tell me what I need to know, show me a corner where I might lie, and I will trouble you no more.'

He stared at me levelly with his startling blue eyes.

'You have been sent to me that I might lift the curse on your family?'

'That is what my grandmother wishes – although the worst

of it has already come to pass. Yet it might comfort her and my still-living cousin to know the curse to be lifted, so mumble what words you must, that I may not lie to them when I tell them you have done what they begged for with their purses to do.'

He glanced for a moment at the pouch I had now set at my feet, then returned his gaze to me. 'You think the worst has come to pass? How little you know this place, or the people whom you claim as yours.'

'I claim no one,' I said. 'I have been claimed, but those who had a right to do so have almost all gone. When I am finished my business here with you, I too will be gone from this country.'

'As if you had never been.'

'As if I had never been.'

He seemed a little reassured by this thought and sat down again on the rock. He motioned towards another, and I sat down and waited. There was a great stillness about him, as if an hour, a day, passed here like this would be as nothing. It was clear he would give me no help: I must begin myself.

'My grandmother and my cousin Deirdre came to you here, did they not?'

He nodded.

'Who else came?'

'No one.'

'My grandmother wished you to give a blessing at Deirdre's wedding, but Deirdre was against it.'

Again he nodded.

'Why did she not want it?'

'They did not argue of it before me. Your cousin may not like our ways, the ways of your grandmother, and of me, but she knows them well and respects them, although she does not fully understand their power. She would not dishonour your grandmother or me by arguing about it openly before me.'

'And yet you know she did not want it?'

He smiled slowly. 'I have spent long years in study of words and of people. You must know a person before you can know the words you must use for them. Ever since I was a child, I have watched people. I watched your uncle, Phelim, your mother too. And when she came here, I watched your cousin. I watched her eyes and the small movements of her face and her body. She did not want what your grandmother wanted. She thinks she can take the road of the new English, and find her place in Ireland. She is wrong. I tried to tell her she was wrong . . .'

'And so my grandmother paid you to do her bidding – to do what?'

'To tell the glories of her family through the generations, to extol her lineage above others, to assert its claims for supremacy in Ulster, to bless this new union that it might further those ends.'

'And of the Blackstones? What were you to say of them?'

'The English ones?'

'The family of the groom,' I said, flatly.

'They were not to be mentioned at all.'

'But the oration you made was something quite different.'

'There are times when the duty of the poet is to point out the errors of his patron, to set him on the right path, to give warning to others that they might not . . .'

'That may well be,' I broke in, 'but that is not what happened at Deirdre's wedding. You were paid by someone to . . .'

He was on his feet. 'Do not insult me.'

'I do not insult you. You know the truth better than I. You have sold the dignity of your calling. My mother schooled me well enough in the understanding of the exalted place of the poets, the years of training required, the honour you were accorded in noble households. Where is your honour to be found now?' I threw the pouch at him. 'At the bottom of a greasy purse.'

'Do not presume to cite me your mother on honour. A whore who abandoned Ireland at the first opportunity. What would she know of noble households, she who rolled in her servant's bed?'

His last words dropped like stones onto the carpet of fallen leaves around us, and lay there heavy and still. A bolt of coldness ran through my body.

'What are you saying?'

'Ask those who remember. I can tell you no more.'

What was he saying? My father had never been a servant. He had been a craftsman, and a soldier. I had not been born until a year after she had returned with him to Banff.

'Are you trying to say I am not my father's son?' I said.

'Is your name truly Seaton? That was the name of the man they said she left with, so you are probably his son.'

Disgust with the poet swamped me; I was growing tired of puzzles and riddles, of things that claimed to be other than what they seemed. I wanted to root out the knowledge I had come for and leave. Remembering the words of the Franciscan, 'Master your anger,' I swallowed down the rising bile. 'Who paid you to curse my family?'

'I was honouring a patron, I was . . .'

'Enough of honour. You were paid. Who did it, and to what end?'

He shook his head. 'You think that I do not know that I am degenerate from my forefathers? Do you think I would be here in this desolate place, selling my talent and my worth, if

I could have the place of my forefathers? We are persecuted by the English, who fear our power over the minds of the people, we are made destitute by the destitution and banishment of our lords, those who once feted us, we are abandoned by those who remain and do not give us succour for fear of falling out of favour with the English masters at whose knees they crawl. So I scrape what living I can with my words and my mind, for I have not been taught any other. But I have my honour and I will not betray my patron to you.'

'You betrayed my grandmother.'

'I spoke only the truth.'

'For a murderer,' I said. 'My cousin is dead and you foretold it.'

'He would have been dead soon enough anyway. Look about you. Look at this country. Listen to what is said. Watch. There will be death. But I tell you this: the person who had me curse your cousin will not be the person who murdered him.'

'How do you know this?'

'I told you, I watch people, and I know love.'

I called from my memory the images of the night of my grandfather's wake. I sought out the poet, as he ate, drank, as he stood to declaim our family's fall. Who had he watched, where had his gaze landed? Faces, faces, faces, all around. But my mind had been taken up entirely with his words, and my memory would not tell me that he had looked on any of them.

His voice broke into my searching. 'You must forget this now. You must learn the lesson of the Cursing Circle: it has no end.'

There was no more to be had from him and I got up in dejection, leaving the money pouch on the ground beside him. I could hear the steady crinkle and splash of a stream running nearby and sought it out, to slake my thirst. The nuts were just bursting from an overhanging hazel and I took them gratefully, with brambles from the bushes. I looked around me for somewhere I might find good shelter and lay my head for the night, but all was damp or jagged underfoot, and would afford me little comfort. I made my way back to the clearing, where Finn O'Rahilly still sat as I had left him, the pouch untouched at his feet.

'My home is in the church,' he said, indicating the ruin from which he had emerged. 'You may spend the night there; there are clean rushes in the corner of the east wall; you will be dry and warm by the hearth. You would not be the first visitor to take rest here before returning to the world. There is a candle and flint in a niche above the bedding. I will not disturb you.'

For want of an option, I thanked him, and sought out a corner for myself in the ruined church. Much of the roof had gone, and what little remained was of old thatch. When the elements were at their worst there can have been few places of true shelter in the shell of the building, but the corner by the hearth protected me from the advances of the east wind, and the night was dry. It was almost dark. I lit the candle I had found in the niche, and lay down amongst the rushes, wishing I had Sean's heavy mantle about me now. I flinched as a bat swooped down from a rotting beam above my head and swept out into the night. I had never liked the creatures. I had always had a terror that they would entangle themselves in my hair. I was glad now of my monk's hood and pulled it up about me. Other creatures scuttled around me, in the rushes, across the stone floor. The noises of the wood seemed to come closer as evening advanced further into night.

O'Rahilly himself sat in the doorway, looking outwards beyond the clearing into the darkness of the wood. I wondered what he was seeing, what he was remembering, the young boy who had sought sanctuary and training with the last of the poets when Phelim was in his prime and my mother in her bloom; what he had known before the cause was lost and the heroes fled, what trials had brought him here, to cling to the last remnants of his dignity in this desolate place. I wondered if he had ever had a family, loved a woman . . . For a while I had thought he might be sleeping, but his eyes were open, and every so often his lips moved in some silent speech. The last remnant of his race.

'Tell me a poem,' I said into the silence.

He did not move and so I asked him again.

'Why do you want to hear a poem?'

'Because I want to know the art of it, the life. I want to know what my forefathers knew, all those generations that will be lost now, in me.'

'Hear then "The Downfall of the Gael".' And the same low, clear, powerful voice that I had heard on the night of my grandfather's wake went out into the night.

My heart is in woe,
And my soul deep in trouble,
For the mighty are low,
And abased are the noble:

The sons of the Gael
Are in exile and mourning,
Worn, weary and pale,
As spent pilgrims returning,

Or men who, in flight
From the field of disaster,
Beseech the black night
On their flight to fall faster;

Or men whom we see
That have got their death-omen –
Such wretches are we
In the chains of our foemen!

Our course is fear,
Our nobility vileness,
Our hope is despair,
And our comeliness foulness.

From Boyne to the Linn
Has the mandate been given,
That the children of Finn
From their country be driven.

The Gael cannot tell,
In the uprooted wildwood
And red ridgy dell,
The old nurse of his childhood:

The nurse of his youth
Is in doubt as she views him,
If the wan wretch in truth,
Be the child of her bosom.

Through the woods let us roam,
Through the wastes wide and barren:

We are strangers at home!
We are exiles in Erin!

And Erin's a bark
O'er the wild waters driven!
And the tempest howls dark,
And her side planks are riven!

And in billows of might
Swell the Saxon before her—
Unite, oh, unite!
Or the billows burst o'er her!

As his voice carried to me, the faces of my family – of those who were dead and gone and those who were now left, in distress and abandoned to fear – came before me. The face of the pilgrims Stephen, and Michael, came before me; Deirdre, with her vision of death; Murchadh and his sons came before me, with Maeve leading their decimated hopes and empty dreams. The memory of myself and Andrew, in our desperate flight to Dunluce, came to me with such force that I had to remind myself that that night was past. I wished I had never spoken.

After a moment, O'Rahilly came back into the church and went to a chest out of which he lifted some garment I could not see. Without so much as turning his head to look at me, he then went out of the door and walked through the circle, crossing himself as he passed the centre stone, and out into the woods. I laid my head down upon the rushes and prayed for that lost man and his lost brothers, and it was all I could do not to forget my religion and ask God's mercy on those of my blood, of this race, who had gone to Him before me.

I closed my eyes and wished for sleep. If it came, it came only lightly, for there was not one moment when I was not aware of the rustling and scuttling of creatures on the ground, the beating and swooping of things in the air, and the creaking of the trees in the wind. And then, into it all, came a sound I had never heard before, but knew; a sound that should not have been in these woods: a howling. I stood up cautiously and quietly snuffed out the candle, which had burnt very low. Hardly daring to breathe, I pressed myself as far back against the wall of the church as I could, and waited. A cloud passed from the face of the moon at the top of the trees, and I watched in a kind of terror as the wolf slowly crossed the circle, pausing at the centre to sniff the air. It howled once again and, looking for a long moment in the direction of the church, walked on, in search of its brothers.

I did not sleep after that, but stood at the edge of the burial ground keeping watch for I knew not what. The bats swirled from tree to tree, an owl hooted somewhere in the woods. I was startled by a movement amongst the stones of the burial ground, but it was nothing more than a solitary fox. I tried to turn my mind from thoughts of what might have happened in this place before the Christianity of Patrick had claimed it for God, but the more I tried to find consolation amongst the scriptures I had by heart, the more my mind ran to the powers of the Devil, to the foul and dreadful deeds committed in his name, to the paganism, the baals, celebrated wherever the light of the gospel did not shine. My mind ran to what Sean had said, long ago now, it seemed, but in truth not so long ago, as I had mocked the superstitions of his people, of my people. He had told me of the attempt made on his life as he rode alone at night, and of his fear then, of the powers of darkness and the spirits of the world beyond, and I had scorned them.

'These forces may have retreated from your land,' he had said, 'but they have a home yet in ours, and they are not ready to be vanquished.' I wished I could have told him now that I understood.

Where Finn O'Rahilly had gone, and if he had encountered the wolf, I did not know. He had had no light with him, taken no staff for travelling, no food or drink that I could see. As my eyes became more accustomed to the darkness, and my ears to the natural sounds of the night, my body began to relax a little, and I could see perhaps how a man for whom the world has little further use might eke out his days in a place such as this. But surely that fate would not be mine; surely my grandmother's madness could not take hold in the minds of reasonable men? I wondered if Finn O'Rahilly had gone to report me to the authorities – whatever authorities there were that would take the word of one such as he – but I saw that the pouch of money lay still on the ground, unopened, where he had left it.

Gradually, I became aware of a new sound in the night, the sound of horses. Not many horses, not the great wolf-hunt that had pursued me from Coleraine, but perhaps two or three beasts and their riders, moving cautiously through the wood, coming closer. I moved quickly and quietly back into the church, found candle and flint again and got myself some light. There was nothing amongst Finn O'Rahilly's few belongings with which I might defend myself, and so I committed myself to prayer.

At last the riders emerged from the forest and came to a silent halt at the edge of the circle. What little I could see of the outline of their forms against the trees told me that these were not the Blackstones, the men of Coleraine. The horses were different, somehow; the set of the men, their clothing different; all three were dressed as Sean had been the first time I had seen him. I was not left long to wonder, for a strong voice rang out, demanding in Irish,

'Show yourself, O'Rahilly. Step out of your sanctuary and meet your fate.'

I emerged from the church into the darkness and held up my light to look into the faces of three men. The two younger sons of Murchadh O'Neill, and another, who by the look of him was a kinsman. For a moment there was silence, even the creatures of the night seemed to stop in their movement, hold their breath. And then the youngest of the three cried out in terror, startling his own horse and those of the others.

'Holy mother of God,' said the lead rider slowly, crossing himself. He regarded me for a long moment and then spoke. 'What are you?'

'I am a man.'

'It is the spirit of Sean risen. Let us leave this place. Ciaran, let us go, before we are damned.'

'This is no spirit.' Ciaran O'Neill turned his eyes once more on me. 'I ask again. What are you?' He edged his horse forward, but those of the two others shied back from the stones and would come no nearer.

'I am Alexander Seaton.'

'You are Sean O'Neill FitzGarrett risen from the dead!'

Again Ciaran chided his young kinsman. He spoke once more to me. 'Whatever your name, you are of the O'Neills. What are you to the O'Neills?'

And so once again, slowly, in English and in a clear voice, I told my lineage.

'Grainne died.'

'Yes,' I said, 'she died. When I was seventeen years old, and she had been safe landed in Scotland eighteen years.'

'And she told no one of your birth?'

'My grandmother . . .'

'That would be right. The old bitch. And now?'

'Now?'

'Who knows of you now?'

'What is that to you?'

'This is not a game, Scotsman, and if it were, the cards would be in my hand. You would do well to answer what you are asked.'

I said nothing and held firm to my staff, as if guarding the church. Beneath my priest's robes, my heart pounded in terror.

Ciaran got down from his horse and the others did the same, careful to keep a pace behind him, casting me glances as if to ascertain that I truly was corporeal. 'You do better to trust me than to make an enemy of me,' he said, venturing a smile at me for the first time. 'I am Ciaran O'Neill, son of Murchadh. We have come for the poet. Stand aside and let us pass.'

'He is not here.' I was glad for a moment for their attention to shift from myself.

'Where is he hiding?'

'I do not know. He left a few hours ago and has not returned.'

It did not take them long to make a search of the ruined church. They cursed their frustration in Irish, and then reverted to English, to treat with me. 'And what are you doing here? Who has sent you?'

'There were things I wished to know from him, information I wished to have.'

One drew a knife from the sheath round his neck, and stepping closer to me slowly raised the blade to my throat. Ciaran did nothing to stop him. 'What is your business with O'Rahilly?'

'I came here to find out who paid him to curse my family.'

'Who brought you here?'

'To Kilcrue?'

'To Ireland.'

'Sean.'

'Safe enough in saying that now, for he is dead.'

I ground out my words. 'He was sent by my grandmother to fetch me from Scotland, with some idea that when he saw me O'Rahilly would lift the curse.'

Ciaran laughed. 'He told you that, did he?'

'Why else would they have brought me here?'

'I would give much to know that, and I suspect my father would also.'

'Our father will know well enough the minute he sees him,' said Padraig, the younger brother. 'Another Franciscan.'

'I am not.'

'Of course not. None of you ever are. But I see the hand of Stephen Mac Cuarta in this.' He had evidently heard enough. 'Come on, we are wasting our time here. The clouds are gathering. We should get out of these woods.'

'You are right,' said Ciaran, turning also from me. 'But first we must find O'Rahilly. Donal, bind him.' And within seconds, before I fully knew what was happening, my arms had been pulled behind my back and my hands bound together with rope. A shove in the back sent me in the direction of the waiting horses, but the shock of it made me stumble, and I caught the side of my face on the centre stone as I fell to the ground. There was nothing I could do but struggle to my feet again and go where they bade me, and I was soon heaved up on to the back of Padraig's mount.

After a short debate they urged their horses not southwards, back to where they had come from, but eastwards, to the part of the wood that I had come through myself a few hours earlier. We had not travelled far on the moonlit paths before the lead horse, under Ciaran, brought us to a halt. It whinnied and tried to turn back, refusing to continue. He dismounted, and proceeded cautiously on foot.

'Damn him to every torment.'

'By God, he did our job for us.'

'Do you think? He will never tell his mysteries now.'

And then I saw it: a few yards ahead of us, arrayed in the magnificent robes of white and gold given to him by my grandmother, hanging by its neck from an ancient hawthorn tree, was the dead body of Finn O'Rahilly. The three men crossed themselves.

'Will we cut him down?'

Ciaran shook his head. 'Let the crows have him. He was a traitor to his race, and his words an outrage to ours. Let his rotting corpse serve as warning to others who might think to do the same.'

He turned to me. 'Think not to pray over him, priest. Save your prayers for us and yourself when we bring you and not O'Rahilly to our father.'

'I have told you, I am no priest.'

They merely laughed in scorn. 'Well, you had better find some God to appeal to before you find yourself before Murchadh.'

'At Carrickfergus?'

'Carrickfergus?' Ciaran smiled grimly. 'No, my friend, he is not at Carrickfergus; we are taking you to Dun-a-Mallaght.'

Within an hour we were out of the woods and riding hard towards the coast once more, trying to outrun the storm which had broken over the hills and was pursuing us down towards the sea. As we approached I saw, encompassed by unbreachable headlands at either end, the broad sweep of a bay, where the sea came in increasingly powerful waves to the shore. I chanced to look back once, when I thought I could keep my balance, and saw a huge bolt of lightning strike right where I imagined Kilcrue to be. In my mind's eye I saw it strike to the heart of the stone – the priest's stone, O'Rahilly had called it – before the storm moved on to seek out the poet himself.

On the headland to my left, watching over the bay, rose a castle. Below, nearer to the shore, was a small town, huddled in darkness from the advancing storm. Further along the bay was another settlement, structured, more formal, but ruined in part. My heart lifted a little when I saw it, and the lights burning in some of its windows. It was a religious house, a church. 'What is that place?' I called in Padraig's ear.

'You know it well enough.'

'Bonamargy?' I said.

'Aye, Bonamargy. Do not excite yourself unduly. This is as close as you'll be getting to it.' He pulled his horse to the left, as his brother had done, and spurred the beast on towards the western edge of the bay, and a strange mound that rose grim and threatening from the earth.

'What is that?' I shouted.

'You are not superstitious, priest?'

'I am not . . . superstitious.'

'That is Dun-a-Mallaght. The Fort of the Curse.'

'I give no credence to your curses.'

He slowed his horse.

'On any other night of the year, neither do I. But it is said that on All Hallows Eve – tonight – the ghosts of the dead walk forth from Dun-a-Mallaght into the world. I would be here on any night other than tonight.'

We forded a narrow river and dismounted. Six yards from

the entrance to the fort Ciaran let up a strange cry, a call, in Irish, that seemed to come from the depths of himself. The cry was returned from inside and bolts pulled back. Doors swung inwards and I found myself walking, just as lightning struck the ground three feet from where I stood, into the lair of Murchadh O'Neill, the Fort of the Curse.

EIGHTEEN

Dun-a-Mallaght

I had a sensation of walking into the depths of the earth. Orpheus entering the Underworld, but I knew not with what purpose. Certainly there was no Eurydice waiting here for me. The passageway was narrow – only room enough for one man to pass at a time. The heavy smell of damp earth suffused the air, but was gradually overpowered by the aroma coming from a peat fire some way ahead. The passageway was lighted every few yards by torches in the wall, and was smooth and dry underfoot. My arms were still tied behind my back and ached as I had never known my limbs to ache before, and it was with great anticipation of relief that I at last saw a pool of light ahead of Ciaran, and soon afterwards found myself stepping into an open space once more.

We had come into a large vaulted chamber, with arched wooden beams supporting the earthen roof. The floor was beaten earth, with rushes spread all around. At the centre was a peat fire, sending blue smoke up through a small hole in the roof, although the rest of the place was filled with smoke also. At the far end of the chamber was a dais, on which I could just make out the forms of a man and a woman sitting. Flickering torches gave intermittent illumination to shapes of men, occasionally women, sitting on the floor.

Ciaran strode towards the dais while the others remained on either side of me, Padraig confiding under his breath that one wrong move would see my throat cut and me at the gates of Hell before dawn.

'Is my father not returned then?'

'We expect him soon. There has been some cause of delay with the old woman at Carrickfergus.'

I lifted my eyes and peered through the gilded gloom; it was Cormac, the oldest of Murchadh's sons, and beside him, like a queen under some enchantment, was Deirdre. She was dressed in a gown of red velvet, the bodice laced tight over a mantle of the purest white linen, sleeves hanging long at the wrists and edged with lace. At her neck hung a crucifix studded with jet, and at her waist a girdle embroidered with gold. On her head was a linen headdress, and beneath it fell locks of burnished copper. The sombre wife of the English burgher was gone: distilled to her essence, every inch the consort of the man beside her, she was magnificent.

Cormac's gaze went beyond his brother's shoulder to where I stood, my cowl still up as it had been against the storm. 'What is this? Is it the poet or a priest you have brought us?'

'Neither, he would have us believe.' I was pushed forward and my hood pulled down. I could feel the shock that echoed round the chamber, the collective drawing-in of breath. Nobody moved for a moment and then, slowly, men started to reach for their weapons as their wives and daughters regarded me in terror. Cormac himself had flinched when he had seen me, and stood up slowly. 'What trickery is this?'

'No trickery, brother, but what the . . .'

He got no further, for Deirdre too had risen from her seat. Her face was suffused with love, and for a moment, forgetful of the reason, the wonder and delight of it caused me to smile back at her. She began to walk, and then to run, towards me, and I realised with a sickening certainty that she had mistaken me. Cormac put out an ineffectual arm to stop her, but she pushed it away. In a moment she was on me, her arms around my neck, tears of joy flowing down her cheeks. The words in Irish came tumbling, one after the other in a torrent of love and thanks to saints I had never heard of.

'Oh my darling, my brother, sent back to me this night. My brother, my darling one.'

I let her hold me, and weep, and gently I put my arms around her and held her, no one trying to stop me. Dun-a-Mallaght held its breath, for a moment, on All Hallows Eve, as a young Irishwoman welcomed her murdered brother back from the dead. Gradually, the heaving of her chest, her sobs, subsided and Cormac stepped forward to lift her hands from my neck; I let my arms fall to my sides, and he drew her tenderly from my embrace.

She looked from one to another of us, her heart willing her mind to believe something she knew was not true.

'What . . . why . . . you would not . . .?' She turned from Cormac to me. 'Sean?'

Slowly, I shook my head, my lips parted to speak but no words came from them.

'Not Sean, but the murdering Scot, Alexander Seaton.'

It was Murchadh O'Neill; and there beside him, at the entrance passageway and looking at me in mute terror, was Roisin, behind them a gathering of his men. He strode forward and took Deirdre firmly by the arm.

'Take her out of here.'

Donal began to lead her towards a side passage away from the main chamber. 'Come, Deirdre, it is not him. You know it is not him.'

She didn't seem to hear him, and looked desperately over her shoulder as he pulled her away. 'Sean,' she called. 'Sean!'

The sight of her tore the heart out of me and I closed my eyes until her cries became distant and dim.

Murchadh had taken Cormac's place on the dais. 'Chain him,' he said, casting the briefest of glances at me. And then, 'O'Rahilly? You found him?'

'We found him all right, hanging from a tree. He has spoken his last curse.'

Murchadh damned the poet to the depths of Hell. He got up and began to stride around the dais, pausing only to fire out questions at his sons.

'Where did you come upon him?'

'Kilcrue.'

'You searched his lair? You found nothing?'

Padraig jabbed a thumb in my direction. 'Only this one.'

'Aye, this one.' Murchadh regarded me a long moment with a look in his eyes that might have been hatred, might have been fear. He stepped down from his platform and began to walk slowly over to where I had been chained to a post at the far end of the chamber, his eyes never leaving my face for a minute. 'Alexander Seaton. The son of Grainne FitzGarrett, cowering in the dirt like a beast.'

I tried to stand up, but found myself pulled back down by my fetters. I lifted my head though, determined that I should look him in the eye.

'I have no fear of you,' I said.

'Do you not now?' He looked around the chamber, his arms outstretched in appeal to his followers. 'The heretic schoolman has no fear of Murchadh O'Neill. He killed his own cousin in cold blood in a deserted Protestant church, so why should he fear me?' He laughed into the uneasy silence and his followers, hesitant at first, did likewise.

He brought his face down close to mine, so close I could

smell the heavy sweat of his night's ride and the stale sourness of wine on his breath. 'You should fear me, schoolman, because I can kill very slowly.'

There was a general murmur of agreement and approval from around the room. 'Do it, Murchadh!' called out one voice.

'Give us some sport!' shouted another, and soon my ears were filled with calls in Irish for many kinds of torturing and a slow death.

Murchadh stood up straight and wiped his hand on his thigh, as if near contact with me was a contamination in itself. 'Calm yourselves, you shall have your sport. The whore's offspring will cross the Irish Sea no more.'

'My mother was no whore!' I had tried to stand up, but was again thwarted by my chains.

Murchadh pushed me by the shoulder back to the ground. 'Your mother had much the same taste as your cousin that's through that door.' Behind him I saw something in Cormac's face, some small flicker in the stone. He turned again to his followers. 'You will have your sport, in good time, but first there are some things I would have of our guest before he loses his tongue.' More laughter from around the chamber, more assured this time.

The laughter was brought to a halt by a shout travelling down the entrance passageway from the watchmen at the door. It was echoed by the watchman to the chamber. 'Strangers coming. Wait – holy men.'

Murchadh's eyes went quickly from the door back to me. 'Take him to the pit. Be quick.' Padraig again took hold of me while Donal loosed my chains. I tried to struggle free from his grip but was rewarded by a tremendous strike into the side of my face by Murchadh's gloved fist. The glove was not quite thick enough to cushion me from the sharp contours of the garnet-studded gold ring he wore on his right hand, and as I staggered to my feet once more I felt a soft trickle of blood begin to make its way down my cheek. Padraig pulled my arm up so tightly behind my back I felt my shoulder burn.

The pit was a small dug-out room set still further into the bowels of the earth. I had to stoop to enter it, almost gagging on the foul human odours that reached my nose and my throat. There was barely enough room in the place to accommodate both Padraig and myself. There was no furnishing or floor covering of any sort, and the only light came from a small grille near the roof, the length and width of the span of my hand, that looked on to the floor level of the main chamber.

'Do not think of trying to get out. And do nothing to attract any attention to yourself; you may not like the attentions we have to offer.' And to my great relief, he left.

As soon as he was gone, I crept to the grille. By craning my neck I could see the floor of the main chamber and feet and the hems of cloaks brushing over it. But I had evidently not been the first unfortunate to find myself here, for on bending down I could see that there was a foothold in the wall, and by pulling myself up to the grille from it I could see much further around the chamber. I could hear too, but the general hubbub was too great for me to be able to distinguish one voice and what it said from another. Then there was a standing to readiness, and all movement in the room stopped. Silence. I could hear my own heart beating, so loud in the silence that I almost feared it would draw someone's attention to me, but I did not dare move from where I was. At last the voice of the watchman echoed through the chamber again, breaking the tension. 'Father Stephen Mac Cuarta of the order of St Francis at Bonamargy seeks audience with Murchadh O'Neill.'

Murchadh was silent, but only for a moment. 'Then let the father enter, and be welcome.'

I shifted position enough that I could see the end of the passageway and, a moment later, Stephen and Michael entered. Stephen gave a blessing in Gaelic to his 'brothers'. There followed murmuring and nodding and general sounds of welcome, before Murchadh spoke again.

'Be welcome, Father. May you bring God's blessing to this place.'

'Amen,' said Michael.

'Indeed,' followed Stephen, 'and on a night such as this it is in need of it. The powers of darkness are at their height in this land tonight.'

'And have been rising some time,' said Murchadh. 'But let us not forget the hospitality due a guest, even on such a night.' His welcome was too quick in coming, his smile too easy. 'Roisin, have the women bring food and drink.'

Stephen watched the girl as she went to the fire at the centre of the chamber, where a hog was being slowly turned and roasted. 'Your daughter has grown up a credit to her mother, God rest her.'

'Amen to that. She will be a credit to Ireland also.'

'I do not doubt it. But,' said Stephen carefully, sitting down on the floor as Murchadh had indicated he should do, 'she will mourn the loss of her betrothed.'

'As do we all,' responded Murchadh, just as carefully.

'It will be a great blow to you also, who had such hopes for the union of your family with that of Maeve O'Neill.'

'Sean was not Maeve's only grandchild, nor Roisin my only child.'

'But Deirdre is already married.'

'There are divorcements, are there not? Besides, that is not the only possibility.'

'Oh?' said Stephen, as casually as if all that concerned him was the comfort of his robes, which he was taking some trouble over rearranging beneath him. 'What other possibilities might there be?'

'Who knows what God will provide? Or has provided?'

'Indeed,' said the priest, setting to now to the steaming platter Roisin had brought him. 'Who knows?'

'Father, should we not thank the Lord?'

Stephen smiled apologetically at Michael. 'Indeed, my friend. You must forgive me: the habits of an old campaigner die hard.' He said the grace and the pair gave their attention to the food and drink they had been brought, chewing slowly and drinking deep. The silence all around them began to weigh heavy on their host, until finally he called on the harper to earn his keep. As the soft music plucked from the strings gradually filled the air, there was the slightest relaxation in the tension around the chamber, but not in Murchadh O'Neill, nor, I noticed as I studied him more closely, in Stephen Mac Cuarta.

Eventually, when the friars had finished and Roisin had brought them a bowl of water in which to wash their hands, Murchadh told the harper to stop. The time had come.

'We have not met in many years, Father.'

'Indeed we have not. Nearly thirty years. Kinsale.'

There was an audible drawing in of breath at the mention of the word, a marked rising in tension. I scrambled through my memory a while until I had it: Kinsale, the last great hope of O'Neill's rebellion against the English, when he and his men had marched the length of Ireland in winter to meet with their Spanish allies, sent by Philip III to help them hound the Virgin Queen from Ireland. But the allies had been relent-lessly besieged, and in open battle on Christmas Eve the expe-dition had ended in ignominy and disaster. As for Murchadh, he had been the last to join in the southern march and the first to abandon his kinsmen and their Spanish brethren to their fates. No one mentioned Kinsale in front of Murchadh O'Neill.

'Aye, Kinsale. A place out of season then, and of no conse-quence now.'

Stephen took great care in the drying of his hands. 'But perhaps it is,' he said at length. 'Perhaps it is of consequence, or should be, if we are not to repeat past failings.'

'And past mistakes,' countered Murchadh.

'Indeed. For such mistakes would cost us all dear, would cost Ireland dear, as they did before.'

Murchadh threw down his goblet and turned on the Fran-ciscan. 'What do you want, priest? State your business now or leave this place. I have business to attend to and no hours to spare on you and your old grievances.'

Stephen looked up, as if he were measuring Murchadh, inch by inch. 'My masters have long memories, but this is no old grievance; it is something of three days' standing I would know of.'

The whole chamber held its breath. My mouth formed the words as Stephen spoke them: 'Who murdered Sean FitzGarrett?'

Two or three of the men around Murchadh stepped forward, ready to draw their swords. Murchadh put up a hand to stop them. 'I am sure you are not here to accuse me, but my men are nervous and see slights where perhaps none was intended. The temper of the times.'

'And always has been,' responded Stephen. 'But no, we are

not here to accuse you. I know it was not you who cut the throat of Sean FitzGarrett, but I believe you know who did. Do not seek to protect him; powers greater than you have an interest in this and will find it out.'

'Then they need no help from me.'

I wondered why, given that both of them knew of my grand-mother's accusations against me, neither of them made any mention of me.

Stephen persisted. 'It will be in the interests of no one to protect Sean's murderer. The news will reach Louvain, and further afield before much more time has passed. You had better show yourselves loyal to our cause or you and all of yours will be swept aside in the onslaught that is to come.'

Murchadh closed in on him. 'I know that your Spanish masters and His Holiness have other plans for the sovereignty of Ireland, but a leader, a figurehead, is needed for Ulster, for the people of Tyrone, of Tyrconnell, of Antrim and all the rest will not be ruled from Louvain, nor Madrid, nor yet Rome. You and your Pope may do as you please with the faith of the people, and the King of Spain may rest assured that Ulster will always give sound bases for his armies – a thorn in England's flank that cannot be removed. That is all they want us for. For the rest, you know as well as I, they will leave us in peace.'

Stephen was struggling to master his ire. 'Dismiss the Church if you must, but you will find that no rebellion will succeed without it. And I would counsel you not to speak of His Majesty of Spain with such contempt: the English will never be driven from Ireland without him.'

'It will take more than another foreign monarch who cares little for Ireland to drive the English out. The people will only rally to one of their own.'

'And that one was to be Sean O'Neill FitzGarrett.'

'My daughter's betrothed.'

'Who is now dead.'

'Who is now dead.'

'And who would you see in his place? Who would the old families and their followers accept?'

'They all knew Sean was to marry Roisin; they all knew my lands were to be joined with FitzGarrett's, that FitzGarrett's wealth was to be used to buy in to more of the old O'Neill patrimony. It is in their minds already.'

Stephen shook his head slowly. 'They will never accept you, Murchadh. Memories are long; distrust has burnt slow: you would be engulfed in their desire for revenge.'

I watched Murchadh, as did everyone else, waiting for an explosion of rage that did not come. 'Truly, you think so, Mac Cuarta? They will not forgive?' His eyes gave out some shadow of sadness, a dawning understanding, at last, that the dreams harboured since his youth would not be fulfilled.

The priest went towards the rebel leader. 'Nor forget, Murchadh.' He laid his hand on the other's forehead and uttered a Gaelic blessing.

All through this, Cormac had watched without moving, without speaking, but the sinews in his arms were stretched to their limit, and a muscle twitching in his jaw gave him away – to me, at least, for no one else had the view that I had.

'There is another,' said Murchadh, at last.

'There is indeed,' said Stephen.

Cormac chose this moment to declare himself. 'And I am ready, Father. Give the word, and our kindred will rally to me; the others will care not that I am your son so much as I am an O'Neill, and a union with Maeve's family . . .'

'You?' said Stephen, as if the idea had not occurred to him.

'If not me, then who else is there?'

A light had come again into Murchadh's eyes, but he said nothing. Stephen exchanged an uneasy glance with Michael.

'No one,' he answered in some bewilderment. 'There is no one.'

'Then give me your hand, Mac Cuarta, as I give you mine, and let us acclaim my son, Cormac O'Neill, as leader of our rising and, God grant it, the liberator of Ulster.'

Stephen's eyes were travelling the hall, where over fifty armed men waited to butcher or to cheer him. He gripped the forearm that was offered to him and Murchadh clasped him around the shoulders as if he were a returning brother. The roar that went up all around them threatened to bring the earthen roof down on all our heads. Cormac was hoisted on to the shoulders of two of his strongest companions and carried in triumph around the hall, shouts of acclamation and the beating of spears on the ground almost deafening me. And through this great moment, through the length of the room from father to son, was a smile as wide as the river Bann and eyes as cold as the water in it.

Eventually, when the cheering had begun to die down, Cormac was set on the ground again and raised a hand for silence. The clamour faded.

'You do me great honour, and place in me a great and sacred trust. Ireland weeps, she has been raped and plundered. She is abandoned by those whose duty it was to protect her. Let the men of Ulster rise to her defence, and where we lead may Leinster, Munster and Connaught follow in our wake!'

More cheering, more stamping, more shouts of acclamation. Again, Cormac let it engulf the room, then again he put up his hand. 'But Ireland has not suffered alone. The Church, our Holy Mother Church, has been brutalised, trampled, stripped by the heretic Saxon horde, and now her bones are gnawed by the avaricious Scot, insatiable in his misery.' This brought much murmured and mumbled assent, wise nodding and deferential inclination of heads towards the Franciscans. It was them that Cormac now addressed. 'And so I ask you to give me your blessing, and to beg the Holy Virgin's intercession on behalf of our enterprise.'

I could almost have admired him. He knew it was not a thing the friars could refuse, and by encompassing their cause in his own, binding it so closely to himself, they, and those in Louvain, in Spain and in Rome in whose name they acted, could not oppose him. Stephen nodded, the slightest movement of the head but it was enough. With Michael at his side, he beckoned Cormac forward. Cormac knelt down before him, his head bowed, and in that action I saw a glimpse of something better than his father, better than the raiding and the brutality of his brothers, something I might have called noble. Michael made the sign of the cross over him, followed by Stephen, who then laid his hand on Cormac's head and began to speak.

'In the name of Mary, Holy Mother of God, I ask God's blessing on you, Cormac O'Neill, in this great enterprise of the liberation of Ireland and of her Church, the Bride of Christ. Grant us the wisdom, oh Lord, to rise, and the strength, to go willingly to an agonising death in defence of our Church and our nation, rather than to bend our necks in the tainted service of a heretic king.'

Fervent amens resounded around the room. From a pouch hanging from his belt Michael drew a small silver casket and held it out towards Stephen. The older Franciscan affected not to notice.

'The ointment, father,' persisted Michael, murmuring under his breath. Stephen looked at him, giving the slightest but unmistakable shake of his head, but Cormac had now looked up, as had one or two of the others, and Stephen was forced, with great reluctance, to take the casket. He opened it slowly, and dipped a finger inside which he then laid on Cormac's forehead in some approximation of the form of the cross. Then he mumbled some words in Latin, the right words, almost, some of them, for a blessing, for an anointing, but in no relation to one another that made any sense to me, and Latin came as easy to me as did my own Scots tongue. Michael glanced uneasily towards him before Stephen again made a cross in the air and called out, clear and with some finality, 'Amen.' All present in the room followed and Cormac stood and thanked the friars, with only the mildest of questioning in his eyes, before accepting once more the acclamation of his followers.

I turned my face from the grille and felt my way to the far corner of my cell, taking care where I put my feet, not knowing what I might find there. The place was cold and damp and told of death. My bones ached with fatigue, and putting up my hood to make some barrier between the dirt and my head, I lay down. I had heard enough tonight of these people and their doings and wanted to hear no more. I had known my cousin briefly, had come to love him and to believe I knew him well, but it appeared now that I had not known him at all, and that this was how he had intended it should be. I felt desolate, more so even than I had done when I had learned that he was dead. And so this was what Andrew had meant when he had alluded to 'what we are constrained to call Sean's "business"'. That Murchadh was at the heart of a planned uprising against King and Church did not surprise me in the least, nor, deluded as she was, did my grandmother's involvement come as a shock. Father Stephen and Michael were also in on it. I began to wonder now whether Andrew had been right when he had questioned the coincidence of Stephen's presence at Armstrong's Bawn, and at Coleraine on the night we were unveiled as impostors and chased from the town, into the waiting embrace of his young, armed, acolyte. What did they want with us? Stephen, who had led me to the Cursing Circle of Kilcrue and abandoned me there to be found by the sons of Murchadh O'Neill, and his cowled and crucifixed brethren to whose supposed mercy, on this All Hallows Eve, I had left the helpless Andrew Boyd?

I could stay awake no longer. If I had the strength in the morning I would get to Deirdre somehow. If I had the strength. I must very soon have been asleep, too exhausted for dreams and too despondent for nightmares. If the spirits of the dead walked Dun-a-Mallaght that night, they left me in peace.

NINETEEN

The Dawning

I did not hear the bolt of my cell drawn back, nor the door open. It was only when I felt the breath on my torn cheek and the voice in my ear that I woke with a start.

'Lie still and keep your mouth shut until I tell you to speak.'

The visitor had brought no light with him, and his back blocked much of the meagre grey light coming through the grille, but I knew by his voice that it was Cormac O'Neill. And coming to from a deep sleep though I was, I understood enough not to disobey his order. I waited, and when he saw that I understood, he continued.

'Where is Boyd?'

I had had no notion that the new-anointed rebel leader had an awareness even of Andrew's existence, and I sought to win some time by this. 'Who?'

He slapped me across the cheek and set the wound his father had made to bleeding again.

'Do not play games with me. Andrew Boyd. I know you left Carrickfergus with him, and that you were travelling with him to Coleraine. Where is he?'

'What is it to you?'

He raised his hand again, but this time I got my arm up in front of my face in time to stop his fist coming down on the broken flesh.

Slowly, he removed my arm from the front of my face. 'You

will answer me, Seaton, or by God you will wish your mother had never met your father. Where is Boyd?'

'I do not know.' It was the truth, almost. I knew where the priest had told me they were taking him, but I did not know if he was there now, and I could not think Cormac O'Neill sought him out of concern for his welfare.

He sat back on his haunches, and told me to sit up. I did so, and in the fine gauze of light that told me it must be daytime, he scrutinised my face. 'There is something in your eyes that was not in his, and in his heart that is not in yours. But you have the same arrogance, by God. The old woman's blood runs strong.' He looked at me a little longer, as if to be absolutely certain that I was not Sean. Then he stood up. 'Enough of him. You are now the matter in question. I know why you say you are in Ireland, and Maeve confirms it, so my father says; it sounds enough like her to be true. But why did you ride to Coleraine, and what is Andrew Boyd in your scheme?'

'I have no scheme. I went to Coleraine because Sean had some suspicion that Deirdre's husband's family might be behind the curse on ours.'

He smiled slightly. '"Ours," you say. I see you claim them as your own now.'

'I have no other,' I replied.

'And what did you find amongst the Blackstones?'

'That they are people of few graces who want their hands on my grandfather's business, but I do not think they would know how to go about treating with Finn O'Rahilly, or have any faith in his powers.'

'Not the slightest. As Sean well knew, and your grandmother too. You went to Coleraine for something else. What was it?'

'I swear to you, before God who knows all, I know of no other reason for me being sent there.'

He began to pace the small cell, thinking. Then an idea evidently came to him. 'Who did you meet with?'

'I told you, the Blackstones, Deirdre's . . .'

'No, not the Blackstones,' he said impatiently. 'Who else? Did you meet with no one on your journey?'

I cast my mind back to the journey of only three days ago. 'We stopped at a poor Scots inn on the road to Broughshane, a widow and her children, friends of . . .' And then I regretted that I had not thought more carefully. Friends of Andrew Boyd, in whom Cormac was so interested, and victims of the brutal roving of Cormac's brothers.

Cormac nodded his head slowly. 'I know the place. Why did Boyd take you there?'

'Because we needed food and our horses rest. And to give the woman some trade.' I looked him straight in the eye. 'They are not far from destitute: armed bands roam the country there and passing travellers keep on their way for fear of their lives; her oldest son and best support was slain by lawless thugs when he would not pay their blackmail.'

'I know all of this,' said Cormac, 'and do not think I take any pride in it. Those responsible were punished. I am sorry for the woman's troubles.'

'Your sorrow does not make her sleep any the easier at night,' I said.

'It should. It has been seen to. The woman has been reassured and recompense made.'

'Such recompense as can be, for the loss of a son.'

'Many women in this land have lost husbands, sons, brothers, seen their children die at their breast for want of nourishment. They have been forced from their homes and the lands of their people to poor and wild places with little hope of sustenance. What recompense can be made has been made, and more if they need it. I have said it, and my word is not doubted.'

I believed him, and, in spite of all the circumstances of our meeting, I began to warm a little to Cormac O'Neill.

'What happened when you were at this woman's place?'

I shrugged. 'She and her daughter served us some broth, the young boy saw to the horses, she and Andrew talked a little of family, we paid her and left. Our stop was brief, for Andrew was anxious to get on.'

Interest flickered in his eyes. 'Get on for where? Did you aim at Coleraine in the one day?'

I shook my head. 'We stopped the night at a bawn beyond Ballymena.'

'Armstrong's Bawn,' he said, quietly, almost to himself. 'And who did you meet with at Armstrong's Bawn?'

'No one.' I hoped the meagre light might cover the lie on my face. I was to be disappointed.

'You simply rested and took meat and drink. All you sought was bed and bread. Is this what I am to believe?'

'Yes,' I said, with some defiance.

'And your bread, tell me, was it well baked? Good bread blessed by the baker?'

I said nothing.

'You met with Stephen Mac Cuarta of the Franciscan order at Bonamargy, did you not?'

'What of it? It was by chance.' I was not sure now that I believed that myself.

'I think not.'

So I told Cormac about the priest's drugging of Andrew and Andrew's distrust of him in return, about how the priest had come to me in the night because he had known nothing of me before he had set eyes on me that day, and this seemed to make him more inclined to believe my pleas of ignorance on our part.

'And what did the priest tell you?'

I kept my recollections to Stephen's reminiscences about Phelim, and my mother, and left out anything he had had to say about Sean or his secret marriage with Macha. I could not tell how far Cormac believed me. 'While Boyd was drugged, and before he knew you were awake, did the priest search your belongings, take anything?'

'No.'

'And you had been given nothing, no note, to pass on to him?'

Again I said no.

'Perhaps, then, you were the message yourself.'

'What do you mean?' I asked.

'I suspect we will find out before another night has passed. But tell me, where have you left Boyd?'

He read the cause of my hesitation.

'I mean him no harm,' he said. 'I have no cause to love him, and some to fear him, but I give you my solemn word that I mean him no harm. I must – I must have some talk with him though. And I must have him brought here. I ask you again, where is he?'

I could not entirely believe that he meant Andrew no harm, or that Cormac O'Neill, anointed leader of a planned Irish rebellion in Ulster, feared the taciturn Scot who had been the companion of my troubles. 'I cannot tell you that,' I said, already bracing myself for another blow. None came, only words, low and earnest.

'I ask you for the sake of your cousin Deirdre, although I would I did not have to. You have seen she suffers already, you know what she has suffered. The strands of her mind and her reason threaten to unravel, as your grandmother's already have done. Grant her this one thing.' He turned his face slightly away from me. 'Grant it to me also.' And then I understood what it was that Cormac O'Neill had to fear from Andrew Boyd.

I made my decision. 'On our flight from Coleraine, we were met and aided by Brother Michael, Father Stephen's young acolyte. Andrew was injured in a fall near Dunluce, and mauled by a hound from the Coleraine wolf-hunt. In the morning he was taken to Bonamargy to have his wounds attended to there.'

'Will he live?' he asked hesitantly.

'If it is God's will. I pray that it may be. He knew not where he was or who he was when last I saw him.'

'Better he is in God's hands than the friars'. And how did you find your way to Kilcrue?'

'Stephen Mac Cuarta brought me there.'

He nodded. 'Father Stephen. He has a habit of appearing, has he not? And the poet told you nothing?'

'Nothing I could make any sense of,' I said.

'Perhaps that will be for the best.' He was pensive a few moments and then strode towards the door. 'Have no fear for your friend on my account, you have my word on that.' He looked towards the grille and the signs of life beginning to stir in the main chamber after the night's debauches. 'Now I must go.'

I halted him at the door. 'I want to see Deirdre'

He took care over his response. 'It would do no good. I think the sight of you again would prove too much for her. She has been in a fever of dreams and hallucinations all through the night, and nothing the women can do will calm her.'

'This since she saw me?'

He shook his head. 'Since the night Sean died. She is almost catatonic when she wakes and like a woman possessed when she sleeps. The friars are with her now: they will be leaving soon for Bonamargy, to seek some compounds from their apothecary that might afford some relief to her mind and spirit.' He glanced towards the grille again. 'I will have food and drink brought to you.'

I was indeed hungry, and parched with thirst; nevertheless, my stomach revolted at the thought of food, for the place I was in was filthy, and the smells reaching me through the bars of the grille were noxious in the extreme: smoke, congealed fat, stale wine and human sweat, blood and, I suspected, other excretions, that had found little outlet save than to my miserable dungeon. I looked down at my hands, cracked and caked in grime, and wondered what I had come to. I sat down again in the corner furthest from the grille and any sharp eyes in the hall, and pulled the old priest's robe as tightly as I could around myself, in a desperate yet futile attempt to stave off the cold that now permeated every part of me.

Some time later the bolt to my prison was again drawn up, and a curt 'On your feet, Seaton,' growled by Padraig.

I did as I was bid, smarting a little at the extra light that now flooded into the room. Padraig had stood back to make room for the woman carrying a tray of food and drink into my cell. She had to stoop a little as she came through the door, but when she lifted her head again I saw that it was Roisin. Some surprise, or recognition, must have shown on my face, for she coloured a little when she noticed it. I mumbled some apology for the condition she found me in.

She kept her eyes lowered and spoke in softly lilting but perfect English. 'Your condition is not of your own making, and necessitates no apology. A visitor should be better treated in our country.'

Her brother responded to her, low and clear, in the Gaelic, and I understood that his every word was intended for me. 'If that visitor has come to our home only to betray us, he is deserving of no hospitality. Your heart is too soft, Roisin, and you no judge of men. Sean . . .'

But he got no further; his sister had spun round, her eyes blazing. 'Do not presume to talk to me of Sean. Never!'

He spread his hands out in supplication towards her. 'Roisin, I . . .'

'I know it, Padraig; I know it. But just leave me now.'

Before doing so, he took the time to address me. 'Do not think to try anything, Seaton: you would be dead before you could ever lay a finger on her.'

I was left alone with Roisin and more conscious now than ever of the disarray of my appearance. She had laid down the food and drink on the floor, and it took all my strength not to drop to my knees in front of her and tear at the food with my filthy hands, but she had also brought a bowl of cold stream water and a cleaning cloth. I plunged my hands instead into the icy water with the intention of washing them. She drew in a slight breath and said, 'No!' I stopped and looked at her, no idea what the matter was.

'Not your hands, not yet,' she said.

I was still dumbfounded as she took a cloth and dipped it into the water. She came closer to me and slowly lifted the rag towards my face. She was tall, taller than I had realised, and her eyes as she looked up into my face came near to the level of my own. Her mouth parted slightly, and she said, 'It is for your wound; first we must clean your wound.'

I stood still, afraid to move, but struggling to control my breathing as she slowly brought the cold wet cloth to my cheek and gently began to dab at the wound her father and brother had made there. I flinched as the movement of the cloth under her fingers caught the edge of the tear and stung me deep. She paused a moment and then returned, more gently and more closely, to her work.

When at last she had finished, I found my voice. 'I am sorry that . . .'

I stopped, not knowing how to continue.

She looked at me directly. 'That what?'

'That I am not Sean.'

Again her lips parted slightly, and then she closed her mouth and her eyes. When she opened them I could see tears hovering on her lashes. 'Sean did not want me anyway.' And then she was gone, leaving me wishing I had never spoken at all.

My ears had accustomed themselves to the rhythms of movement of Dun-a-Mallaght, and I realised it must be evening time when Stephen and Michael finally returned from the friary.

'So, Murchadh, we have brought the medicine for the girl.'

'You were long enough about it. She could have been to the Devil in this time.'

'The preparation had to be made up. The simples were ready, but the decoctions take time; there is little room for error in their preparation.'

Stephen was permitted to go, with Cormac and Padraig in attendance, to administer the medicines to my cousin. Roisin, I assumed, was already with her. As they left, I saw the priest glance towards my grille and Michael, following his eyes, do the same.

When at length they returned, Cormac's face was ashen, and even in the dim and flickering yellow light, I could see the darkened circles beneath his eyes.

'How fares the girl?' asked our host and jailer.

'She is a little more settled, but she is still fevered, and easily frightened. It is not good having too many in the room with her,' answered Stephen

'She cannot be left alone.'

'No, but Roisin is all that is needed – she has knowledge enough already, and as for the rest, I have shown her what to do. Have your men stand guard outside her door by all means, but it is not seemly that they should be in her chamber, and they disturb the balance of her mind.'

Murchadh looked to Cormac, who readily assented, and went to clear the guards out of Deirdre's room. The glance between Michael and Stephen made me uneasy.

'And now,' said Stephen, 'that goodly business attended to, my young friend and I should no longer trespass on your hospitality, and indeed the offices at the friary require our attention . . .' His face was breaking into a grin, his eyes dancing.

'But surely you would not think to leave us so soon,' said his host.

'Well,' said Stephen, rubbing his hands and inclining his head in the direction of the spit, where a hog had been several hours turning, 'it is a cold night for all that, and Michael and I haven't had a morsel since the morning; we will have long missed our poor supper at the friary by now.'

Michael attempted a jovial smile in agreement, but he was not so practised in deception as was the older brother, and the nervous grin of a boy was all he could offer. This seemed to please Murchadh even more.

'Then indeed you will stay. Let it never be said that Murchadh O'Neill sent servants of our Holy Mother Church out into a cold night, with dry throats and empty bellies.'

Music had started up again, and all around, men were bringing out dice and dealing cards. The pig on the spit surrendered at last to the appetites of Murchadh's followers, and the noise of people forgetting their troubles and their coming trials grew to such a pitch that I wondered that Deirdre or any human creature could sleep through it.

I watched the priests eat and drink, Michael initially with some hesitation and then with less caution; Stephen heartily. Michael was very soon drunk, and found himself assailed by the charms of a pretty young serving girl. The harper had been called for, and a poet also – no Finn O'Rahilly this, but an aged and revered fellow who had known better days for his patrons and caste – who having lamented the passing of the great days of the O'Neills, and looked forward to their resurrection under Cormac, was applauded and dismissed. A pipe was taken up, and then another. They were joined by a flute, the sound strange and discordant at first to my ears, and then the bodhran came, soon followed by the bones. If ever there was heathen music, music of another age, I was hearing it now. The speed of the playing increased, the dexterity of the players incredible. It was not possible that a man should be clear in his mind with such music. I felt my foot beat on the hard earth, my body move in time to the building rhythm and power of the sound that filled every part of my cell and seeped into my every sinew. I poured the last draught of wine from the jug Roisin had left me, but that did nothing to clear my thoughts or form in me any good resolve. I should have known that it couldn't.

If I was set on a dangerous path, few in the chamber were far behind me. Those who were not at dice or cards flew in pairs and sixes and eights around those who were. Murchadh himself made the lustiest dancer of all, young girls throughout the hall trying to hide their terror in affectation of delight.

Only one person in the place seemed cut off from the exhilaration, the incipient danger, the sense of approaching abandon: Cormac sat alone on his dais, brooding, with the look of one who watches but does not see what he watches. As his father caught a young girl and buried his face in her torn bodice, Cormac drained his cup and, his face set in resolve, left his place and strode towards a doorway at the other side of the chamber, and a corridor I could not see.

It was a few moments later that I saw Roisin: she was standing, hesitantly, with her back to the door Cormac had disappeared through. Her pallor and stillness called to me through the orgy of movement, of reddened faces and sweating bodies that separated us, and it seemed through the smoke and the movement, the daemonic bacchanal of the music, that she looked directly at me. I felt the heat of the place pass through me, and shut my eyes against the knowledge of what I wanted, of what I was. But I did not step back; I did not lay myself down on the cold, bare earth as I should have done. I opened my eyes and continued to look on her.

She was standing in a shaft of light. Her pale blonde hair fell loose down her back and over her deep blue velvet gown. At her neck she wore a single white pearl, pearls hung also in diamond-encrusted drops at her ears. Everything about her was clean, pure. A harper was called to the space by her; a certain Diarmuid was called for, and the hall fell silent as the harper began to pluck at his strings and the young man opened his mouth in a lament I knew well, for my mother had often sung it to me, a song of longing and promise for her homeland: *Roisin Dubh*, Dark Rosaleen. A lover promised help would come from across the sea to his abandoned virgin bride; help from the Pope, wine from Spain; that the woe and pain and sadness of the dark Rosaleen would soon be over, every step homewards of the unresting lover was taken that his love would be lifted again to her sovereign throne. The singer's voice was fine, the object of his performance filled with grace, but she was no *Roisin Dubh*, no Dark Rosaleen, for that, I knew, was Ireland herself. The final verse had always frightened me:

> O! the Erne shall run red
> With redundance of blood,
> The earth shall rock beneath our tread,
> And flames wrap hill and wood,
> And gun-peal, and slogan cry,
> Wake many a glen serene.
> Ere you shall fade, ere you shall die,
> My Dark Rosaleen!
> My own Rosaleen!
> The Judgement Hour must first be nigh,
> Ere you can fade, ere you can die,
> My Dark Rosaleen!

The complete silence that followed the rendition spoke every hope and fear of the men who might soon be marching with their guns and their cries through those glens, whose blood might soon run into the rivers of Ulster. And then, slowly, Stephen began to clap, and Michael, and Murchadh himself, until the whole chamber shook with the noise of it, and I thought the reverberations would bring the earthen roof crashing down upon us. Murchadh threw coins of gold to the singer and the harper, and caught his daughter in a tight embrace, before turning her and showing her, with pride, to his men. 'May the women of Ulster carry the hope of Ireland in their wombs!'

Released at last by her father, Roisin had begun to move

away a little, but her father stopped her and said something for only her to hear. At first he had been laughing, and she affected a smile, but then she shook her head and his laughter stopped. He took her by the shoulders and held her firm and spoke to her insistently. She mouthed something to him, three or four times, slowly, with real distress in her eyes, but he just spoke at her all the harder. All around this dumb show, the fever and pace of music never let up, but they might have been in a glass box for all that reached them. I looked over to where Father Stephen stood, and saw he had dropped his mask of joviality and begun to move closer towards them, but the crowd got in his way. He assumed again the mantle of every man's friend, but now and then he cast a glance of unease in the direction of Roisin and her father until the young woman nodded in submission to Murchadh and disappeared through the door from which she had emerged.

It was not very much later that the door of my cell opened, and two of Murchadh's men came in. Only one of them spoke, and he in a gruff and thick Irish tongue, but I understood that I was to leave this place and go with them. Again my hands were tied. The corridor I was led down was just as dank and narrow as the place I had come from, but better lit. I counted three doorways as we passed, and then, at the end, we stopped outside a fourth. My leading captor opened it and I soon found myself in another hollowed-out earthen room, with wooden supports to the roof and a beaten floor, but this one had torches burning on the walls to either side, and a small fire in the middle. Towards the rear of the room were rushes laid on the floor, such as I knew the Irish preferred to sleep on. There was a pail of clean water by the door, and a clean robe hanging from a wooden peg beside it. A tray bearing oat bread, cheese and wine had been set down over by the rush bedding. I looked to my two guards for explanation but was given none. They untied my hands and left without a word to me, only pausing to indicate the water and the robe and taking care, though, to bolt the door behind them.

I stood alone in the silence, letting my eyes grow used to the greater light. Though the music reached even here, there was no grille in wall or door. I had found myself in a place of luxury in comparison with my late holding-place, but I felt a great loneliness, more cut off now than ever from any human contact. I was sickened of this place and these people. I longed for the cold, sharp certainties of my life – the grey stone college, my students, the sermon. I longed also for the warm promise of Sarah. I saw how these people took what they wanted, and I cursed the two years I had let waste. Two years when I had scarcely touched her. I longed for the clean cool sheets of my college bed, a world away from a pallet of straw upon the bare earth.

Slowly, I removed my priest's robe, the coarse woollen garment that I had begun to become accustomed to. I took the rag that was there and began to wash myself, finding something purifying in the cold, clean water. The garment hanging by the door was of a much finer stuff than that I had discarded, a short blue tunic of the finest linen, bound at the waist by a cord of white silk. The trousers – for that was what those garments were, so favoured by the Irish rather than our hose, gave me a little greater difficulty, but soon I was fully attired again, arrayed fit to be a companion for Cormac O'Neill himself, and with my beard grown, and my hair long and lanky, none would have taken me for any other than the high-born Irishman I might have been. Of the low-born Scottish craftsman's son who was a teacher of philosophy in a reformed northern university, there was not the least remnant.

I sat cross-legged on the ground by the fire and began to eat, and drink. The wine was good, warmed and spiced, and much better than the vinegar I had earlier been given. When I had had my fill I let warmth and calmness course through me, and the music pass over me. I did not sleep, but lay as in a dream. I tried to push away the image that part of me was reaching out for. I tried to picture Sarah in my mind, but Sarah would not come to me here. Her place was somewhere warm, comfortable, familiar, not somewhere dark, strange, cold. Not here. Struggle though I did to bring her face before my eyes, I could not find her here. Her hair was not the pale, almost white blonde that came into my vision. I tried to pray, but prayer would not come, so I took more of the deep red wine that had been set out for me and willed myself to sleep.

The fire had sunk to embers and the candles burned far down when I heard Roisin softly enter the room. She hesitated, seeing me, as she thought, sleeping, and knelt quietly down by the round hearth and laid another turf of peat upon it. She was watching me, I knew, and I opened my eyes fully, that she might not be deceived. She swallowed, looked away, then back again. I sat up and held my hand out towards her. She took it and let me draw her closer, and laid her head in my lap. As I stroked the silken hair away from her face I felt the slight moisture of the tears on her cheek. My hand moved over her brow, down the side of her face. There was an anger in me that I could scarcely master: anger at Sean, whom I had loved, and she had loved, and who had not loved her; anger at her father, who had sent her here to me, who saw only Maeve O'Neill's grandson, and cared not which one it was, nor if his daughter did either; anger at myself for the weakness that was in me, the lack of constancy, the sin I knew I would succumb to.

'Why have they sent you?' I asked eventually.

She did not lift her head, 'It is only my father; Cormac does not know that I am here.'

'This is some policy of your father's alone?'

She raised her head and I brought her up closer, in to my chest. 'I think so, I think he is no readier to accept that Cormac should lead this rebellion than he was that Sean should.'

'Do you think your father killed Sean? Had him killed?'

'He would not have dared. Sean was his best hope of acceptance by the Irish outside our own kin. If I had married Sean, and produced a child, then my father could have taken the fosterage: he would have been untouchable.'

'But now with Cormac . . .?'

'Cormac is his own man. He has always been his own man. Since his youngest boyhood he has burned with shame at my father's pandering to the English while others who would not succumb to their blandishments were abandoned to their fates. My father will never control Cormac; he will be as an old stallion put out to grass, not fit for the race or the hunt or the siring any more. My father will not accept living like that; there will be a reckoning between him and Cormac, whether before or after the rising, I do not know.'

'But none of that explains why you are here.'

'I am here because it is the time of my fertility. The women keep an eye on these matters, and they tell my father.'

'And he has sent you here . . .'

She looked away. 'Any child born of this night he would pass off as Sean's: it would have a right to the patrimony. Or even as your own – by the brehon laws, it would be as if I had married Sean himself.'

'Have you . . . were you ever with Sean?'

'I have never been with any man.'

'Will they know? If you have lain with me or not?'

She shook her head. 'They will not force me to that indignity.'

'Then before you leave — if you stay till morning — we could cut my wound once more — let some of the blood drop upon your dress . . .'

'Yes,' she said. 'That is what we could do.'

I spread out the rushes on the floor a little more, and took down the priest's robe again, to be a cover over us — it was coarse, but warm. She laid herself down, her head on my chest, as I held her close in the near-darkness, and wished her good-night. Her breathing was even, but I knew she was not asleep. A tear ran down her cheek and I felt the wetness of it on my bare chest, where my robe had begun to come loose. I brushed her cheek and kissed her head again. She moved slightly and looked up at me. I lowered my head and kissed her again, gently, on the mouth. She responded and I did it again, less gently this time, pushing the crucifix at my neck to the side, desire taking over my senses. I knew it was wrong, and I knew it was not me that she wanted, but I had not been with a woman in three years, and in the darkness of that God-forsaken place, I submitted to her heartbroken passion and to my every carnal desire.

TWENTY

The Brothers of Bonamargy

It was almost dawn when I woke, Roisin still entwined in my arms, the lingering scent of rose oil from her hair drifting into my senses. The fire had gone out and the room was cold. The dark mass of guilt had found me, as I had known it would. I felt it weigh me down like a rock on my stomach. I looked down at her as she moved slightly and murmured in her sleep. Oh God, that Sarah would never know of this. I lifted Fintan's cloak from where it had slipped to the floor and covered the girl's bare shoulders with it, and prayed for forgiveness. Suddenly the cell door crashed open. I sat up quickly, trying to shield Roisin with my back, and was only a little relieved when I saw Father Stephen Mac Cuarta stride into the room.

He took in the scene in less than a second. 'So, it is like that then. Like the rest of the O'Neills: weak in the flesh.'

I struggled to say something, but he put up a hand to stay me. 'Save it for your prayers. There is no time.' He quickly gathered the clothes I had put on the night before that were now strewn around me. 'Quick, put these on. Time is scarce.'

Roisin was stirring now, but he crouched down near her and laid a hand on her head. 'Sshh, sleep on, child. When they come, tell them you woke and he was gone, that you know no more.' Taking a moment to understand what he said, she looked from him to me, then nodded her head. She lay slowly back down on the pallet, pulling the robe to her, and watched quietly as I dressed. Stephen strode around the room impatiently as I fumbled with the belt to my tunic and the trousers.

'Come on, come on, man! Did your mother always dress you?'

'I am not used to this clothing,' I said, eventually triumphing over my leg wear and casting around the room for my boots, which, I was thankful, they had not made me exchange for a pair of priest's sandals.

'Here they are,' said Stephen, thrusting them towards me. 'Now be quick!'

'But where . . .?' I began.

'For the love of God, will you *move*?'

A moment later I was ready and Stephen made for the door. I looked at him and then at Roisin, and understanding, he relented a little. 'One minute,' he said, raising a finger, 'and not one second more.'

I nodded and, muttering something under his breath, he went out.

I went over to Roisin, crouched down, took her hands. 'I am sorry,' I said, 'that I am not of your world. May you find someone who is worthy of you.'

She smiled. 'Perhaps I did. I will not forget you.'

I bent down and kissed her, one last time, then left, without looking back.

'Thank the Lord for that,' said Stephen, in some exasperation. 'Now can we go?'

'Yes,' I said, 'but go where? What is happening? Where are the guards?'

'The guards are all drunker than lords, and will have heads like balls of lead when they come to in the morning. The apothecary at Bonamargy has many talents.'

'You drugged them?' I said in disbelief.

He smiled grimly, and with a relish that almost disturbed me. 'Every last one of the devils, from Murchadh himself down to the boy who empties his piss pot.'

'But how? You were drunk yourselves.'

'Were we indeed?' He allowed himself a low laugh. 'You think those fools strutting about the stage in Coleraine the other night are the only men in Ireland who can act? No, my young friend, we were not drunk. But I think you would do well to take a lesson from your friend Andrew Boyd, and inspect very carefully any drink handed to you by an Irishman.'

'How so? I was not drugged to sleep.'

'Not to sleep, no, indeed not to sleep, but there was more stuff in the goblet you had by you in yonder room than any vintner ever put there.'

'What stuff?'

'How should I know? A man of my calling has no need for such arts, and indeed does better to stay away from them, but there were the dregs of something that was not of the grape in that.'

So I had indeed been drugged, given some aphrodisiac, at the instance of Murchadh, no doubt. His daughter would not even have known about it. This should perhaps have assuaged in me something of my guilt, but it could not, for I had wanted her last night, as I knew I had the very first time I had laid eyes on her.

Passing the main chamber, a quick glance confirmed Stephen's story: it was like some enchantment in a child's fairytale, as men, women and boys lay in attitudes of satisfaction and great contentment in utterly drunken slumber. We stepped with caution over the guards at one end of the corridor and then, with more apprehension, over those at the entrance to Dun-a-Mallaght itself.

Day was breaking as I emerged at last from my earthen prison. I stretched out my arms and breathed deep the fresh air of early morning.

'No time for that,' said Stephen, turning eastwards, where the sun had just begun to rise over the sea.

'What of Deirdre? I will not leave her.'

'She is there already, and a damned sight less trouble than you she was, too, let me tell you.'

'Where is she?'

'For the love of all things holy! Bonamargy, where else? Now come on, or I'll leave you to Murchadh's dogs.'

I had had enough of dogs and took my warning, following him in a steady trot towards his friary, which I could already see emerging out of the morning grey.

In a matter of a few minutes we had left Murchadh's subterranean fortress well behind us, and had come within the precincts of the small friary, near the mouth of the river. My own college, my own haven, the Marischal College in Aberdeen, had once been a place of friars, a cloistered ornament to a debased way of life, put to better use in the service of God following the reformation of religion in my country. Despite the darkness and depravities of the place I had just left, I was apprehensive at entering this place that declared itself dedicated, in its misguided way, to the service of God.

'Don't look so pious, Presbyterian,' said Stephen, 'it sits not well on the countenance of one who spent last night as you did.'

Bereft of anything to say in my defence, I cast my eyes to the ground and braced myself for yet more of the rituals of their superstitions. We were welcomed by an old friar at the gatehouse, who greeted Stephen with a blessing and a prayer of thanks for his safe return 'from that evil place', and cast a suspicious glance in my direction. He did not question Stephen, though. I was beginning to realise that few people questioned Stephen Mac Cuarta, and those who did rarely received answers it did not suit him to give.

'How many are you here?' I asked, as a means out of the silence.

'Six. Only six of us friars. And a nun: Julia. You'll not see her if she's not in the humour for it, and she's rarely in the humour.'

'A very small community.'

'Aye, and has been scarcely that sometimes.'

The church was long and low, with a cloister walk that continued down its east range, beside the domestic quarters we were headed towards. 'The chapterhouse and refectory,' explained Stephen. 'The dormitory is above. Julia has her own cell, separate from us of course, and the kitchens are in there.' He indicated a small limestone building with thatched roof, tacked on to the end of the eastern range. I had always imagined that friaries, or monasteries, must have been hives of activity, communities at work and prayer, every skill represented and followed behind their cloistered walls. But it was evidently not thus at Bonamargy. The authorities vacillated between banishment and toleration of the Catholic churchmen, and only the protection of the Earl of Antrim stood between this small knot of men with their spiritual sister and eviction. The place had a desolate air of emptiness and silence, as if its time was well past and it was just waiting for those within its walls to acknowledge that truth and die.

'We have not been a constant community here,' said Stephen, reading my face as I surveyed the place. 'But it makes a base for us here, we who have returned from the continent, for our mission, our work.'

Their work. Stephen would have had me believe that he was returned to Ireland for the capture of souls, the solace and encouragement of the remaining faithful on his island. He did not know I had heard any of what had passed at Dun-a-Mallaght, that I knew what his work was. I knew from his own lips that Stephen Mac Cuarta was a man who would say mass at dawn and kill a man at noon, a soldier for Ireland and a soldier for God being all one in his eyes. I had not the opportunity to say anything, for we had entered the friary building by a door in the east range, and Michael was waiting there to meet us.

'God be praised! You got away, then?'

'Only just.' Stephen afforded me a grudging sideways glance.

Michael raised his eyebrows in curiosity, but did not pursue the matter, as Stephen was bustling past him through a long vaulted room, evidently the refectory, to some place beyond.

I spoke to Michael as we followed after him. 'Will they not think to follow us here?'

Michael's face was set, grim. 'Even Murchadh will not think you will have been stupid enough to come to so close and obvious a place.'

'Then they will not come after us?'

'Oh, they'll come after you all right, eventually. And first we will deny all knowledge of you and your escape, and then, after Ciaran has tortured me a little, I will break and tell him Stephen organised a boat that took you across to Rathlin, from where you will flee back to Scotland, taking Deirdre with you.'

'Torture?' He spoke of it with such composure, such casual certainty.

He glanced at me sideways and smiled. 'I have been trained to withstand it, to the necessary point.'

We could say nothing more, for we had now arrived in a

small, vaulted chamber that I took to be a chapter room or sacristy. 'The girl?' Stephen had asked as soon as he was through the door.

'Julia has her in her cell,' said Michael. 'Gerard is attending to her.'

'And the Scotsman?'

I had seen no sign of Andrew since we had entered the precincts of the friary.

Michael pointed upwards. 'In the dormitory.'

'And the others?'

'Out in the burial ground. Digging for all they are worth. Time presses on.'

I felt my heart drop within me, a nauseating hollow appear at the pit of my stomach. 'For Andrew?' I managed to say.

'There is little enough time to do it before Murchadh and Cormac appear here. It must be done before then.'

I sank to the bench below me, desolate. He had been a man cheated by time, cheated by life, in life, and in his thirty-four years he had been a better man than all who had cheated him. I thought of what I had only started to glimpse through breaches in his defences he had allowed himself with me, and of the girl who was hovering at the edges of sanity in some small room above me. I put my head in my hands and let despair take me.

It was Stephen who noticed first. 'What in the name . . .?'

An old friar who'd been sitting in the corner came over, knelt before me, took my hands from my face. 'No, my child, you have it wrong. He is not dead. Your friend lives, and will live.'

'Then why?' I began.

'Because we know Cormac seeks him, and knows he was brought here.'

Because I had told him. I cursed myself.

'And when Cormac comes here and demands to know where Andrew Boyd is, he will be shown to that freshly dug ground, and asked to pray for a lost soul.'

I did not know whether to laugh at their ingenuity or recoil from their blasphemy, but relief swept over me like the tide over a rock.

'Come on,' said Stephen, less gruff now than he had been. 'Let us go to your friend.' He took me out into a passageway and up a stair to the dormitory above.

There were six beds, flimsy-looking wooden cots, set under six windows, three down each side of the room. The floor was completely bare, and the walls were without adornment, save for the wooden crucifix above each bed. Of Andrew there was no sign. Father Stephen was behind me, at the top of the stairs; I stepped back, fearing a trap.

'What is the matter?' he said, advancing towards me.

I stepped back again. 'Where is Andrew?'

He looked to the one disturbed bed in the dormitory and saw that it was empty. 'At the latrine, if nowhere else.' He indicated a small door off to the left, at the end of the long chamber. 'We are not altogether savages.'

I sat down on the bed he had declared to be Andrew's, and watched the latrine door. I jumped when another door at the very end of the dormitory opened, and a black-clad figure moved through it.

'Well, Stephen, so you are returned from your carousing.'

'I am that, Julia,' he said. 'And not alone.'

She looked down upon me for the first time, and her face froze for a moment. She crossed herself. 'Holy Mother of God.'

'Be at ease, Julia: it is not Sean FitzGarrett.'

'I know who it is and is not,' she said. 'I had not known Grainne had another child.'

I looked at her in incomprehension, and then to Stephen, awaiting his correction: it did not come. 'Julia . . .' he said, his voice full of warning.

'I am not in the business of deceit, Stephen Mac Cuarta. And if you had not been either, this would be a different day and Sean FitzGarrett might yet walk among us.' She looked then to me. 'You may go in to Deirdre, but remember: she is not fit to be disturbed by the conversation of men.' She gave Stephen a look that would have frozen iron, and swept through the dormitory and down the stairs.

'What did she mean?'

'Alexander,' he began.

I rose to my feet and I could feel my voice rise in anger. 'No more of your lies, your half-truths, your rationing of information, priest. What did she mean?'

'You must understand,' he said.

'Understand?' I shouted. 'Understand? I have been hounded by dogs, dressed as a priest, bound in shackles and left in a stinking cell; my own grandmother noises it abroad that I have murdered my cousin; I have heard my mother called a whore by those who were not fit to look at her, and now there is talk of Grainne's "other child". And you tell me to understand? Well, tell me why, priest, for I want nothing more than to understand.'

Suddenly, before he could answer, the door to Julia MacQuillan's cell opened again and Andrew came through it, leaning on a crutch for support. 'Alexander,' he said, his ravaged face breaking into a broad smile of relief. He came over and grasped my arm in affection, as of a long-remembered friend. 'I thought never to see you again.'

'Nor I you,' I said, embracing him, then quickly releasing him as he winced at the pain of his bruised bones. 'You were nearer death than life the last time I saw you.'

'I rambled a great deal, they tell me.'

'I could not make out a word of it.'

A look of relief passed over his face. 'Then I am glad. The brothers have also told me I said nothing to offend. They have been mending me well.' He grinned. 'I will never be so pretty as I once was, but I believe my scars will lend me some distinction.'

'A great deal,' I said.

'Truly, it is good to see you again, Alexander.' Then he glanced at Stephen with less distrust than had been his wont. 'But whatever the cause of dispute between you, you must have it out elsewhere. The Sister tolerates no disturbance. You will waken Deirdre with your rumpus.'

I felt the rage in me subside a little at the mention of my cousin. I turned to Stephen. 'Later. We will have this out later, but I will be deceived no longer.'

The nun's cell was tiny, and only a poor grey light seeped through its one small north-facing window. On a stool, dropping some liquid from a tiny phial into the barely parted lips of my cousin, was another friar, whom I took to be Gerard, the doctor-apothecary. The figure on the bed, covered by blankets pulled tight and a warm, clean, sheep's fleece, was so thin and pale as to be like a wraith, almost without substance. I stood in the doorway a moment, unable to move, struck by a sudden terror that she was dead. I held my breath until at last I saw the cover at her chest rise and fall a little.

'How long has she been here?'

'Less than an hour. Michael brought her just before dawn. I thought I was dreaming. They brought her straight to the nun's room, and Gerard has been attending to her ever since.'

'How is she, Father?' I asked in a low voice.

'I cannot tell. She has no fever; there is no vomiting or effusion, and her blood beats slow in her veins. I think she has had a great shock, and her mind has closed her eyes and ears to the knowledge of it.'

'You mean she does not want to wake up.'

'Yes, I think that is exactly what it is: she does not want to wake up.'

We sat a long time watching her, Andrew and I, each of us bound to her as if she was the only link between us and everything around us. And if that link should break, we would each of us be set loose in a land where we had no place. I looked across the bed and saw in him anger, hurt, rage, tenderness. At one point he reached out a hand to touch her, just for a moment, and in that moment I saw the tale of a man who has loved too long. When at last she began to show some signs of stirring, he left the bedside and went to stand by the door.

'Alexander,' she said, as her eyes opened on the grey dawn. Some of the apprehension that had been building up for the last hour left me: the delusion was over. Her lips were cracked and dry, and speech came to her only with great difficulty. 'You should not have gone, Alexander. I begged you not to go.'

'Ssh,' I said. 'Rest now. Time enough to talk of this later.'

But she grabbed me fiercely by the wrist. 'No. Sean is dead. You are in danger now. The curse has found us.'

'No curse, Deirdre, but a killer, and I will not leave Ulster until I have found him out, and I will not leave you.'

As she sank backwards again, she caught sight at last of Andrew, standing behind me. She closed her eyes, turned her head away on the pillow and groaned. 'Oh God, oh God, oh no.'

Andrew looked at her a moment, then something in him broke, and he left us.

I waited longer with her as she drifted back to sleep, shutting herself off from the world she had found herself in and the knowledge of its dreadful truths, and I almost wished I could join her. But I could not, and the time of my hiding from the truth was over. I left the doctor to his vigil and went in search of Stephen.

I found him, eventually, in the church. The nave was dark, much darker than I had expected, but I found my way to the east end where a finely carved wooden screen led to the chancel. Through the screen doors a transforming light flooded from the east in a myriad of colours. I walked towards it in a kind of wonder, feeling a tinge of unfamiliar regret that such beauties of man's creation had been destroyed in my homeland. So entranced was I for a moment by the jewels of colour sent out by the great east window that I did not at first notice him. I had been looking straight ahead of me, and upwards. There was enough of my vision to tell me that there was no one in any of the wooden stalls to either side of the aisle. But then my eye was taken by the altar, and what lay beneath it spread out on the floor.

His head was at the edge of the step and his arms flung out to either side of him. He was not moving, but as I drew closer I could hear a low sort of groaning coming from his throat. I started to bend down towards him, but hardly had I stretched out my hand to his shoulder than I found myself flat on my back, my head only just having missed the edge of the stone step, and the old Franciscan pinning me down with one hand while he held a knife to my throat with the other. We stared at one another for what seemed an eternity but what in truth must have been less than two seconds, until something odd came on to Stephen Mac Cuarta's face, and he started to laugh as if he would never stop. He released his hold on me and sat back, wiping tears from his eyes with the hand that less than a moment before had been on the verge of slitting my throat. He laughed and wheezed and took a deep breath to steady himself, and then wiped away some more tears.

'Alexander Seaton, is it? O'Neill, more like. They never taught you to creep about like that in your heretic seminary, I'll tell you that. That is in your blood, and let no one tell you otherwise. Phelim himself could not have got closer. By God, you were near enough to getting yourself filleted; I took you for one of Murchadh's crew.'

'I thought you were injured,' I said, still shaken, 'or dead.'

'No,' he said, recovering his composure at last, 'not dead, but praying.'

'A heartfelt prayer, by the look of it.'

'Oh, yes: it is all that. I pray God's forgiveness for the injustice I have done you, that others who loved you have done you also. And that perhaps, if God so grants it, you would forgive me too.'

I rubbed my arm where he had twisted it behind my back. 'You must tell me first what it is that I am to forgive. The truth, with no more deception.'

He looked away a moment, searching for words he did not wish to speak. Eventually he was ready. 'You must understand that the lies, the deceit I have practised upon you, were at the instance of those who had a greater call on my loyalty, aye and on my love, than yourself. Promises made nearly thirty years ago, but as fresh to me as if I had made them this very morning, and it grieves me to break them now, but I see I must. First, though, I'll get my old bones off this floor, if you don't mind.' He got up from his crouching position, and indeed, for the first time it seemed to me that he felt something of his age as he stretched and straightened himself. He took up a seat in one of the wondrously carved oak stalls of the chancel and waited until I had settled myself properly on the step by the altar.

'Now,' he said, assuming some of his accustomed heartiness. 'Where to begin? Here, now? Or then.'

'I think you had better begin with "then".'

'Aye, perhaps so.' He leaned forward a little in his stall, beginning to move his hands outwards, then taking them back in, folding them in his lap. He did not know what to do with them; he did not know how to start.

'My mother,' I said, at last.

He bit his bottom lip, and began. 'Your mother, yes: Grainne. You were how old when she died?'

'I was seventeen.'

'Seventeen. So she would have been not yet forty. Her beauty would not yet have been quite gone.'

'No,' I said quietly. 'It had not. Only at the end.'

'And not even then, in the eyes of God. She had all your grandmother's beauty, but more grace, and none of her coldness.'

I would have liked to acknowledge this too, but my mind had gone often in the last week to the bitterness towards my father that she had tried so hard and failed to hide from him or from me. I had hidden the knowledge of it away somewhere beyond memory, but it had found its way back somehow, unlocked by the sight of my grandmother. I said nothing to the priest of any of this, and if he noticed my abstraction, he did not comment on it.

'She was the light of your grandfather's world, and they were difficult times for him, for Tyrone was in open rebellion against the English, and your grandfather's wealth was based on his trade with the English at the garrison in Carrickfergus and in their few outposts in the North. Many of the Irish with whom he did business lost their lands or their wealth, whichever side they were on, in one way or another. Worse for him was that Phelim had gone into rebellion with Tyrone. It could have been no other way: Maeve had suckled her son on tales of the greatness and pride of the O'Neills, and she had made her arrangements for his fosterage in a sept very close to Tyrone with the greatest care and forethought. But to Grainne, your grandmother paid very little heed. Grainne had a little too much of the FitzGarrett in her for Maeve's liking – it was as if she had believed the call of her own blood to be so strong that it never occurred to her that her children might inherit something from their father. So, save for an understanding that one day she would be married to Murchadh – an ambition that your grandfather was implacably opposed to – Grainne was all but neglected by her mother, and consequently spent more and more time at her father's side, learning to understand the business, the world that he lived in and that he had come from. You are following me?'

'Nothing you have said so far has occasioned any great surprise. Go on.'

His face became uncomfortable again, as he searched for the right words, if there could have been such words, for what he was next to tell me. He did not look at me as he spoke, but at some point beyond my left shoulder, almost as if he was looking through the wall. 'It was inevitable, then, that she should have found herself much in company with her father's steward.'

'Andrew's father,' I said, my breath almost catching in my throat.

'No, not Boyd. Yes, he had arrived from Scotland by then,

and was in your grandfather's employ, but as his agent along the coast. There was another man – his name does not matter – older than Grainne by five years or so. This man had a liveliness to him that was like an infection, but he was wayward too. He and Grainne, beneath the eyes of your grandfather – who did not see it, thinking it a natural thing that everyone who set his eyes upon his daughter should love her – fell in love. She told me, time and again, that the man was not to blame, that he had done everything save leave Ireland to keep away from her, but strong and lively as he was, he was a lonely young man – and remember that he too was young, younger than you are now – and he loved her.

'Maeve found out about the affair, and her fury was terrible. Grainne was dispatched to relatives in Donegal, and not brought back for a year; your grandfather was almost beside himself – he knew nothing of the relationship – but was persuaded at last that it was for the girl's safety, that she might be too easy a target for English ire if left in Carrickfergus. By the time she returned, Maeve had almost managed to get rid of the young steward, dispatching him to Dublin, as your grandfather's agent there. It was not long before false accusations were raised against him – anonymously, of course – and he was hanged at Dublin Castle for treason. When Grainne returned, to be followed shortly afterwards by the boy whom Maeve presented to everyone as the fruit of Phelim's marriage, no one guessed that Sean was not his, but his sister's child, for like you, he was the image of his uncle. When, three years later, a troop of Scots arrived in port, making their way home with their master from exile in France, Grainne found she could bear life in her mother's house no longer, and left with them, abandoning her own child as she did so.'

I could not move. I wanted to speak, but the muscles in my

face were frozen. Behind my forehead, behind my eyes, there was a rush, a roaring of words, of denial, of a young boy yelling that it was not so; it could not be so. I felt my arms begin to shiver and my lips tremble; the more I struggled to master myself, the more my limbs shook. Stephen, looking at me now rather than beyond me, rose from his stall and crossed over to the altar. He sat down by me and put a strong arm round my shoulder and pressed hard.

'Now, son; it is all right; it is all right.'

'But then ... Sean was my brother.' I could hold off no more, and felt myself crumple inwards, collapsing into myself in the onslaught of loss.

We were there a long time, I think; I was conscious only of a steady murmur of words in Latin from the priest and the softly changing colours of the light on the floor of the chancel as the sun played upon its window. In each colour, each gem of light before it changed, disappeared, merged into another, was an image of my lost brother, lost to me now and in all the years that had gone before, all the years of my life, when he had not been there, all the times my mother must have held me and thought of the other she could not hold. There was Sean smiling, always smiling, laughing, Sean picking me up as I fell, Sean outstripping me in races, in climbs, Sean gradually letting me go to Archie, who would have followed and adored him. Sean bidding me farewell that early morning five days ago as I left Carrickfergus, until we should meet again. The sun slowly passed behind a cloud, the light grew dim, the colours went, leaving only the bare stone behind them. I looked up at the priest and nodded slowly. 'Yes,' I said, 'I am all right.'

TWENTY-ONE

Defiled Sanctuary

Stephen sat a while with me, on the altar steps, and prayed. I had not the heart to join him, but took comfort in the rhythm of his murmured words until suddenly the sound of voices at the gate broke into the calm of the friary. He scrambled to his feet. 'Murchadh,' he said, and then, as to himself, 'There is no time.'

He cast his eyes around him quickly, the closest I had seen him to a panic. He bit his bottom lip, calculating, calculating as ever. At last his eye lit on something. 'The altar! Quick. Get you beneath it.'

I did not need two tellings and within a moment had laid myself under the sacrifice table of the church. Stephen had gone to a cupboard in the wall and brought out a heavy linen altar cloth, bordered in fine Flemish lace. He threw it hastily over the altar and I heard the sound of two large pewter candlesticks being moved to hold it down. 'Now,' he hissed, 'pray for all you are worth. Pray to all the saints, and do not move from here if you value your life!'

And then he left me. The door of the chancel banged heavily shut behind him, and I was alone. The stone was cold and clean under my cheek. I tried not to think about the century of abominations committed on the altar above me, or the bones of the dead who lay buried in the church itself and were all I now had for company. I tried to think of my mother, but I could not bring a vision of her to life. All I could see was the single headstone, mottled already by creeping moss and the harsh blasts of salt and wind from the North Sea, that stood in St Mary's kirkyard in Banff, where she had died but where, as I now realised, the woman who had been Grainne Fitz-Garrett had scarcely lived.

I had not much longer for reflection before the door from the east range opened again, and I heard the sound of sandalled feet scuttle quickly into the church and to the stalls. They settled themselves hastily and then voices rose in unison, no organ or music of any sort in accompaniment, in what I knew to be the 'Salve mater'. A clear, young voice took the lead – Michael, I guessed – and was followed by other, older voices, the strong taking care not to overpower the weak, in a purity of sound that, as my friend the music master in Banff had often tried, in vain, to persuade me, could touch the soul. I stopped listening to the words, and sought some place of peace in the music.

But that peace was short-lived: before the friars had brought their devotion to its end, the noise of heavy boots coming down the stair from the dormitory found its way to the chancel, and was soon followed by that of curses unseemly in any house of God. I recognised the voices of Murchadh and his sons, and others I had heard at Dun-a-Mallaght. The door was kicked open with little ceremony, the holy voices fell away and the intruders clattered into the silence of the church.

'And so, you skulk in here, Mac Cuarta. I wonder that you dare to show your face.'

Stephen must have risen from his stall. His voice was full, and there was no hesitation in it. 'I skulk nowhere, Murchadh; this is the house of God.'

'It is a den of vipers and thieves. Where is Seaton?'

'I do not know.'

'Do you lie in my face at the very altar, Mac Cuarta?' Murchadh was consumed with rage. 'You left my house in the night, and you took Seaton and the girl, Deirdre, with you. Now where are they?'

Again, I heard Stephen say, 'I do not know.' But this time it was no voice but the sickening, quick, drawing of a sword from its sheath that answered him.

'I will fillet you from top to bottom and feed my dogs from your belly. Where is she?' It was Cormac, all his habitual self-control gone.

Then I heard Ciaran's voice. 'Put your sword away, Cormac. You'll get nothing from him: he's too long in the saddle and the tooth to fear what we might do. But now, let me see . . .'

There was a pause, and I was in a terror that the altar cloth would be lifted the next moment, for the feet of the incursors were very near me. Then Ciaran spoke again; his very voice was smiling, and something in it sickened me. 'That one; we will take that one.'

There was a flurry of movement, the scuffing of feet on the floor, the sound of flight, pursuit, capture, and ultimately, of Michael crying, 'No, please no.' But they took him anyway, as he and his brothers had known they would. 'Take me instead,' shouted one I had heard called Brian, but they didn't even answer him.

'He is just a boy,' said Stephen, 'just a young boy.' And I knew there was no dissembling or pretence in the sorrow in his voice.

Two sets of booted feet had dragged Michael back up the aisle and out of a south door in the church. But Murchadh and others, Cormac with them, remained. 'So,' he continued, 'five of you here and one out there – no one missing then, save for that withered old bitch Julia Mac Quillan up the stairs there. I see her temper is no better now than it was fifty years ago. A poisonous child who grew up into a poisonous old woman, which her robes and her rosary can do little to mask.'

'She was not greatly pleased to see you then?' There was amusement in Stephen's voice, in spite of the circumstances.

'You would have thought we were there to rape her. God forbid. I would rather spend a night in St Patrick's Purgatory than enter that chamber of hers.'

Relief coursed through me, and thanks for the redoubtable old nun: they had not got past her to Deirdre. But what of Andrew?

Others had the same question in mind. 'Where is Boyd, the Scot who travelled with Seaton? You, apothecary, you were treating him. Where is he?'

'He is not here.'

The sound of a hard slap. And Brian again coming angrily to his feet.

'Sit down, priest. You will have your turn, when I have finished with your brother here. Now, apothecary, I ask you again: where is Andrew Boyd?'

'You will find him there, in the earth, near MacDonnell's chapel. My poor skills were too little, and came too late to keep him longer from his Creator. He passed from this world yesterday, a little before dusk.'

'There is a fresh-dug grave out there,' said one of the men.

'You are not lying to me, old man, in this your house of God, before His altar?' and a fist smashed down on the place above my head.

The apothecary's voice was low but clear. 'I am not lying to you.'

And then Cormac breathed a great sigh, as if some burden

had been taken from him, and I realised that all he had wanted to know was that Andrew was dead.

'Well, enough of such trifles,' said Murchadh. 'Would you not spare your boy, Mac Cuarta, for he has a pretty face, and I know how in these cold dark cloisters you churchmen value a pretty face.'

'You disgust me.'

'And you me, for it is but two nights ago that we pledged in the unity of our cause to support my son, and now you have taken from my care the two living grandchildren of Maeve O'Neill.'

'I have taken nothing from your care, and I am as true to the cause I was sent on as the day I left Louvain. I rejoice, though, that the grandchildren of Maeve O'Neill are "in your care" no longer, for I doubt that they would be living much longer if they were.'

'They have no cause to fear me.'

'You beat and bound one of them, and took the other from the keeping of her family.'

Cormac spoke. 'It was necessary. It was not safe for Deirdre to remain where she was.'

'And her cousin? The Scot?'

'He might have met the same fate as Sean.'

'And it was necessary to bind and beat him to prevent it?'

'He had been in commune with Finn O'Rahilly.'

'You know as well as I do that Alexander Seaton never set foot on this island before that curse was laid.'

'Aye,' said Cormac, 'and very convenient that was, too.'

Stephen had started to make some response, but his words fell away as a horrible, animal, cry came through the oak doors, the stones, the cracks in the stones of the church, searching in desperation for some relief from its pain.

'Oh, God, dear God . . .'

'Michael!' cried Brian. I heard a scuffle as he was forced back down into his stall.

The cry came again, scarcely human. I was not worth this; whatever Stephen thought, or might want me for, I was not worth this. I turned from my side and began to push myself from the floor. Deirdre was safe, for even if they found her, Cormac would let no one lay a finger on her, and it was me they wanted. My hand was on the overhanging altar cloth, ready to pull it away, when Stephen shouted, 'Stop! I will tell you.'

'Say that again,' said Murchadh.

There was a sound of some sort of whimpering now, very close to the south door.

'I will tell you,' repeated Stephen, utterly defeated. 'They took ship two hours ago, the pair of them, for Rathlin. Seaton had left money with Boyd and came here to get it. It was still among the fellow's belongings. He prayed at his companion's grave a few minutes, and then hired some fishermen to row himself and Deirdre out to Rathlin. They were to wait there for a boat to Scotland, a small merchant vessel returning from Coleraine. I pleaded with him to leave the girl here, with us, but he would not listen, and she wandered so much in her mind she thought she was with her brother. I wish to God I had never set eyes on him.'

'You may wish such a thing indeed,' said Murchadh. He called to his torturers to bring Michael in. The door was opened and there was the sound of a heavy weight being dragged across the floor. They left it lying before the altar, inches from my face. I looked upon the thing, and suppressed a retch; I shut my eyes and turned my head away for fear I would vomit. Michael had told them he had seen nothing; they had taken out his eyes.

They did not hold back the friars this time as they left their stalls and went to their stricken brother. They had had what they wanted from here and would move on. I heard Murchadh's men tramp out of the desecrated church, but he could not resist one last cruelty before he left. 'Learn to tell the truth, boy, or next time it will be your tongue.'

Stephen went after them while Brian and another friar cradled Michael gently and the old apothecary bent over him, murmuring to himself about what he would need, what he was to do. Cormac had been the last to leave. I heard his voice as he hesitated at the door.

'Stephen, believe me, that should not have happened.'

'You will have to rein in your father, boy, or the shambles of '15 will be as nothing to the disaster he will preside over.'

'I will do it; have no fear, I will win over him. But first I must find Deirdre.'

'Cormac, leave Deirdre. If it is meant to be, it will be. Leave her for now: you have greater things to attend to.'

'I cannot. I am sorry about the boy, Stephen. I will send messengers to you soon.'

The door swung shut, and they were gone.

I waited until the brothers had lifted their young companion and carried him out of the church to the chapterhouse, where the apothecary would seek to do what he could for him. I was too ashamed to look at them, to present myself as the cause for which that vibrant, good young man had been so mutilated. When I was sure they had gone, I dragged myself out from beneath the altar, but could not bring myself to stand up. I sat there, wretched, on the floor, and watched, uncaring, as the rays of light sent their colours to play about my feet. A wooden crucifix, the body of Christ carved out upon it in ivory, had been knocked from the altar during some of what had just passed. I took it in my hand and examined it. Our saviour, in his agonies, brutalised and tormented by those so unfit to look upon him. Some of Michael's blood was smeared on it. The cruelty of man to his fellow man. I pressed the cold ivory to my forehead and prayed, hopelessly, like a child: O Lord, let this not be; dear God, I will do anything, just let this not be.

I was like that when Stephen found me. He knew my state of mind, I think, better than I did myself. 'Come now, it is a hard thing, but it has happened, and cannot be undone.' He took the cross from my hand and set it back in its place, then set about persuading me to my feet. I got up heavily, reluctantly, and stood before him, waiting. I had nothing to say.

He breathed deep. 'They have struck out for Rathlin, and will be back before dusk when they discover I have lied to them.'

'And what will they do here then?'

'Nothing if they have yet any of the sense they were born with. This friary is under the protection of Randall MacDonnell, Earl of Antrim. Murchadh has gone too far already, in the sacrilege he has perpetrated here today; anything further would be more than MacDonnell could tolerate, and Cormac would lose the one great support he must have if his rising is to succeed. It is not necessary that MacDonnell openly joins with his cause, just that he does not openly condemn it.'

'And when is this rebellion to be?'

'It was not to have been been until the spring, when the worst of the winter storms would have passed and help could have been sent from abroad. The death of Sean has changed things.' He said this last to himself as much as to me. 'But suffi- cient unto the day is the evil thereof. We have more pressing concerns today than the Irish rising. I must get you and Deirdre away from here before Murchadh and Cormac return.'

'And Andrew Boyd also.'

He smiled. 'I had forgotten. I have never in my life before known Gerard to lie: when he told Murchadh that Andrew was buried yonder in the churchyard, I think I believed him myself.'

TWENTY-TWO

Ardclinnis

It was not long before we were on the move again. The fishermen at the shore would have nothing to do with us, for they had seen Murchadh's party leave for Rathlin, and had a good idea as to who they were after, and so we had to take the small boat belonging to the friary itself.

I was greatly relieved to see Andrew.

'The old nun had hidden me under her bed. She was a thing to behold when the raiding party came to the door of her chamber. I have rarely seen such vitriol. She has no liking for Murchadh.'

'Then she judges well, for the man is a vessel of evil.' I told him what had happened to Michael.

'Dear God,' he said slowly, 'this curse spreads, it contaminates everything.'

I did not question his superstition, I did not argue with him, for I knew it; I felt the contamination in every part of me, in everything I touched. No matter how far or how fast we ran from it, it came with us.

The friar, Brian, had helped me carry Deirdre in a litter from Julia's cell down to the shore. He did not look at me, addressed not a word to me, and I knew the anger in his mind – for this, Michael was blinded. Deirdre was sleeping still, but not at peace. What her reaction to Andrew had signalled, I did not know. She must know of Cormac's feelings for her, of Murchadh's plans for her, and in their schemes there was but one place for Andrew Boyd, and that was the place they thought they had left him – under six feet of earth in an unmarked grave at Bonamargy. He had been insistent that he would take his turn in carrying the litter, but Stephen had been equally insistent that he should not. 'You have more need of it yourself.'

The old nun had told Andrew, in a manner that brooked no argument, to forget such foolishness, but she had warned Stephen too that he had only the strength of a man. 'A mortal man, and even you are mortal, Stephen Mac Cuarta. Your time is coming, but there are tasks required of you first.'

Stephen did not laugh off her words and her tone as I had expected him to, but looked at her suddenly, as if caught in a lie that even he had begun to believe. 'That is the way of it, is it, Julia?'

'For all men, eventually.' She blessed him, and dismissed him with a kiss on either cheek. It was a parting of people who knew they would not meet again.

I looked at my companion at the other end of the litter.

'They say she has the sight,' he said. It was the only conversation that passed between us, and it discomfited me.

As I positioned myself at the oars, Stephen tried to assist me, but I began to think it was as if those who had taken Michael's eyes had taken his strength, for a light had gone out of him, and his body was hunched. Yet his will was great, and the force of it overpowered the complaints of his limbs and drove him on. He raised a sail, the wind caught it from the west and began to blow us along the coast.

'Where are we going?'

'Ardclinnis.'

I had never heard the name. 'Is it another gathering place for those in your rising?'

'It is a refuge.' We were a good few miles down the coast before it came to me who would be waiting for us at this new refuge; it was the one I had forgotten in all that had happened: Macha. If Murchadh had even begun to work out Finn O'Rahilly's allusion to 'the bastard child', there would be no safety for Sean's wife even within the walls of Bonamargy.

As we rowed, I cast many anxious glances behind me at the slowly receding Rathlin Island, looking for the boat carrying Cormac and Murchadh in their duped rage, a boat that I knew must surely come. We rounded Tor Head, and I remembered this was where Sean had been riding, alone, when the shot had been fired that nearly sent him over the cliffs. I remembered too the odd way he had said it: 'I was riding home . . . I had been visiting — friends.' This had been his call to me, this how he had brought me in, when his tale of the curse had left me unaffected, this reality of an assault, a threat made manifest on my mother's family. And I knew now who those friends were — Murchadh and his crew — and what business Sean had been on. And if there had been such a shot, there can have been little doubt that it was one amongst Murchadh's followers who had fired it.

The wind dwindled and we had been going two hours or more before Andrew desisted from his attempts to take the oars from the old priest.

'What, do you think me so shameless that I would sit back while a man half-eaten by dogs ferries me to my home? See to your woman.'

We passed the burnt-out MacDonnell castle at Red Bay, and could see ahead of us the promontory of Garron Point; it seemed impossible that Stephen could pull another stroke, when at last he said, 'Praise be to God; take her to the shore — we are at Ardclinnis.'

As we brought the boat up to the small expanse of shingle shore, I could at first see little to distinguish this place from so many other inlets we had passed on our voyage – bog and moss and heather and clumps of trees banding together up the hillside. Massive stones, tumbled on the slopes as if dropped by a forgetful God. But then, from beyond a swathe of birch and willow, at the side of the burn a hundred yards or so from where it ran into the sea I saw a welcome breath of grey smoke curl into the sky. I looked more closely and saw that dotted around the trees were not only rocks and boulders, but head-stones, and behind them a squat and ancient church.

Stephen inhaled deeply as he stepped onto the shore, grate-fully stretching his arms and his chest. 'Smell that air, Alexander. Did you ever smell anything so clean and pure in all of God's creation?'

And indeed, beyond the constant smell of brine that had attended us from Bonamargy, made more rank at the shore by the seaweeds abandoned by the tide, the rich verdant earth of Ardclinnis was something that spoke to me of the first days, before God's earth had been sullied by man.

Stephen said, 'I will go ahead and warn Macha of our arrival; you see to our invalids.'

Deirdre was fully awake now and Andrew was readying himself to carry her to the shore.

'Let me,' I said quietly, and he did not argue.

I lifted her from the boat and onto the shore.

'Can you walk at all?'

'Yes,' she said, 'but I will need some help.' She looked directly at Andrew, who had been waiting a few yards ahead of us, scanning the horizon for signs of Murchadh.

'You see to the boat,' he said to me, any notion of master and servant between us long since forgotten. He put his arm carefully around Deirdre's back, holding the hand at the other side. 'Can you manage?' he said, so quietly I could barely hear him.

She let her head rest on his shoulder. 'Yes, I can manage,' and there was a softening in his eyes, the suggestion of a smile on his lips as they made their way to the church, the one wounded in body, the other in heart and mind.

As I watched them go, and thought of Father Stephen in his church, preparing Macha for our arrival, for the hurt of the first sight of me, a desire began to crawl through me to turn about and get back in the boat, to take the oars once more and row for Scotland, for Sarah, and what was home, to be away from this place or to drown in the attempt. And if Murchadh and Cormac should apprehend me, that would be the will of God, and if my suffering would be great it would not be long.

I had half turned when Stephen's voice stopped me. 'Alexander, we have everything we need from the boat.' He watched me with a strange curiosity, waiting, and with great reluctance I turned my back to the sea and followed him.

He took me first into the church, a ruin long before he or I had ever drawn breath. 'Will you make your devotions with me here, Alexander? We might be of two faiths, but there is the one God and it is He who has delivered us. Will you pray with me?'

I looked around the tiny chapel, bare of all furnishing save the simple altar below what remained of the east window. 'I will.'

He knelt, and I stood, and we prayed to our God in silence together, and then aloud, in the words our Saviour had taught us, he in Gaelic, I in Scots. To the one God. And in this place, where God had been so long before man, there was no place for dogma, for doctrine, for words or forms that might have claimed one of us as right and the other wrong. He blessed me at the end and led the way through a small doorway to what evidently served as his home.

As I was bending my head to pass through the low archway, a glint of something to my right, just below the west window, caught my eye and my breath. It was a crozier, a staff such as I had seen in stained-glass windows and stone effigies, in the hands of bishops and saints. The base of the shaft was of simple wood, cleanly carved, but at the neck it was bracketed in gold, and its curved head was covered entirely in gold, intricately engraved with symbols of the earliest Christian days, and set with precious stones of black, green, red and turquoise. I had never been so close to an object so beautiful. It was a piece for a cathedral, not a lonely and abandoned church of the Culdees.

Stephen stopped ahead of me and looked back. 'Alexander?'

'What is that?'

'The crozier? It has been here many lifetimes, left in the care of the church by an early saint. It will be here long after I am gone. A truth that has been touched by the hands of a saint, and will not be defiled.'

'What do you mean?'

'It is believed that this staff is a repository of God's judgement, a rod of truth. If any man, or woman, be accused of a crime and deny that crime, should he swear his innocence on this crozier, and yet be a liar, his mouth will twist and freeze in its deformity. If he be innocent, he will go on his way unmarked.'

'A man must tell the truth before this staff?'

'A man must tell the truth, always.'

'Then will you come before this staff, and tell the truth to me?'

He spread his hands before me. 'Alexander . . .'

'You have put me off long enough, priest. Stand before your piece of wood, and tell me why I am here.'

His head dropped and his body sagged. 'I will then, I will. Just let us have some rest and warmth, some sustenance for the body. I will tell you all, just let us have some rest.'

He was an old man now. A sick old man. Every step he had taken from Bonamargy, every pull on the oars, had been to bring him here, and now that he was home, Death would not be long in gathering him. I could not deny his request. 'I will see you on your knees in front of that staff before nightfall.'

'You have my very word on it.' He coughed, and steadied himself in the doorway. 'I am a man not far from my maker. My word is of greater worth than most.'

We found Andrew and Deirdre in a room so tiny it was little more than a cell. Deirdre was seated by a small fire beside which, tending a skillet with frying fish, crouched a heavily pregnant girl. She straightened herself when we came in, and I knew then why Sean could never have loved Roisin O'Neill. The girl into whose momentarily startled eyes I looked was every part the equal of my cousin. Long chestnut hair hung in loose ringlets about her face and down her back. Her brows formed perfect arches above eyes of the warmest brown and the hesitant smile lit up a face that was full of life and kindness. I felt I had always known her. I knew Stephen had forewarned her, but her shock at the sight of me registered a moment before she composed herself. She stepped forward and greeted me in Irish, extending both hands towards mine and kissing me on the cheek.

'I am greatly sorrowed by your loss,' I said. 'If there is anything I can do for your help or comfort you must ask me as you would a brother.'

'He told me it would be so when he went for you. He always knew it might end in this way, as did I. I have his child and he has taken care that his legacy might be fulfilled. No more can we ask.'

I looked to Stephen, but he avoided my eye, and I sat down with some discomfort beside Andrew.

'And so, Deirdre,' said Stephen, affecting some of his old heartiness, 'you have met your sister-in-law.'

My cousin looked up at Macha, smiling. 'God has blessed us where we thought he had forsaken us. That I will soon see the face of my brother's child lightens the sorrow in my heart.'

'As it will your grandmother's too,' said Stephen.

Her face clouded, the smile fell away. She looked to Andrew and to me. 'Must my grandmother know?'

'There is no need . . .' began Andrew.

'Surely she must know, it is the child's birthright . . .'

Deirdre looked pleadingly at the priest. 'But you know what will happen; you know what she will do: the child will have no life!'

Stephen began to speak, his voice raised, but his breath failed him and he swayed on his feet, only a wheeze escaping his throat. I steadied him and Macha brought forth a small stool for him to sit upon. Once recovered, he tried again. 'Your grandmother knows what is the child's birthright. She will teach him what he must know, as she did Sean.'

'Who is dead now, murdered . . .'

Andrew put out an arm to calm her but she shook it off. 'You condemn this child.'

'There are those who will protect him. We will be better prepared, the time is soon . . .'

'The time is gone. Will none of you see it? The time is gone!'

She pushed past him into the church, from where the sounds of her grief wrenched the heart of me. Andrew would have followed her, but Stephen held him back. 'Give her this time for her anger. She has held it too long, and now she will give it up to our Holy Mother. Let her have this time.'

Macha brought us the food on simple wooden platters. Despite her bulk, she moved with grace, and there was little in her to suggest she had known a life of servitude. 'She is of a family in Down,' Stephen had told me. 'They fell foul of your grandmother's family many generations ago. The certainty of Maeve's wrath added to the attraction for Sean, I think. In truth, though, I cannot see that he would have married any other woman. And her lineage was every bit the match of his own. She will hold her own with your grandmother, and the old woman will take to her in spite of herself.' I watched the girl as I ate, and knew the priest was right.

The cooked fish were coated in oatmeal and in an instant took me home, the softness of the flesh melting on my tongue, the small hard balls of the oatmeal cracking like crisp hot nuts on my teeth. Could I have done, I would have willed myself back there now, to Mistress Youngson's kitchen in Banff, the austerity of her countenance matched only by the warmth of her welcome, the safety of her home.

In the poor light of the room it was difficult to see whether Stephen improved with the rest and nourishment, but soon Macha was chiding him gently for not having eaten enough, and had warmed a bowl of goat's milk to tempt him.

'He seemed strong as an ox,' said Andrew. 'Invincible.'

'I think the trials of the last few days have proved too much for him. And who knows how long he has been living and travelling on reserved strength? He must have used what little fortitude was left to him to reach this place.'

'It was his home, the girl told me. When he was a young boy, he was servant to the priest here. It was believed he was his father. I think he has come back here to die.'

'We cannot linger here long. Murchadh and Cormac will be after us soon, and we must get the women to safety somewhere.'

'We must get them to Carrickfergus.'

I nodded. 'Rest now – I will need what strength you have tomorrow. We will make up a pallet for the priest in the boat and take him with us. Deirdre improves a little, thank God, but with Macha too it will be slow progress. We will start at dawn.'

Andrew looked over to the priest, who was sipping at the bowl of milk and smiling at Macha as if he were only doing it to indulge her. 'I doubt he will make it to the dawn.'

Stephen finally nodded off to sleep and Andrew went to bring Deirdre back from the cold church. Macha knelt beside me, getting down to her knees with some difficulty.

'He is much agitated and has made me promise I will waken him after he has slept an hour. I know he has business of some sort with you, but can it not wait until the morning, until he is better able for it?'

'I do not think it can,' I said.

'Then I will make up a fire through there, for he insists he will speak to you only before the crozier.'

'Let me do it,' I said. 'You cannot be long from your time.'

'I do not think it will be many days now until my husband's son cries his first upon this earth.' I forced myself not to dwell on thoughts of what Sean would never hear, never see.

'You are so sure it will be a son?'

'I know it. It was promised and foretold.'

'By whom?'

'By Julia MacQuillan, at Bonamargy. She has the sight; she is never wrong. I shall bear my husband a son.'

In my homeland, such things would not have been spoken so freely, and I had trained myself for many years to pay no heed to them, but here, tonight, I knew that the old nun could not be doubted, that I would soon hold in my arms my brother's son, and that Stephen Mac Cuarta would be dead by morning. I laid a fire of wood and peats before the crozier, beneath the west window of the church. Neither Andrew nor Deirdre questioned what I was doing, and I was glad to see the two women lie down soon after on clean straw in the priest's cell, with rugs laid carefully over them. Andrew did not sleep for a long time, but watched them, as I had known he would. I waited until he, too, had finally dozed off and then quietly woke the priest. He seemed to come to with some relief, for his sleep had been a restless one, and once or twice he had muttered, as if struggling in a dream.

I supported him through to the church, for although it did not matter to me now where we spoke, it was he who insisted that we should do it there. The fire had lent what warmth it could to the crumbling building, and two large candles, mass candles, burned on the altar. Through a hole in the rafters where there was no thatch I could see the stars.

I eased Stephen down on to a pallet of straw covered in an old sheepskin, and waited. His breath came hard and heavy, but eased off at last when the exertion of walking from his cell passed. He bent his head towards the crozier and kissed it.

'You do not need to do that,' I said. 'Your word is enough.'

'For you, perhaps. But I have made many bargains with my God, and may He forgive me, I have not kept them all. He shall know by this that I tell the truth.'

'He knows anyway.'

'Perhaps. But indulge the beliefs of an old man, and pray that He might also.'

'I have spent much of the night in prayer for you.'

He inclined his head a little towards me. 'Thank you. Now, tell me where you wish me to begin.'

'At the beginning.'

He almost managed a laugh. 'The beginning? There is no beginning to Ireland, save the day of creation when God filled her with his bounty and then said, "Come, fight it out."'

I did not like the blasphemy, and we had no time for humour. 'Tell me when you became involved in the treachery of Murchadh O'Neill, what my cousin's place in his scheme was, and why he brought me here.'

'There is no treachery . . .'

'Do not lie to me; I heard you at Dun-a-Mallaght. You plan rebellion against the king. You boast of continental powers . . .'

'There is no treachery and there is no boast. We fight for the Holy Roman Mother Church and her daughter, Ireland. We cannot be traitors to a king to whom we have never bent the knee. Our people are paupers in their own land. Men like Murchadh, heads of great families, revered through all Ulster, forced to till the land like beasts or peasants.'

'But there is peace,' I said. 'And Murchadh has prospered in this peace. Many have told me so – he has made his bargains with the English and has done well of it.'

'And is held in distrust and contempt by the Irish because of it, and do you think he does not know that? He wanted Roisin to marry Sean to gain some of the affection and esteem in which your grandmother's family is held, as well as to build up his lands.'

'But surely that could have been achieved without rebellion?'

'He can only properly establish himself by wresting power from his English masters.'

'But why did you join with him? You saw what he did to Michael; you know what he has done to others.' My mind went back to the shabby Scots inn where Andrew and I had taken rest and sustenance, where a widow and her children lived in the shadow of a murdered son.

He breathed deep. 'I made common cause with Murchadh for a greater purpose than his: a cause whose ends could not be achieved in opposition to his, so must needs join with them. But it was never Murchadh who was to lead the struggle, it was to have been Sean. Murchadh does what generations of his sort in Ireland, leaders of septs, have done through time – he fights for himself. He has used the English to further his own ends, and has no notion of leading a rising for the sake of the Irish. Throughout time, for centuries, our poets have called for a leader who would put an end to rivalries, unite Ireland, and protect her against the foreign invader. It was to have been Sean. Did you think for a minute your cousin was involved with Murchadh for personal gain? Sean was all that a leader should have been, and with access to Murchadh's power base, much might have been achieved. And he was faithful, too. Faithful to the Church and to Rome.'

It made sense now, the talk of powerful friends, of Louvain, Madrid. 'And this is why you came back from the continent? To put your Franciscan mission in the hands of the king of Spain, and wrench Ireland from King Charles's hands in the name of Rome?'

'You think I had done better to stay in my college in Louvain and simply pray for Ireland?'

'Better than to have joined with a butcher like Murchadh.'

'Butchery, is it? Let me tell you something of butchery, my young Scottish friend. When Chichester burned and destroyed the whole of Ulster, when you were a babe safe in your mother's arms in Scotland, and Sean had been abandoned by her, starving children were found with their hands in the innards of their dead mother; old women enticed boys and girls away from their play, to murder and eat them. And you would disdain Murchadh for making his peace with the English whilst hoping to raise himself once more? Those whom the earls left behind in their flight – brothers, sons – were rounded up, imprisoned, for the very fact of their existing, and some rot in the Tower of London still, children once, now men, grown to manhood in their chains. They will never see the blue of an Irish sky nor drink the clear water of a mountain burn again. Others, who took ship for England to plead their case with their king, their Celtic king, son of a faithful daughter of Rome, never saw his face before they were shipped to Virginia, to be murdered by savages or die of disease in his colonies. Say what you will about Murchadh, but he remains an Irishman, holding his land on Irish soil, and as such gives hope to other, better men, who do not.'

The effort of this speech had cost him much, and he lay back a moment with his eyes closed. I offered him a little water and he took it gratefully.

'But I will die in Ireland. Unlike your uncle, Tyrone, Tyrconnell, so many others that I left with, so many years ago. I have seen the sun rise and set once again on the land of my birth, and for that I give thanks to God.'

'And that is why you came back now? Because you knew you were dying?' There was little point in sentiment, or dissembling. He had seen the last sunset of which he spoke.

He raised the familiar grin, and the trace of a sparkle came into his eyes. 'The timing of that is merely a stroke of good fortune. Many powerful men on the continent take an interest in the affairs of Ireland. Tales of Murchadh's planned rising came to their ears – through MacDonnell, I am certain – at about the same time that Sean's letters on the same subject came to me.'

'Good news for you,' I said.

His eyes were quick. 'No: the worst. Murchadh is unmeasured, hot-headed. He lacks discretion. We all feared a repeat of the debacle of '15.'

'What happened then?'

'I forget you have lived your life in such blissful ignorance. In 1615, plans were laid for a rising against the English, to free prisoners – Tyrone's own son amongst them – and to drive the English, those who were not put to the sword, from Ulster.'

'And it failed?'

'Failed? It never even began. The leader, Rory O'Cahan, did little but drink and brag the country round for weeks what he was to do. The English heard of it, of course, and he was caught, tried and hanged, with six others, a Franciscan priest among them, before flame was lit or sword lifted. The Spanish stood ready then, as they do now, to help. But they will brook no more Rory O'Cahans, and Murchadh is such a one. I was sent here to assess the readiness of the English in their settlements – not just the towns like Coleraine, but the bawns too – to meet our attacks, and to gauge the level of supplies we might garner from them. But I was also sent to protect Sean, and to rein in Murchadh. I have failed in my second object, but God willing, will not do so in my third.'

'I think Cormac has greater honour than his father ever did, but his determination upon Deirdre threatens to blind him to all other concerns. He is no Sean.'

'No,' he said, looking at me as if by the concentration of his mind alone he could pierce my heart, 'he is no Sean.'

It was cold enough in the crumbling church, and what heat the fire had first offered could do little against the advancing frost of the night, but the shiver that passed down my spine under his gaze had little to do with the air around us. I looked away, pretending to make a start on gathering up the straw.

'Look at me, Alexander.'

'It is very late. We have an early start in the morning. We should go back to your . . .'

'I will go nowhere in the morning, as you know, save to the place of atonement for my sins.'

'You may go where you will, if you believe in such places. I have need of sleep.'

I bent down to lift him to his feet, but he shook his head. 'I will see my last of this world here.' He gazed up through the hole in the rafters. 'The stars in their firmament were never more beautiful than they are here, tonight.' Then he looked back at me. 'You know now why you are here, don't you?'

'I am going to my bed,' I said.

He reached up and gripped my arm, a terrifying grip from a man so close to death.

'You know why Sean brought you here, don't you?'

'The nonsense of the curse . . .'

He shook his head, impatient. 'Sean no more believed that than you do. But Deirdre does, and more importantly Maeve. When the curse was laid and Maeve told him he had a cousin . . .'

'He never knew we were brothers?'

'Perhaps he suspected, who knows? But I don't think he ever asked. I have heard from your grandmother's priest that when Maeve sent him to fetch you to lift this curse, he took it as a message from God that our prayers had been answered, that a help had been found to us in our fight. One of Murchadh's men, acting out of a misplaced enthusiasm and a misunderstanding of his master's mind, made an attempt on Sean's life not long ago. The attempt, as you know, failed, and the man paid for it with his own, but Sean knew he might never live to see the rising's beginning, still less its end, and he knew what would happen to it and all our hopes should he die, without an appointed successor . . .'

I backed away. 'I am a Scot, a teacher, and no follower of Rome. You were as well to get a dog to lead your rising as me.'

'Do you tell me you cannot handle a sword?'

'Of course I can handle a sword.'

'That you are not the grandson of Maeve O'Neill?'

'You have told me I am.'

'And do you tell me I have not seen you finger that cross at your neck for comfort? Do you tell me I have not seen you on your knees, praying at our altars?'

The shock of his words stopped me where I stood. A denial was ready in my mouth, but I could not deny what he had said; I knew it myself. How had it come to this, that I had so easily lost sight of my own faith when surrounded by the snares of idolatry? I forced the words through gritted teeth at last. 'I am no follower of Rome.'

'Alexander, you were born to this. You have Irish blood enough for those who would ask it, if you have a heart to do what it is that they ask of you.'

His breathing was coming short and fast now. I put out a

hand to calm him. 'Do not agitate yourself over this. God's will will be done. There is no more you can do.'

He did not calm himself, but by a supreme effort hauled himself up so that his eyes were almost level with mine. In the thin golden light that found its way to us from the altar, they were red, and shining. 'Alexander, I beg of you. Take up Sean's mantle. Do not leave them to Murchadh, all will be lost. MacDonnell will support you. They have my letter at Dunluce already, naming you your cousin's successor . . .' A pain seized him and he fell back down, clutching at his heart.

'Alexander, I beg you,' he gasped.

I ran for Macha and she was there in a moment, cradling his head in her lap. A smile of immense peace passed over his face. 'I can hear the child's heart beating,' he murmured.

'Hush, do not talk,' said the girl, a tear falling from her cheek and splashing onto his face. 'Do not leave me.'

He brought a hand up to cover hers. 'Do not weep, my child. The stars in God's heaven wait for me, it is my time, for as the Preacher says: "To everything there is a season . . ."'

But he hadn't the strength to go on. I took up the words for him:

'And a time to every purpose under the heaven;
A time to be born, and a time to die;
A time to kill, and a time to heal;
A time to weep, and a time to laugh;
A time to mourn, and a time to dance;
A time to love, and a time to hate;
A time of war, and a time of peace.'

I let the words die in the room, and then his voice came, in a hoarse whisper. 'I have loved and I have laughed; I have wept and I have danced; I have waged war and have craved peace. Do not mourn for me: it is my time.'

At that moment, the light in the church changed, and the darkness gradually receded in the face of a glory of reds and yellows and greens, as the sun rose and sent its magnificent rays through the east window of Ardclinnis, to light for the last time on the face of Father Stephen Mac Cuarta.

I dug the grave, while Andrew kept watch at the shore, for the sea was calm and would not have detained Cormac and Murchadh long at Rathlin.

I had chosen a place close to the church, by the hawthorn, the fairy tree, and we buried him there with some words from me and prayers from the women. Andrew intoned the forty-sixth psalm. There was no time for a headstone, or even to carve out a wooden cross, but Macha had taken a slip of a wild rose and planted it at the head of the grave to mark the place. 'It will grow, and I will bring my son here,' she said.

'Where do we run to now?' asked Deirdre.

'Carrickfergus,' I said warily, for I knew she would not like it.

'You cannot go to Carrickfergus. You know what my grandmother in her delusions accuses you of.'

Andrew took up my argument. 'We will plead our innocence and clear our names, but we can do it in no other place, although we must call first at Ballygally.' I shot him a quizzical glance, but he chose not to notice it. As we walked to the boat he stopped me.

'You are sure you wish to go south?'

His question surprised me. 'Where else would I go? There is no other safe way for me to reach home to Scotland, and I certainly cannot go north.'

'Not even to Dunluce?' He was watching me carefully.

'Andrew, what are you asking me?'

He looked away, to the sea. 'I heard you speaking with the priest, in the night. I had long suspected something of what Sean's business was, although I would not have thought him honourable, and now I believe he was. But now I know also what brought you here. . .'

'I had no knowledge of it. It was the talk of the curse.'

'The curse. And where is the curse now?'

'With its maker, who hangs from a tree in the hills above Ballycastle.'

'Is it? We neither of us know that.'

'I thought you did not believe in it.'

'And neither do I, but I believe in the evil intent in whoever paid Finn O'Rahilly to lay it, and so should you.'

I looked back at Ardclinnis, a slow mist rising from the ground beginning to envelop it, to take it back upon itself, away from the eyes of mortal men. 'There is evil everywhere in this land, Andrew. I cannot concern myself with that I do not know, only with present danger. And that danger lies in Murchadh, and Cormac, to say nothing of the Blackstones, who may even now be in Carrickfergus ahead of us, adding their accusations to my grandmother's.' In my mind I heard the sound of Michael's pistol shot, and saw again the horse that crashed down on its rider within sight of the walls of Coleraine.

'Then you were not persuaded by the priest? You will not take Sean's place at the head of their rising?'

'I am not the man they seek. I am not the man he was.'

'I think perhaps he was a better man than I knew.'

'He was a better man than I am,' I said at last. 'I will not fill his place, have no fears on that. Come, we have little time

to lose.' And within minutes we were pulling away from the
shore, from Ardclinnis, and from the last earthly resting place
of the man who had so mistaken what I was. I cast a glance
behind me as we rounded the headland. A boat, long and dark,
bearing a standard I knew to be Murchadh's, was powering
down the coast from the north. I committed our party to God
and rowed for all I was worth.

TWENTY-THREE

Ballygally Castle

It was the mist that saved us, and they could not see us. Or their need to search Ardclinnis, that bought us time. Or God in His Providence, who had not finished with us yet. Whatever the cause, we got away from the search party of Murchadh O'Neill and before midday had won to the safety of Ballygally.

'Sir James Shaw is a Scot, well affected to the king and the Protestant cause. We will find sanctuary there, and a place of rest for the women.'

The latter was becoming a pressing concern: Macha was in a deal of discomfort, and the constant movement and exposure to the elements were playing hard on Deirdre's weakened state of health. Her sleep last night had been restless, and full of terrors she could not name on waking. She had murmured of Sean, of the poet, and of Maeve MacQuillan, and I wondered if she was seeing again in her mind's eye that vision of a death foretold.

She insisted on sitting up in the boat, on keeping watch, although we had told her there was no need to. 'You will not watch properly,' she said. 'You will not see what I see.' Her hair blew wild in the wind, and her eyes looked far into something that I knew in truth I could not see. She might have been a daughter of the legends of another age, fleeing from powers that had come to call her back to them.

Andrew watched her. 'She loved me, Alexander. Like fire. Like a storm.'

'She loves you still.'

'I have lost her once already, to the English, to her own pride. But she can no longer hide from her roots: the Irish blood is too strong in her. Cormac knows this, and I think he knows her. He has bided his time, and waited, and I will lose her now to him.'

'I have watched her with you, Andrew, and I have seen her with Cormac: she still loves you.'

'I could only keep her while she is broken, and I will not do that.' I did not argue with him, for he knew my cousin better than I did, and I knew him: he would not see atrophy that which he loved. And if Cormac's rising did not fail then perhaps Deirdre would find her place in Ireland after all, the place that Andrew knew he could never give her.

We had kept close to the shore most of the way, but when the mist lifted, and Andrew pointed landwards, I thought we must have drifted across the narrows to the southern tip of Scotland. Only yards from the shore was a castle, a Scots castle, like so many I had spent time in as the friend of Archibald Hay.

It rose perhaps five storeys, looking directly across the sea to the land where it had its roots. The roof was steep, and turreted windows at the corners gave views to the west and the east, from where trouble or assistance might be expected to come. A high outer wall reached almost to the sea, where a small river met the shore. Loopholes in the walls allowed for musketry. Everything was clean and new, and it took me home, to the castles of Mar, like a miniature, a fragment of Castle Fraser, or Craigievar.

Before we had pulled the boat up on to the sand, a musket

was sticking through a loophole in the castle wall, and a voice challenging us to state our business.

'Tell Sir James it is Andrew Boyd. Tell him I bring news of Madeira, and seek shelter from rebels against the king.'

That was it, no explanation of who 'Andrew Boyd' might be, a direct appeal, with some shadow of a familiarity, to the master himself. Before I could ask what nonsense he spoke of 'Madeira', the musket had been lowered, and the huge oak gate in the outer wall was opening in before us. Andrew called for assistance for the women, and soon four men were hastening down the sand and helping them from the boat, as I was thrust by my companion towards the castle and told to get myself within its walls. A carving in the stone over the entrance portal showed its master's initials and crest, along with those of his wife, Isabella Brisbane, with a date of 1625, the legend proclaiming God's Providence to be his inheritance. 'And mine also,' I thought.

An attempt had been made, when we entered, to take Macha down to the kitchens with the servants, but Deirdre's eyes had flashed fire: 'She is my brother's wife.' And from that moment, there was no further suggestion that Macha should be handled as a servant.

It was evident, from the manner of their greeting, that Andrew Boyd and Sir James Shaw were not strangers. 'I am sorry to see you injured, Boyd, but glad that you have gained safe to my house. You do credit to your master, and,' his eyes drifted to me, 'to his grandson. But perhaps you, sir,' and now he was addressing me, 'would be more comfortable in some fresh clothing.'

The fine garments I had been provided with for my night with Roisin at Dun-a-Mallaght had not fared well since I had left that cursed place. I opened my mouth to protest that

Andrew was in greater need of attention than I was, but was silenced by a look from my companion that brooked no argument, so I went reluctantly with the two guards whom Shaw deemed it necessary to attend to my dressing. Only then did it occur to me that my host believed me to be Sean.

Less than an hour later, after some vigorous scrubbing in a tub set out by the stream that ran through the inner courtyard, and arrayed in the serviceable clothing of a Scots servant, I was brought once more to the great hall, where a welcome fire burned. Shaw and Andrew had been deep in conference as I'd entered, but lifted their heads from some papers as soon as they heard me. A momentary hesitation in Andrew's eyes was quickly replaced by relief, and Shaw, distrust now gone, strode towards me, his hand outstretched.

'Mr Seaton. You must forgive the coolness in my manner earlier. You are so much like your cousin that although I had heard him reported dead, the sight of you made me think the reports mistaken. Be welcome to my house as a fellow countryman and one of my own faith.'

I took his hand gladly as Andrew took up the explanation. 'Sir James was an associate of your grandfather's. He is a staunch supporter of the king, and of the Protestant faith. I have apprised him of your true identity, and of what has brought you to Ireland.'

'Damnable superstition,' the older Scot interceded, 'but you do honour to your family in coming to their aid. It is the tragedy of some that they will not be helped.' I did not ask him what he meant, but visions of my grandmother passed through my mind. 'And you have garnered little thanks and much hardship for your troubles, I hear. But no matter, that will be put to rights. First though, you will rest and sup here, now, before we come to business.' He banged a great gong by the fireplace and within moments, a light quick step was on the stairs. Glad of the fire, I attended only to it until the girl's voice made me turn around and look towards the doorway where she stood.

'You wish something from the kitchens, sir?'

'I wish my wife. Where the Devil is she? Our visitors are half-starved.'

'She is with the ladies yet. I will go and fetch her.' I looked to Andrew in astonishment; I knew beyond a doubt that it was Margaret, the girl from the poor roadside inn, daughter to a widowed mother and sister to a murdered brother.

Andrew registered the cause of my surprise and his face broke into a broad smile. 'Yes, it is Margaret. You recall when we last saw her, she asked if I could do anything to help her find some position of service, that she might be a charge on her mother no longer, and might perhaps earn something to help her with? I wrote a testimonial for her and she took herself to Carrickfergus to find work. That very day.'

'And indeed, it was our good fortune that she did. My wife had gone in despair to the town, thinking a trustworthy girl was not to be had in the country. Young Margaret is quick, and careful, and minds her tongue. My wife is much easier in her own house to have such a girl by her.'

In a country where I had known only bad news, and worse, this was something truly to be welcomed, and for the first time in many days I felt a gladness in my heart.

Margaret soon returned, begging Sir James's pardon, but Lady Isabella was much preoccupied with seeing to the comfort of the ladies, and might she be of service instead?

He ordered her to have sent up whatever food the kitchens might have ready. In no time, a hearty quantity of food had made its way from the kitchens to the hall. I could see Andrew took genuine pleasure to see Margaret in her new situation, and I hoped something might come of it, when the time was right. That time, I knew, would be a while off yet, because he would never abandon Deirdre or thoughts of her until she was ready to abandon him. Margaret mastered her emotions well, and I doubt her new employers could have guessed at any feeling between the pair, but she could not mask them so well that I, who knew already, could not see what her feelings for him still were.

Margaret bent to attend to the fire and Sir James moved from one side of the hearth to the other. 'And so to business,' he said. 'You are accused of your cousin's murder. I am blunt of necessity, for time presses and the niceties are not to our purpose here.'

Margaret could not help but look up at me, her face a study in shock. Andrew put a hand on her shoulder. 'Don't be afraid,' he said. 'Whoever murdered Sean, it was not Alexander. He was nowhere near Carrickfergus at the time: he was with me, and we have the witnesses to prove it.' She regained a little of her usual composure, and attempted a smile in my direction, but she still looked far from assured on the matter.

Sir James continued. 'The accusation, as you know, has come from your grandmother. There are few who believe her, however loud she proclaims it, but it must be addressed all the same. Now, Boyd here tells me you were together, taking shelter in Armstrong's Bawn, on the road to Ballymena, on the night of your cousin's murder. Is that correct?'

'They tell me my cousin was murdered on the night of my grandfather's funeral?'

He gave a curt nod, watching me carefully.

'Then that is correct,' I said.

'Good, then there will be little difficulty in proving your

innocence, as not only Andrew but others can vouch for your presence there. We must get you to Carrickfergus, to the safety of the garrison, and state your case to the governor.'

'We need to get the women back too, as soon as possible, to the safety of my grandmother's house.'

'Murchadh O'Neill is after you, and his son also?'

'Yes. Murchadh would like to get his hands on me, I think, one way or the other, but Cormac's only interest is in Deirdre.'

'And yet, from what Boyd has told me, it will go ill for your cousin's wife should they come upon her.'

I did not want to think about what they would do to Macha and her unborn child should they realise who she was. 'I think we must leave here soon.'

'We cannot all go together. Murchadh will know our party, and once we have left the protection of the castle we will be at risk of capture, at least until we reach Olderfleet.'

Sir James was not disposed to be much put out of his plans by fear of the O'Neills. 'I am not as young as I was, but I am not ready to bide my time at the hearth, sucking on my gums, quite yet. You and the Irish girl, Sean's wife, must leave tomorrow, early.' It was Andrew he addressed himself to. 'My steward takes a consignment of hides to Olderfleet. You will travel with him, in the guise of a Scots servant and his pregnant wife.'

'No great disguise required for that, I think.'

'Indeed. If they do not know of the girl or that she is with you, you should not be troubled on your way. No one will be searching for a servant with a pregnant wife.'

'And what of Deirdre, and Alexander?'

'They will travel later in the day, with me, and by God, let O'Neill try his hand and he will soon see what a Scotsman can do!'

'The man is ruthless,' said Andrew bluntly.

'Oh, never fear, for I know that well enough, and if I did not, there is Margaret here could have told me.' The girl, who had been refilling our plates and glasses, lowered her eyes. I remembered how I had felt at the sight of Finn O'Rahilly hanging from a tree, and wondered how much worse it had been for her to so find her own brother. 'No, I can be ruthless myself, and have had cause to be so before now, and will be again, if need be. But I have cunning too, and I think, unlike so many of his race, that is what our friend Murchadh lacks. They will have to halve their numbers if they choose to go in pursuit of both of us. Margaret here will take on the role of lady's maid, and we will have eight of my strongest men with us. It is no great distance from here to Olderfleet, and from there we will be accompanied by a detachment from the garrison to Carrickfergus. Let him try to approach us!'

And so the thing was decided.

I took my leave of our host and went in search of Deirdre and Macha. As I mounted the stone turnpike stair, I glimpsed, through open doorways and at windows, men standing, muskets at their sides, eyes trained on the sea. They were watching for Murchadh. It was a place awaiting attack, preparing for a siege.

While we had waited for our food, James Shaw had sent for one of his men and entrusted him with some commission. He was striding towards the stable, fully dressed now for a late autumn ride, and making for the saddled horse that stood in readiness. Before he mounted, I saw him place a paper in the saddlebag of his horse. I could not tell, but felt sure it was the same paper over which Andrew and James Shaw had been bent when I had first come upon them in the hall. Within moments, he was through the gates and riding for all he was worth, towards Carrickfergus. I felt a chill that was little to do with the coldness of the early November air, and wondered whether I truly knew Andrew Boyd at all.

Deirdre and Macha were in a small room almost at the top of the castle. Lady Isabella welcomed me. 'Your cousin will be pleased to see you.'

'And I her,' I said, smiling at Deirdre, who was looking up at me from a stool by the fire, registering the relief of a child who has been left amongst strangers, and whose parent has finally come.

'You look better already,' I said.

'Lady Isabella is kind, and I feel safe here. How long are we to stay?'

'We leave for Carrickfergus tomorrow.' The disappointment registered in her face.

'And Macha?' She looked at her sister-in-law, who was asleep on the bed.

'We must take her with us.'

'Must it be so? Could not they stay here, anonymous? What good could it do to place Sean's child in my grandmother's hands? She can only destroy.' She looked away and into the fire. 'She can only destroy.'

I knelt down in front of her, taking both her hands in my own.

'There will be no more destruction in this family. This child is a chance to end it. Trust me, Deirdre, and believe in this chance.'

'Do you believe God gives us second chances?'

'I believe in His grace. I have known His grace.'

'And what about love? Have you ever loved?'

'I have loved twice.'

She drew a pattern in the ashes. 'It is a sad thing to love twice. What happened to your first love?'

'I had no courage, and was eaten up with selfishness. By the time I realised what I had lost it was too late; she had married another.'

She nodded, as if this came as no surprise to her. 'This family does not know how to love properly.' Then she laughed. 'Apart from Maeve. Maeve truly loved. She loved our grandfather, and poisoned us all because of it. But I think you lie when you talk of a second love. You cannot love a second time.'

'I do, Deirdre, and if I ever manage to leave this country, and if God forgives me my transgressions, I will not lose her.'

'God will not forgive me mine.'

I brushed the hair back from her face; the colour had returned a little to her cheeks, and her eyes were as alive as any I had ever known. 'What transgressions could you have to your account?'

'I have dishonoured myself. I have dishonoured my family.'

'Because you married a man and found you did not love him?'

'I knew at the start I did not love him.'

'And now? Do you plan to go with Cormac?'

She looked up at me as if I had said something that had never occurred to her. 'I do not love Cormac. And anyhow, he will die in the same cause as my father did. He is less free even than Sean was. You know who I love.'

'Yes, I think I do.'

She was silent for a few moments and then spoke to me again. 'Was Grainne happy?'

'My mother?'

'Yes.'

'No. She was not happy.'

'Then there isn't much left to me, is there?'

'There is your brother's child. He will need you.'

A determination I had seldom seen on any human face came into her eyes. 'And I will not fail him. Before God and all who will judge me, I will not fail him.'

I held her to me, feeling her life, her breathing against me, my cousin, my dead brother's sister, my trust.

Darkness was drawing in on the castle as I descended the stairs. What little blue there had been in the afternoon sky retreated in the face of the advancing dark clouds sent from Scotland, a Presbyterian anger at this unsettled land. The tide, pale silver at its eastern edge, was at a low ebb, and quiet, as if it too was waiting, and little stirred across the broad bay of Ballygally.

I found Andrew in the kitchens, talking with Margaret. Again the light in her eyes, the smile on her lips, died at the sight of me. I wondered when I had become the object of such fear and mistrust. She went to attend to a sauce bubbling in a pot. Andrew saw her discomfort, and the cause of it, and affected a brightness all three of us knew him not to possess.

'We are to have fine fare tonight, Alexander. Sir James's table rivals that of your grandmother's house.'

'I hope we can stomach it, after so many days of existing in such simplicity.'

I had not meant my words to come out so harsh, and yet I had had enough of being mistaken in what I was. If I made the girl uncomfortable, it was no fault or concern of mine. Andrew read my mood and gave up on his attempt to lighten it.

He changed his tack. 'How is Macha?'

'She sleeps. Lady Isabella is very attentive to her.'

'And Deirdre?'

I watched Margaret for some reaction, but there was none. So she did not know of Andrew's feelings for my cousin.

Perhaps it was better that way. Women did not always forget these things, and if she and Andrew were ever to be happy, it was a thing she would have to forget.

'Deirdre is . . . calm. She is weary, still, but a little stronger in body.'

We ate late – Sir James did not intend to sleep that night and there was nothing, he insisted, better at keeping a man from sleep than a good dinner eaten late. We had eels in a pickle of vegetables, mopped up with fresh baked bread, and slabs of venison that would have fed twice our number for three days. 'There is nothing like a fine piece of venison, and yet the Irish do not prize it. They reckon nothing worth the praise and eating unless it be slathered in that infernal cheese. I am settled here twenty years and more now, and I have never yet got a taste for it.' He lifted another slab on to his own plate, and to mine, before dousing it in the sauce Margaret had been busy at in the kitchens. 'But this,' he said, inhaling at the ladle with evident pleasure, 'this they do better than any. Do not be mistaken in thinking this sauce to be the muck of the French – a man would need a stomach of iron to survive a month in that country. Smell it.' He proffered me the ladle and I breathed deep. It was as I had thought.

'Whisky?'

'I have it brought down from Bushmills. If something from your own glens can be got now and again, well and good, but there is little that will surpass this.'

James Shaw was a genial host, and free and blunt with his opinions – too free, perhaps, as his wife often cautioned him.

'James! Your tongue will lose you your head one of these days.'

'Ach, hush, woman. Only if I waggle it at someone with a

mind to carry its tales to the wrong ears. And those are not our guests tonight, or I am no judge of my own table.'

And so we talked late into the night, of the state of Ireland, of Ulster, of the state of religion in Scotland and the perils it faced.

'Mark me, the king will have cause to regret his dabblings with prayer books and kneelings. Why does he meddle in something that needs no meddling with? It is that wife of his, no doubt. The French.' And he poured himself another glass of wine to swallow his disgust. 'But I'll tell you, he'll never find a nation more loyal than Scotland, as long as he will leave to us our religion.'

And in such a vein it went on, and I began to understand why Lady Isabella feared for her husband's head.

At intervals, Sir James sent for reports from the walls, and always the answer came back the same: nothing. There was nothing to be seen, from sea or land; nothing coming to the castle. A little after eleven the lady of the house excused herself, and an hour later, when the castle bell tolled midnight, he told us to go to our beds also. And we did, leaving this Scottish soldier, this Presbyterian adventurer, watching the sea, thinking to hold it back alone.

I saw that Andrew did not sleep easy. I would have asked him what troubled him, but I did not think he would tell me. Since we had left Ardclinnis, something between us had been broken. His bible had given him little comfort from the agitation of his mind. I myself had little trouble in surrendering my body and mind to a few hours of respite; I was too tired even to dream.

It had been better that I had dreamt, for I awoke to a chorus of shouts from the walls and through the castle; the

O'Neills had come. Not by sea – they must have returned to Dun-a-Mallaght when they could not find us at Ardclinnis, and now, mounted, they had come overland. They were lined up to the west, torches in their hands, perhaps fifty of them. Swordsmen, musketmen, archers, whose arrow dipped in a flame could, well-landed, turn the castle and its yards to an inferno. Every man around the walls of Ballygally, at the windows and loopholes of the house itself, had his weapon trained on the party which had drawn itself up perhaps a hundred yards away, little more. Murchadh rode forward, his three sons at his side.

'What do you want, O'Neill, that you disturb a Christian's rest?' called Sir James.

'I have come here in peace, for Deirdre FitzGarrett, who is held against her will by Alexander Seaton, her cousin and treacherous murderer of her brother.'

Shaw laughed, a hearty bellow that corralled the place round and must have reached Murchadh with as much power as it had left his throat. 'Against her will? She was released from imprisonment in your bestial lair only three days ago, and her cousin her greatest support. You will prise neither of them from my gates. You had better go tend to your cattle than disturb my sleep or theirs.'

'Seaton is an accused murderer!'

'Seaton is wickedly maligned by an old woman whose mind is so badly mangled by superstition and treachery that she hardly knows what she says.'

'She knows what she says, and he will answer to it.'

'As will he, but to the proper authorities, and in the proper place. Go back to your bogs; you have no business here.'

Cormac detached himself from his father and brothers, and rode closer in beneath the walls of Ballygally than any sane man should have done. Ten muskets now, that I could see, were trained on him.

'Give me Deirdre, and do what you will with the Scotsman; I have no quarrel with him.'

'And I no duty to you. An inch closer, and I'll have your head blown from your body.' Shaw meant it. He was standing now on his own walls, and had raised a musket himself.

Cormac ignored the threat. 'Seaton,' he shouted. 'Seaton, can you hear me? You know I will do her no harm. You know she has need of me. Seaton!'

I took a step closer to the edge of the wall from which Andrew and I watched, but I felt his arm pull me back.

'Don't do this, Alexander. You cannot give her to them.'

'What will become of her in my grandmother's house?'

'A chance, for life.'

'He would give her that chance. At least she would have a position and respect.'

He looked me straight in the eye. 'Alexander, if you let her go with Cormac she will be hanging by the neck from Carrick-fergus Castle before a month is out.'

'You cannot know that.'

'I know it.'

He looked into my eyes, hard, a moment longer, and I stepped back from the edge of the wall, trying to ignore the shouts of my name until the crack of a gun startled Cormac's horse and sent its rider back to join his father. We watched as they conversed a few moments, before wheeling their horses round and retreating to the woods. But they did not leave. Torches glowed amongst the branches of the trees, and then swiftly moving shapes began to emerge from the glen behind us – shapes that were men, unencumbered by munitions or mounts, almost silently jumping burns, scaling rocks, flitting through trees. They had no guns, these men, but swords, or bows on their backs. And for every ten of them, one carried a flaming torch. Within a very little time, the castle was surrounded on three sides, the sea alone offering some chance of escape. And then, as I tried in a desperate way to understand how we might make use of that, a line of boats appeared, snaking down the still water from the west, a dozen men and a burning brazier in each one.

'Oh, dear God!'

James Shaw turned to his wife. 'Get back to the women, Isabella; this is no place for you.'

'We will burn in our beds.'

'Did you hear me, woman?'

He turned to Andrew and myself. 'You, too, should go back. There is nothing you can do here, but these Irish dogs are cunning, and thrive on the ways of the night. If one should find his way undetected into the castle . . . Go inside. Bring the women down to the great hall: you can guard them closely there, and there will be greater chance of egress than from my wife's chamber should the place take light.'

We did not need to be told twice. The noise had woken both Deirdre and Macha, and they were glad to see us. In Macha's eyes was a truly hunted look. She held her hands across her belly, the last defence of her unborn child.

I went to her, put a blanket around her shoulders. 'It is all right. They still do not know about you. I will see that no harm comes to you.'

I had spoken to her in English, but she answered me in Gaelic. 'You can have no knowledge of the brutality of these men, what they can do. For Sean's sake, save his child.' I remembered Michael, lying beaten and blinded by the altar at Bonamargy, and I prayed to God for His mercy on these innocents.

Lady Isabella refused to lie down, but took up a seat by the window in the great hall, watching through the night at the deadly show of light in the woods beyond the castle. A servant had brought rugs and blankets, which we put in front of the hearth. Deirdre and Macha both, in the ways of the Irish that I had come to know, were used enough to sleeping on the ground, with little to cover them, and exhaustion soon won out over anxiety and took them to their sleep. Andrew and I sat on the carved oak chairs at either side of the fire; he watched me intently.

'You have to make your choice, Alexander. The time is coming when we must all make our choice and trust to God.'

'I am here, am I not?'

'But your heart is not entirely.'

'I learned long ago to bridle my heart.'

Nothing more was said between us as the hours of the night advanced, and the candles burned down in their sconces. Margaret tried to persuade her mistress to rest. The older woman shook her head kindly and continued to gaze out of the window, from where salvation or eternity might come.

It was about an hour before dawn that the first of the arrows was launched from the edges of the woods and into the castle yard. It formed a perfect blazing arc in the sky before dipping, assuredly, into the thatched roof of one of the byres. A rush of men and buckets was running for the byre when the second arrow hit – this time landing close to the pond. Ducks and geese screeched horribly and took flight, flapping in the faces of those who sought to douse the arrow in the water. A third arrow came, taking the shoulder of a guard on the inner wall. The man's screams were quickly muffled by the comrade who launched himself at him, flattening him to the ground and putting out the fire. The flames on the roof of the byre had taken hold now, and the whole was ablaze. A chain of men and women passed bucket after bucket from the stream to the flames, while others released and sought to calm the terrified and bellowing beasts. Another arrow came, and found the brewhouse.

I surveyed the scene from the windows. 'There is no way out,' I said.

'No way but surrender,' said Andrew.

Lady Isabella's face was drawn, hardly moving. 'My husband will never surrender.'

I had not planned for such a death as this. I summoned images of Sarah and Zander, as if I could hold them, keep them before my eyes to take me through whatever was now to pass.

'Then we must commit ourselves to the mercy of God.' It was Deirdre, she was on her knees. Macha soon joined her, and I heard the words I had come to know so well over these last weeks, the words that begged intercession from Mary, the holy mother of God. My hand again was at the crucifix at my throat, still there. Andrew watched me carefully, as if waiting to see if I would bend the knee and join them. I fought the urge to do so, and tried to summon in myself the strength and faith that He had given me. I reached up my hand to pull at the chain around my neck, thinking to break it once and for all.

As I felt the cold metal at my fingers, a shout went up from outside, a shout that rose above the clamour of the flames, the sloshing of the water, the terror of the yard. Andrew ran to the window. I was quickly at his shoulder.

'What is happening?'

It was a moment before he was able to make sense, through

the smoke and the last dark before the approaching dawn, of what he was seeing.

'They are leaving,' he said at last. 'Thanks be to God: they are leaving.'

TWENTY-FOUR

A Homecoming

'It was a messenger. On foot. One of my tenants saw him coming over Ballygally Head a little before dawn. He was running like the wind. My man knew it was a native the moment he saw him. By the time he had saddled his horse to go in pursuit, the fellow was almost here. The men on the walls saw him from here – they took aim, but none hit him thank God – or we might all be ashes now.'

We were standing in the burnt-out remains of the inner courtyard of Ballygally Castle, an hour after unknown tidings from the fleet-footed messenger had caused Murchadh and his men to lift their siege and beat a hasty retreat to the north. The fires had all been doused, and what had yesterday been a picture of well-ordered industry was now a blackened and sodden mess. Animals had been calmed, and word had come from the nearby pastures that it was safe to let the beasts out once more.

'It is a miracle, a blessing of God. Only six injured and none killed, and the house still standing. I doubt you will come closer to death without meeting it than you did last night, Mr Seaton.'

'Your hospitality to us has cost you dearly, Sir James.'

'It has cost me nothing that cannot be mended. Fore-knowledge of the events of last night would not have made me refuse you. But I think the time when my hospitality was a protection has waned, and we must get you all to Carrick-fergus before Murchadh has dealt with his other business and returns.'

I was a little uneasy now, at the prospect of leaving Macha in Andrew's care, but there was no option, and to separate would give at least one of us a chance of getting through to Carrickfergus, regardless of the fate of the other. Andrew took time to speak alone with Deirdre before he left, and then came to me. 'Whatever you do, promise me you will not hand her over to Cormac. Give her a chance, at least, to come back to herself. With him she will have none.'

'I will do nothing to put her at risk.' It was not the answer he wanted, but he did not press me for another. I wished him well and gave him my hand, like a man, whereas two days ago I had embraced him as a brother. I turned away, and was back within the castle before the gates had opened. I watched with Deirdre at a window as they left.

'I have driven him away,' she said.

'No. He only goes to get Macha to safety in Carrickfergus. We will meet with them again before nightfall.'

'He will not give the child to my grandmother? Sean's child must be free.'

'We will decide on the safest place for them once we get there, once Sir James has spoken to your grandmother.'

It was as if she was not listening. 'She must not have him,' she said, and continued to watch after Andrew and Macha until the steward's cart disappeared from sight. Lady Isabella tried to send me to my bed, but I told her what was the truth – I could scarcely remember when I had last had more than three hours' sleep, and I feared what visions my mind would conjure for me when I shut my eyes again.

A little before midday Sir James declared that we should set forth soon, or lose the end of our journey to the darkness. Before we had even reached to Olderfleet, we were passed by a troop from the English garrison, heading north, and on the road to Carrickfergus, English soldiers were more in evidence than traders or labourers in the field. Lady Isabella commented upon it.

'Something is afoot.'

'It would appear so,' was her husband's only response.

Deirdre did not appear to notice, but Margaret, who took pains to look after her on the journey, was nervous and unsettled, looking around her all the time, as did the guards Sir James had riding with us.

Little over three miles from our destination, a detachment on the road counselled us to make haste, as word had come to Carrickfergus of a planned Irish rising from the North. They warned us too of two Scots fugitives from justice who had fled Coleraine a week ago, leaving one of their pursuing party paralysed and like to die. Sir James hazarded a glance at me and assured them that he would inform the governor at Carrickfergus should he chance upon such dangerous wretches on the road.

'They are not in the town, of that we are certain, for the party in pursuit of them has searched every inch of it. No, they are in tow somewhere with those damned Franciscans the Earl of Antrim harbours.'

Sir James's views on the Earl of Antrim's loyalties had been made a little too openly and a little too volubly at dinner on the previous evening for his wife's comfort, but out on the road he kept these views to himself, even amongst common soldiers. But it was of no comfort to me to know that the Blackstones had passed this way already, and that further tales of outlawry on my part would have reached Carrickfergus before me.

We approached the town from the Scots Quarter. If I had felt apprehension on leaving Carrickfergus only a week ago, I felt more now, about to re-enter it. Rather than a place of sanctuary and safety, what waited for me behind those walls might be imprisonment, condemnation, death. While Sir James might argue my innocence of involvement in the murder of my cousin, there was nothing he could do against the charges the Blackstones would level against Andrew and me over the injury to their companion, crushed by his horse when Michael shot at them as we fled from Coleraine. And Andrew had entered the town already, with no Sir James to speak for him.

The apprehension, anticipation of some evil to come, that I felt, was in the air all around us as we proceeded down through the Scots Quarter. There was stillness everywhere. A dog barked on the empty street, beasts snorted and jostled for position in the backlands, frustrated at being brought in and tethered so early in the day. Doors were shut; windows, where there were any, were boarded. There was not one human soul to be seen or heard upon the street or from the houses within.

I looked on the mean thatched dwellings that we passed, and thought of the damage that had been done to Ballygally the previous night. Sir James spoke my thoughts.

'The savages will burn everything they have.'

Sir James was well known to the guards, and soon I found myself walking the streets of Carrickfergus in daylight for the first time. A beard of a week's growth and the severe haircut Sir James's barber had given me that morning afforded my only disguise, save the helmet of coarse brown wool and the hood of the short cloak I wore in common with his other men. Once within the gates, he took me aside and indicated two of his men. 'Go now with those two. They will take you to the safe house where you will find Boyd. Tell him we are arrived safely, and purpose to go immediately to your grand-mother's house. Time is pressing. We must get you off the streets before you are seen. Once we have dealt with Maeve I will take you to the castle myself and argue your case there, although only God in His Heaven knows how I am to extricate you from this business at Coleraine.'

This business at Coleraine. How succinctly he put it. Four words to cover a night that had begun for the Blackstones in merriment and anticipation of a play, an entertainment, and ended with their younger son dead under his horse and Andrew and myself fleeing the town in the darkness with the help of renegade priests.

'We should have told you of it, but . . .'

He held up a hand. 'Enough for now. Go and fetch Boyd and the Irish girl that I might get your cousin to her grand-mother's before she collapses. We will meet with you at the marketplace.'

I was able to see Deirdre properly for the first time in several miles now, and it was evident that the news that her father-in-law and his party were also in the town had greatly shaken her. I went closer to her and looked in her face, to make sure that she listened to me. 'It will not be long now, and you will be in a place of safety.'

'No,' she said, looking past me, 'it will not be long now.'

Sir James's men led me up a street behind the tholsel, past the palace of Joymount and on to Back Lane, where a nervous-looking young boy opened the door.

'Where is your father?'

'He is taking his turn on the walls,' answered the boy.

'Are you alone here?'

'No. Yes. You are from Sir James?'

'We are.'

At first I could see no one in the murky living area of the house, and then I was aware of a slight stirring in the corner farthest from the door. It was Macha.

I took a step towards her, my hand outstretched, but she shrank back, her eyes filled with fear; in the near-dark of the interior my disguise was too good. I pulled down my hood and removed the woollen helmet.

'Where is Andrew?' I asked her in her own tongue.

She began to answer, but she was anxious and upset and spoke too quickly; I had to ask her to slow down, so I could translate for Sir James's men.

'Men came, English men, not long after we arrived. A party from Coleraine. They were filthy brutes, I could see it. They only let me alone because this boy's father told them I was his wife. They were looking for you both. Andrew was out in the backland, washing. He heard what was being said and was over the back wall and away before they could even get out there. It was a few hours ago; I have not seen him since.'

The boy confirmed her story. The Englishmen from Coleraine sought us by name – Andrew Boyd and Alexander Seaton. They charged us with the murder of Henry Blackstone, Deirdre's husband's brother.

Andrew knew the town well, but where could he go? He was known everywhere. And his wounds would need attention again soon. There was little I could do for him now save offer up a silent prayer. I bent down towards the girl and this time she did take my hand.

'Come,' I said. 'You are nearly home.'

'I have never been here before,' she said. 'Strange to think it will be my home.'

We went quickly up Back Lane and down North Street to

the marketplace. I had my first proper sighting in daylight of St Nicholas church, and felt a sudden longing to go through its doors, to reaffirm for myself my faith, my Protestant faith, so shaken by my times of sanctuary in other places. I felt against my skin the crucifix, put round my neck at Dunluce and never yet taken off, and recalled to myself with a sweep of nausea that St Nicholas church had been the site of Sean's murder.

Sir James's party was waiting for us in the marketplace, just in front of my grandmother's tower house.

'She will not let you in?' I asked, incredulous.

He smiled. 'The old woman is not as bad as that, do you think? No, I have not yet sought entry. It seemed right that I should wait for you. But where is Andrew Boyd?'

I quickly told him, and his face became troubled. He urged his horse a few steps forward, and taking a halberd from one of his men, banged with it upon the door.

I was not altogether surprised to see my grandmother herself appear on the parapet, Eachan beside her, searching the crowd below for any sign of danger to his mistress.

Sir James looked up. 'I am Sir James Shaw of Ballygally and I bring here to seek sanctuary with Maeve O'Neill their grandmother Deirdre FitzGarrett and Alexander Seaton, and another who is of her kin and has a claim upon her hospitality.'

Maeve stepped closer to the edge of the parapet and narrowed her eyes, but it was evident they were too poor and she could not see us properly. Eachan was also looking, and spoke urgently to my grandmother. She shook her head, and again he spoke urgent words in her ear. Eventually she murmured something to him and he gave orders that we should be let in.

It was strange to enter my grandmother's house from the front, openly, rather than as a thief in the night as I had done on my first arrival in Carrickfergus. And yet then I had been a figure waited for, welcomed; now I came as one reviled. I walked ahead of Sir James, ahead of the two women, with my shorn head and my unkempt beard, into a place that looked the same as it had done the first time I had seen it, but where everything had changed.

They were in the great hall, waiting for us. Maeve did not look at Deirdre, or Macha; she ignored Sir James; she looked only at me.

'You foul thing; you filth. Do you dare to come into my house? Unnatural child of a wanton, ungrateful daughter. You murdered your brother.'

Whether she had intended to shock me by the revelation, I could not tell. 'Grandmother, I . . .'

'You are no grandson of mine. I cast you off! I disavow you! I curse the womb that bore you! That Finn O'Rahilly had only known of you before he laid his curse on me!' Her voice had risen to a shout, and the effort of it winded her. A servant helped her to a seat, and she did something I doubt she had ever done in her life before: she wept. I was about to go towards her, but Sir James stopped me.

'Madam, I knew your husband well these last twenty years. He trusted me and I him. I ask you to trust me now also, when I tell you that your grandson here, Alexander Seaton, did not murder his . . .' he hesitated, looking from Maeve to myself. Neither of us said anything. 'His cousin. He cannot have murdered his cousin in Carrickfergus as you have claimed, for I have it on good authority, that will stand in any court of law, that he spent the whole of that night, from dusk to the next dawn, at Armstrong's Bawn on the road from Ballymena to Coleraine. He was there in the company of Andrew Boyd, a young man of your household whom I know well, and whose word I would trust before almost any other.'

Maeve stared bleakly at her hands.

'And where is Andrew Boyd now?'

Her voice hung heavy with accusation.

I spoke reluctantly. 'I don't know. We know he reached Carrickfergus in safety, but that a party from Coleraine has been searching the town for him and for me. He went into hiding when he heard of it.'

An odd little smile appeared upon her lips. 'From Coleraine. Those English that you entangled us with, Deirdre. Your husband's brother, you know, is dead.' They were the first words she had uttered to her granddaughter since we had entered the house. 'They tell me he did not even have the sense to get out from under his own horse.' And then she laughed, a horrible laugh, quiet, to herself.

Deirdre broke the dreadful silence that followed.

'Can I sit down, Grandmother?'

'You can please yourself; you always did,' said the old woman, her poise gone, but her venom intact.

Sir James, at a loss for anything else, brought Macha forward from where she had been obscuring herself behind him.

'And what trollop is this?' said my grandmother, but before she could say more, Eachan had let out a sound of joy, and gone to Macha, and taken her into his strong, hardy arms. He held her close and wept, a torrent of thanks falling from his lips.

'Blessed be the Holy Virgin, the Holy Mother of God that has brought you here. Mistress,' he said, talking to Maeve, 'this is Sean's wife.'

'Sean had no wife.'

I spoke again. 'Sean was married to this girl by Father Stephen Mac Cuarta of Bonamargy, on the way to Deirdre's wedding. Eachan was there and witnessed. This is your grandson's wife and she is carrying his child.'

Deirdre let out a low groan and crumpled in her chair. Maeve ignored her and looked instead to me, the light that had gone coming back into her eyes. 'How do you know this?'

'Stephen Mac Cuarta himself told me.'

'Mac Cuarta.' Her voice was a mixture of bitterness and sadness. 'He lived while my son died. His robes protected him, I suppose. But he wishes our family well, that cannot be denied. Where is he now? Why is he not here?'

'Because he died two nights ago. He is buried at Ardclinnis.'

'May the Lord have mercy upon his immortal soul,' she murmured. 'He will be a long time in Purgatory.' Then she addressed herself to Macha. 'Come forward, girl, that I might see what my son rejected Roisin O'Neill for.' Macha went towards her, not hesitantly, but surely. She had been told all there was to tell of Maeve by Sean, by Deirdre, yet she had no fear of her, and the old woman liked that. 'What is your family?'

'The Magennises of Down.'

'It cannot be helped, I suppose.' Maeve walked around her slowly, looking in her eyes, feeling her arm, the width of her hips. 'You are strong. He always knew how to pick a good mare.' And then she came to her belly, and placed her hand on the swell beneath Macha's woollen dress. 'The child will come soon. You have eaten well?'

Macha nodded.

'You have prayed for a safe delivery?'

Again the girl affirmed that she had.

'And for a son?'

'I know the child will be a boy.'

'How do you know it?'

'Julia MacQuillan told me. And it was confirmed by Finn O'Rahilly.'

At the mention of the poet's name, Maeve recoiled from the girl, her hand dropping to her side.

'When did you see him?' I asked.

'After Sean left for Scotland, when I was with the brothers at Bonamargy. I feared for Sean, and I wanted O'Rahilly to bless my child, so I went to see him one afternoon. But he said he could not. He only told me it would be a boy, and worthy of his father. I went on my way. I did not tell Stephen, for he did not trust the poet.'

Maeve seemed a little more at ease, Deirdre a little less so now.

'And he will be worthy of his father, and of his grandfather, and of all the generations that came before, and gloried in the name of O'Neill.'

'No!' Deirdre had stood up. 'You will not do it to him! You will not steal his life as you did those of my father and my brother, to fuel your own fantasy! Those days are gone, Grandmother. Please, I beg of you, let Sean's child be.'

Maeve afforded her a look of ice. 'Look you to your own life, that you do not end it as his mother did.' This indicating me. 'And go down on your knees to pray God for widowhood, pray that your husband might soon join his dead brother, that He would give you another chance. Now get to your bedchamber and make yourself decent. It cannot be long before Cormac O'Neill rides into this town at his father's side, and you will not refuse him in my house.'

I tried to go after my cousin, but was stopped by my grandmother.

'You have done all you will do in this house. Do not think to set your foot over its door again.'

'Grandmother, will you not believe me? I did not kill Sean.' I looked in appeal to Eachan, but he was already guiding Macha to what had been Sean's chamber and would now be hers: he had no further interest in me. Maeve made to follow them, pausing only for a moment to answer me.

'If Sean were not dead, what you have done now would have killed him anyway.'

I could have torn my hair in frustration. 'Woman, I do not know what you mean! Tell me, what have I done?'

'You have betrayed our cause. Tell me why, if you were with Stephen Mac Cuarta, are you not with his people yet? Do not tell me that he did not ask you to join with them. Why have you brought Deirdre back here, away from Cormac, from Murchadh, whose protection she was in? Why do you come here, with this Scot from Ballygally, when I know, and all the town knows, that messengers rode yesterday from Ballygally to the governor of the castle here, to warn the English of the planned uprising?'

I began to stammer. 'I told no one, I . . .'

'If not you, who? You have betrayed everything your cousin lived for, and I pray God that you may soon drown in your own blood.' And with these words, my mother's mother sent me from her house.

All the short way from the FitzGarrett tower house to the castle, I asked myself the same question, 'If not you, who?' but there could be only one answer, and I knew that already. It had been Andrew. Andrew, who had listened in the night to my talk with Father Stephen while I had thought he slept; Andrew, whom I had found deep in conversation with Sir James soon after our arrival at Ballygally. I felt I had been betrayed. Yet why should I feel that? He had done no more than any honest citizen of the town of Carrickfergus would have done; he had done the duty of any honest subject of the king. And yet . . . And yet . . . He had betrayed Stephen, and Michael, and Sean, and Cormac, and me. He had not told me what he was going to do; he did not trust me. But I could not feel betrayed in that. He was right not to trust me. While I had refused to fight for them, I could not have gone against them. I could not have said, even now, that I would not have tried to get a warning to Cormac, somehow. Alexander Seaton: a man of no principles, of no commitment. Such a man cannot be betrayed, and yet I felt abandoned by Andrew, cast adrift and left behind.

TWENTY-FIVE

Carrickfergus Castle

As we approached the gatehouse of the castle I was gripped by a cold apprehension, for it was in this massive, terrible foothold of the English Crown on foreign soil that I would see my name cleared or damned.

Archers and musketmen patrolled the parapet and the overhang beyond it. The occasional glint of a weapon could also be seen through arrow slits set in the walls. Unarmed, my head protected only by a hood, and dressed in the clothing of one of Sir James's servants, I felt exposed and certain that for every three weapons I saw edge through the walls, one was trained on me. But on Sir James making himself known, the bridge was let down and first one portcullis and then the other lifted. At the gateway I glanced upwards with some trepidation, mindful of Sean's tales of the gruesome fates of many who'd passed beneath the murder hole above my head, but there were no bowmen there, no soldiers readying boiling oil to pour over me. A moment later I was within the outer ward of Carrickfergus Castle; I should have felt safe there, but I did not.

A soldier escorted us to an upper room in the western tower of the gatehouse, where the constable was greeted by Sir James as an old friend.

'Ronald, I see you are much busied.'

'Busied? I have not slept since we received your letters, and neither has half the garrison. I have sent troops of men to hunt down O'Neill, and have had to make the castle ready for attack should we fail to find him. And this,' he said, looking beyond Sir James to where I stood, slightly stooped beneath the doorway, 'this, I am assuming, is Richard FitzGarrett's other grandson.'

It was the first time since my arrival in Ulster that anyone had identified me by the name FitzGarrett – it was always O'Neill: Sean's cousin, Grainne's son, above all Maeve's grandson, but to the constable, I was FitzGarrett, and that could only have been because Sir James had announced me as such. It was, I suspected, a shrewd move, and it gave me some hope.

'Well, James, there has been a stir and a half here about this one, and Boyd also since the Blackstones thundered down from Coleraine. You know Matthew Blackstone's younger son is dead, and Seaton here and Boyd said to be the cause?'

Sir James chose his words carefully. 'I had heard something of it, but have not had the time to get to the bottom of it.'

'And no more do I, my friend. What do you say, Mr Seaton? Did you and Boyd leave Coleraine with the shouts of murderers in your ears?'

'We did, but we murdered no one. We . . .'

He held up a hand. 'I have not the time. James, do you vouch for him or not?'

My countryman looked at me carefully. 'I vouch for Andrew Boyd, and he for Seaton here.'

'Then that will have to do. I leave him under your guard until I can attend to the matter. See you don't let him out of your sight. Now, your wife has been spirited away by my own dear lady. You will find them in our quarters somewhere, gossiping even now, no doubt.'

As we were about to leave his room, the constable called us back. 'James. Where is Andrew Boyd?'

'I do not know. He came safe to the town, but then went into hiding from the Blackstones.'

'Then we must pray we find him before they do. Matthew Blackstone is as a bull enraged. If he finds him or Seaton here, he has sworn to tear them limb from limb.'

Our escort took us to the inner ward, and finally the castle keep itself, having first checked with his constable that he was sure I was not to be warded in the sea tower prison instead. He made little attempt to mask his disappointment when told I was not to be, and led us away mumbling that I had 'the very face of a rebel'.

It was evident that my company was not looked for in the great hall of the keep, and I went gladly to the small chamber next to the basement kitchen, where Sir James's men were quartered and where I could be watched. Margaret brought me some food and drink. As had become her way, she avoided my eye, and spoke little to me.

In another place, in another circumstance, I would have left her to her silences. I had little interest in pursuing the society of those who did not wish mine. But we were bound by deaths, this girl and I, and bound by friendship with another.

'Margaret, I wish you would look at me.'

She lifted her eyes but lowered them again. 'Why?'

As was often the case when speaking to women, I found the words that came to my mouth inadequate. 'Because I am Andrew's friend, or have been, and I know that you care for him. There is no cause for hostility between us; I wish you would trust me.'

'You do not know what you are talking about.'

'Margaret, I killed no one. I never lifted a hand to my cousin, and I killed no one at Coleraine.'

'I care nothing for Coleraine or what you did there.'

'You cannot think I had a hand in the murder of Sean? I swear to you, I loved him as a brother.' As a brother. I breathed deep. 'Margaret, he was my brother.'

She looked at me now. She did not flinch, or turn away, but looked at me as if I were at last other than she had thought me to be. 'Your brother?'

'He never knew it; I never got to call him so, but he was my brother, for we shared a mother. Sean O'Neill FitzGarrett was my brother, and you who have also lost a brother must know what I feel.'

She stared at me a few moments longer. 'Do not think to tell me what I know, or feel.' She left and I knew, however well I might wish her, that she would never accept friendship from me.

I was disturbed only by the cooks coming in and out of the room for stores. What passed for my bed was an arrangement of sacks on the floor, but it was better than what I had laid myself down upon on several nights just past, and I slept with some ease. At some hour well before dawn I became aware of a stirring of activity, and anxious voices in the kitchens. The door of the storeroom was opened and light brought in.

'He's still here,' said a harsh voice, whose owner I could not see.

'Then see that you keep him there. He is not to be allowed near the other one. Who knows what plots they have on hand.'

'The constable thinks the other had himself caught simply to get to where this one is.'

'They are sly, every one of them, and it may be so.'

I struggled to my feet as the man closed the door again and the storeroom became dark once more. I tried to open the door, but it had been locked on the outside. I banged on it, provoking curses from my guard and shrieks of terror from the women in the kitchens.

'Who have you taken? Who is it? Tell me who you have brought here!'

The door was wrenched open, and an angry face leered at me out of the darkness. 'Hold your tongue and your noise while you still can: you'll get to sing your song soon enough.' He shoved me backwards into the storeroom and I heard the bolt brought to again.

And so I waited through the night, as the castle settled in on itself again, and it waited too. The servants in the kitchens, the dogs in the hall, returned to their sleep, but like the guards that walked the parapets above us and the curtain wall around us, I did not sleep. There was no attack, or sound of attack; no noise of skirmishing or fighting, no sounds of fire or panic from the town. Who had they brought in?

Perhaps two hours later I heard Sir James's voice in the kitchen, and soon my door was opened again and the light brought in. Sir James took the candle, but ushered the guard away. He sat down on a flour sack and, with little ceremony, got to his point.

'What do you know of Cormac O'Neill?'

Cormac? I had not thought it would be Cormac.

'Cormac O'Neill . . . I . . . he is the son of Murchadh O'Neill.'

'Murchadh, yes, who held you against your will, and pursued you to my home, which he then set alight.'

'Yes.'

'And Cormac, his eldest son, pursued your cousin Deirdre to my home, and begged that we should turn her over to him.'

'Yes.'

'This same Cormac who, I am informed, given the death of your cousin Sean, is designated leader of the planned rising.'

I did not ask him how he knew. Andrew: Andrew had told him everything.

'If you know it all, there can be no need to ask me.'

'Can there not? Then there is no need to ask why Cormac O'Neill should take pains to exonerate you from any wrong-doing in the death of Henry Blackstone?'

I was dumbfounded. There was nothing sensible I could say. The words that came to my mind were 'Cormac wasn't there,' but some sense of self-preservation stopped me.

'Well, have you no answer?'

I shook my head. 'I have none. I do not know why Cormac would do that.'

'But he has. He has sworn this night before the constable and myself and the governor's deputy that you and Andrew Boyd played no part in the murder of Henry Blackstone; that when they reached Coleraine with your grandmother's false accusations, you left the town to come back here and clear your name, that you fell in with a Franciscan priest, a consort of the rebel Stephen Mac Cuarta, who caused Blackstone's death and brought you to Murchadh O'Neill. Is this the truth?'

Almost, it was almost the truth. But why should Cormac have chosen to tell it? Why should he offer to myself and Andrew a way out of our predicament where before there had been none? 'Yes,' I said, 'it is the truth. Can I see him?'

'The governor thought you might make such a request. You can see him, for ten minutes, and not alone. Come, we will do it now, before the dawn of a new day brings its own troubles upon us.'

The embers in the kitchen hearths still glowed. A kitchen boy, curled up with a hound before the hearth, stirred as we passed, but everyone else slept on. Out in the courtyard, guards were waiting for us and torches lit our way to the middle ward and then out towards the sea tower, jutting from the walls to the north and west, musket men guarding it. We entered by the guardroom at the basement, and a ladder was put up to the cell above. I heaved myself through the hatch and into a dank, foul-smelling room with little light or furnishing save a few sodden rushes on the floor. The place stank of seaweed and rot.

Cormac was in the corner, hunched, his feet shackled, his wrists bound. He did not look up, and I watched him a moment, feeling no triumph in the reversal of our roles.

'Cormac.'

His handsome face broke into a momentary smile, then faded. 'Have they taken you, too?'

'I am not a prisoner, at least . . . I do not think so.'

'Then I am glad of it.'

'What happened?'

'They took me last night, after I entered the town.'

'Alone?'

'My father and brothers have gone to Dun-a-Mallaght. Others of our men have gone to Tullahogue; we cannot wait any longer for Stephen's help from abroad.'

'Stephen is dead,' I said.

'I know. We found his grave.'

'His great fear was that your father would be precipitate.'

'My father has waited twenty years. Those who talked of helping us have had long enough.'

'And you think Murchadh will come for you?'

Cormac laughed, a low laugh with little humour in it. 'They will hang me before my father is halfway to his horse. I won't see the sun reach its height in the sky today, nor go down in the sea again.' It was a statement of fact, and I did not attempt to argue with him.

'But why did you come into the town on your own?'

'I was coming for her.'

For Deirdre. Of course.

'Did you get as far as my grandmother's house?'

'I was in sight of it, almost within the shelter of the door, when the mob of Coleraine, with her husband and his father at its head, came on me. To be caught by such as these. It will be a wonder if the hangman gets his rope around my neck before I die of shame.'

'Cormac, she will not go back to her husband.'

'I knew that already. But who is there to protect her now? Your grandfather, Sean, both gone. You will leave this place as soon as you are able, I know that, and even the servant Boyd is dead.'

The words reached me from a nightmare. Andrew was dead. He could not be found, because he was dead. The knowledge sank like a stone on my stomach. 'Was it you or the Blackstones?'

He looked at me strangely. 'Was what?'

'Was it you or the Blackstones that killed him?'

'What are you talking about? He died at Bonamargy. We saw his gr—' And then his face broke into a broad, unaccustomed smile. 'By God. Well, by God! Were we taken in by that? You have Sean's guile, Seaton.'

'It was not I, but the friars who thought of it. They had the grave dug before I ever got there.'

'And where did you hide him? We searched every inch of that place, apart from the old nun's cell.'

I said nothing.

'He was in there?' Again he laughed. 'My father said he would rather pass through the gates of Hell than cross that threshold. Well! The old woman has nerve. But I know it was

Mac Cuarta we found at Ardclinnis. It is for the best. He would not have liked what he might have lived to see.'

I remembered Stephen telling me of the debacle of the planned rising of 1615, ended before it was begun by the drunkenness and swagger of its leaders. It had taken him and others thirteen years to persuade powers abroad that the Irish could be trusted again. With Sean, with Cormac, he might have been right, but with Murchadh? Cormac was right – it was as well Stephen had not lived to see what was going to happen now. But it was not Murchadh's swagger that had ended it for them this time: this time the English had learned of their plans through Sir James Shaw. Through Andrew Boyd. Through me.

It was as if Cormac could read my thoughts. 'And Boyd lives, you tell me?'

'I do not know. I have not seen him since Ballygally. He came into Carrickfergus a few hours before me, but has not been seen since.'

'He is not at your grandmother's?'

'Not when I was last there. But I cannot go back. She knows now I did not murder Sean, but I do not think she can forgive me that I live while he is dead.'

'And you did not murder him? I am a dead man: you can tell the truth to me.'

'It is the truth. Why should I have wanted Sean dead? That I might take his place? That I might have what is his? I *have* a life.' My voice was rising and I could hear the guard at the ladder. 'I had a life, and I do not want his.'

He tried to reach a hand towards me, but the bindings stopped him. 'It is all right. I believe you, for what such credence is worth. And you do not know who murdered Sean?'

I was losing patience. 'Cormac, who else could it have been but your father? Who else had cause to want him dead?'

'It was not my father,' he said quietly. 'He never left Maeve's house that whole night.'

'Then who? Who did?'

'Ach! How should I know? Half the country was in the house. How could anyone keep note of comings and goings?' He grew angry in his frustration. He might as well have said, 'How could I have noticed anyone else, when I could look at no one but Deirdre?'

'And Deirdre did not come into any danger? She did not go after him?'

'No! She did not go after him. Deirdre was unwell; she had been distraught since O'Rahilly's appearance the night before. She left the hall only to rest. This has nothing to do with Deirdre.' And then I began to see it, through his vehemence, through his anger, through his desperation; I saw the reason for his desire to believe that I had killed Sean, for his anger on being questioned on the events of that night, for his determination to get Deirdre away from Carrickfergus, to keep her hidden away: Cormac feared that my cousin, the woman he loved, had murdered her brother.

He looked directly at me. 'You must take care of her now.'

'You cannot think she murdered him.'

'No. But she is so lost I . . . You must take care of her now. I have done what I could to clear your name over Henry Blackstone's death. Keep yourself clear of further trouble.' That was why he had done it: so that there might be someone to watch over her when he was gone.

He said something in Gaelic that I did not understand. I do not think he had meant me to hear, but I asked him to repeat it.

'She is my Deirdre of the Sorrows. Did you never hear of Deirdre of the Sorrows?'

'No.'

'A long time ago, so the bards have it, a child was born whose name and fate had been decreed before she ever left the womb. She would be called Deirdre, and so great would be her beauty that it would be the ruin of Ulster, tearing the kingdom asunder and resulting in the death of three brothers, its finest warriors. As she grew, all that had been predicted came to pass – Deirdre was indeed beautiful; she was to marry a king, an older man whom she did not love, but she fell in love instead with Naoise, a handsome young warrior with whom, with the help of his two brothers, she eloped. The king pursued and harried them, and finally captured them by an act of treachery. The kingdom was ripped asunder by discord, and the girl's lover and his two brothers put to death.' He looked away from me. 'Your cousin is my Deirdre of the Sorrows. She always has been.'

'I will take care of her,' I said. 'But you should know: I would have done it anyway. There is something, though, that I want from you in return.'

He raised an eyebrow in question.

'Tell me who laid the curse on my family.'

He was weary now, and longing, I think, for me to be gone. 'Finn O'Rahilly laid the curse on your family.'

'At whose behest?'

'Does it matter, now?'

'It matters to me.' I asked him again. 'Do you know who laid the curse on my family?'

'What did the poet tell you?'

'He told me nothing.'

'He said nothing to you; he did not speak?'

'He spoke to me, but he refused to tell me who had commissioned him in this work; he seemed to think he retained some remnant of honour in doing so.'

'Then perhaps he did. You might follow his example.'

'It was the curse that brought me over here, and before I leave this place – if, God willing, I ever leave this place – I will know who is behind it.'

'And if such knowledge harms you?'

'I must know it anyway.'

'Then think on his words, if you must, but you will call down upon yourself whatever griefs may follow.'

I nodded and turned to the hatch, ready to descend from this freezing, miserable place to the world of free men.

'Do one thing more for me, Seaton: tell her goodbye. And tell her I would have loved her better than any man who has walked this earth.'

Cormac O'Neill had finished with me now. And whatever dreams he might have had, they too were finished: he might have been a hero, in other times.

Sir James was waiting for me outside, talking with the guard. 'The stench in that place would make a man vomit. You have finished your business with O'Neill?'

'Yes, it is finished.'

'A better man than his father, they say.' He was awkward a moment, but it passed. 'Ah well, we must run with the tide, and if we do not, we get caught. The constable wishes to see you. I have spoken up for you as far as I am able. For the rest, you must shift for yourself. Also, he has news for you of a sort you may not like. If that is the case, I counsel you to keep your misliking of it to yourself.'

The constable was waiting for us in a state of evident agitation.

'He has been to see O'Neill? And?'

'Nothing of substance. Some talk of the FitzGarrett girl, and their nonsense of poets, little more.'

We had kept our voices low, and the guard had been able to hear little.

The constable turned his eyes on me. 'The matter of your cousin's murder is unresolved, but witnesses at Armstrong's Bawn have spoken for you, and of that, at least, you are clear now.'

'I have always known I was clear of that atrocity.'

'What you know and what you are called to answer for may not always be the same thing.' He looked at me silently for a moment, before returning to his papers. 'It is not usual, you understand, that I take the word of a professed rebel over that of a settled Englishman. And yet there are reasons why I am prepared to accord some faith to the words of Cormac O'Neill in the matter of the killing of Henry Blackstone. I have considered that it might be in O'Neill's interest, if you are of his mind, to have you free to roam and communicate with his father, but the tale he tells seems likely enough. I have decided to allow you liberty, within the town but no further. Should you take it into your head to leave Carrickfergus there will be a patrol of my men on your tail with orders to show no leniency. Do you understand?'

'I understand.' I had hardly known a moment's freedom since I had set foot in this country. To be allowed the liberty of the town was an unimaginable boon.

But the constable had not finished. 'You have not asked why I should take O'Neill's word over Blackstone's. Perhaps you already know.'

I suspect from my face he registered that I had no idea what he meant.

He hesitated and looked to Sir James, who nodded for him to go on. 'Andrew Boyd, under the supervision and instruction of your grandfather for some years now, has been an agent of the king in these parts.'

He'd as well have told me Andrew was an agent of the Pope. I did not believe him, and looked from one to the other for some explanation.

'Your grandfather was one of the most trusted of the Old English subjects of the Crown in Ireland. Despite his marriage to your grandmother, the treachery of his son, and his clinging to the old religion, he was never anything other than a true and loyal servant of the king. When King James of his grace gave his blessing to the plantation of our northern counties, he had great need of such men, and your grandfather's trading connections made him the ideal man for keeping an eye on the new merchants and planters in the North. There have been many others, of course, but few so well established as Richard FitzGarrett. As age overtook him he turned to his late steward's son, who had grown up in his house, to aid him in this invaluable work.'

I had heard of such things, of course, but I could not believe it of the old man whose hand I had briefly held just over a week ago, or of the companion of my trials in the days since then.

'You wish me to believe that my grandfather used Andrew Boyd to spy on his own wife and grandson?' I could not keep the anger out of my voice.

The constable was unmoved. 'Cool your passions and *listen*. Richard FitzGarrett was employed to report upon the planters, the new English settlers of Coleraine and Londonderry. He did from time to time transmit information about Murchadh to the king, but there were others whose primary function was to do that. Many of the planters who have gone to the escheated counties from England have become duplicitous, greedy. They think not of the higher purpose of the plantation, which is to civilise these parts with men of our own speech and religion, to break the dependency of the Irish on their kin, and to bring them under our laws. Some of these planters aim only at their own profit, plunder the rivers, denude the forests; they keep their workers ill-supplied and ill-paid, so that many of the best craftsmen will not come. Worse, they lease great portions of the land with which they have been entrusted not to decent English Protestants, or even Scots, but to the native Irish who will pay the highest rents for lands they once thought their own. Under such circumstances, the plantation will fail. And it has been getting worse of late, for the planters are falling out amongst themselves, bickering over their rights and sending conflicting tales to the king. Men like Andrew Boyd, paid by the Crown and with no interest in the plantation themselves, or like Sir James here, a loyal campaigner of long standing, have become more and more important for the gathering of intelligence to be sent back to London.'

I looked to Sir James. 'And my grandmother, Sean, Deirdre – they knew nothing of Andrew's activities?'

'Do you think your grandmother would have had him in the house a moment after she knew of it? And as to Sean – if he had known of it, Andrew Boyd would not have lived to draw another breath.'

I sought to defend my cousin. 'No, Sean wouldn't . . .' but the constable stopped me.

'Your cousin was in league with Murchadh O'Neill. What country is it you think you have come to? Have you learned nothing of it yet? In this place, men have to make choices. There is no room for nobility in friendship that will compromise a man's loyalty. I do not doubt your cousin was a man of honour – indeed, I know him to have been so, for all his faults – but he could only have one loyalty, and that loyalty was not to the king. He would not have waited for word from

Murchadh or Cormac: he would have slit Andrew Boyd's throat himself had he known.'

And Deirdre? How much of it might Deirdre have known? There could be no doubt now that Andrew had reported to Sir James all he had heard – where? At Armstrong's Bawn, as I'd thought he slept, drugged? At Dunluce, between the priests? But no, he had been too far gone in his injury, and even I had been able to make out little that was said there. He had not been with me to Kilcrue, to the Cursing Circle, where Finn O'Rahilly had told me little enough anyway. He had not been to Dun-a-Mallaght, but how much had I told him of what had passed there? How much had he seen and understood of what passed at Bonamargy? But it didn't matter, for he had been at Ardclinnis, and as he had not hidden from me himself, he had heard every word that had passed between Stephen and me on that last night. Andrew Boyd knew everything about the planned rising that I knew myself, and now everyone in it was being hunted down by the English authorities. But what was there for him to tell of Deirdre? And Macha? Macha, who carried Sean's child.

'Is my family to be arrested?'

'Do you think they ought to be?'

The constable had talked of loyalty, of choices: he had mistaken the one I'd made. 'They should be left in peace.'

He appraised me a while. 'For the time being, they will be, for I have enough on my hands with tracking down Murchadh's rabble, and trying to get MacDonnell to deal with these accursed Franciscans of his. By God, I'll hang the lot of them if I can. And then there are the Blackstones.'

'Cormac told you what happened to their son,' I said carefully.

'It's not that business I'm talking about. When Boyd was in

Coleraine, he collected documents proving Matthew Black-stone's son Edward, your cousin's husband, has been avoiding customs, having secret landings and sailings of goods from creeks and bays along the coast, outside the jurisdiction of Londonderry or Coleraine. We had our suspicions, but he over-reached himself when he intrigued to bring in weapons for the rebels, all for profit.'

The avoidance of customs, the secret landings, I could believe, for such things were common enough near any major port, but this last, this bringing in of weapons for enemies of the king, could have one name only: treason.

I cleared my throat. 'He was dealing with Murchadh?'

'Not Murchadh: Blackstone was too closely watched; the only connection he had with the rebels was through your family. He was dealing with someone, but it was not Murchadh.'

'You think Sean?'

'That is not our information.'

'You cannot think Deirdre had a hand in it?'

He shook his head. 'She has always made her sympathies clear. She has never been suspected of favouring rebellion.'

'Then who?'

'Who is left?'

Maeve. Only Maeve. Ready at last to play her own part in the story of the O'Neills. 'My grandmother.' My voice was flat. For all she had done to me and to others that I cared for, I could not wish her the fate that would befall her should she be found a rebel against the king. But yes; Sean had told me how she'd raged against Deirdre's marriage into the Blackstones, then gone into an unaccustomed silence on the matter. I recalled his words now, and wondered just how much Sean had known about her dealings with them: 'in the end I think she may have come to believe that it was in her interests to let the match go ahead in any case.' She had not gone to Coleraine with Deirdre to make preparations for a wedding she had no interest in: she had gone to buy guns.

The constable sighed. 'We believe so, but we have not the evidence, and to take one of her age and standing in for . . . questioning' – he had not meant questioning; I knew what he had meant. 'To take her in for questioning without evidence would have caused more uproar than I have the men to deal with.'

I straightened a little at this, sensing some hope. 'And what have you got?'

'We have the papers Andrew Boyd received at Coleraine, sent from London, detailing Blackstone's contraband shipment of weapons and when and how they were to be landed.'

'The crates of slate,' I said, almost to myself. Under my own eyes, Matthew Blackstone had taken delivery of the guns they were to sell to my grandmother. And under his eyes had been landed the very letters that would condemn him, 'and the Madeira.'

Sir James raised a good-humoured eyebrow. 'I believe a cask of that sort played its part. The papers were sealed in an internal compartment, with no damage to the liquid goods either, I am glad to say. It is a blessing on a man of fine tastes that these coopers know their trade.'

'And that is why the Blackstones are so keen to hunt Andrew down.'

The constable nodded.

'But Andrew does not have the papers. I am certain of it. I saw him half-drowned, stripped, treated and clothed all on the night of our flight from Coleraine: he had no papers with him.'

'He knows better than to carry such papers on him. Shortly after the cask was landed, he checked its contents. Within an hour it was in the hands of another of our agents there, a man very close to the centre of Blackstone's operations . . .'

'The master of the brickworks,' I said.

'I cannot say. The man is still in the field. Let us say simply that within another hour, that cask was on the back of a cart of goods and on its way to me at Ballygally.'

I marvelled at the ingenuity of it, and at how easily duped I had been, I who had suspected nothing. 'So, you had much news to convey to the castle here.' The news of English treachery contained in the letters, the word of the coming rising, out of Andrew's own mouth.

'Much. Andrew Boyd has saved many English lives, and Scots. Not just in the towns like Coleraine. Londonderry and Carrick-fergus, but out on the plantations, in the bawns. Like the one in which you yourselves spent the night.'

'Armstrong's Bawn?'

The constable nodded. 'There were rumours that Franciscan agents were infiltrating the settlements, gathering intelligence in preparation for the planned attacks. Andrew was able to verify this for us.'

And so it had been no great work of coincidence that saw Andrew and me put up for the night in the very bawn where Stephen Mac Cuarta was gathering his information in the guise of an Irish baker. Andrew had indeed saved many lives, but how many Irish lives had he betrayed? Would he have betrayed me, had I answered Stephen differently that last night at Ardclinnis? I knew that answer already. One choice, one loyalty, as the constable had told me.

I had heard enough, and asked if I might rest awhile again

in the kitchen storeroom before trying again at my grandmother's house to make my peace.

'Rest here as long as you wish, but, after all that I have told you here, you cannot go to your grandmother's house.'

I returned wearily to my sacking bed, seeking nothing more than blissful oblivion.

Sleep came, but the sought-for oblivion did not. I knew myself to be standing on the shore beneath the castle, looking across the water to Scotland, from where voices I knew I could not hear were calling to me: Sarah, Jaffray, my father, little Zander. I kept trying to step into the water, to go to them, but a hand held tight to my wrist, pulling me back. It was my grandmother. She pointed with her other hand to some shapeless thing in the water, some shapeless thing in a white shift, and with my mother's flowing black hair. Deirdre and Roisin were on either side of the thing, trying to pull it up, while my grandmother intoned again and again in my ear: 'Better for you she had drowned. Better for you she had drowned.'

I didn't know when the note was pushed under the door; I didn't know who had left it. No one in the kitchens knew: they all denied having seen anyone. I told them it was of no matter when they started to wonder about calling a guard, and went back to my resting place to look at it again.

Alexander, for the love of God and our friendship, meet me tonight, at seven, in the church of St Nicholas. Tell no one, if you value my life.
Andrew

It was not his usual careful hand, but something more hurried and scrabbled. A man in fear of his life does not take as much care over his letters as he does when setting a line of accounts. I went back out to the kitchen and threw the paper into the fire.

TWENTY-SIX

Chichester's Tomb

I had been so much in my own company, in hiding places, watching, listening, waiting, that I craved noise, hubbub, light. I felt a desire to walk the streets openly, to hear the laughter of others.

As I went down into the town, towards the marketplace, I could see lights blazing in the windows of the FitzGarrett tower house. I had promised Cormac I would look after Deirdre, but I knew with a certainty that my grandmother would not allow me entry to her house, and the constable had warned me away from there anyway. Who was there in that place now who would care for her? Maeve had barely looked at her once she had understood who Macha was and what her condition meant, and Eachan was not the man to treat my cousin's fragile soul. 'Deirdre of the Sorrows' Cormac had called her. I was not sure I understood what he meant. Her husband might be in there even now – pleading with her, intriguing with Maeve. I had not the time to concern myself with the Blackstones tonight – wherever they might be in the town, they would be joining Cormac O'Neill in the castle prison soon enough.

Much of the air of apprehension that had cloaked Carrick-fergus yesterday had lifted; word of Cormac's capture, and the disarray of the rebels had begun to circulate in town and countryside and people were going about the usual business of their lives. The marketplace, the scene of so many entertainments for me as I had watched from my incarceration in my grand-mother's house, was cleared, business for the day being finished, and quiet. The life of the town now was behind doors and walls, in taverns and houses up winding lanes and darkened back streets, where families and companionship and friendship might be found. There was safety in these streets, up those lanes, where people simply lived and did not dedicate their lives to plot or policy, revenge and unattainable dreams. Between the uncertainties of the sea on one side and the unknowable expanse of Ulster stretching out in the darkness beyond the walls, there was the possibility of something I would have recognised as normality.

But it was not yet time for me to enter back into that world, and I turned my steps up the narrow street behind my grand-mother's house and towards St Nicholas church. The slate-grey sky of the day was giving way to dusk, and so little light escaped from windows or doors in this part of town that I found it difficult to see my way once I entered the churchyard. A light breeze had got up, and dry leaves were swirling around the paths, paving and gravestones. I wondered if any of my own forebears were buried here, and if they watched me now. It was difficult to cast such superstition from my mind as I made my uncertain way between tombs and headstones that seemed to rise up from the ground and lean towards me. The nocturnal stirrings of the churchyard made my heart beat faster. Bats swooped from the trees and from the eaves of the roof. I pulled my hood up against them, these messengers of the coming darkness, manifestations of the night. The wind caused the occasional creaking amongst the near-bare branches, and I was glad to reach the portal of the church, where the merest sliver of light edged the not-quite-shut door within the porch. I hesitated now; for the last few days, churches had been places of sanctuary, places of hiding, places of brutality: I did not know what might await me here. For all his secretiveness, his duplicity, I could not believe Andrew meant me harm, but I think I knew then I had been foolish in telling no one of the contents of the note. It was too late for these thoughts – a bell nearby started to toll the hour of seven and I pushed open the door of the church.

Inside the porch, all was darkness, only the faintest glow of light emanating from the nave, allowing me to find my way up the steps and under the stone archway into the church proper. There was not a sound anywhere save my own foot-falls echoing in the vast building, and the creaking, high above, of the roof beams in the wind. I called out his name, but my call found no response and, in the gloom, I could see no sign of Andrew anywhere.

I made my way up the nave towards the chancel. What shapes my straining eyes could make out were large, solid, inanimate – the preacher's lectern, the stalls of the choir and, at the very far end, the altar itself. I reached the crossing where the transepts cut nave and chancel, and saw, through a gap in the carved wooden screen, that there was a light, a single candle, burning at the end of the aisle to my left. I called Andrew's name again, and this time the silence that returned it seemed deeper. Slowly, I ascended the steps up to the aisle and began to walk towards the glimmering light. The sound of my boots on the tiled floor was unnaturally loud in my ears, and I could hear my own clothing rustle as if the wind were blowing through them. Every stirring, every noise in the place was emanating from me, and yet I knew that I was not alone. And I knew now where I was going: up ahead of me, rising out of the darkness in marble and alabaster, was the monument above Chichester's tomb, that ornate manifestation of man's earthly pride. I had been called to the altar upon which my cousin's life blood had run and his dream of Ireland perished.

I reached out my hand and touched the creamy stone: it was pure and smooth and clean. Sir Arthur Chichester, late governor of Carrickfergus and Lord Deputy of Ireland, and his wife, Letitia, praying in effigy over the body of their baby son. I read the epitaphs carved into the stone beside them, of how Chichester had made the land flourish in peace, how he had subdued the wildest rebels, and through justice, gained an honoured name. 'Now though he in heaven with angels be, Let us on earth still love his memory.' I remembered what Sean had told me of Chichester's justice, his road to peace – that he had burnt the homes of the Irish, destroyed their crops to render them starving, and slaughtered the people, without regard for age, sex or quality. I felt within me a quiet fury that my cousin had had to die with this man's image before his eyes. I spoke again through gritted teeth, quietly at first.

'Andrew, are you here?'

Nothing.

Louder, then. 'Andrew? This is no time or place for games. Andrew, I . . .'

Even as my words were echoing, unfinished, about me, I saw it: a flash of movement, of something shining out of something white. And then before I could understand it there was the sharp, cold tip of the knife in my neck and slicing to the bone. I grabbed out with my left hand, clutching fruitlessly at the sarcophagus as I fell. There was shouting, Andrew shouting my name; his voice was distant but coming closer. He was thundering down the nave, shouting out my name. I was helpless to do anything other than watch my own blood trickle down the creamy marble to the floor, and see the knife fall from the girl's hand as she ran.

TWENTY-SEVEN

'Now these are the judgements'

I thought he was bringing me home. There were no carvings, jewelled staffs or candlesticks here: no distraction from the worship of the Lord; no kaleidoscope of colours in the glass, enticing thoughts of understanding that were beyond the capacity of man. Here were just bare walls and floors, plain windows and simple benches, and the sound that rose out of the near-darkness around me was a call to God.

But my arrival, as Andrew staggered through the door with me in his arms, disrupted that moment of pure worship. Words faltered and stopped as the notes fell away. Women's voices exclaimed in shock, the men quickly turned to organisation, and a way was cleared for us to the preacher's dais. One man went for the sergeant, another for the doctor. A cloth was pulled from the altar and strips torn for my throat. An old woman bent towards me to do the work while the strong arms of the preacher bore me up beneath the shoulders. The old woman drew back slightly, just a moment.

'He has the look of the debauch, the merchant Richard FitzGarrett's grandson, but he is dead.'

'It is the other grandson. A Scot, and one of our faith.'

'Then what is this in his hand?' asked the precentor, forcing open my fingers to reveal the crucifix gripped between them. I looked in confusion at my own palm, bloodied, where I had put my hand up at the last second to grab at the knife and had clutched instead at the crucifix, causing Margaret's knife to slip from the place where it should have entered my neck. I tried but failed to speak, and the women hushed me.

'There will be time for that later,' said Andrew, and then to the precentor, 'Believe that he is no Papist. Now I must go and find the girl before she brings harm on herself.' He paused a moment to look at me, but where I could make no words heard, he could not find the right ones. He left me to the ministrations of the Presbyterians of Carrickfergus in their meeting house, and went out into the night to hunt for Margaret.

It was morning before they moved me from the meeting house. One of the congregation, not knowing of my relations with my grandmother, had sent word to let her know I lay gravely injured in their care, but that I could be brought to her home when the doctor had finished with me. The messenger returned in a very short time, with the comforting words from Maeve that if they would do her some service, they might tell her when I was dead. But he also brought with him a note, secretly penned by Deirdre, telling them precisely when to bring me to the back entrance of my grandmother's house, what they were to say, and who they were and were not to speak to when they got there.

And so it was that a little before ten the next morning, I found myself once more in the backyard of the FitzGarrett town house, seeking secret entry as I had done only two weeks ago, newly arrived from Scotland. I had been borne on a litter and helped to walk the last few yards. At precisely ten, one of my escort knocked hard three times on the door, and it was opened at once by Deirdre. She brought me quickly inside and shut the door, putting her finger to her lips in warning.

Then she started up the back stairs, indicating that I should follow her. But I was weak from loss of blood and unsteady on my feet, and after the first two steps swayed to the side and slumped down the wall. I tried to stand up again but the effort was beyond me: I could only crawl. She struggled as best she could to help me, but it was almost fifteen minutes before we reached the safety of Andrew's chamber.

Deirdre encouraged me to lie back so that she might examine my bandages. 'I cannot trust any of the women, and the arrival of the doctor would attract too much curiosity. I will have to change them myself.'

And so she did, lifting the wrappings as gently as she could from my neck, but it was still an agony when she came to the last, where the dried blood had fused the fabric to my skin and the gaping flesh below. I clamped my mouth tight shut to stifle the pain. She cleaned the wound, dried and dressed it. 'You were fortunate, thank God. A little to the left and you would have bled to death before Andrew had ever got you out of the church. But if her aim had been better . . .'

'Her aim was true enough,' I said. 'I was saved by a . . .' I could not call it a trinket, as once disparagingly I had done. 'I was saved by this.' I held towards her the crucifix that had caused Margaret's knife, at the last moment, to slip.

She lifted it to her lips and kissed it. 'Your faith is stronger than the curse. Promise me you will keep this.'

I promised her. I would have promised her anything in that moment.

'I cannot stay long: I have sent the servants on errands in the town and at the quayside. They will be back soon. Maeve is at mass in the priest's room with Macha; Eachan is guarding them.'

'And Andrew?'

Her words came slow, as if she feared invoking some misfortune by uttering them. 'He has not yet returned.'

The effort of the last half-hour had been almost more than she was equal to, and I saw that she had little more strength than I had myself. I did not attempt to keep her longer, and I think I was asleep before she had left the room.

Images of the poet, of his circle and the ancient cross at Kilcrue came to my dreaming mind and I tried to push them away. Finn O'Rahilly was talking to me, but in Irish, and I did not want to hear it. I tossed and turned through many hours in my efforts to throw him off, until a cold hand was placed on my forehead, water began to run down my face, and I woke up.

It was not my grandmother's priest, but Andrew who stood above me now, a dripping cloth in his hand; he pressed it to my dry and cracked lips.

'Did you find her?'

His face was grey; he looked as if he had not slept in two days.

'I found her.'

'Where was she?'

'On the road to Glenoe.'

He sat down and put his head in his hands. They were grazed, and burnt on the palms, as if he had been working, struggling desperately at something. They were like the burns from a rope. He spoke blankly. 'It was dawn before I came upon her. I had searched through the town, places where people might know her, but no one had seen her. And then I thought that, despite the night and the darkness, she might have tried to get home. I was lucky at the first gate. A young girl, distracted and wild-looking, had left the town not long after seven. They had warned her of the darkness and the dangers, but she told them she had more to fear from the light. They let her go; they had been given no instruction to prevent a Scots girl passing out of the town on her way homewards. But she did not go home – I don't think she had ever intended to go home. She just wanted to be with her brother. So she did it herself.'

I did not ask him how he had found her at last, if she had already been dead before he had managed to cut her down, whether he had carried her home, what he could have said to her mother. Neither of us would have been the better for talking of those things, but there was one thing I could not help but ask him.

'Did she . . . did she give any explanation? Was there any message? A letter?'

He understood what I meant. 'There was a message: coins in a leather pouch suspended from her neck, and a portion of scripture, along with a note. Ten words: "Tell the O'Neills: we do not want their blood-money."'

'Blood-money?'

'When her brother David was murdered, at first it was treated like any other such killing by the kerne. But when I heard of it, I lost my control and let rage get the better of my judgement. Even then, I had some suspicion of what Sean was, what Murchadh planned for him, though I did not know for certain and I did not know then that neither Sean nor Cormac rode with the kerne. I took my rage and poured out my disgust to Sean. He swore he had not known of it. He took my report to Cormac, who dealt with those responsible – his own brothers among them. Then Sean took money to her mother, in compensation.'

'Sean?'

'I never knew that until we were at Ballygally and she told

me so herself. Say what I might, she would not dissociate him in her mind from those who had murdered her brother. And then I began to wonder if it had been Margaret who paid Finn O'Rahilly to lay the curse on your family.'

'It never occurred to me,' I said. 'Not for one moment. But how did she pay for it, if she refused Sean's money?'

'She did not – pay for it, I mean. She laughed when I suggested it. She said she knew nothing of the poet or his curse, that she had better things to do than traipse through bogs looking for half-mad Irish seers. I believed her; I still believe her. But once my mind had started running down that path, it would not stop. Do you recall, Alexander, when we arrived at Ballygally and found Margaret there? Do you remember we learned she had gone to Carrickfergus in search of work on the very day we visited her mother's cottage, the very day of your grandfather's funeral?'

I remembered. So she had been there the night Sean had been murdered. 'And yet it might have been little more than coincidence.'

He nodded. 'Perhaps. That is what I told myself. I might have believed it, too, had it not been for her bible.'

'Her bible?'

'Not long after I had brought Macha in to town, the Blackstones arrived at the safe house, searching for me.' He looked up at me, evidently uncomfortable. 'It has been me, all along, that they have pursued, not you.'

'I know; the constable told me,' I said. 'Go on.'

'I managed to get away, through the back yards, to the Presbyterian meeting house where I knew I would be given shelter for as long as I needed it, as long as it took to clear my name of having killed Henry Blackstone.'

'It is cleared already.'

'How so?'

'Cormac O'Neill cleared both our names of the charge.'

'Cormac? I do not understand.'

'His love for Deirdre is stronger than his concern for himself, or any petty jealousies he might have of you. He cleared our names that there might be someone left whom he could trust to care for her, as he could do no longer. Whatever you might think, he is an honourable man.'

Andrew was silent a few moments, not shame-faced but regretful. 'He was an honourable man. He is no more; Cormac O'Neill was executed in the castle yard an hour before dawn.'

I had known it could not end for him any other way: he had chosen his path and that was what had lain at the end of it, and yet I wished it might have been different. A man who should have been a prince: at least he had had the dignity in death of not being made a public spectacle for the crowd.

'And what has this to do with Margaret?'

'Margaret? Yes. The Blackstones. I took shelter from them in the Presbyterian meeting house. Whenever the weather is too severe for me to walk out to Templecorran, and the Scots congregation there, I worship with our English brethren in the town. On my first night there, there was divine service. I felt sorely in need of hearing the Word, after our days surrounded by the trappings and practices of idolatry.'

'Which saved your life,' I sought to remind him, but he had stayed firmer than had I, and was quick in his riposte.

'No, Alexander. Never that, only God, always God. The priests and the nun and all their places were but the instruments of God's Grace to us: they were not the cause of it.'

I should have been ashamed that my own faith had been so easily swayed, but I could not be, and so said nothing in my defence.

'Anyhow, I attended the service, and was glad to see Margaret there too, and to learn that she and you had found safe quarters in the castle. I had nothing with me – not so much as a change of clothes, and certainly no bible – and so we shared Margaret's. Despite their poverty, she and her brothers were taught to read and write, and she has always prized her bible above all things. I wish I could have loved her.'

'That might have come,' I said.

'No,' he said. 'I will love only once.' He breathed deep. 'The psalms were strong that night, assured of God's power in the face of all that might assault his people. They recalled the struggle of Israel with the Philistines, and gave much hope to the congregation, I think, for the days of danger to come. We shared her bible, Margaret and I, as the reader took us through the passages on which the minister was to preach. We followed him line for line as he intoned them for all the congregation. But as we turned the pages, I noticed that one was torn. It was in the Book of Exodus. Chapter 21 had been torn out.'

'"Now these are the judgements which thou shalt set before them."'

He handed me a thin, crumpled piece of paper. Had I not been able to read it, I would have known instantly by the feel of it that it was a page from a bible.

'This was the scripture you found in her pouch?'

He nodded.

I smoothed out the paper, and my eye was drawn instantly to the words scored under in ink: '"if a man come presumptuously upon his neighbour, to slay him with guile; thou shalt take him from mine altar, that he may die."'

Andrew continued where the passage had also been marked. '"Eye for eye, tooth for tooth, hand for hand, foot for foot."'

'Brother for brother,' I said.

He looked up. 'It does not say that in the scriptures.'

'No, but it might well have done. She killed Sean near the altar because she thought he was one of those who had murdered her brother, and she sought to murder me because I had told her I knew what it was to lose a brother, for Sean had been mine.'

He sat down, his face drained of what little colour it had. 'When did you tell her this, Alexander?'

'Yesterday, in the castle kitchens. I knew she had some great hostility towards me; I wanted to build some bridge of trust, of fellowship between us, and I believed that would do it.'

He rubbed his eyes and looked to the heavens. 'I have been a fool, such a fool.'

'What do you mean?'

'The very first time Margaret saw you, in her mother's cottage – you remember?'

'I remember.'

'She thought for a moment you were Sean. She could not believe that I had brought him to their home. I assured her you were not, and tried to tell her he had had nothing to do with the murder of her brother. I thought I had convinced her, for she left that subject but told me I must be mistaken in you, that no two men could look so much alike who were not brothers. I laughed at her, Alexander, I was almost going to tell you, but I forgot about it soon after we left their place. And then when I heard what Stephen had told you of your mother, and Sean, and that you were his brother, I did not think of Margaret's words but of what it meant for you. Even when I saw the torn passage in her bible, I did not realise what she was going to do.'

'You could not have been expected to.'

'But I should have done.'

'Andrew, whatever else has happened between us, last night you saved my life.'

'A moment later, and I would have been too late. I had been so certain that Murchadh had had Sean killed that I did not think to look elsewhere. I only followed Margaret last night because I was worried about her, her manner had become strange. I saw her enter the church, and thought perhaps she wished a moment's quiet prayer. When I saw a man moving through the graveyard towards the door, I became anxious, and then when you stepped beneath the portal and I saw in the light from the door that it was you, doors began to unlock in my mind. It did not make sense that you should have an assignation, you who were so much like Sean, and she who hated him so much. Even as you walked through the door, your very walk was his. It was a moment before it came to me, a sight of something I had not seen – of Sean going through that same door on the night of his death. And then I knew. I ran through the churchyard, not caring whose bones I stood upon, and only just got to the door in time to see her lift her arm. I am sorry, Alexander. I could have stopped it if I had not been so slow.'

He was genuinely distraught that he had not prevented the attack.

'Why did you stop her?' I managed to say at last.

'Alexander . . .'

'Would it not have been better,' I paused to gather my strength a little. 'Would it not have been better to have let her kill me?'

He shook his head slowly, his face the image of incomprehension. 'After all we had been through, even had I not been a Christian, why would I have let her kill you when I could do anything to stop it?'

'Because you have doubted me for some time now, have you not?'

He looked away and then back at me. 'Perhaps. Yes, I have doubted you. Since Ardclinnis; before that, even. Since they took you alone to Dun-a-Mallaght. I think that was why Sean brought you to Ireland.'

'I think so too, but I was never for a moment tempted to take his place. This is not my world, and these are not my people.'

'Are you certain of that?'

I had thought long and hard on this for the last few days. 'Had I been born, raised here; had I been brought up in their faith, then yes, perhaps it would be different. But I was not; a man cannot live in two worlds; he must choose. You told me so yourself.'

'And you have chosen?'

'Yes, I have chosen. And I would leave here this very day, if I had the strength, but I have not yet the strength, and there is one thing I must know before I go.'

He looked at me expectantly, as if it was from him that I waited for my answer.

'The curse,' I said. 'Pretext or no for bringing me over here, it was real enough, its intent real enough, and much of the harm predicted in it has come to pass. It was not Margaret who was behind it, nor Cormac. Finn O'Rahilly is dead, but his patron I believe is still alive, and I cannot leave Deirdre and Macha here until I have found that person out. I owe as much to Sean, and to the love that I bear them both, and to my nephew yet unborn.'

He laid a hand on my arm. 'And I will be with you in that quest, Alexander. And when we have discovered who it is, and we have dealt with them, I will be here and look after those you love, long after you have returned to that other life you have chosen. But I must go to the sheriff, and tell them of Margaret, and bring these evidences to them, and then see what further orders they might have for me at the castle. Rest now, and gather your strength and your thoughts, for what it remains for us to do. Finn O'Rahilly can tell us nothing more than you already learned from him. When you are better recovered, we must plunder your mind for the answers he can no longer give.'

Andrew left me then, and left the FitzGarrett house, a servant no more.

TWENTY-EIGHT

The Curse's Circle

'Do not even consider walking through that door. I will have it bolted from the outside if you do not give me your word that you will stay in here.'

It was the following morning, and Andrew had found me standing at the end of my bed and with intent to go further. A night's rest in sheets rather than straw had restored enough of my strength that I could walk a few steps unsupported without fear of falling. The pain from my wound was sharper, more insistent now though. Deirdre had done what she could, but it was clear some sort of infection was setting in. Remembering one of Jaffray's methods, when all other means were lacking, I had asked him last night for a little *whisky* to clean the wound, but he had thought I was in jest, and had in a similar vein admonished me that I had been too much amongst my cousin's associates and that abstinence from vice would do for me what drink and other things could not. I had had neither the energy nor the wit to explain to him properly, and I was paying for it now. I tugged at the bandages.

'I think it has become infected.'

He lifted the dressing carefully, and this time it was he who winced when he saw what lay beneath. 'I will send for the doctor.'

'What about my grandmother? She will know I am here.'

'Word of Margaret's death and her guilt in Sean's murder is

all around the town. Your grandmother was up much of the night, busied in commending that girl's soul to all the punishments of the damned. She is not yet ready to acknowledge your innocence, but she will. You are safe here now.'

The doctor arrived within the hour, and did little more than raise his eyebrows when told the cause of my wound. 'It is in the blood, it would seem. I treated your cousin, and your uncle before him, for woundings of this nature on more than one occasion. You will be left with a scar that will more than match that on your forehead. Do not tell me that a young girl gave you that too?'

It took me a moment to understand what he was talking about.

'No, not a young girl. A powerfully-built man with a rock in his hand and an intention to embed it in my skull gifted me that,' I said, rubbing at the deep gouge in my temple carved out by the provost of Banff, over two years ago.

'Do you O'Neills never consider the peaceful resolution of disputes?' he asked, as he steadied his hand to thread the needle that would soon be drawing together the skin at the gash in my neck.

I attempted a smile. 'I did not know I was an O'Neill, then.'

Later, as darkness was drawing in, Andrew came again to see me, bringing with him a bowl of broth and some bread, 'and the eager wishes of Deirdre and Macha to see you. Your grandmother will not hear of it. Macha she will not let out of her sight, and she holds Deirdre in scarcely less contempt than she does you.' He was silent for a moment. 'She blames her for the death of Cormac.'

'But that is ridiculous. How could she . . .?'

'However ridiculous, Deirdre has joined her in the certainty of her own guilt. I have tried to reason with her but she will have none of it. She says if she had but done what Maeve wanted her to do in the first place, none of this would have happened.'

'She cannot believe that is true.'

'More than that, she cries out about the curse, that it is her fault, that she has brought it down upon us.'

'Andrew, that is madness.'

'I know it is madness, but she is beyond telling. I begin to fear it might truly send her mad. She says that her only consolation is that she has seen Maeve MacQuillan, and must surely join Sean and Cormac soon.'

'And my grandmother?'

'She stokes the fire of her delusions, goads her on, with accusation after accusation.'

She was engulfed in a storm, this cousin, this girl whom I had sworn to Sean and to Cormac that I would protect, and I did not know how to get her to safety; it seemed that here there was no way out for her, no possibility of shelter.

'What can we do, Andrew?'

'We? There is nothing we can do until we know for certain that she will allow it to be done.'

A loud banging on the outer door beneath us interrupted our conversation. Andrew ran to look out over the machicolation and I attempted to hobble after him.

'It is the Blackstones; I must alert them at the castle,' he said, before rushing down the stairs.

I saw that he was right. Deirdre's husband Edward was there, and his father Matthew with him. They had in attendance a rabble of men – not the hunting party that had pursued us to Dunluce, but an ill-mounted assortment of what I thought must be brick-makers, builders, tenants, all men in Matthew

Blackstone's pay with little option but to do his bidding. The genial Englishman at whose table Andrew and I had dined a few nights ago was gone, his place taken by an enraged, blustering bull of a man. His own son looked to be in fear of him.

'Let us in, you conniving whore, or I will break these doors down.'

A servant's voice replied. 'You will gain no entrance here. Go back where you came from, if you value your liberty.'

'Liberty? I will have no liberty; your man Boyd has seen to that with his creeping about, setting spies amongst my own men, when the greatest culprit, the greatest traitor to the king, was reared within these walls by that bog-nurtured old bitch you take your coin from.' He turned to his men. 'Break it down.' And the rabble set to with a pole they had brought with them, which they began to ram with increasing force against the door.

I left my position at the window and made my way to the stairway down to the balcony above my grandmother's great hall. I reached the bottom just as two doors burst open – the one on the ground floor, having finally succumbed with a sickening crack and splintering of wood to the Englishmen's blows; and the other, the small door that I knew led to my cousin Deirdre's chamber. She appeared, pale and insubstantial, like a ghost of herself, in the doorway. I held up a hand to stop her, and taking advantage of the noise and confusion below, crossed the balcony as quickly as I could to where she stood. I did not know if she had thoughts of going down to her husband, but I could not see – in her father-in-law's frame of mind – that any good would come of that. I took her by the arm, and began to lead her back towards the safe hiding place of Andrew Boyd's chamber.

We had not covered half the distance, at my halting pace,

before the intruders had made their way into the house and up to the hall where my grandmother, attended only by her steward, was waiting for them. There was no sign of Eachan; he would be with Macha, protecting Sean's unborn child. I pulled Deirdre with me behind the pillar from where I had watched my grandfather's wake. Gone were the groaning tables, the musicians, the servants and mourners. Gone too were Sean, Cormac – Murchadh also by now, perhaps. There was only a defiant old woman, with her steward, standing in her empty hall, the glories of the past hung in faded colours all around her.

She was the first to speak, her voice careful, soft. 'So, Englishman, you come uninvited to my house. You must forgive my want of hospitality: I had not looked for visitors at this hour.'

'Your hospitality be damned. I will have what I am owed.'

'You are owed nothing. Murchadh O'Neill and his son paid you every penny that was agreed for what arms you supplied to them. And you will see not a penny more from my husband's coffers.'

'I do not talk of money, woman.'

She raised an eyebrow, mocking even now. 'But I have heard you speak of little else. I had not known you to concern your-self with other matters.'

This was too much for him, and the rage he had been trying to master exploded out of him. 'My son, you murderous bitch. My son!'

Although the steward had moved forward a little, to stand in front of my grandmother, she herself had not so much as blinked.

'I see your son beside you there,' she said. 'Will one lumbering oaf not do you as well as another?'

Edward Blackstone restrained his father. 'My brother Henry was murdered by Andrew Boyd and by your own grandson, the Scot, who masqueraded in our house in the guise of your other and took my mother's hospitality.'

This time a look of astonishment. 'Your mother's hospitality? I congratulate him most heartily on finding it; I had not thought him so resourceful. As to the question of your brother's dispatch, I am sorry to say that neither my grandson nor Andrew Boyd can claim the credit in that. Another more honourable has cleared their names of that deed.'

Matthew Blackstone had again to be restrained, while all courage and intent seemed to be draining from his son. The younger man's shoulders sank, and his voice dropped.

'Where is Deirdre? Where is my wife?'

This time the old woman actually laughed. 'A fine specimen of a man, who does not even know where his wife is. Little wonder she went so easily to a servant's bed.'

I glanced at my cousin, but she seemed to be observing the exchange as a conversation between strangers.

'I want you to tell me where my wife is. I must know she is safe.'

'Oh, she is safe enough,' said my grandmother, unconcernedly. 'I have little use for her now, and she has turned her back on those she should have served. You may take her as you wish.'

The steward glanced swiftly up to our watching place, and then towards the door to the machicolation. I put my arm more firmly around my cousin and began to move her away from the balustrade and towards the door. I heard Blackstone order his people to search the house, and the steward protest to no avail. I had only just pulled the door shut behind us when I heard the footsteps of two or three men, having taken the stairs, start to clatter on to the balcony. I tried to hurry

Deirdre, but she was in little haste herself and my weakness made our progress slow. I turned halfway up the steps and saw, to my horror, the doorknob turn. I thought it was over for us both, but at that very moment a furious shouting came from out in the yard and the lower floors of the house as the castle guard stormed through the already broken door and demanded the submission of Matthew Blackstone and all who were with him. I recovered my wits quickly, and almost dragged Deirdre up the remaining steps and along the corridor to the tiny room where I thought we might be safe awhile.

Once I had her inside, I bolted the door and pulled Andrew's heavy chest across it before slumping down on the floor to try to catch my breath. Deirdre said nothing for a moment, looking in some astonishment at me.

'Where is he, Alexander?'

'He went to alert the men at the castle. I think he will be here soon; he is probably already in the house.'

'My father-in-law wants to kill him.'

'I know that.'

'My husband too, for other reasons. But they will not. Andrew is a better man than either of them.'

'Yes.'

She sat down on the bed, smoothing out the linen with her hand.

'He is a better man than my grandmother would ever acknowledge.'

'Yes, he is.'

'Will he have me now, do you think?'

'I cannot answer for him, Deirdre, but I know he loves you.'

'Oh, he always loved me,' she said. 'I knew that. I always knew it. And I him, but other things mattered more, then.'

I waited, but she appeared to think no further explanation

necessary. After a while, she became aware of my silence.

'I often thought of your mother, you know, when I was growing up.' Her face brightened. 'They tell me I look like her.'

I smiled. 'You do.'

'I used to think of her, picture her, lying with her dead love at the bottom of the sea, her hair entangled in seaweeds and a smile of perfect peace on her face. I envied her her freedom.'

'Her life was not as you thought,' I said.

She stood by the small table at the end of Andrew's bed, and started to examine the pieces on the chessboard there. She fingered the white queen awhile, picked her up, looked at her and set her down again somewhere else on the board, without giving much consideration to where she had positioned her. She turned her attention then to the black pieces, picked up a knight, put him down in his place again, and then moved the other. She carried on in this way, touching the pieces, considering them as objects, and then moving them in a way that had some logic in it that was clear to her, but unfathomable to me.

'Did Sean ever try to get you to play Fidchell?' she said, after some time, when it looked impossible that the white queen should survive a move longer.

'No, I have never heard of it.'

'A pity,' she said, 'but perhaps not. It was a game of the ancients. No one really knows how to play it now. But Sean wanted to know and Maeve had a board and set made for him, from as much information as could be gleaned from the old stories. It was beautiful, the board a pale wood inlaid with markings of gold, the pieces a white stone carved by the finest craftsmen. We knew very little of the rules, only some idea that the king should claim and keep his throne, and that to win at Fidchell, you had to play very well. Sean studied all the stories, and made up his own rules. He tried to teach them to me, but I could never understand it, and I always lost.'

The white queen was now impossibly compromised and had nowhere to go. Deirdre had entirely abandoned any attempt at protecting either king. She studied the board a moment and then knocked the pieces over, one by one. 'I was never any good at games. I should have remembered that.' She held up one of the white knights. 'I should have married Cormac, as she wanted me to – God knows, many a woman would dream of such a man, but I would not enmesh myself further with the O'Neills. And then he was too good for me and he would not see it. And now I have brought death to him years before it should have come.'

'Cormac's death is not your fault, Deirdre. You cannot blame yourself for all that has happened.'

'Can I not? I have made many mistakes, believed that many things could be that I have learned could never have been. I didn't even understand my own brother.'

'He loved you dearly.'

'And I him, but I did not understand him. I could scarcely believe it when I realised that he would fall in with Maeve's plans, with Murchadh's, that he would marry Roisin and throw it all at my grandmother's feet; everything my grandfather had worked for, his wealth and our name, to be squandered in a cause that was long lost.' She looked away. 'I could not believe he would not listen to me. So I determined to set myself at the furthest extreme from their world that I knew. I had tried to get away from Maeve before; I went once, you know, to our grandfather's people in the Pale, but they would not have me. So I married the son of a wealthy English planter.' She laughed. 'What an insult to Cormac, to Andrew too, to have married such a man. I would have done anything to stop Maeve, but it made no difference, and still Sean would not listen to me. And now my grandfather is dead, and Sean is dead, and Cormac is dead. The poet, too, is dead.' Her voice trailed off. 'I was never any good at games. And you have been brought here, where I know you do not wish to be, because of me.'

'I came here because Sean asked me to come. I came to help lift the curse.'

'The curse cannot be lifted. He tried to tell me that, and I only laughed at him. But now I know it and it is too late.'

'Who told you, Deirdre?' I reached out to take her hands in my own. 'Who told you?'

'He told me himself, of course,' she said, her eyes shining with a strange brilliance.

At that moment there was a thud against the door and an oath that surprised me, for I had rarely known Andrew lose control of his tongue.

'Alexander? Alexander!' he shouted. 'Alexander, are you there? Where is Deirdre? Let me in before I break the door down.'

I got up and put all my strength against the side of the chest, which had moved more easily in one direction than it would in the other. Another thud threatened injury only to the attacker. 'Andrew, for the love of God!'

Eventually, I had the thing shifted and managed to unbolt the door. He almost fell through it.

'Why did you not answer me?'

'I did,' I croaked, pointing at my own neck. 'You were making too much noise yourself to hear me.'

He saw past me then to Deirdre, and that she was safe, and without ceremony took her tight into his arms.

'You came back for me.'

'I will not leave you, Deirdre. You will stay with me now, and I will not leave you.'

To my astonishment, Sir James Shaw was through the door behind him.

'The men from Coleraine have all been taken to the castle. Their hired thugs will be released before long, I am sure – the constable has not the room nor the inclination to hold them – but Matthew Blackstone and his son will be in the Tower before the month is out. They will be shown no mercy for their treachery in selling arms to rebels against the king.'

'What about his wife and daughters?' I asked.

'He is no fool – he would not have told them what he was about, and they will fare the better for it. Unless it be found that they colluded in his business, they will be left in peace.'

'To fend for themselves,' I said. 'And what about Deirdre?'

He looked from me to Andrew and and back to me. 'Your cousin cannot be assured of safety here. She has too many ties to too many people who have been involved in plotting against the king. Your grandmother will not lift a finger to help her.' He spoke now to Deirdre herself. 'I think you must leave Ireland, and as soon as possible.'

A shout from one of his men below called him away, and a moment later only his words remained where he had been.

'Leave Ireland?' she said, as if the thought had never before occurred to her. 'But where could I go?'

The words were out of my mouth before I knew I had thought them. 'To Scotland, with me.'

She shook her head. 'I will not leave Andrew again. He is all there is left, he and my brother's child.'

'I am coming too,' he said. 'There is a boat leaving for Ayr tomorrow, at five o'clock in the evening. I have this afternoon purchased passage for all three of us. Alexander can return home and you and I, Deirdre — we can begin life anew, away from here.'

She smiled. 'Is it possible? Is it really possible?'

'It is possible. There is nothing for us here any more. I am sickened of this country. I have money for land and for trade. We can buy our way into some town . . .'

'I have friends in Aberdeen who can help you,' I said, picturing already the friendship that I knew would form between Andrew and William Cargill, the bond of sisterhood between Deirdre and Sarah, the healing there would be.

'Truly, you can help us?' said Andrew.

'I have a friend who is a lawyer, well thought of in Aberdeen. The town and the countryside around are full of those looking for someone with money to invest. Even a small amount of capital is welcomed. And your experience in my grandfather's business would help you to similar work soon enough, if you needed it. I am sure of it.'

'It is so far away,' said Deirdre.

'A world away,' I said. 'From rebellions, and kindreds, and feuding, and poets and curses. A world away from our grandmother and from here.'

'Where we might start again, where we might live our lives as others live them.'

'Yes,' said Andrew gently. 'As others live them.'

'But the child,' she said.

We looked, uncomprehending, at each other, and then at her. I think Andrew was in some fears that she carried Edward Blackstone's child, or even Cormac's.

'Sean's child,' she said.

'We cannot take Sean's child. It is yet to be born, and we must leave for Scotland tomorrow. I do not know how much longer you will be safe here. And besides,' he took her hand tenderly, 'it is Macha's child, too, and she will never leave Ireland.'

'But who will protect him?' She looked frightened now, her eyes darting from one to the other of us.

'Macha is stronger than you think. And Eachan . . .'

'My brother had Eachan, and now he is dead. Besides, Eachan can do nothing against my grandmother. We must get the child away from her. We must protect it from her. She will poison his life as she did my father's, Sean's, mine. She will fill his head with nothing but dreams of the O'Neills, of the old Ireland, of leading rebellion. She will live out her last days through him.'

There was nothing I could say against this. I knew she was right.

'We cannot take him from his mother, Deirdre, and his mother will never leave here; I am not sure that her dreams are so different from Maeve's anyhow. She loved Sean for what he was, but for all he planned to do also.'

'Then she should not have him either.'

'Deirdre . . .'

'She should not, she should not.' She was beating her hands against Andrew's chest as she wept.

Deirdre's outburst had exhausted her, and we laid her down on Andrew's bed to sleep. He went below, and returned with the news that Maeve believed Deirdre to have gone to the castle with Sir James, where she assumed I would be also. She was too taken up with the imminent birth of her great-grand-child to give much thought to either of us. Macha was now in what had been my grandfather's room, awaiting her childbed, with Eachan in constant attendance, swearing death on almost any who came near her. Still traversing a dark valley of grief for Sean, his devotion was channelled now to the protection of his dead master's wife and child. Once born, there would have been no hope of spiriting the child away from its mother, even had Andrew or myself had the slightest desire to do so. Neither of us did. We agreed that Deirdre must be persuaded to come away without him.

I lay down on the bed across from my cousin and watched her sleep, counting with every breath the moments passing until we could leave this place on tomorrow's tide. She had spoken of my mother, but the life she was fleeing to would not be as my mother's had been; my father had been a good man, a decent man, but he had not had the vision, or indeed the means, of Andrew Boyd. Deirdre would not have the endless work to do that had been my mother's lot, would not grow to resent her husband's lack of learning, his satisfaction with his position in the world, as my mother had done. It would be a different life, a different future for them. Andrew, again condemned to a pallet of straw while I slept on feathers, laid himself down on the floor of his own room and was soon asleep.

These two, at least, would escape Finn O'Rahilly's curse. But would I, who had not been encompassed by it? A fear was growing within me that it had already reached out, beyond these shores, to the place I had come from, the place I wished to return to, and begun to poison everything there for me. It had brought me here, that curse, entangled me in the lives of those it damned, and I could not escape untarnished. It had drawn back veils I had not known were there and shown almost everyone I had come to know in Ulster to be something other than I had supposed them to be. And yet I was still no closer to discovering who had hired the lips of Finn O'Rahilly to unleash those words in the first place. I fell asleep with the image of the poet in my mind.

I would have slept until dawn, had not the sounds of a living nightmare pierced my consciousness somewhere in the darkest hours of the night. It was a woman screaming, a scream of such terror and agony as I had never heard from a human throat before. I fumbled for flint and lit the candle as I tried to get out of bed. Deirdre's place was empty: she was nowhere in the room. Andrew was already on his feet.

'In God's name, Alexander, what is that?'

'I don't know. She is gone.'

He looked now at the empty bed, grabbed the candle from me and was out of the door within seconds. I had not the strength to follow him at speed and could only fumble my way along the darkened corridor until a crack of light showed me the door to the stairs. The screaming continued, but through it, Cormac O'Neill's voice came to me again, as he had tried to warn me of pursuing the curse, '. . . may think on his words if you must, but you will call down upon yourself whatever griefs follow.' And those griefs were calling in my ears, ringing in them now. When I had asked him, Finn O'Rahilly had told me that no one else had come to see him about the blessing that became a curse – no one but Deirdre and my grand-mother – and he had not lied. And only tonight, Deirdre herself had told me she would do anything, anything, to put an end to Maeve's endless dreaming of a triumphant resurgence of the O'Neills in an Ireland that could be no more. Having no faith in the powers of poets herself, she had believed she could play upon the superstitions of her grandmother, warn, manipulate a woman who had spent a lifetime manipulating others. She had instigated the cursing of her own family and it was too late now, as the poet had told her it would be, to undo what had followed. I redoubled my efforts and ran the remaining distance to the room whence Macha's screams, as she brought my cousin's child into the world, reverberated through the house and into the night.

Andrew was there already, slumped out of breath beside the door, the candle still in his hand and a look of sheer relief on his face.

'It is only Macha, Alexander, only Macha. The child will be born soon. All is well.'

'No,' I said. 'Where is Deirdre?'

'She is in there with her.'

'I must get in.'

But the powerful arm of Eachan barred the door. 'No one gets in but the women and the doctor. Cross that door and it will be the last step you take.'

'Eachan, you do not understand.'

'It is you who does not understand: I will . . .'

But he was stopped by a silence, and then a cry, a different cry from a woman's agonies, the cry of a human child entering into the world. We held our breath a moment, we three men, and then Andrew broke into the broadest of smiles and I thought I saw a tear in the old Irishman's eye. I took my chance and was through the door before he knew I had passed him.

I only had a moment to take in the scene. The room was ablaze with light – candles lit all around the walls, along the mantelpiece and in the hands of two servant girls on either side of the bed. A doctor was washing his hands in a bowl and congratulating my grandmother. The old woman paid him little attention, lost in an unwonted moment of tenderness, lovingly stroking Macha's brow; and the midwife, having cleaned and swaddled the child, was handing him not to his mother but to my cousin Deirdre.

I took a step forward, opened my mouth to shout, and the last thing I felt before I went down was the huge fist of Eachan

slam into the side of my face. There was nothing but blackness and startling lights in my head, and for a moment I think,
for several moments, I succumbed to them. Eventually I forced
myself up. By the time I had done so, the room had changed.
It was still ablaze with light and fire, but almost all the people
had gone save the midwife, a servant and the distraught girl
on the bed crying out in Irish for her child. There was no
Andrew, no Eachan, no Maeve and no Deirdre. And there was
no child.

Lunging from one piece of furniture to the next, I reached
the corridor. I could see them now, across the balcony, at the
head of the stairs that led down to the great hall. Eachan was
in a stupor almost, his hands at his sides, tears rolling down
his face, repeating over and over again some Gaelic impreca-
tion. Maeve was frozen, like an effigy of herself, dawning
comprehension robbing her of the power of speech. Andrew
was standing perhaps three feet from Deirdre, very still, but his
eyes moving and his mind, I knew, calculating. In the hall
below, hurriedly but quietly, servants were laying down cush-
ions, mattresses, pillows: anything that would soften a fall. And
there, by the head of the stairs itself, was Deirdre. Beautiful,
her eyes shining, her hair tumbled loose over her shoulders, in
the pale blue gown she had lain down to sleep in, holding
close to her cheek and murmuring soft words of comfort into
the ear of her brother's child.

'Give me the child, Deirdre,' said my grandmother at last.

Deirdre only smiled, and continued to whisper into the
baby's ear, and to kiss its soft cheek.

'Give me the child,' my grandmother repeated.

'No. I will not do that, grandmother. You would destroy
him, as you destroyed my father, my brother. You will not
destroy this child. I will keep him safe.'

The old woman was getting desperate. 'I will not. I will send them away, tomorrow. The child and his mother. I will send them away, and Eachan with them to protect them. And money. I will give them money. I will never see them again.'

Deirdre shook her head, smiling at the child and not looking at her grandmother. 'No, you lie. You have always lied. Ever since I was a child. Before that even. You told my grandfather his daughter was dead, but look, there is her son Alexander, here in this house, too late.'

'Please, Deirdre,' I said.

She continued to smile, at me now. 'No, Alexander, it is too late. It was always too late.'

Andrew took a step towards her as she spoke, but she shrank back, drawing the child closer to herself.

'It is too late,' she repeated.

'But we will go, as we planned. We will go with Alexander, make a new life for ourselves, and take the child. You will allow that, will you not, Maeve? We can take Macha with us even.'

My grandmother nodded in desperate acquiescence but still Deirdre shook her head. 'No, you are lying to me too, Andrew. I heard you both last night. You will not let me take him. But I have to. No one else will protect him from her. I am taking him to his father.'

She moved closer to the edge of the balcony and what happened next was done so quickly I hardly knew where it began. She lifted the baby high in the air, Maeve screamed and Eachan, come to himself, started to run. But Andrew was closest and lunged for the child, only wrenching it from her arms as she hurled herself backwards over the balcony rail.

She seemed to fall for ever, her arms outstretched, her hair flowing behind her, a look of supreme peace on her face. Falling into the arms of those who had gone before her, she broke her neck on the hard stone floor below. There was silence, utter silence for a moment, and then the child started to cry. Andrew held him tight and tried to soothe him, but as his grip strengthened, his teeth gritted and his eyes became a film of tears, I feared he would crush the breath out of the tiny bundle in his arms. I made my way over to him and gently took it from him, handing him to my grandmother who, ashen-faced, went quietly with him towards Macha's bedroom. And then I held Andrew as he succumbed to his overwhelming grief.

TWENTY-NINE

Parting

I had all but pleaded with him, but he would not come with me. We had parted at Ayr. I think he took something of me with him, and I something of him with me, and yet it was a lack I felt, an absence.

'You could make the new life we talked of. You could have that new beginning.'

'It was a dream, Alexander, of another time. It is gone now.'

'I know it cannot be how it was to have been . . .'

'No, she is dead.'

'Yes, she is dead. And she can no more be in Dumfriesshire than she could in Aberdeen. There is nothing for you to the south that you would not find in the north.'

'I have family there, in the borders. My father's family.'

'Whom you never knew and who will scarce remember him even.'

He looked sharply at me, a fragment of an old antagonism in his face. 'Do you think it only for you that kin matters?'

'No, Andrew, but I know you. And I know what I would be bringing you to if you came with me. You have my friendship, and will have it always, wherever we might be. But you will also have it of those who are my friends, for my sake and in a very little time for your own. I know the life you could make there.'

'I am going, Alexander, where I will not see one story play

itself out in my mind while I am forced to live another. If I came with you, every day I would be haunted by the life she and I might have had there, together. Everywhere I turned, there would be signs of what could have been. I will go where she never was, in her dreams or mine, and I might keep my mind that way.'

'But Andrew . . .'

'No, Alexander! Good God, man, do you not see it? Every time I look at your face I can see them all again, all the O'Neills and what they made her, what they took from me. I never had a friend in my life before, and I love you dearly, but for the love of God and for your own sake and mine, understand this: I cannot bear to look upon your face.'

And so we had struck out, one for the south, the other for the north. And I do not think he looked back once, as I did, at the dark blue shape across the water, the island of Ireland, receding with every step I took, into its own sky, its own sea, to its own world where we would play our parts no longer, Eirinn cloaking herself in memory once more, from the eyes of unworthy men. I did not know if I would ever look on her again.

And as I walked on, I left also my grandmother and her great-grandson, my two living blood relatives in this world. Macha was there too, and Eachan of course, and would be until his last breath left him. But it was in the old woman and the newborn child that the fate of those I had left behind in Ulster, and the names that had gone before them, would rest: I knew that.

Maeve was free, still free, saved from certain trial and execution for treachery by Murchadh O'Neill, in one final act of pride. When at last taken with his two younger sons; when, after much bloodshed and courage, Dun-a-Mallaght had finally fallen, Murchadh had scorned the idea that a woman, even such a woman as Maeve O'Neill, had intrigued with the English to bring arms into Ireland for a rebellion against those Englishmen's own king. He, Murchadh, and no other, had led and directed all. And by that his name had salvaged some honour, at the point of death, that he had never managed to attain to through his life. But no poets were left now to sing the praises of Murchadh, to glorify his family and his deeds. And as our boat had left Ulster for Scotland and passed beneath the walls of Carrickfergus, the severed head of Murchadh O'Neill, along with those of his three sons, looked out from the stakes on which they had been impaled, over me and across the sea that might have brought them aid. Already, the gulls had begun to peck at their eyes, and in a few days, or weeks perhaps, they would be eaten or rotted, and only their skulls, and some story of a rising that had never been, left to remember them.

And Roisin, for Roisin had not been found, she had not been taken. Eachan said she would have gone to Bonamargy; that Julia MacQuillan would have taken her; that she would be got away to the continent like so many others of her standing before her, that she would become a nun. My grandmother thought the Earl of Antrim would have found her and got her away to safety with his MacDonnell kin in Scotland. Macha prayed that the girl who had also loved Sean and should have been his wife might find welcome and rest somewhere in the west, with some of her own people.

It was a respite that Deirdre had never found, for she had not known who or what her own people were. But she was at rest now, Deirdre of the Sorrows. She lay with her brother in a grave on the Knocagh Hill, high over Carrickfergus, looking out over Belfast Lough to a Scotland she would now never see. We had gone there and buried her two days after her death. No feasting, no great gathering of mourning guests. Just a small and quiet procession of those who had known her best and loved her. My grandmother, showing her age, and something else, perhaps, at last, had allowed herself to rest on my arm as we had mounted to the place where Sean already lay. The priest had intoned his words, and I did not try to shut them out as I might have done before. Andrew had taken a ring that had been his mother's and placed it in the grave with her. At a small movement of Maeve's hand, Macha had begun to sing a beautiful lament, words that lifted and filled the breeze and were carried like fallen leaves on the air and away from us.

The lions of the hill are gone,
And I am left alone – alone –
Dig the grave both wide and deep,
For I am sick and fain would sleep!

The falcons of the wood are flown,
And I am left alone – alone –
Dig the grave both deep and wide,
And let us slumber side by side.

And as the words went on, verse by verse, I realised that the lament was not only for Deirdre, or not even just for Sean, but for Murchadh's sons, all three, for Father Stephen, for all those who had died in their dream of Ireland and what they might have been.

At last the song came to its end, and we men covered my cousin in the earth of her country, returned to it, part of it at last, the girl who had so feared it that she had laid a curse on her own family, on herself. Deirdre had thought to use the words of a poet she did not believe in to drive a fissure in the union of her brother and grandmother with Murchadh O'Neill and his plans. She had thought to spare her family the destruction and disgrace that she had known would follow. She had thought, with her grandfather's inheritance safe in her hands, to guide them to a place in a new Ireland that she had not understood they could never accept. The understanding, at last, that she herself had no place in that new Ireland, and the knowledge of the curse she had unleashed, had driven her to madness. As I dropped the last sod of turf over my cousin's body, I prayed, in the manner of my forefathers, that God might grant mercy, rest and peace unto her eternal soul.

She had asked them to leave her a few minutes, to give her a few moments alone, and they had done so. Alexander hung back behind the others, a little way off; it was solitude enough for her. The sight of him was like a knife through her heart, every time she looked at him, for there was Phelim, there was Sean, there was Grainne's second son. Grainne: her place of pain. Her son had come to them at last, across the water, but he had come too late.

As the wind whipped over the bleak hillside, she reached her hand out to the stone, Sean's stone, and traced with her fingers the words of the epitaph freshly carved out beneath an engraved sword:

I am in blood and power better than the best of them . . .
My ancestors were Kings of Ulster, Ulster was theirs,
And shall be mine . . . with this sword I won them,
With this sword I will keep them. This is my answer.

And Maeve O'Neill swore to her God that she would take her great-grandson here often, and that she would not rest until her work at last was done.

Epilogue

Aberdeen, late November 1628

The guards at the quayside were hesitant about letting me pass into the town, and I could scarcely blame them: the man who had disembarked from the *Nathaniel* and called himself Alexander Seaton bore little resemblance to the teacher of philosophy last seen in the burgh over two months ago. Sean's beaten hide travelling jacket and trousers, the heavy new mantle trimmed with beaver, gifted me by my grandmother, and the fine leather boots, did not speak of a man from this town. My cropped hair and my beard aged a face and features hardened by their fresh scars.

'I tell you again, I am who I claim to be,' I said. 'I have a testimonial, here, in my pocket, from the constable of Carrick-fergus Castle, in Ireland, for the eyes of Principal Dun; it will confirm my identity and explain my absence.' I held it out to them and they looked a moment at the seal and then again at me.

A merchant taking delivery of his goods called over, 'That is Mr Seaton, you dolts. Can a man not grow a beard?'

The guards grumbled that it was difficult to see in the darkness, and they had to do their duty. I waved my thanks at the merchant.

'Do you go to the college, Mr Seaton? I am headed that

way – you might ride up with me that far in the cart once these goods are loaded. You look wearied from your travels.'

I thanked him, but declined his offer. 'No, there is somewhere else I must go first. A thing that will not keep till the morning.'

He smiled, and turned back to the loading of his sacks, and I went on my way. The town was like a spectre, a cathedral of the dead, rising out of a hard frost that looked not to have lifted for days. Nothing moved, no cats, dogs, scarce any humans, on streets and paths silent with tiny crystals of ice sparkling into the night. I could see my breath in front of me as I walked.

All was quiet at William's house, everything shut up and in darkness, the last smoke having curled its way from the chimney hours since. I went up the pend at the side to the backland. Nothing stirred. I thought to wash my hands and face at the well, but the water in it was frozen hard. They would have to see me as I was.

I lifted my hand and knocked, lightly at first, on the door. Bracken began to bark inside. I heard no other movement and knocked louder. This time there were sounds on the stairs, and from beyond the kitchen. Soon I was banging hard on the door.

'Who is it?' came Davy's voice, a little tremulousness in the old man's tone.

Then there was William. 'Get back, Davy, I'll see to this.'

'But Mr Cargill . . .'

'You go and see to your mistress . . . Elizabeth! For the love of God, woman, will you get back up those stairs.'

I started to shout. 'William. Will you let me in? William! You must let me in.'

A moment later the bolt was drawn back and my friend stood before me in his nightclothes, his sword in his hand, and the whole household behind him. The dog rushed past him and was over me with joy in a moment.

'Alexander.' William's face was ashen. 'We had thought you dead.'

I could say nothing. The dog calmed itself eventually and William's sword hung loose in his hand. I went past him, and past Davy, who had the two children gripped firmly under his hands, past Elizabeth, to where Sarah stood, motionless, at the foot of the stairs. She was staring at me as at a risen ghost, and began slowly to shake her head. 'No,' she said. 'No.'

'Sarah,' I said, putting a hand out to her.

She stepped back. 'No. It is not you. It is not you.'

'Sarah.' I put my hands on her shoulders. She struggled to get free and said once more, 'No!' And then her fists were raining blows down on my chest as her voice rose. 'No, No.' She was crying, bringing her fists down in turn with each repeated word. I let it go on until the strength started to go out of her, and then I pulled her in close to me and held her until the sobs died down. I closed my eyes and murmured into her hair that I would never leave her again.

Extracts and quotations

Epigraph – Fynes Moryson, quoted in Caesar Litton Falkiner, *Illustrations of Irish History and Topography: mainly of the seventeenth century* (London, 1904), Part II, contemporary accounts of Ireland in the seventeenth century, 247–8.

Chapter 16 – 'The Downfall of the Gael', by Fearflatha O'Gnive (fl. 1562), translation by Samuel Ferguson in Kathleen Hoagland (ed.), *1000 Years of Irish Poetry: the Gaelic and Anglo-Irish Poets from Pagan Times to the Present* (Connecticut, 1947).

Chapter 18 – 'Roisin Dubh', Anonymous (attr. 16th century), translation by James Clarence Mangan in Hoagland (ed.), *1000 years of Irish Poetry*.

Chapter 25 – Excerpt from Chichester's epitaph transcribed from the Chichester Memorial, Donegall Aisle, St Nicholas church, Carrickfergus.

Chapter 28 – 'Deirdre's Lament for the Sons of Usnagh', from the Red Branch Cycle, 12th century, translation by Samuel Ferguson in Hoagland (ed.), *1000 Years of Irish Poetry*.

Chapter 28 – Sean's epitaph, taken from letter of Shane O'N 'The Proud', to Sir Henry Sidney, 1565. Quoted i Bardon, *A History of Ulster* (Belfast, 2001), 7

Acknowledgements

I would like to thank Judith Murray of Greene and Heaton for her friendship and encouragement, and Jane Wood at Quercus for her perceptive and tactful editing. In researching this book I was fortunate to be able to consult the libraries of Queen's University, Belfast, and the University of Aberdeen. The Custodians of St Nicholas' Church, Carrickfergus kindly let me see round their beautiful church and explained many of its features to me – the events I have portrayed as taking place there are purely fictional. I would especially like to thank my husband's family in Northern Ireland for all their hospitality, babysitting, ferrying around and sharing of local knowledge during my research trips for this book. Most of all I would like to say thank you to James, for taking me there in the first place.